Alison Weir is one of the ???????? historians in the United Kingdom, and has sold ??????????????????? wide. She has written sixteen histo?????????????????? *Wives of Henry VIII, Elizabeth the* ????????????????? in the 7?????? *The Fall* ??????????? *Boleyn: The Great and In?????? Who* ???? ???? ???? published four historical novels: *A Dangerous Inheritance, Innocent Traitor, The Lady Elizabeth* and *The Captive Queen.*

ALISON WEIR

A NOVEL OF ELIZABETH I

The Marriage Game

HUTCHINSON
LONDON

Published by Hutchinson 2014

2 4 6 8 10 9 7 5 3 1

First published in Great Britain in 2014 by
Hutchinson
Random House, 20 Vauxhall Bridge Road,
London SW1V 2SA

www.randomhouse.co.uk

Addresses for companies within The Random House Group Limited can be found at:
www.randomhouse.co.uk/offices.htm

The Random House Group Limited Reg. No. 954009

A CIP catalogue record for this book
is available from the British Library

ISBN 9780091926250 (Hardback)
ISBN 9780091930868 (Trade paperback)

The Random House Group Limited supports the Forest Stewardship
Council® (FSC®), the leading international forest-certification organisation.
Our books carrying the FSC label are printed on FSC®-certified paper.
FSC is the only forest-certification scheme supported by the leading
environmental organisations, including Greenpeace. Our paper procurement
policy can be found at www.randomhouse.co.uk/environment

Typeset in Bell MT Std by Palimpsest Book Production Limited,
Falkirk, Stirlingshire

Printed and bound in Great Britain by
Clays Ltd, St Ives plc

This book is dedicated to the happy memory of
Nick Hubbard
and to his devoted wife, Jean,
dear and beloved friends,
and to their wonderful family, into which I have been
warmly enfolded,
Philippa, Dave and Alice,
Lizzie, Scott and Sebastian.

When I was fair and young, and favour graced me,
Of many was I sought, their mistress for to be;
But I did scorn them all, and answered them therefore,
'Go, go, go seek some otherwhere!
Importune me no more!'

Elizabeth I

1558

She had put on the black mourning gown. Even though her heart was singing for joy, she must appear decently to mourn the sister she had feared and come to hate, and it was thus attired – jet glistening on her tight black bodice, on her long train, and at her ears, and with her red hair coiled up under a peaked cap – that on that crisp November afternoon of her accession day she made her stately, smiling way through the ranks of eager courtiers who thronged the palace of Hatfield to the soaring great hall. Hastily hung with damask, it was to serve as her council chamber, and upon the dais there was set a rich chair beneath a canopy of estate of cloth of gold, emblazoned with the royal arms of England. The lords assembled along the polished oak board bowed low as she strode in briskly and took her place – her rightful place, she told herself – on her throne. The seat of government, she reflected, smiling at the expectant men, and now I know what it is to be charged with the sacred care of my people.

Immediately after they had come upon her in the park with the momentous news that she was now, by the grace of God, queen of England, Elizabeth had hastened back through the patchy November mist to the palace of Hatfield to give thanks to God for this, the most manifold of His blessings. He should not have cause to regret it, she vowed. She would do her duty and more. She would put an end to the strife and bloodshed over religion and the succession. She would be a mother to all her subjects, loving and cherishing them as if they were truly her children, and guiding them in the way they ought to go. She would win and keep their love and their respect, and they would be her shield against the enemies who would surely beset her.

1

She surveyed the men who would serve her, a mere woman, her eyes bright and dancing, her narrow pointed face alive with triumph. She had accomplished it! She had survived! And now she would rule. Briefly, she wished her father, great Harry the Eighth, could have lived to see this day. All her life she had craved his approval, and yet it had never occurred to him that his daughters might be capable of ruling England. All he had wanted, for most of his long reign, was a son to succeed him. For that he had married six times. Would he be proud to see Elizabeth seated in this chair of estate he had once occupied? She hoped so.

She thought too of her mother. That the disgraced Anne Boleyn's bastardised infant should have come through so many perils and inherited the throne was surely a sign of God's approval. Anne had been vindicated at last. If there was exultation in Heaven, this was surely the occasion for it. Maybe Anne knew now that her blood, cruelly shed by an executioner's sword, had not been spilt in vain.

Elizabeth shivered, and not just because the lofty hall was chilly. She felt quite overcome with gratitude to God, who had brought her safely to this place. She was twenty-five, and all but two of her years in this world had been testing. But she had been honed from fine steel. She had survived bastardy, scandal, controversy and accusations of treason and heresy. Converted to the true, Protestant faith in childhood, she had steered herself steadily through the stormy waters stirred up by her Catholic sister, the late Queen, and come at last to a safe harbour. Who would have thought that she, the least of King Henry's children, would one day wear a crown?

Sir William Cecil, faithful, clever friend throughout the years of trial and testing, took his place at Elizabeth's right hand, laying before her the accession proclamation for approval. It would be cried in every town and city in the land, and sent to royal and princely courts throughout Christendom.

'Thank you, William,' she said, twinkling at him. An unwonted smile creased his long, serious face, and he bowed his head, stroking his beard. A stout Protestant of thirty-eight, and a clever lawyer, he had effortlessly slipped into place as her chief adviser; she knew she could trust his wisdom, his ability and his fidelity. He was a man who liked simple pleasures, hard-working and discreet, and above all trustworthy. He had proved himself in the dark days of her sister's reign by his quiet but constant support.

'Madam, there is the matter of public mourning for the late Queen.'

'Three days should suffice,' she told him. She doubted that many would mourn Mary for long, not after her savage persecution of heresy. Mary had sent three hundred Protestant souls to the stake. That must now stop. Elizabeth had already given the order sparing all the poor wretches who yet remained in prison awaiting a dreadful death. She would never have her subjects, even Catholics, burned for their beliefs. She would not make windows into men's souls, so long as they showed themselves faithful and obedient.

'Next.'

'Your Majesty, we must remove to London as soon as possible. So many have come here that there are no lodgings to be found for them.' They had been arriving for days, a steady stream of courtiers who had abandoned the dying Mary to seek favour with her successor. Elizabeth shuddered. Heaven forbid that that should one day happen to her, when she saw death approaching.

Cecil was going through his agenda. 'There is your Majesty's coronation to be planned, but we can discuss that anon. As for shifting the court, and all your Majesty's household and stuff, I would advise the urgent appointment of a Master of Horse.'

Elizabeth's eyes scanned the expectant men seated around the table. Sombrely but richly clad like herself, they were all substantial persons of rank and breeding, hard-headed and ambitious. She realised that, as a woman, it would take all her skill to manipulate them to her will; but there were ways of handling that, she smiled to herself. She would ration her favours so that they would be all the more prized, make her servants work hard for their rewards, and lead them on to live in hope. Her mother had done it, even with her awe-inspiring father, and so therefore would she. Some of these lords had served Queen Mary, reluctantly at times, she knew. There sat the earls of Winchester and Sussex, who had escorted Elizabeth to the Tower in the dark days of 1554, clearly contrary to their will and better instincts. She did not hold it against them, for they had shown her all the kindness they dared. There too were Throckmorton and Knollys, staunch Protestants both, now able to profess their faith without fear; and Shrewsbury, Arundel, Pembroke and Derby, shrewd men of experience who had turned their coats to the wind more than once; the clever lawyer Nicholas Bacon; William Parr, brother to the late Queen Katherine, whom Elizabeth had loved but wronged, she remembered painfully; and Lord Robert Dudley.

Robert, magnificently dressed and making his usual extravagant impression, had been seated astride his white charger, waiting to greet Elizabeth as she strode into the courtyard at Hatfield, exultation in her heart. She would forever associate him with that glorious moment. They had known each other since childhood, been prisoners in the Tower at the same time, for Robert, the son and grandson of traitors, had himself come under suspicion. His father, the Duke of Northumberland, had been beheaded by Queen Mary for setting up the usurper, Jane Grey, in her place, and the Dudley family had duly fallen. After his release, Robert had clawed his way back into favour, proving his loyalty and his prowess on the battlefield.

He was opinionated and a braggart, and some found him insufferable, but Elizabeth had always been fond of him, for she knew there was kindness, loyalty and a serious mind beneath the bravado. There was an inner man whom few knew, who had robustly espoused the Protestant cause, was fascinated by science, geometry, mathematics, astronomy, maps and navigation, had read the classics and could speak fluent French and

Italian. Robert had also distinguished himself gallantly in the tiltyard and in war, yet what most people saw was a showily dressed young man who rode a horse as magnificently as he jousted, who danced and sang divinely, and was expert at tennis and archery. But what counted most to Elizabeth was that he had been a good friend to her throughout the dark days of Mary's reign, even to the extent of impoverishing himself for her sake. It was for that kindness that she was now about to reward him.

She might have allowed herself to like him better had he not been married. It had been a carnal marriage, Cecil had told her, a touch disapprovingly, and founded more on lust than good sense, but she doubted the lust had lasted. Amy Robsart was pretty and graceful, but Elizabeth had reason to believe that she lacked the skills to keep a man captivated.

She thought back to that forbidden moment in the Tower when, briefly, she had snatched some conversation with Robert and known instinctively that he wanted her. They had not been supposed to meet, but she had been permitted to walk in the fresh air, and there he had been, looking down on the garden from his vantage point on the wall walk. They had called softly to each other, their shared predicament lending the moment a kind of intimacy. After two or three contrived encounters, Elizabeth had little doubt that Robert had a fancy for her, and knew that she was powerfully attracted to him. Then their gaolers realised what was going on, and the meetings ceased. Later on, after both Elizabeth and Robert had been released, he from the Tower, she from months of house arrest at Woodstock, they had rarely seen each other, for he was away soldiering, and she was away from court as often as possible, avoiding the enmity of her sister, Queen Mary. It was as well, in the circumstances, she had thought . . .

Now her eyes came to rest on Robert's dark, saturnine features, which had earned him his nickname, the Gypsy, although it was never used to his face. Despite her misgivings, she found herself wanting to feast her eyes on him. His tall, muscular stature, lean visage, red-brown hair and neat beard were of a type that vastly appealed to her. They reminded her of— No, she must not think of *him*, today of all days. That way lay horror and fear.

'Lord Robert shall be my Master of Horse,' she announced, keeping command of herself. 'There is none more skilled with horses than he, and I have no doubt that he will also excel at organising my coronation procession and entertainments for my court.' There was a murmur of discontent. By virtue of his duties, the Master of Horse would often be in company with the Queen, and therefore in an enormously influential position. Robert was grinning broadly, not heeding the discomfiture and unconcealed jealousy surrounding him. Elizabeth ignored it too. She was the Queen, and she would have about her a man who was congenial to her.

Later, when they had all dispersed and she was in her privy chamber, impatiently signing her way through a mountain of state papers, Cecil came to her.

'Your Majesty, forgive me, but was that wise? There are many more worthy. People have not forgotten the ambition of the Dudleys, or where it led. Think of that harvest of heads that followed Northumberland's fall.'

'Robert is loyal and he has the requisite qualifications for the post,' Elizabeth insisted. 'Those who criticise him are merely envious.'

'Madam, I pray you, be governed by me, or some other wise person. With respect, you are a woman and in need of masculine guidance.'

Elizabeth suppressed a smile. She was well aware of Cecil's views on the frailty of women. 'Why should that be so, William?' she asked sweetly.

Cecil's thin face flushed. 'God gave men the power and wisdom to wield dominion over mankind. Your Majesty has most rightfully succeeded to the throne of your forefathers, and yet – forgive me if I speak plainly – the weakness of your sex makes it incumbent upon you to accept advice and guidance from your humble servants, who are able to give it on account of their experience and their – ah – superior intellect. Book learning, in which your Majesty is notably well versed, is not enough. This is a turbulent and dangerous world we live in.'

Elizabeth frowned, but she acknowledged the truth of Cecil's last words. The old order was dying; Christendom was divided, with the might of Catholic Europe set against Protestant states that had dared to break away from Rome. England, now that Elizabeth ruled, was about to become one of them; already she had many enemies, some of whom might be showing a friendly countenance for their own ends. She was aware that most of Christendom regarded her as the bastard of a public strumpet, a heretic who had no right to the throne she occupied. And soon, when her new Anglican Church was established, as she was determined it would be, she and her island kingdom would stand in ever greater peril.

'Despite my womanly weaknesses, and my *inferior intellect*, my sex cannot diminish my prestige,' Elizabeth reproved him, then quickly relented. 'You mean well, old friend. I am well aware of the perils that will beset my path, but I mean to govern myself – with the benefit of your wisdom, of course. Talking of fathers,' and she turned around to look at the portrait of Henry VIII in all his fearsome glory behind her, 'would you have spoken thus to mine?'

'Er, no, Madam.' Cecil had to smile, knowing she had bested him. 'But his late Majesty was not a woman!' Elizabeth threw back her head and laughed, but she resolved to make it plain to everyone that she was made of no ordinary female clay.

Three days later, she sat enthroned in the great hall at Hatfield beneath a royal canopy of estate brought by the deserting rats from St James's Palace in London. The lords had formally made obeisance to her as queen, and now she was to announce the names of those who would serve as her councillors and chief advisers. She had prepared a speech. She knew herself to have an eloquent style and some talent with her pen, and she had worked hard on this, her first oration as queen. Reading it over, she was proud of this particular result of her efforts.

Smiling, she summoned Cecil to step forward.

'William, my good servant, I appoint you my Secretary of State, the greatest office that I can bestow,' she told him. 'I give you this charge so that you shall head my Privy Council and take pains for me and my realm. This judgement I have of you: that you will not be corrupted with gifts, and that you will be faithful to the state; and that' – her lips twitched – 'without respect of my private will, you will give me that counsel which you think best.' Cecil bowed, his normally impassive face registering some emotion.

One by one the men came forward, each to be given his office: rotund, thick-lipped, astute Bacon to be Lord Keeper of the Great Seal; beetle-browed, respected Throckmorton to be Chamberlain of the Exchequer, others to be admitted to the Privy Council. Parr showed himself humbly grateful to be restored to the peerage, after being out of favour under Queen Mary. Knollys, the new Vice Chamberlain of the Queen's Household, was similarly thankful. His wife was gentle, self-effacing Katherine Carey, whom Elizabeth loved, not least because she was her cousin – and indeed her half-sister, although that was supposed to be a secret. Yet there was little mistaking Lady Knollys's strong resemblance to the late King, and many knew she was Henry VIII's love-child by Mary Boleyn, Elizabeth's aunt. Under Queen Mary, the Knollyses had been forced into exile because of their firm Protestant convictions, and they were overjoyed to be home and back in royal favour.

For Robert Dudley there was no seat on the Council, and when all the names had been read out he looked somewhat crestfallen. Although he was loyal, a sound Protestant and an intelligent man, Elizabeth had borne in mind Cecil's caveat. Well, she thought, let Robert prove himself, and I will reconsider anon.

The honours and offices dispensed, she spoke from the throne. 'Good people, the burden that has fallen upon me leaves me amazed. But I am God's creature, bound to obey Him, and I yield to His appointment, praying with your help to make a good account to Him. I mean to direct all my actions by wise advice and counsel. I require of you nothing more than faithful hearts, and then you shall not doubt of my good will, so you use yourselves as loving subjects.'

With applause ringing in her ears, she left the hall, her train of ladies following, and walked through her apartments – those same apartments that she had used since infancy – to her bedchamber. Here, she found Kat Astley, her former governess, now puffed up with pride at having been made first lady of the bedchamber and mistress of the robes. Dear Kat, who had taught Elizabeth her first lessons, said her prayers with her every night, suffered with her through the terrors and tribulations of the past years, and even been imprisoned in the Tower for her sake. Kat had been as a mother to her, in place of the mother of whom she had been cruelly deprived, and now she would have her reward. It was comfortingly strange to see the homely Kat so finely dressed in silks. It brought home to Elizabeth that her years of peril were at last behind her.

'To your duties, ladies. The Queen's Majesty awaits,' Kat cried, rustling forward, the ladies-in-waiting, maids-of-honour and chamberers hastening to assist her in changing their mistress's attire for tonight's dinner, which would, of course, be a subdued affair, for the court was in mourning. So it would be another black gown, but of velvet this time, with a high-standing collar – and very becoming too. Kate Knollys began untying the ribbons that secured Elizabeth's sleeves to her bodice. When Kate had arrived at Hatfield, Elizabeth had wept as she embraced her. She had never enjoyed such a rewarding relationship with her other half-sister, Queen Mary, after she had left her childhood behind her. Mary had loved Elizabeth when she was little, because Mary adored children and had always prayed – in vain – for a child of her own. But later there had been nothing but resentment and jealousy. So it was wonderful to have someone closely related and sympathetic in attendance. Elizabeth was pleased too that her niece Lettice, Katherine's enchanting, flame-haired young daughter, was also to serve her, and Mary, Lady Sidney, Robert Dudley's beautiful sister; she held both girls in high esteem.

There was only one notable absentee, whom Elizabeth had been glad to leave behind in the outer chamber: her pale, sullen cousin, Lady Katherine Grey, whose sister Jane had gone to the block for usurping Queen Mary's throne.

The memory of Jane's fate always gave Elizabeth pause for thought. They had shared a common zeal for the new religion, but Jane had had the makings of a fanatic, and she had died for it. Given the chance to save herself by converting to Catholicism, she had said no, and no again – and suffered the consequences. Elizabeth still shuddered at the thought of her seventeen-year-old cousin lying broken and bleeding on the scaffold. She had had nightmares about it at the time, and had feared – and with good reason – that she herself would be next.

Elizabeth was not sure if she would have had the kind of courage that Jane had shown, and that made her feel uncomfortable. But Katherine, Jane's little sister, had converted to the old faith without a qualm – no 'no, and no again' from her – and had won the warm favour of Queen Mary, who had made her a lady of the bedchamber. It was now safe, of course, for Katherine to convert back to the religion in which she had been raised. I expect it of her, Elizabeth fumed, angry that the girl remained obstinately Catholic. Until she herself bore an heir, Katherine was next in line to the throne – a truth that Elizabeth had no intention of acknowledging – and therefore she should openly be professing the Protestant faith.

Elizabeth knew, of course, why the little hussy was holding back. She had seen Katherine tête-à-tête with the Spanish ambassador, no doubt sweet-talking King Philip into championing her as the Catholic claimant; or maybe it was a ploy to galvanise the Queen into naming her as her successor. Whatever it was,

Elizabeth smelt a rat, and she was furious with Katherine for daring to meddle in dangerous matters that should not concern her. More than that, she was scared; she admitted it. Unlike herself, Katherine was unquestionably legitimate, and she had been born in the realm, which could not be said for their mutual cousin, Mary, Queen of Scots, who had been excluded from the succession by Parliament. Katherine had the potential to prove a deadly threat to Elizabeth's security. It was for this reason that Elizabeth had demoted her to the rank of lady of the presence chamber. She hoped that would put an end to her forward cousin's pretensions.

As the women unlaced and unhooked her gown, Elizabeth gave Kate Knollys an affectionate squeeze.

'Dear cousin, I cannot let you out of my sight again,' she declared. 'You must be in attendance on me as often as possible, as one I love much.'

'I should be honoured, Madam,' Kate said, but she looked a touch downcast.

'And what of her children, Bess?' put in Blanche Parry, Elizabeth's old nurse, who spoke her mind from force of long habit and privilege. 'Who will look to them when their mother is dancing attendance on you? And that fine husband of hers will be jealous of you if you keep him from her!'

Kate flushed.

'Go to, Blanche!' Elizabeth cried. 'Kate does not mind. She may see her children, aye, and bring them to court from time to time. As for you, I love you too much to send you to the Tower, so I mind to put you in charge of my books, to keep you quiet. I know you love learning.'

Blanche subsided, a happy expression on her old face. But Kate's smile was forced. She loved her husband and little ones, and could not bear to be apart from them for long. Yet her love for Elizabeth was such that she would never desert her. She, who had been with her sister in her darkest moments, knew how much she needed her. For Elizabeth had no other close kin, and here she was, in her exalted position, set apart from ordinary mortals, isolated and untouchable. How could Kate deny her?

The next morning Elizabeth was up early, eager to be out in the crisp fresh air after days spent cooped up with her ministers. Zealous in his new duties, Robert Dudley had a fine mount ready saddled and waiting for her, and one for himself too, for her Master of Horse must accompany her whenever she went riding or travelled anywhere. He had put off his mourning and looked splendid in forest-green velvet, his riding cloak swirling jauntily from his shoulders. Elizabeth's eyes were drawn again to his fine-boned features – the high-bridged nose and prominent cheekbones were compellingly attractive – and his shapely legs encased in tight white hose. There was no denying that he was a most handsome man.

He bowed at her approach, doffing his feathered bonnet, and she smiled graciously, realising that her heart was pounding. She was tall for a woman, but when Robert stood up he towered above her. She rather liked that. What she did not like was this new formality between them. They had been friends since childhood, and more than that, surely, not so very long ago. Now she was queen, and Robert was obliged to distance himself and pay her the proper courtesy. She found herself missing the old familiarity they had once enjoyed.

'Madam, allow me,' Robert said, as he stood by the mounting block and cupped his hands so that she could place her foot in them and heave herself into the saddle.

'Do not madam me, Robin,' she chided him playfully. 'We are old friends, are we not?'

'I had hoped that your Majesty would remember that,' he smiled.

'How could I forget it?' she teased. 'You used to call me Bess when we were children. Do not call me Madam, Robin. We know each other better than that.'

'It seems strange to address the Queen's Majesty as Bess, as I did once.'

'How should such strangeness be between friends? I hope we *are* still friends, as before,' Elizabeth said, thinking how debonair Robert looked with his dark hair tousled in the breeze.

'I hope that too – and for more,' he said, bold as the bear on his family's badge.

'Then you may hope!' she said lightly, her heart singing.

Robert's dark eyes lit up. 'I would hope for much, were I permitted.'

She looked down at him. 'I like a brave man!' she declared.

He mounted his own steed and they rode forth, letting the horses break into a canter across the park. The air was cold but the sun was rising. It was going to be a fine winter day. Elizabeth loved the rush of the wind against her cheeks, the heady excitement of jolting along at speed beside Robert, for they were equally fine riders. There was no one in sight for what seemed like miles. More than that, she relished the freedom to relax and be herself with someone who had known her since childhood.

Presently they slowed to a trot, passing through a stretch of woodland, the trees bare above their heads.

'How do you like living in Norfolk, Robin?' Elizabeth asked.

'It is quiet, Madam,' he answered with a grin. 'I prefer to be at court.'

'What, this glittering misery, full of malice and spite?' she teased.

'It cannot be so when it has your Majesty in it,' he replied gallantly.

'Bess,' she said firmly.

'Bess,' he repeated. His tone was tender.

'And your good lady? Does she like it?' She was surprised to find herself suffering a pang of jealousy at the thought of Amy Dudley.

'Well enough.' He seemed not to want to talk about his wife. Well, neither did Elizabeth. She would not mention her again unless he did. In fact, she decided, she would make it clear that she did not want to hear anything about Lady Dudley.

'I trust that the apartment allocated to the Master of Horse is comfortable?' she asked, changing the subject.

'Excellent, Madam – I mean Bess – thank you. It is a great honour to be lodged at court near you.' The intensity in Robert's eyes suggested that this was not mere flattery. 'I would sleep in a cupboard for that.'

'You are too bold, Robin!' Elizabeth reproved, laughing.

'And prepared to be more so,' he riposted.

'Pish!' She was really enjoying herself. She loved nothing more than flirting, and there had been too little of it in her life so far. 'Be serious, Robin! I meant to discuss my coronation. There is much to plan.'

'Then I am at your Majesty's disposal.' The eyes were warm now. She knew that his meaning did not encompass coronations, but she deftly steered the conversation on to that subject. It occurred to her that the old, easy relationship between them had been replaced by something else. They were not children now, or prisoners in the Tower. She was queen, and he was her loyal servant. They were re-encountering each other in these new roles, and the balance of supremacy in their dealings with each other had shifted. If she had been desirable to him in adversity, how much more so must she appear now. Power drew many men like a lodestone, and Robert was overtly greedy for it. And yet, she realised, there was a long-suppressed attraction between them, which had suddenly burgeoned again, there was no denying it. She must be careful, for her heart was in danger of falling captive to his charm and his ambition, and a queen must never be ruled by her heart.

When they returned to the palace, Robert leapt from his horse and led Elizabeth's mount to the riding block. As she slipped down from her saddle, he caught her by the waist and turned her to face him. The feel of his strong hands through the thick stuff of her gown and corset came as a shock to her. They stood there, close together, their eyes locked, for a moment too long – until Robert let her go. She did not reprove him.

*

Dark and handsome, his fine features aligned to a dazzling smile, Count de Feria, the Spanish ambassador, stood before the Queen. His master, King Philip, had sent him to London when Queen Mary lay dying. Mary had been Philip's wife, but in forsaking England when it became clear that she was barren, he had broken her heart. Before then he had championed Elizabeth, even betrayed a less than brotherly interest in her, and that had only inflamed Mary's well-rooted jealousy of her sister. But Philip was a devout Catholic, Elizabeth an enlightened Protestant; there could never be any common meeting ground between them.

Feria, his blue eyes warm, offered his congratulations to the Queen on her accession. 'Your Majesty is no doubt grateful that King Philip's influence has brought you a crown,' he purred.

'My gratitude is due solely to my people,' Elizabeth said crisply, 'but I thank my good brother for his kind words.' She must not alienate Philip, for she needed his friendship. Danger threatened her – from France, from Scotland, from Spain, from Rome, from every Catholic in Christendom. Already the King of France had proclaimed his daughter-in-law, Elizabeth's cousin Mary, Queen of Scots, as the true Queen of England; Mary was married to the Dauphin, heir to the French throne, and, with the might of France behind her, represented the most chilling threat. But Elizabeth was confident that she could steer her ship of state carefully through the stormy seas of European diplomacy. She knew she needed to take on board all the friends she could cozen, and she meant to keep them sweet by promises. She might as well begin now by making overtures to Spain, France's great enemy!

'Your Majesty,' Feria ventured, 'I have come to discuss a delicate matter, that of your Majesty's marriage.'

Elizabeth frowned. This was an unlooked-for complication. She did not want to think of marriage. There came unbidden the memory of a pair of dark, lascivious eyes, long dulled in death . . . 'Pray speak,' she said, a trifle sharply.

Feria cleared his throat, wondering why he suddenly felt so

nervous in the face of this young woman. 'Naturally your Majesty could not contemplate ruling alone, without a husband to guide and support you, and be a father to your children. Maybe you will give some thought to a suitable choice. My master, King Philip, is happy to advise you.'

No, thought Elizabeth, and no again. I need no advice, and I will not be Philip's puppet. 'I am not contemplating marriage just now,' she said, as pleasantly as she could. 'It may suit me better to remain unwed. I have too much work to do in this kingdom to think of wedding.' And, ignoring the astonishment on Feria's face, she swept on briskly to the subject of the aggravating French, their mutual enemy.

Alone with Kat in her chamber, she gave vent to her fury. 'There is a strong idea in the world that a woman cannot live unless she is married!'

Kat, who knew better than most why Elizabeth did not want to marry, said soothingly, 'None can force you to wed.' Heaven knew they had tried in Queen Mary's day. Elizabeth had felt buried alive under the pressure to take first this Catholic prince, then that one, or even another.

'I will never marry!' she declared. She had been saying it since she was eight years old, and she said it again later, when Cecil proposed raising the matter of the succession in council. 'Your Majesty must look to the future security of yourself and the realm,' he reminded her, a touch severely, as if he thought she was being frivolous.

'Must?' she echoed. 'Do you say must to me, William?'

'Madam, marriage is your only surety. That you should wish to remain a maid is not natural.'

'I am not natural!' she retorted. 'I know it.'

'A husband would share the cares and labours of government,' Cecil persisted, ignoring her. 'He would father the heirs who will carry on your Majesty's line.'

'Aye, and relegate me to the nursery!' Elizabeth said, tart. 'No, I will not suffer a man to rule me and usurp my power.'

16

Cecil sighed. 'King Philip may ask for your hand. Feria has been dropping hints.'

'So I heard. Well, let Philip live in hope.' She thought of those calculating but lustful eyes, that cold character, those full but disdainful lips, and inwardly shuddered. To be certain, he had wanted her. But never, never could she even consider . . . Besides, there was the insurmountable obstacle of religion. 'We will keep him sweet with promises, William. You must accept, though, that I am determined to be governed by no one.'

'I am sure that a settlement acceptable to your Majesty can be arranged,' Cecil said smoothly. Elizabeth left it. He would see that she meant what she said.

Her new Archbishop of Canterbury – good Matthew Parker, who had been her mother's chaplain – asked to see her. Cecil had sent him, she suspected – but it seemed that she was wrong.

'Madam, I bear a most holy charge,' the Archbishop told her. 'Your late mother, our sainted Queen Anne, not three days before her arrest sought me out and besought me to look to your welfare should evil befall her.'

Elizabeth said nothing for a few moments. 'She knew, then,' she whispered. 'She sensed what was coming.' She could imagine how her mother must have felt. She had been there herself, a prisoner in the Tower, anticipating death. For Anne it had become a reality.

Parker's homely face creased in distress. 'She knew something was badly amiss, and that her enemies were uniting in an unholy alliance. She feared there would be some move against her. But I doubt she ever envisaged what actually happened, poor lady. She was braver than a lion.'

'And my father?' She had never been able to bring herself to believe that the father she revered had signed her mother's death warrant merely so that he could marry Jane Seymour.

'Suborned and wickedly misled,' said Parker firmly.

'That has been my understanding,' Elizabeth told him, reassured. 'He was a great king, but sometimes ill served.'

'Aye, Madam, he was.' The Archbishop paused. 'I came to speak more of that charge laid on me by your lady mother. Madam, in looking to your welfare, like a father, as it were, I must advise you that it would be to your safety and comfort to enter the holy estate of matrimony.'

So Cecil *had* sent him! Elizabeth rounded on him. 'Good Parker, I know your worth, but *you* know not of what you speak. Think you, with the examples of my mother and my stepmothers before me, that I can see marriage as a secure and comfortable estate? I have no good reason to believe it!' Her tone was bitter. 'Think of my father's marriages. Some say one was unlawful, some that another was not, and that the child of it is a bastard; some say other, and so they go to and fro, as they favour or mislike. My own mother was falsely accused of adultery, as you well know. There are too many doubts, and so I hesitate to enter into marriage, for I fear the controversy it might engender. How then can it be called a holy estate?'

Parker looked shocked, but Elizabeth gave him no room to speak. 'If I marry,' she went on, 'my husband might purpose to carry out some evil wish. My lord, you have had the good fortune never to have been in the Tower – but I have been a prisoner there. I assure you that the prospect of the axe cleaving into my neck was so terrible to me during those anxious days that I even resolved to ask that a French swordsman be sent for, to dispatch me as my mother had been dispatched. I can never forget it. Do you think I could lay myself open to that again?'

'Calm yourself, dear Madam,' Parker soothed, his brow troubled. 'You are queen now. None may gainsay you or make you do what you do not wish to do. And your Majesty is loved by all. No loyal subject would allow harm to come to you, even from a husband.'

'Enough! The matter is threadbare!' Elizabeth snapped. 'I do not want to hear the word "husband" again!'

When the next council meeting broke up, Cecil handed Elizabeth a letter.

'This arrived today,' he said. 'It is not official business but something personal to your Majesty, which you may prefer to read in private.' His voice was gentle, his eyes kind.

Elizabeth took the letter. A sense of foreboding filled her.

'What does it treat of?'

'It comes from a Scottish divine, Alexander Aless, who lives in Saxony. He was in England in 1536, and acquainted not only with the late King Henry, but also with Master Secretary Cromwell and Archbishop Cranmer. The letter contains information he felt he should disclose to you about your mother, Queen Anne.'

At the mention of Cromwell, Elizabeth shivered. He had been the man responsible for her mother's fall, and the bogeyman of her childhood dreams, who had lurked in dark places, in cupboards, tree trunks, behind doors or under the bed. For as long as she could remember, the name Cromwell had had the power to disturb her. And yet, as a ruler herself, she recognised that he had been an administrator without peer and a tireless servant to his royal master – except for spinning a web of lies about his master's wife!

Cecil was watching her compassionately. 'I am sorry if this letter distresses you,' he said. 'I thought hard about whether I should show it to you, but decided I had no right to keep it from you. Would you like me to stay while you read it?'

'No, William,' Elizabeth said. 'Leave me now.' Cecil departed, telling the ladies waiting in the outer chamber that the Queen would call when she was ready.

Slowly she unfolded the letter. The spiky black writing danced before her eyes as she steeled herself to make sense of it.

Aless wrote vividly – too vividly, it would prove. He took Christ to witness that he spoke the truth, a truth he felt the Queen of England should hear. And he went on to describe how, at sunrise on the day on which Queen Anne was beheaded – although he had not known that that was to happen – he had had a dream or vision; he knew not if he had been sleeping or waking, but in this dream or vision he had seen the Queen's neck, after her head had been cut off. It was so clear to him that he could count the nerves, the veins and the arteries . . .

Elizabeth felt sick. She realised that she was trembling, and rose to pour a little watered wine to steady herself. She was not squeamish by any means, and had seen blood shed in her time, but this was her mother of whom the insensitive Dr Aless had written. And although he had seen this horror in a dream – she could not credit that he had been vouchsafed a vision – he had described what would have become reality only hours later.

She did not know if she could read any more. But she had to, of course. She had to know the truth.

Aless wrote that he had been so terrified by the dream that he immediately arose from his bed and crossed the Thames to the Archbishop of Canterbury's palace at Lambeth, hoping to see Cranmer and ask for a spiritual view of it. He found him walking in the garden; he too had had trouble sleeping. Elizabeth knew that Cranmer had been one of her mother's most ardent supporters, a chaplain to the Boleyns, and a great advocate of church reform, as Anne herself had been. Small wonder that he was disturbed in his mind.

The Archbishop asked Aless why he had come so early, for the clock had not yet struck four. When Aless answered that he had been horrified in his sleep, and told him of the dream, Cranmer had continued in silent wonder for a while. Then he asked, 'Do you not know what is to happen today?' Aless answered that he had remained at home since the Queen's arrest, and knew nothing of what had occurred since. The Archbishop raised his eyes to the sky and said, 'She who has been the Queen of England upon Earth will today become a queen in Heaven.' So great was his grief that he could say nothing more, and burst into tears. Shaken by what he had learned, Aless had returned to London, sorrowing.

His landlord, a servant of Cromwell, told him not to attempt to attend the execution, as foreigners were not being admitted to the Tower. But he could not have borne anyway to witness the butchery of such an illustrious lady, especially as he believed her to be innocent of the crimes for which she was condemned. However, his landlord went, and after he returned home at noon, he gave an account of what he had seen, which Aless could now impart to Anne's daughter.

The Queen, he wrote, had covered her own eyes with a kerchief, kneeling upright on the scaffold before two thousand spectators. She had prayed aloud, beseeching God to receive her soul, then commanded the executioner to strike, which he did quickly. It had all been over in an instant. She could not have suffered much pain.

Elizabeth drained the wine, fighting back tears. She had long ago trained herself not to dwell upon Anne's brutal end. As a girl she had been hungry for details, had consumed them greedily, and then felt sick when they were too unpalatable to ingest. Aless's letter had made her confront the truth once more. She stumbled to her bedchamber and found a handkerchief, then sat on the bed going over and over in her mind what he had written. When Kat came to lay out the Queen's clothes for the evening, she found her sitting there in darkness.

'Why, Bess, what are you doing here?' she asked, reverting to the familiarity of long, affectionate service, as they were alone. Then she saw the letter lying on the bed.

'Read it,' Elizabeth said. Kat read. Then she sat down heavily beside her mistress, and suddenly Elizabeth was a little child again, sobbing her heart out on Kat's plump breast, crying for the mother she had never known and yet still so sorely missed in many ways.

'France is our enemy,' Cecil told the Council. 'We are in a poor case to fight any wars. The treasury is empty, the realm impoverished. Our continued friendship with Spain is an imperative.' He looked meaningfully at Elizabeth.

'We will warmly consider any approaches from King Philip,' she said. 'In the meantime, my lords, I would welcome your advice on a sensitive matter. When Queen Mary came to the throne, she had Parliament repeal the Act declaring her mother's marriage unlawful and herself a bastard. My own mother's marriage was annulled, and I too declared a bastard. I wish to reverse that.'

There was a silence. The councillors looked at each other uncomfortably. Then Bacon spoke. 'I would advise against it, Madam. Queen Anne, God rest her soul, was unjustly condemned; but there are still many who dispute that, particularly the Catholics. The crimes of which she was accused were monstrous and sensational, even though the accusations were certainly false. To rake up the events of 1536 would be to court controversy and give your enemies more opportunities for calumny. Indeed, that would be more hazardous than the taint of bastardy. My advice is to let your lady mother rest in peace.'

Elizabeth found herself perilously near to tears. 'It is a sad state of affairs when, even as queen, I cannot rehabilitate her memory,' she said bitterly.

'Madam, leave well alone,' the Earl of Sussex advised. Balding and narrow-eyed, he was a man of great experience. The others nodded sagely.

'The truth will out!' Elizabeth said, rising. 'Mark what I say. My mother's name will not be covered in ignominy for ever.' And in an angry rustling of silks she left the room and hastened to her bedchamber. Two startled maidens bent hurriedly to their curtseys, but she dismissed them. She had dreamed of this day for years, looked forward to the moment when she could clear her mother's name of scandal and herself of the stain of bastardy. But she knew that Bacon had spoken the truth. Anne Boleyn had been accused of adultery, incest and treason, and for over twenty years her reputation had been steeped in infamy. In Europe, she was still reviled. Should Elizabeth arouse the sleeping dogs of gossip, there would be many to say: like mother, like daughter. And that she could not afford. All the same, she was resolved upon two things: she would take for her motto as queen the one her mother had chosen: *Semper eadem* – Always the same; and for her badge she would have Anne's crowned white falcon perched on a tree stump flowering with Tudor roses. To Elizabeth, that stump was symbolic of her mother being cut down before her time.

She stood before Anne Boleyn's portrait, one of her most prized possessions. She had come upon it years ago, hidden in an attic; now it hung opposite her bed. Save that her mother was dark and had a straight nose, there was a strong resemblance to Elizabeth herself: the same slender figure, the same slim face, the same dancing eyes that drew men on. Oh yes, it was easy to see why people had believed ill of Anne. And yet, Elizabeth had heard, she had been most careful of her honour, even as she had flirted and danced with the men in her circle. She had known she was watched by hostile eyes. Above all, she had been a religious woman, keen in the cause of reform. True faith had flourished in England under her patronage. Elizabeth wished she had known her better. All she had of her mother was the portrait, a set of virginals, four pendants in the shape of Anne's initials with drop pearls, and the blurred memory of a black-clad lady with furred sleeves and musky perfume who sang to her and appeared to have a halo around her head. It had been an illusion, of course. The halo would have been Anne's French hood, a daring fashion in its day because it had exposed the hair – but how elegant! Even so, the impression of a halo had led the child Elizabeth to believe that her dead mother had been destined for Heaven.

She smoothed her gown and resolved to think of something else. Pinching her cheeks to bring out a blush, she stared at herself in the mirror, turning this way and that to admire her reflection in the burnished silver. It occurred to her that her habitual black clothing, of rich stuff but plain, did not become a queen, and that she did not have to dress so soberly any more, especially now that there was no longer any need for her to be subtle in proclaiming her Protestant faith to the world. For nearly ten years she had worn the plain, unadorned garb of a godly Protestant maiden, and latterly made the lavishly dressed Queen Mary look like a graven idol by contrast.

But the truth was that Elizabeth had adopted her severe clothing years before there was any need to blazon her faith; she had done it to emphasise her virtue, at a time when there had been a very pressing need to do so. She did not want to think of that time now. Few knew her secret, and they would never talk.

She would put aside her dull attire and wear her long, wavy hair curled. She would still display her faith in colours of black, white and silver, but magnificently, in silks, velvets, taffeta or cloth of gold, with delicate lace ruffs, gauzy veils, intricate embroideries, and the vast collection of jewels and pearls she had inherited. Her imagination leaping ahead of her, she resolved to adorn her clothing with emblems proclaiming who and what she was – Tudor roses for her House, ears of wheat for her faith in Christ, mulberries for her wisdom, suns to personify a ruler directed by God, and pansies, her favourite flower; and there would be symbols, too – an ermine for purity, a pelican for maternal love and sacrifice, a sieve for prudence, and a phoenix for immortality. By these symbols her people would know her and what she stood for. She felt quite elated at the thought. She would summon her tailors and her embroiderers right away! And – there was no point in spending money unnecessarily – she would have Queen Mary's sumptuous coronation gown altered to fit her for her own crowning.

She also desired to have men admire her, which they could not fail to do because she was a queen and she had her mother's gift of making them believe that she was beautiful. And she wanted to look beautiful for one man in particular. She wanted Robert Dudley to gaze on her enraptured as she processed through the court, a glorious being something more than human! She realised that she was thinking more and more of Robert as the days passed. She loved their daily rides, the easy banter, the flirtatious game of cat and mouse they played. All harmless fun, but if she was honest with herself, it was coming to mean more than that to her. And to Robert too, she was sure. She often sensed that he was reining himself in.

There was another portrait on the wall by the door. It always drew her eye, for it showed Henry VIII in all his magnificence, painted by Master Holbein. He had been a king among kings, and Elizabeth was proud to be his daughter. She always thought of herself as the lion's cub, a lioness in Henry VIII's mould. She knew, of course, that majesty was not just about outward display. She would be another ruler such as her father, but merciful, not as severe. Yet for all his cruelties, the religious changes he had brought about, and his unhappy marriages, Henry had retained the love of his subjects, and was still spoken of with awe and affection. The English, Elizabeth had concluded, liked strong kings. In his youth, she had heard, her father had been a golden hero, warlike and accomplished, the embodiment of the old royal blood of the realm, and he had been hugely popular. He had had the common touch, and she would follow his example. It came easily to those born with Tudor blood.

She looked at his painted, well-remembered face: the shrewd eyes, the high Roman nose, the small, sensual mouth. How she had longed for his smiles, his fatherly caresses, his praise. He had been a distant, god-like figure for much of her childhood, but when the mood took him he could be loving and playful and kind. Those had been the best times. He might have had her declared bastard when he had his marriage to her mother annulled, but he had been proud of her, she knew it; and she knew he had recognised in her something of himself.

That was a comforting thought, because all her life there had been rumours that she was not his daughter but the fruit of her mother's adultery with one of her so-called lovers. Even her sister had come to believe it. Mary had commented several times on the resemblance between Elizabeth and Mark Smeaton, the lute player who had perished with Anne. Well, it had suited Mary to believe that. She had come to hate and fear the prospect of Elizabeth inheriting the throne. But her comments had hurt, as no doubt she had intended.

I *am* my father's daughter, Elizabeth had said firmly to herself on many occasions. King Henry himself had never doubted it. He had always acknowledged her as his own. Many people had remarked – and still did – upon Elizabeth's strong likeness to him, especially in her red-gold colouring and her noble profile, and some had even said that she looked more like him than Mary did. But often she would find herself gazing at his portraits looking for evidence of that likeness. Then she would pull herself up, recalling that her father had restored her to the succession, something he would never have done had he entertained the slightest doubt about her paternity.

She had grown up idolising Henry VIII, and now she revered his memory. Already she had proudly taken to describing him as 'her Majesty's dearest father' in official documents. She knew beyond doubt that he had always loved her, whatever he had come to believe of her mother, whom he had also loved profoundly once – and beyond reason, it had been said. How she wished – as countless times she had wished before – that that love had never been cruelly turned to hatred.

As queen, and with her coronation imminent, Elizabeth needed to be in London, her capital city. By the time her great procession reached its walls, her ears were ringing with the tumult of cheering along the frost-rimed road south from Hatfield. Crowds had lined the way, running to catch a glimpse of her, emerging alike from humble farmsteads and timbered houses glittering with diamond-paned windows. She found herself seeing the landscape anew, from the vantage point of one who ruled this kingdom, and marvelled at the broad expanses of green fields, the scattered villages clustered around soaring churches, the bustling little towns with their packed narrow streets and busy shops, and the tranquil glories of great mansions glimpsed beyond brick walls and hunting parks. This was her England, and these were her subjects.

'Elizabeth! Elizabeth! God save our Queen Elizabeth!' they had cried, again and again, falling to their knees in the dust as she passed. She was touched to her soul, and inwardly vowed anew to serve her people well and deserve their love. They should have peace, aye, and the freedom to worship as they pleased.

And here was my Lord Mayor in his scarlet robes, come with his aldermen and sheriffs to welcome her to her capital. She dismounted and extended her hand to be kissed, before raising them all lovingly from their knees; and then she espied the advancing figure of Bishop Bonner, 'Bloody' Bonner, who had been so avid for the burning of heretics. There were hisses and boos as he knelt before her – and cheers when she deliberately turned her face away from him.

Now, with a thousand people attending on her, and herself magnificent in royal purple, she was riding towards the looming walls of the Tower, where she was – reluctantly – to lodge until Whitehall Palace was ready to receive her. Ahead of her rode the Lord Mayor, the Garter King of Arms, and the Earl of Pembroke carrying aloft the sword of state; and right behind her, much to her content, the splendidly attired Robert Dudley on an equally splendid black horse. Progress was slow, as Elizabeth would keep pausing to smile and wave at her people, or stoop to exchange a word or jest, receive a humble gift lovingly offered or hear a grievance. All might come forward, she commanded. Soon everyone was extolling her for her condescension, her common touch and her care for her people. Let foreign princes threaten me, she thought exultantly: I have my people's love, and that is worth more than a thousand armies.

At the Tower she reined in her mount, steeling herself to enter the fortress where she had suffered three terrible months of incarceration, not five years ago. She forced herself to smile; she would not think of the past.

'When last I was here, good people,' she addressed the crowds, 'it was as a prisoner, unjustly suspected of treason, and in fear of death. Now I give most hearty thanks to Almighty God who has spared me to behold this day!'

She said no word about her mother, whose blood *had* been shed here these twenty-two years past, but Anne Boleyn was much in her thoughts, and later that day she insisted on entering the Queen's lodgings, which were the very rooms that Anne had occupied before her coronation and then, three short years later, in the days leading up to her execution. Here, in this same lodging, Elizabeth herself had languished during those desperate weeks when she had expected daily to be summoned to the scaffold. She had always believed that her sister, knowing where Anne had been held, had deliberately intended that Elizabeth should suffer this added refinement to her punishment. And Elizabeth had been permitted – nay, encouraged – to take the air along the wall walk that overlooked the scaffold before the House of Ordnance, a scaffold built for Lady Jane Grey on the exact place where Anne Boleyn had perished; Elizabeth vividly remembered praying each day for it to be taken down.

The apartments had been cleaned, sweetened and made luxurious with rich hangings and furnishings, but an air of misery pervaded them, and Elizabeth was glad to close the door on their faded antique grandeur, gratified to be staying in the former King's chambers in the old royal apartments. These had been hung with silk tapestries threaded with gold and silver, and furnished with a magnificent canopy of estate edged with seed pearls and a great bed made up with rich stuffs. Beneath the canopy was a throne made for her father, Henry VIII – she recognised the pattern of the green damask – and there too was his footstool, on which he had once rested his poor diseased legs. God rest him, she thought, momentarily overcome by the poignant sight.

Lying wakeful at night in the vast bed, Elizabeth's thoughts inevitably strayed to her mother and the grim pageant of traitors who had perished within these walls. It was only a short walk from the palace to the Chapel of St Peter ad Vincula, where Anne lay ignominiously buried in an unmarked grave. Elizabeth wished she could have the poor remains translated to Westminster Abbey and given honourable burial in a fine marble tomb. But she remembered what Bacon had said. It would not be politic. It would be raking up matters best left forgotten.

She tossed, turned, curled up, then stretched, time after time. She could not sleep, her mind would not stop racing, and she could not abide the stink and noises that drifted through the draughty casement from the Tower menagerie. In the end, she rose from her bed, pulled on a heavy robe over her nightgown, pushed her feet into velvet slippers and wrapped herself in a dark cloak. The maid on the pallet bed stirred, but Elizabeth bade her go back to sleep. She descended a small spiral stair and found herself in the freezing night air in the courtyard below the White Tower, which loomed massively above her. To her right was the Jewel House, and to her left the great bulk of the King's Hall, where Anne had been tried and condemned to death. This night Elizabeth would honour her mother, as she had never had the chance to do before.

The yeomen of the guard keeping watch in the courtyard were astonished to see their Queen abroad, unattended, in the dark hours before dawn, but they jumped to obey her determined command to open the great Coldharbour Gate, the only way out of the inmost ward that housed the palace complex. She bade them await her return, then set off with purposeful strides across Tower Green to St Peter ad Vincula, which stood solid and lonely next to the great House of Ordnance. The door creaked as she pushed it open.

Inside, all was still. The only light came from the moonlit windows and from the solitary flame in the sanctuary signifying the constant, reassuring presence of God. Elizabeth walked across the flagstones down the empty nave, a colonnade of pillars to her left. Ahead lay the altar steps. Reaching them, she knelt. She had been told that her mother and Katherine Howard had been buried before the altar, with the beheaded dukes of Somerset and Northumberland between them. She wished she knew which side Anne Boleyn lay. Never mind. Somewhere, just inches below her, was the arrow chest of elm in which her mother's mangled remains had been interred on that tragic spring day in 1536.

As a good Protestant, Elizabeth was not supposed to pray for the dead. The practice had been condemned under her brother, the short-lived, zealous Edward VI, Jane Seymour's son. But Elizabeth still preferred Archbishop Cranmer's earlier version of the Book of Common Prayer, which did provide for such prayers, just as she was determined to keep the jewelled crucifixes in her chapels, which some hard-line reformers and Puritans had denounced as graven idols. She would do, she had resolved, as her conscience dictated. Was it wrong to derive some comfort from praying for the dead? Who knew, it might do the dead some good. And so she folded her hands, composed her mind to tranquillity, and recited over and over again Cranmer's beautiful prose: 'I commend into Thy mercy Thy servant Anne, who is departed hence from us with the sign of faith and now doth rest in the sleep of peace: grant unto her, I beseech Thee, Thy mercy and everlasting peace.'

It felt strangely comforting to be here, near to the mother she could barely remember. Kat had told Elizabeth many times how Anne had loved her and taken pride in her. How terrible it must have been for her — nay, beyond terrible — to leave behind her little child, not knowing what that child would come to believe of her; and knowing that she would not be there to shield and protect Elizabeth from the troubles that would arise from being declared a bastard and left motherless. Anne's marriage to the King had been declared invalid just two days before her execution, so she had gone to the scaffold knowing of the terrible legacy she had bequeathed to her daughter. Kat reckoned that, having been condemned to be burned or beheaded at the King's pleasure, she had been offered the kinder death in return for her consent to her marriage being dissolved. And who could have blamed her for accepting?

A wondrous sense of peace stole over Elizabeth as she knelt on the altar steps, as unexpected as it was comforting. It was as if someone unseen knelt beside her, emanating love and acceptance and joy. It had been her willing imagination, she told herself as she walked back to the palace, yet there remained a strong conviction in her heart that God had answered her prayers, and that it had been her mother who had come to her, bringing healing and peace to her troubled soul.

1559

In January Elizabeth went to her crowning in Westminster
Abbey. The day before, she had gone in procession through
the teeming streets of London to the rejoicing of the citizens
who had thronged to see her. Every house had been hung with
tapestries, painted cloths or garlands of evergreens; all the
church bells rang out, music echoed from every street corner,
and the crowds were dense. Lord Robert had organised the
procession, the ceremonies and the lavish pageants set up along
the way for the Queen's entertainment. Bless him, he had even
arranged for the life-like figures of her parents, King Henry
and Queen Anne, to be displayed in a tableau exalting her royal
descent. She blinked away tears from her eyes at that – and
when a man pointed at her and cried, 'Remember old Harry
the Eighth? Here he is, come back to us!' Again and again she
thanked the citizens for their warm welcome. 'I shall be as
good to you as ever queen was to her people,' she promised,
and they loved her for it.

It was snowing when she walked to the Abbey wearing a
heavy mantle of embroidered silk lined with ermine over her
coronation robes, those same robes her sister had worn five years
before. Hundreds of candles illuminated the distinguished
throng and flashed fire on the jewels of the regalia and the
gold threads in her father's priceless tapestries, commissioned
from the great painter Raphael, which hung in the church.
When the bishops presented Elizabeth to her subjects, there
were such shouts of acclaim and such a crescendo of sound
from the organ and trumpets that the ancient building almost
shook to its foundations. Symbolically chosen, sworn and
anointed, Elizabeth was lifted up into the ancient coronation

chair and the crown was raised above her. As it was placed upon her head, she thought of both her father and her mother, and knew a moment of indescribable exultation. She was truly a queen now, invested by God to rule. This crown had been hard-won, and none should ever take it from her.

Ten days later, again wearing her coronation robes, Elizabeth opened her first Parliament, seated majestically in a chair padded with cloth-of-gold cushions beneath the royal canopy of estate. But it seemed that barely had she taken off those robes afterwards, having left both houses to their debating, than the Speaker and a deputation from the House of Commons were begging an audience at Whitehall.

Reluctantly she came to her presence chamber. Its walls and pillars were carved and gilded with gold leaf, its black-and-white marble floor spread with the costliest of Turkey carpets. Against this magnificent backdrop Elizabeth made a striking contrast in her carefully chosen dress of virginal white. As she ascended her throne, looking like a goddess, the members of Parliament fell to their knees in awe before her.

'Sir Thomas Gargrave,' she said, indicating to the Speaker that she was ready to listen to him. As ready, that was, as she would ever be. Love her commons she did, but her Commons might prove another matter!

'Your Majesty, we come to present a petition from the House of Commons,' he replied, looking nervous. He swallowed audibly. 'We believe it would be best for you and your kingdom if you were to marry a consort who could relieve you of those duties that are fit only for men.'

Elizabeth bridled, but said nothing. Out of the corner of her eye she noticed Robert Dudley standing among the watching courtiers, gazing at her intently, and Cecil, frowning and nodding. Her irritation increased.

Sir Thomas advanced into the fray, unheeding of his sovereign's mutinous look. 'Princes are mortal, but kingdoms are immortal. If your Majesty remains unmarried and, ah, a Vestal Virgin, so to speak, it would be contrary to the public interest.'

Elizabeth forced herself to be civil, although the Speaker's assertion that her royal duties were fit only for men had made her see red, and she was fighting down the urge to box the man's ears.

'This is a matter most unpleasing to me,' she said, 'but what does please me is the good will of you, my faithful Commons, and all my people.' She glanced again at Dudley and Cecil, noting that both were listening avidly. 'I have chosen to stay unwed, even though great princes have sought my hand. I consider myself already bound to a husband, which is the kingdom of England.' As she extended her finger with her coronation ring elegantly displayed, her fiery gaze encompassed all in the room. 'Every one of you, and indeed all Englishmen, are children and kinsmen to me. Sirs, I will do as God directs me. I have never been inclined towards marriage, but I do not rule it out completely. I promise you, this realm shall not remain destitute of an heir. But in the end, this may be sufficient for me, that a marble stone shall declare that a queen, having reigned such and such a time, lived and died a virgin.'

So saying, she nodded to the kneeling deputation and left the presence chamber without giving the Speaker the chance to answer her. Cecil watched her retreating back, detecting in every sweeping movement her barely contained fury. He knew that he must go after her and, whether she liked it or not, remind her of the desperate jeopardy in which she would find herself if she did not marry soon. This course she had chosen was madness!

He caught up with her in the gallery that led to her private lodgings.

'Madam, Madam,' he sighed in some agitation, 'a word if I may.'

Elizabeth led the way into the deserted council chamber.

'Yes, William?' Her eyes were wary. She knew what was coming.

'Madam, if you do not marry, there will be no heirs of your body to carry on the succession.'

'And if I do, William, any son of my body would not lack for supporters who might conspire to overthrow me, who am a mere woman – and who would trouble to gainsay him?' Her eyes bored into those of Cecil, who was unable to answer her.

'Madam, I beg of you, please consider. If you do not bear children, who will succeed you? This Parliament will turn England Protestant. I need not remind you that your nearest heirs are Catholics.' Elizabeth glared at him, but she knew he was right. There was Mary, Queen of Scots, now calling herself queen of England, with the might of France behind her, even though she was a foreigner and could never by law succeed here. But the French would not care for such niceties. Elizabeth conceded – although nothing would make her admit it openly – that Lady Katherine Grey had the better claim, but she was a dangerous nuisance, flirting with Spain, so obviously hoping that King Philip would press Elizabeth to name her her successor.

As if he could read her thoughts, Cecil said, 'Do you want Lady Katherine Grey to succeed you?'

'Never!' Elizabeth snapped. 'She is naught but a pretty flower that bends with the wind. No brain and no principles.'

'My thoughts exactly, Madam. At least we agree on something.' Cecil made a rueful face. 'My dearest prayer is that God will send you a husband, and by and by a son.'

'So that England has a king again!' Elizabeth exploded. 'William, you are as transparent as air. Like most men, you see it as unnatural for a woman to rule. You want me consigned to the nursery so that my husband can rule in my name. Well, again I say, never!'

Cecil flushed. 'Madam, I protest, I want no such thing. I am your most loyal subject. Did I not help you to secure your throne?'

'Aye, you did, and for that I am grateful. Never think I am not.'

'Then strengthen your position and take a husband, Madam!'

Elizabeth's eyes were like steel, her mouth set obstinately. 'And whom do you suggest?'

'King Philip may ask for your hand.'

'Have you already forgotten how he was hated by my sister's subjects? How he dragged England into his own ruinous wars, those same wars that cost us Calais, our last possession in France? Think how cruelly he abandoned Queen Mary!'

'I do not say you should accept his suit, Madam, only that some great prince might be found, one who is prepared to forsake his country for yours and who would be your champion in matters of religion.'

'That rather narrows the field,' Elizabeth observed tartly. 'There are few eligible Protestant princes in Europe. And if none suitable can be found, then I suppose you would have me marry a subject! What dangerous rivalries that would cause at court! Besides, it would demean my blood to stoop so low.'

Cecil sighed again. 'Then, Madam, how do you propose solving the problem of the succession?'

'God, and time, will solve it, believe me,' she replied, fizzing with irritation. 'I have enough to deal with without your pestering me constantly with this – this trifle! I have a church to establish; the Catholics and Puritans are making trouble; the French threaten us; the Protestants in Scotland urgently need my help; the Queen of Scots and Katherine Grey want my crown, and the treasury is still empty! I don't have time to think of marriage!'

Fear was coursing through her blood. There were good and pressing reasons why she should stay single, but the very mention of marriage terrified her. There was only one person who came near to understanding, but even he, who had known her since she was eight, was not aware of the whole story.

'Walk with me awhile, Robin,' she said, tapping Dudley on the shoulder after coming across him idling in a gallery hung with maps and portraits. He willingly abandoned his scrutiny of Sebastian Cabot's map of his North American discoveries, and followed her out of her lodgings as she strode into the privy garden, which was colourful with plants even at this time of year. Here, among the forest of painted columns surmounted by gilded heraldic beasts, with her shivering, fur-clad ladies keeping a discreet distance, they could be private together. Elizabeth did not feel the cold; she loved being out in all weathers.

'You heard what my Commons said,' she began, as she and Robert strolled along a path that led down towards the River Thames. 'God's blood, I do not see how I can marry and stay a queen! The husband holds dominion over the wife, the queen holds dominion over her subjects.' She turned to face him. 'Robert, you know better than most what my life was like before God brought me a crown. I am free at last of all those who put me in danger or forced me to do what I did not want to do. I do not have to tread warily any more. I like my power. I feel liberated. But what power, what freedom would I have if I married, tell me?'

'That would depend on whom you married,' Robert said, after considering for a moment. 'Some men would consider themselves sufficiently lucky to win your sacred person, and would not ask for more.'

'Knowing men, I doubt it,' Elizabeth snorted.

'Then, Bess, may I suggest that you have not known the right men,' Robert ventured.

'Aye, maybe I have not,' she said, considering, refusing to take his bait. 'But I need my councillors to understand that I have found the celibate life to be rather agreeable – and perhaps, Robin, as one who knows them well, you could convey that for me – and repeat it whenever the opportunity arises. I grow weary of wrangling with Cecil on the issue.'

'He cannot comprehend why you do not wish to wed, Bess. And, to be plain, neither can I.'

Elizabeth stopped. She looked distressed. 'I cannot explain, Robin. I can only say that I would rather enter a convent or suffer death than be forced to renounce my virginity.'

Robert looked at her with sympathy, but there was a degree of scepticism in his gaze. There had been gossip that she was no virgin. He had wondered about that, the prospect arousing excitement in him rather than disapproval. Now here she was, saying she would rather die than marry – and she was not joking.

'Sit with me, Bess,' he invited, offering his arm and leading her to a bench in an arbour that would be shady in spring. 'You have confided in me thus far, and you know I would never betray that confidence. What is it you fear?'

'There are reasons I could not divulge to my twin soul,' Elizabeth said. She was trembling, and not with cold.

'Bess, we two are twin souls. We have both been through so much. I know what you have suffered.'

'Not all of it,' she retorted.

'Of course not. Who can look into another's heart? And I suspect this goes back a long way. I remember when you were eight, and told me then that you would never marry.'

'That was when my third stepmother, Katherine Howard, was executed. Young as I was, I knew what adultery and treason were. I had been early schooled in such matters.' Her tone was bitter.

'Because of your mother.'

'Yes. You were a man when your father went to the block, Robin. I was not three years old when my mother died, and not much older when I found out the reasons why. It was a hard burden to grow up with. I shudder to remember the nightmares I had. And when Katherine Howard was executed, the horror of it hit me all over again and I fell to thinking once more about my mother, only my thoughts were more gruesome than before, as there was plenty of talk and gossip to bring home to me the reality of beheading. And if *I* felt bad, think of my father! He suffered all kinds of trials and torments with his marriages. I had stepmother after stepmother. Two died in childbed. Others in my family, and among my nobility, have been entangled in matrimonial disputes. Surely you can see why it is impossible for me to regard marriage with equanimity or see it as a secure state.'

'Do you fear childbirth?'

'Aye, I don't mind admitting that.' It seemed the most natural thing to be discussing such matters with Robin. 'My physician once told me that it would not be easy for me. Ever since then . . .' She shied from the humiliating memory; Dr Huick had terrified her to the point where she felt she could never risk a pregnancy. 'I also fear that bearing children would put a bridle on my queenship. I would be out of action, out of control. Others might try to wrest power from me.'

'That fear is understandable,' Robert said. He laid his hand gently on hers. 'But I for one would not let them, and I know I speak for many.' He squeezed her fingers for emphasis, then regarded her with compassion − and something else. 'Bess, what is it you will not − or cannot − admit?'

'*That* I will not tell you or anyone else.' Reluctantly, Elizabeth moved her hand away.

'Is it the act of procreation?' he asked. She turned her head sharply towards him.

'Robin, you presume too much!'

'Come, Bess, you were ever plain in your speech, and no shrinking maiden. I have heard you swear with the best of them. If I presume, it is because I want to help you.'

She felt as if she was melting inside. For all her fears, there was something very wonderful about having Robert comfort her like this. How easy it would be to lay her head on his broad brocaded shoulder and surrender to his reassurances. It occurred to her that she would not protest − or not very much − if he attempted to kiss her. Despite herself, his talk of sex excited her. She wanted him − even as she feared him. But confide in him she could not. She dared trust no one, even Robin. There remained in her head the memory of that other − another dark-eyed charmer.

'You *have* helped me,' she said firmly. 'And now I must go and give audience to the Spanish ambassador.'

*

Count de Feria stood again before her, bowing low. She had done her best to avoid him these past weeks, to make it clear she would not be ruled by Spain, but she could not go on doing that for ever. King Philip must not be offended.

She had chosen to receive the Count in her privy chamber. It was a privilege, for access was permitted only to those sufficiently great or favoured, and most ambassadors never got beyond the presence chamber next door. But behind the throne in the privy chamber was Hans Holbein's massive mural of Elizabeth's immediate forebears: her grandparents, Henry VII with Elizabeth of York, for whom she was named; and, in the foreground, her father, Henry VIII, with Jane Seymour, who had borne him his longed-for son, Edward VI. The majestic figure of King Henry loomed massively over the room, over-awing all who beheld it. One visitor had confessed to the Queen that he had felt abashed and annihilated standing before it. That was just how Elizabeth intended Feria to feel.

'Your Majesty, I bring a very special message from my master,' he began, looking up nervously at the wall behind her, as if he expected Bluff King Hal to come leaping out of it, roaring his disapproval of an alliance between England and Spain and brandishing an order for Feria's arrest.

Oh no, Elizabeth thought, even as she smiled in apparently joyful anticipation of the special message.

Feria recovered himself and spoke with a flourish: 'King Philip hopes that your Majesty will see fit to continue in the alliance between our two kingdoms, and that you will consent to become his wife.'

Elizabeth was not often at a loss for words, but she struggled to find them now, and to keep the smile fixed on her face. Feria was staring at her, clearly disconcerted by her silence and trying not to look at the terrifying figure of her father.

'I am overwhelmed by his Majesty's proposal, and I thank him for it,' she said at last. 'He must understand, however, that I am torn between the need to marry and my desire to maintain my virginity. There are many great and good reasons for this alliance, so I will give the matter due consideration, after taking advice from my councillors. But it may be that God will direct me to live a virtuous but celibate life.'

Feria was now looking angry, but Elizabeth stood her ground. If he thought she was going to enlarge on the honour Philip thought he was doing her, he was mistaken. Bed with that cold haddock? Never!

'If your Majesty does not marry and produce an heir to sit on England's throne,' the ambassador said bluntly, 'the King of France will surely rise against you and place Mary Stuart there instead.'

'God's teeth,' Elizabeth exploded, rising to her feet, and looking very much like her august sire above her. 'I will teach King Henri a lesson if he so much as dares to try, and that mewling daughter-in-law of his as well. The French and the Scots have never given up conspiring against England. Why should I fear them? Have you forgotten how we trounced them at Agincourt and Flodden? Let them come, and be humiliated before Christendom!' She was breathless with indignation, and sank down into her chair. Feria was astounded: were all Englishwomen this savage? He thought nervously of his feisty new English wife, wondering if she might turn out like this. On balance, he thought not. It was probably not being married that did it. He wished he could go home.

'I need time to consider King Philip's proposal,' Elizabeth said, calmer now. 'I will speak with you again in a few days.' And she left the ambassador quaking in his elegant Spanish leather shoes.

Although Elizabeth knew that she should be considering Philip's offer, she found her thoughts constantly straying to Robert Dudley. Seated on her chair of estate and constrained by the formality of her presence chamber, she found her eyes wandering in his direction. Her heart now raced when she saw him about the court, and she felt ridiculously disappointed when he did not attend her or seek her out. On the few-and-far-between occasions when he begged leave to make a brief visit to his wife, she was unaccountably consumed with jealousy, and often made a fuss about keeping him at court.

She took to summoning him to her privy chamber on the pretext of discussing some affair of state or other, and when it pleased her she took his advice. Cecil did not like it; he hated Dudley. The fellow was above himself already, and he had no official position to merit his advice being given.

'He is the son and grandson of traitors,' he warned Elizabeth, 'and he is ambitious. Mark me, Madam, he will make trouble for you!'

'Poof,' scorned Elizabeth. 'Think you I know not how to handle him? I have every right to ask my advisers for their opinions. I summon you at night and ask you for yours, William, don't I?'

Cecil gave a sigh of exasperation. 'Madam, by your good grace, I am one of your councillors; Lord Robert is not. The advice I give you is for the good of yourself and your realm, as you enjoined me. Robert Dudley's advice will be for the benefit of Robert Dudley.'

'God's blood, William, allow me some good judgement of my own!' Elizabeth erupted. 'You let your prejudice against Robert colour your perceptions. I assure you, he is very warm to my service.'

'And would be in other ways,' Cecil could not resist adding.

'I know not of what you speak,' she retorted. But she did – and the knowledge that others believed that Robert desired her made her heart glow.

Feria's manner was stiff when Elizabeth next summoned him to her presence. She pretended not to notice.

'There are difficulties with this marriage,' she said briskly. 'King Philip was my sister's husband. That places us within the forbidden degrees of consanguinity.'

'His Majesty anticipates that his Holiness the Pope would be accommodating in that respect,' Feria said smoothly.

Elizabeth had no intention of allowing the Pope to involve himself in English affairs. Even now, Parliament was preparing the legislation that would establish the Protestant Church of England, with herself, and not the Pontiff, as its Supreme Governor. Her realm would never again bend the knee to Rome. For now, though, she must be diplomatic. Who knew whether the forces of Catholic Europe would rise against her?

'My lord Count, you are forgetting that in England, such unions are forbidden,' she pointed out. 'My father, of blessed memory, put away Katherine of Aragon because she had been his brother's wife, and the English Church declared their union to be incestuous and unlawful. Thus it is likely that this marriage would be disputed here, and I would never accept a Papal decree that contravened the word of God. So you see, I could not marry my sister's husband without dishonouring my father's memory.'

Feria clearly did not see, judging by his expression.

'All is not lost,' Elizabeth went on, more kindly. 'You have my promise that I will lay the matter before Parliament. In the meantime, I should like you to assure King Philip that, if I marry at all, I should prefer to take him before all others.' Unbidden, Robert Dudley's face came to mind. She thrust the image aside. *That* could never be.

As she had expected, her councillors were hot against the Spanish marriage.

'How can your Majesty even contemplate it?'

'It was your sister's undoing!'

'Madam, it provoked a rebellion that nearly cost Queen Mary her crown, and yours is by no means secure.' That was Cecil.

Elizabeth did her best to calm them all. 'I will do nothing contrary to England's interests,' she assured them. 'My father and mother were mere English, and not of Spain, as my late sister was. Surely you agree that it would not be politic to turn down King Philip when we need his friendship in the face of French hostility? Let us give Feria cause to hope that he may receive a favourable answer.'

*

When Robert next returned to court after a rare visit to his wife, Elizabeth, come in procession from the Chapel Royal to her presence chamber following Sunday morning service, saw at once that he was downcast.

'What ails you, Robin?' she asked. 'You were not paying attention to the sermon, and that is not like you.'

'It is nothing, Madam,' he replied.

'Nothing does not wear a gloomy frown and a sad countenance,' she said.

'Believe me, Madam, it is nothing,' Robert repeated, a touch irritable.

Elizabeth walked away, chin high, heart sinking. He did not want her any more. His wife had used her wiles on him, no doubt. She wondered, as she had so often wondered before, how things stood between those two. Robert had been spending so much time at court that she had come to believe that Amy meant no more to him than his favourite horse, but maybe she had been wrong. Maybe ambition overcame all other considerations, and his wife understood that he had to be at court in order to seek rewards and preferment, and to perform his official duties. Maybe – God forbid – he loved his wife!

She tried to settle with a book. It was her habit, if she could snatch the time, to spend three hours each day reading about history, and it was one of her great pleasures, but today Herodotus's words merely danced before her eyes, so that she feared she might be coming down with a megrim.

She felt deeply agitated. She had to know what was troubling Robert, she could not leave it. Laying her book down, she summoned a very dubious Kat and bade her accompany her to Lord Robert's lodging. His face when he opened the door was a joy to behold.

'Bess!' he said unthinkingly, his eyes lighting up. 'This is a great honour.'

'Oh, poof,' she retorted. 'I came to have the truth from you. Something is wrong. Kat, wait here while I talk with Lord

Robert.' And she shut the door in Kat's disapproving – and now outraged – face.

Courtier lodgings were always cramped, and although Robert's was one of the best, it was packed with his furniture and gear, leaving little room to move; but there was a fine oak chair and Elizabeth appropriated it, removing the Protestant tract that lay open there and leaving her host to perch on a stool.

'Calvin, I see,' she said. '*Institutes of the Christian Religion.*'

'It is about attaining salvation, and a vindication of those who have died for their faith,' Robert told her.

'I know. I have read it. I do not agree with all his points.'

'No, but they are worthy of debate.'

There was a pause.

'Now,' she said, 'the truth.'

'I fear my wife is very ill,' Robert said, after some hesitation. 'I did not like to trouble you with my personal affairs, seeing that you carry so many burdens of your own.'

'You are my good friend, Robert. Whatever affects you affects me. What ails your wife?'

'A malady in her breast,' he replied. 'There is a lump. It has been getting larger for some time, but now it looks very nasty and is causing her much pain. She has lost weight, and she is terrified lest her sickness is mortal. She cries constantly. I do not know what to say to her.'

Elizabeth had known two women who'd suffered from such an illness, and both of them had died. Could Amy Dudley be dying? God forgive me, she thought, shocked at her inward – and uncharitable – response to Robert's words. I must not exult in my rival's illness. Her rival? She pulled herself up mentally. Had it come to that?

'Has she seen a physician?' she asked.

'She refuses, although I have begged her.'

'Then I will send Dr Huicke to her.'

'Bess, she will not see him. She is too terrified of what any doctor might say. And if this is what she and I both fear it is, then there is no remedy.' He buried his face in his hands.

'I am sorry for you both,' Elizabeth said, and laid her hand gently on his shoulder. The effect was astonishing. Robert looked up; his eyes met hers; and then she was in his arms and he was kissing her hungrily, as if he would devour her. No man had kissed her like that these ten years and more. It felt sublime – as if she had been born for this moment. She wanted it to go on for ever . . . And then her body responded, quite naturally, and, in fright, she drew back.

'Forgive me, Bess,' Robert breathed, startled. 'I presumed too much, but you were so kind – and I was so fraught that I forgot myself . . .'

'There is nothing to forgive,' Elizabeth said, dismayed at the conflict within herself.

Robert's eyes held hers, even as his arms still encircled her. 'I have loved you for so long,' he breathed. 'Ever since that day I saw you in the Tower, when we were both prisoners. But I know I have no right. You are the Queen, and far above me now; and I am married.'

'The one is surmountable, if I will it so; the other is not.' She was horrified to feel a treacherous sense of relief at that.

'I am not in love with Amy,' Robert said. 'I was when we married – she was different then, young and fair and merry – but that was a long time ago. She has not been a proper wife to me for many months. Even so, I care for her, and would never do her any hurt.'

'And yet you just kissed me,' Elizabeth said, her heart exulting even as her body had shied away from the prospect of a greater intimacy.

'I love you,' Robert declared. 'I would be more to you than a friend, but I cannot say that because I am not free.'

'Not free to offer me marriage, is that what you mean? Have you not been listening? I do not wish to marry, Robin, so comfort yourself.'

'I hear you, Bess – but do you wish to love?'

Elizabeth recoiled slightly. 'That would depend on what you mean by love.'

Robert smiled at her. 'You are the Queen. I cannot pay court to you as my mistress, for people would talk. You have your reputation to protect.'

Perversely she now wanted him to pursue her. 'A thousand eyes see all I do,' she protested. 'I am rarely unattended. Scandal could not fasten on me for ever.'

'You are here unattended now. Heaven knows what Mistress Astley is thinking behind that door. Did it not occur to you that it was irregular to come to my chamber like this?'

'I came to console you, as a friend. Had you attempted to ravish me, Kat was within earshot.'

Robert grinned. 'Well I did attempt it, but I did not notice you calling for help.'

'That was because I enjoyed it,' Elizabeth said lightly, suppressing the warring tumult inside her. 'Robin, if I choose to favour you, none can gainsay me.'

'Are you saying I may take you for my chosen lady?' His eyes were full of hope.

'Oh, Robin, you must not say such things to me,' Elizabeth breathed, then belied her words by falling again into his arms, knowing herself safe from any commitment beyond that which she was prepared to give.

A second marriage proposal had come, on behalf of the Archduke Ferdinand, younger son of the Holy Roman Emperor.

'It would be a prestigious match, Madam,' Cecil said hopefully. 'The Emperor might be a Catholic, but he is the most powerful ruler in Europe, and with his backing England would be much more secure, especially against threats from France.'

'France and the Empire are enemies on principle, and ever will be,' Bacon smiled.

'It is an offer worth considering,' Sussex put in. It was the Emperor who ruled Germany, Austria, Hungary, Bohemia, and God knew how many other states. He was uncle and ally to King Philip.

'Do you think my people will approve of my marrying a

Catholic?' Elizabeth asked. 'When Parliament sits, England will turn Protestant. It is never easy to reconcile religious differences. I suppose there is no question of the Archduke changing his faith?'

'The Emperor would never permit it!' Bacon observed.

'His ambassador seems to think that your Majesty will end up being guided by Ferdinand in matters of religion,' Cecil said drily.

'His ambassador may think again!' she retorted.

'A compromise on religion might be reached with the Archduke,' he said, 'but never with King Philip. You do realise, Madam, that the new religious settlement will be a bar to your marrying King Philip and prevent you from maintaining the pretence that you are considering his offer? He will never consent to it when he hears that you have broken with Rome. He is the greatest champion of the old faith in Europe.'

'But we need Philip's good will and friendship,' Elizabeth sighed. 'Before I consider this new proposal, I will see Feria.'

Feria arrived with hope in his eyes, delighted that this infuriatingly contrary Queen had at last come to her senses.

'Alas, my lord Count,' she said, dashing that hope, 'I have to tell you that I cannot marry his Majesty because in his eyes I am a heretic.'

'Madam, Madam, do not distress yourself,' Feria hastened to reassure her. 'I promise you, neither his Majesty nor myself regard you thus. We do not believe you will sanction these bills that are now before Parliament.'

Elizabeth's eyes gleamed. 'Count de Feria, I am a committed Protestant, and I will never change my views.'

Feria's face changed; his tone was lofty. 'Then, I fear, your Majesty is right to see the difficulties. My master will not change his religion for all the kingdoms in the world.'

'Then much less would he do it for a woman!' Elizabeth answered, tart, and ended the interview.

Elizabeth was now in Robert's company every day; often he attended her in his capacity as her Master of Horse, accompanying her when she went riding. At other times he attended her because she wanted him to. She was now openly quoting his opinions on political and religious matters, which left Cecil spluttering with rage. He was appalled to realise that Dudley, who still held no political office (and never would if he, Cecil, had anything to do with it), might grow influential in matters of state, just because he had the Queen's ear. But it pleased Elizabeth to have Robert at her side constantly, and late at night, when she, wakeful as usual, was working and wont to summon her advisers from their beds to give her their opinions, he was called often to her privy chamber. There, her women and footmen dismissed, and she in the unadorned and strangely becoming black gown she liked to wear when she was not on display, they could be alone. Inevitably matters of state led to matters of the heart, and to kissing and fondling – and Elizabeth drawing a halt. She wanted Robert, but she feared having him more. And she dared not – *just dared not* – risk becoming pregnant. She could not go through that again.

Headily involved with him as she now was, for he filled her thoughts and her senses, her wits had not entirely forsaken her. She knew that she was insecure on her throne, and that any scandal could topple her; her enemies were legion, and already, in spite of the phalanx of yeomen of the guard and gentlemen pensioners whose duty it was to protect her, she lived in fear of the assassin's dagger or the poisoned cup. A queen must be above reproach; she knew that, none better. So she and Robin kissed and clung and became entwined, but that was all she would permit. It left them both breathless, and him aching for more.

'Madam,' Kat fretted, 'it is said you are visiting Lord Robert's chamber by day and by night. There is talk.'

'Not since that one time, when you were just outside, and I have done nothing *wrong*,' Elizabeth protested.

'Not according to the gossips,' Kat persisted. 'Madam, he is married. People say you are waiting for his wife to die so that you can wed him.'

'How dare they!' Elizabeth shouted. 'I have no wish to marry any man. I have said it countless times. Why does no one believe me?'

'Because they think it is mere maidenly modesty, Madam.'

'They can't have it both ways – am I a modest maiden or Lord Robert's whore?'

'Madam,' Kat cried in distress, 'I say these things only for your good. You have your reputation to consider. Remember what happened before.'

'How could I forget?' Elizabeth snarled. 'Enough, Kat! Just go. I have papers to deal with.'

She read Philip's letter. It was kindly put, but to the point. He regretted the fact that they could find no common meeting ground, but hoped that, with good friendship, they could maintain their alliance.

She was dumbfounded, therefore, to learn that, with unflattering promptitude, he had announced his marriage to the French King's daughter. Feria, who imparted the news, feared that Elizabeth might fall into a frenzy.

'An alliance with France, our common enemy? He cannot!' she stormed. 'He was negotiating to marry me!'

'But your Majesty turned him down.'

Elizabeth was so angry that she was barely rational. 'He kept me waiting before he proposed. He wasn't even prepared to give me more time to think about it. Obviously he was not as much in love with me as either of us seemed to imagine!'

'In love?' Feria did not remember saying the word. Esteem had been mentioned, and affection, but what had love to do with royal marriages? She was laughing at him, surely – or trying to save face.

'My master understood that your Majesty was unwilling to accept his proposal,' he said. 'He means no slight to you. He will remain as good a brother to you as before, and render you any service in the matter of your marriage.'

'You have mishandled this, Count,' Elizabeth fumed. She

regretted her decisive curtness at Feria's last audience. She had wanted to keep Philip in hope for some time to come. It was Feria's fault that he had taken her at her word, and now Philip was allied to France. She was heartily relieved when Feria was immediately recalled to Spain and replaced with a new ambassador, Bishop de Quadra. Just to be on the safe side, she instructed her ministers to treat for peace with the French.

Elizabeth was enjoying some flirtatious sparring with Robert in her presence chamber when Bishop de Quadra was announced. Robert was leaning down and whispering something naughty in her ear, for which she tapped him playfully with her fan. Her face was flushed as she turned towards the Bishop, whose expression was taut with disapproval. He was a portly man of middle years, urbane and cultivated, she had been told. Wily too, if she was any judge of men, and a gossip, it was already rumoured. He had brought with him a dark-visaged, dapper man whom he introduced as Baron von Breuner, the Imperial envoy. Both men stiffened at the sight of Robert standing so close to the Queen's chair of estate, but the Baron remembered his manners, bowed and presented a letter from the Emperor.

Elizabeth's face did not change as she read it. His Imperial Majesty very much regretted that he could no longer press the suit of his son, Ferdinand. Instead he was offering her his younger son, the Archduke Charles.

She had known that this was coming, known – thanks to Cecil's far-flung spy network – that the Emperor had just found out that Ferdinand had got himself secretly, and unsuitably, married; known too that some of her advisers believed Charles of Habsburg to be malleable and ready to convert to the Protestant faith if she accepted him.

'I thank his Imperial Majesty for deeming me worthy of another of his sons,' she declared. 'However, although my subjects continually exhort me to wed, I have never set my heart upon, nor wished to marry, anyone in the world.' She glimpsed Robert Dudley's studiedly inscrutable face – and then there came into her head, unbidden, another face, almost as dark, and handsome too. Worms' meat now, these ten years . . . Thrusting the horrible thought from her, she smiled. 'But I might be persuaded to change my mind, for I am but human.'

'The Archduke may agree to leave the Catholic Church,' the Bishop said. His smile was strained, for had he not just seen with his own eyes proof that this heretic Queen standing before him was the licentious harlot she was reputed to be?

'Ah, my lord, I would rather be a nun than marry, so it might be for nothing,' she said mischievously. Bishop de Quadra's expression was sceptical, as if he was trying – and failing – to imagine her in a convent, but poor Breuner looked utterly perplexed at this turn of events. He had come bearing a great and honourable proposal, far beyond – in Catholic eyes at least – the merits of one who was a bastard, heretic *and* usurper, and was clearly puzzled as to why Elizabeth had not said yes thrice over, with appropriate enthusiasm, and preferably in an attitude of supplication. She decided to unsettle him further. 'I have heard that the Archduke has an abnormally large head, which rather concerns me.' Breuner squirmed visibly.

'Nay, Madam,' Quadra reassured her. 'He is a most personable gentleman, all that your Majesty could wish for in a husband. His portrait is on its way to you from Vienna.'

'I have had no faith in portrait painters since Holbein misrepresented Anne of Cleves, and misled my father into marrying her,' Elizabeth said dismissively.

'A sad case, Madam, to be sure, but this portrait is very life-like, as the Baron here can attest.'

Elizabeth knew that she had to play for time. While the Emperor was in hope of her as a daughter-in-law, he would not be hostile to a Protestant kingdom. 'Hmm,' she murmured. 'I fear, good sirs, that I can never marry unless it is to a man of worth whom I have seen and spoken to. Maybe the Archduke could come to England? Would the Emperor agree to it?'

Quadra frowned. 'Madam, assuredly he would send him out of love for your Majesty, but not *on approval*, as it were. He would not risk his son being publicly rejected, and thereby humiliated.'

'It *is* an unusual request, Madam,' Breuner protested. Elizabeth was aware of that. It pleased her to make difficulties. They could only prolong negotiations and keep the Emperor sweetly disposed towards her in hope of an alliance.

'He could come in disguise,' she suggested brightly.

'That would be contrary to custom, and his dignity,' Quadra sniffed.

'Madam, I know the Archduke,' said Breuner, who was clearly tiring of this nonsense. 'He will not agree to come until a marriage contract has been signed.'

'Then I must think on the matter,' Elizabeth promised, and dismissed them.

Later, in council, she faced her lords. 'I will take your advice and wed,' she told them, 'but only on condition that I can see and know the man who is to be my husband before accepting any offer of marriage.' That should prolong things indefinitely, she thought, pleased with herself.

'So your Majesty is seriously considering the Archduke?' Cecil asked, brightening.

'No, William. I am *considering*. And I am in no mind to marry at all for the present. God, with Whom all things are possible, might change my mind in the future. I will write to the Emperor myself, explaining the situation, so that he shall not be offended. And I will charm and flatter the Baron, and let him live in hope.'

There now arrived at court a Swedish envoy armed with a marriage proposal from his master, Prince Erik. The desire of men was the breath of life to Elizabeth, even if their approach was through diplomatic channels. It pleased her inordinately to be the object of such speculation; and she loved, and thrived on, being courted. How she was enjoying herself! She was even more thrilled when the Swedish envoy presented her with the ardently hopeful Erik's gifts: gorgeous tapestries, fine ermines

– and his portrait. It was then that her face almost fell. That slack mouth! Those spindly legs! But she praised it loudly, within earshot of Breuner, who was most put out.

Erik, for all his physical deficiencies, was the perfect suitor. Unlike King Philip and the Archduke, he sent her passionate love letters, which she made a point of reading aloud to her courtiers when Breuner was in attendance. Oh, she revelled in teasing the man! The courtiers sniggered, enjoying the pantomime. The Swedish envoy began to look uncomfortable, fearing that he had made himself and his master appear ridiculous.

In council, all frivolity vanished. 'Prince Erik must undertake to forsake his country entirely if I agree to marry him,' Elizabeth insisted, 'because I will not leave mine for any consideration in the world.'

'Madam, he is his father's heir, in line for the throne,' Cecil said.

'Then turn him down,' Elizabeth said. 'King Philip was his father's heir when he married my sister. He was always itching to be off back to Spain. We don't want another such as he.'

'A wise decision, Madam. And all is not lost. We have today received envoys from the Duke of Saxony and the Duke of Holstein, each of whom seeks your Majesty in marriage.'

'We will consider both proposals in good time,' Elizabeth replied, already planning yet another campaign of deferral.

Cecil's sigh was heartfelt.

To Elizabeth's amusement, there were two rival courtiers who were determined that she would choose a husband much closer to home. She found it hard to stop herself from laughing when the middle-aged Earl of Arundel took it upon himself to come a-courting. He was flabby, awkward and unprepossessing, and she had always thought him rather silly. He was at least twenty years older than Elizabeth, a widower with grown daughters, but now here he was, paying his addresses somewhat breathlessly, like any young buck.

'Madam, ye need a good man to assist ye,' he told her. 'Why

bother with yon furriners? A pox on 'em all. What your Majesty needs is a good, stout Englishman to bed with ye.'

Stout was the word, Elizabeth thought. She knew, with mounting dread, what was coming.

'Aye, I'll not beat about the bush, Madam. If ye'll have me, I'll do right by ye. My line goes all the way back to the Norman Conquest, and I am rich, and willing to put all my wealth at your Majesty's disposal. And I can offer ye a goodly palace to lodge in when the fancy takes ye. Ye love Nonsuch, that I know well.'

Offer her Nonsuch? She herself had leased it to Arundel. But no matter. It was all she could do to keep a straight face.

'My lord, I thank you for your offer. I will think on it.' And, hiding her smile behind her fan, she dismissed him.

Then there was the tall, lithe, gallant and handsome Sir William Pickering, who had served Elizabeth faithfully during Queen Mary's time, before he had been forced into exile. On his return she had spent hours closeted with this old, good friend, catching up on news, enjoying the easy pleasures of companionship with such an attractive man, and toying with the idea of a flirtation with him. In gratitude for his loyalty, and the inconvenience he had suffered on her behalf, she had assigned him apartments in the palace. But now she became aware that her courtiers and councillors alike were gossiping about them and fawning over Pickering, who was living in hope, and that Robert was jealous. The black looks he was casting in his rival's direction suggested that he thought hanging, drawing and quartering too good for him.

Pickering had never married, but he had no distinguished ancestry, only his diplomatic skills and his popularity to commend him – and his fine library, which Elizabeth secretly coveted; but these were not nearly enough for her to consider marrying him. She watched in amusement as he swallowed the gossip whole, gave himself airs and graces, appeared at court in increasingly magnificent – and ruinously expensive – suits of clothing, and hosted elaborate dinners over which he presided

like the royalty he desperately desired to be. Elizabeth's attendants told her that bets were being laid in London that Pickering
would soon be king.

Not to be outdone, Arundel also began swaggering – or
rather waddling – around the court in new finery. He gave
costly jewels to the Queen's ladies, begging them to sing his
praises in her ear. He seized every opportunity to belittle and
disparage the ignoble Pickering. He even challenged him to a
duel, but Pickering declined to accept on the insulting grounds
that Arundel was the weaker man. The court held its sides
and rocked with mirth.

Not so Robert Dudley.

'How can you encourage those buffoons?' he complained.

'It pleases me to do so,' Elizabeth replied, enjoying teasing
him.

'Pleases your vanity, you mean, as you have no intention of
accepting either of them.'

'At least they are free to offer me marriage,' she taunted,
popping a sweetmeat into her mouth.

'You said you would never be married, and that it mattered
not that I was.'

'Ah, but I might change my mind!' She laughed gaily. 'Poor
Robin. I am cruel to you. I beg your forgiveness. Do not glower
at me like that, especially as I have a surprise for you. Come
with me.' Helping herself to another sweetmeat, she rose and
led him along the privy gallery to a fine suite of apartments
that she had had furnished especially for him. His jaw dropped
when he saw the gilded friezes, the exquisite tapestries and
the fine furnishings with which they were adorned. There was
nothing lacking here that any prince could desire, but what
was more, a door to her own bedchamber led off them.

Robert stared in wonder. His mind was racing ahead of him.
'Does this mean what I hope it does?' he asked, his voice hoarse.

'It means nothing!' Elizabeth said playfully, and tapped him
with her fan. 'I could not have my sweet Robin cramped in
that evil lodging.'

'And will you leave your door unlocked for him at night?' he ventured, desire rising in his eyes.

'Why would I do that?' she asked lightly. He bent to kiss her, but she moved away.

'All this,' he said, indicating the sumptuous apartment, almost at a loss for words. 'Most people at court would kill to have this favour at your hands. How can I thank you?'

'I will think of a way!' She gave him a frolicsome smile.

Cecil stood before her, his face grave.

'Madam, I must beg of you again, do not encourage Lord Robert. He is a married man, and tongues are wagging.'

'Let them wag,' Elizabeth said. 'I have nothing with which to reproach myself.'

'Madam, I cannot put this strongly enough. Your reputation is at stake here. It is said – forgive me – that Dudley is your lover, that you often visit his rooms alone, and worse.'

'That is a vile calumny!' she seethed. 'I enjoy his company. That is all.'

'Madam, the Spanish ambassador sees Lord Robert as a threat to negotiations for your marriage to the Archduke.'

'William, I am attended at all times by my ladies. I am careful of my honour. Let those who impugn it dare say so to my face! I am relying on you to make the truth plain. Lord Robert is a faithful friend. He has a way with him that I much like. If I see him often, it is because he is my Master of Horse. You cannot deny that he is zealous in the performance of his duties, or that he is marvellously talented when it comes to arranging entertainments and jousts. God's blood, why should I not enjoy the company of such a one?'

'There is no reason, clearly, Madam, so long as it is just friendship, but again, I do urge you to be circumspect,' Cecil enjoined her.

'I assure you, William, that I value my good name as much as my soul. And *I* will be the judge of what is circumspect.'

*

Elizabeth's door remained firmly locked at night, but by day there were plenty of opportunities for seeing Robert – and for flirting and more. They rode out together and hunted whenever possible; in the evenings, they often played chess or gambled at cards or dice.

'You always beat me,' Robert would groan.

'I am the Queen!' Elizabeth laughed. 'Of course I should win. But I gave you a fair fight.'

Sometimes they enjoyed lively debates on religion and philosophy, or danced in the Queen's spacious privy chamber. There was a daring new dance from Italy called *La Volta*, which she could never perform in public because it allowed too much physical contact with a male partner. The dance had been condemned by several shocked preachers as the cause of much debauchery, and even murder, but behind closed doors, with only her ladies and musicians present, it thrilled her to have Robert lift her high in the air, one hand placed firmly on her busk below her breasts, the other on her back, with his muscular thighs supporting hers as she descended.

Always she wanted his touch, his attention, his admiration.

'Do I look well in this gown?' she asked him one day. It was of forest-green velvet, but she thought its bunched skirts made her look fat.

'You would look better without it!' Robert said boldly, winking at her, at which she slapped him.

'Go to!' she sniffed. 'I asked if I looked well *in* it?' She was determined to have an answer.

'Not as well as in other gowns,' he told her.

'That is what I thought,' she said. 'I will have it altered.'

On another occasion she was having her period.

'I feel lousy,' she complained, needing reassurance, 'and I look terrible.'

'You look beautiful to me, Bess,' Robert said, kissing her hand. It was all she needed to hear.

When St George's Day came, she made him a Knight of the Garter, and thrilled to see him looking so tall and splendid in his velvet robes. The other peers selected for the honour – the Duke of Norfolk and the earls of Rutland and Northampton – looked down their disdainful noses as Dudley knelt before the Queen, hauteur in every bone of his body. Were good looks and a fine seat in the saddle all it now took to secure the highest order of knighthood that her Majesty had to bestow?

Elizabeth ignored them. She cared little for their opinions. She gave Robert a fine mansion, the Dairy House, at Kew, and other lands, along with grants of money. She kept him constantly at her side. In the light of these visible signs of her favour, there was frantic speculation that she would marry him. Courtiers came flocking, seeking Robert's patronage, bringing him gifts, hoping he could secure them favours and preferment. He revelled in it all.

'I see you are become very popular,' Elizabeth observed to him one day, as they walked through the grounds of Greenwich Palace towards the bowling alley.

'If I am, it is because you have made me so,' Robert answered. 'I would be nothing without you.'

'You mean much to me, Robin,' she replied, 'but take care. I will not have you rule me.'

'I would never presume to do so,' he said. She sensed that he was riled, and she was right. He could not contain himself. 'But I wish that you esteemed and trusted me sufficiently to give me some high office – maybe a seat on the Privy Council,' he went on.

'Do you not ride high enough as my Master of Horse, Robin? I would have you know that it suits me to keep you where you are, an influential presence at my court and in my counsels. You are my eyes, ever watchful on my behalf. Yes, I like to think that, and I shall call you my Eyes, because you are – and because yours are very fine!'

Robert forced a smile. It was no compensation, she knew, for not being raised to any formal political role. She could not explain that her decision was for his own good. Aware that her nobles thought him an upstart who had got much above himself, she knew it was wiser not to advance him further just yet. But there were other ways in which favour could be shown.

That night, Robert was awoken by his servant.

'What time is it?' he groaned, rubbing sleep from his eyes.

'One o'clock, Sir. The Queen has commanded that you attend her.'

The Queen! Was this yet another late-night summons to discuss some matter of state that was troubling her? Surely it was too late for that. Or – and he hardly dared hope – was she summoning him to her bed at last? He all but leapt to his feet and hastened to dress.

Mistress Astley admitted him to the royal apartments, her face wearing its usual mask of disapproval, and led him to a small panelled closet where Elizabeth sat writing at a table of mother-of-pearl. As he entered and made his courtly bow, she looked up, laid down her quill and smiled.

'Robin, my Eyes! Forgive my late summons. I find I come more clearly to decisions in the middle of the night, and I would have your advice on the proposals of marriage I have received. Thank you, Kat. That will be all.' Kat withdrew with a vicious swish of damask skirts. The door closed reproachfully behind her.

Robert's eyes met Elizabeth's, and they both started laughing.

'She does not like me,' he said.

'She would not approve if Our Lord himself descended from Heaven and began paying court to me,' Elizabeth said. 'Be at peace, Robin. She is like a mother hen protecting her chick. She sees all men as predators.' And had every reason to do so, she realised.

'I trust you tell her that my intentions are honourable,' he said.

'Indeed I do, but I tell her nothing about mine!' she smiled.

'You will pray tell me, though,' he pleaded.

'Not tonight, sweet Robin. We must get down to business,'

Elizabeth said. 'The business of my marriage. Of all my advisers, your opinion is the one I would most appreciate.' There was a faint flush on her cheeks.

'You might not like it, Bess.' Robert took a step closer to her, near enough to catch the faint scent of rose-water and marjoram that she always carried with her.

'Don't tell me, you think I should have accepted Philip!' she countered.

'You think that I, of all people, would advise that, my Queen? No, of course, I see you but jest.' He grinned.

'But what is your advice, dear Eyes?'

Robert bent and pulled her to him, clasping her in his arms. 'That you marry *me*,' he said boldly, staring searchingly into her eyes and seeing there a response that reflected surprise, desire – and something less welcome. Was it a flicker of fear?

Again Elizabeth had the feeling that she was melting into this man who was almost her lover; he was pressed so close to her that she could feel his urgency through the stiffened fabric of their clothing. She had not expected him to be so bold, and the sudden reaction of her heart – and, to her surprise, her body – had left her breathless with need. How easy it should be to give in to it. But she had learned long ago to have mastery over herself, and she knew well that lust could overcome all sense of reason. She must conquer it therefore, and remember why she could never again compromise her honour – especially with a married man.

She kissed Robert gently on the lips, then drew back in his arms – and now it was his turn to look surprised. Oh, he was aptly nicknamed 'Gypsy': his eyes were so dark and beautiful, like deep pools of desire. When she spoke, her voice was hoarse. 'Robin – bonny, sweet Robin – if I meant to wed, and could follow my heart, I would choose you before all others. But it cannot be.'

Robert let her go. His heavy-lidded eyes were now cold with disappointment. Elizabeth felt a constriction in her chest, like her heart breaking.

'You have a wife,' she said.

'She is dying,' he reminded her.

'But she yet lives, and until you are free, there can be no talk of marriage between us.'

'But if I were free, then you would consider it?'

'There would still be difficulties, Robin.'

'We can overcome them, Bess. What you need is a strong man to support you, a firm Protestant, one who is unfettered by foreign ties, and who is devoted to your interests. One who truly loves you. I am that man. Can you not see it? Which of those foreign princes you dangle like puppets can offer you all those things?'

'Do you truly love me, Robin?' Elizabeth asked, sidestepping the question.

'With all my heart,' he replied, holding her gaze. 'Did you need to ask?'

'Nay, but I wanted to hear you say it!' she laughed. 'As well as all the other things.'

He pulled her into his arms again. 'I love you, Bess. I am *in* love with you.'

'With me or my crown?' she teased.

'Oh, with your crown, most definitely!' he riposted, then his face grew solemn. 'Now it is your turn.'

'Ah, sweet Robin, how could you doubt it? I love you as I have loved no man.'

'Even there you are ambiguous!' he protested. 'For all I know, you have loved no man!'

A shadow crossed Elizabeth's face. She disengaged herself and sank down into her chair. He had inveigled her into a corner, and now she had no choice but to tell him the truth. She realised that she owed it to him.

'There was someone once,' she said. 'I was very young. Surely you have heard talk of it. He was my stepfather.'

'Thomas Seymour, the Lord Admiral,' Robert said. 'I too was young when I heard the rumours. I gave them no credence.'

'For that I thank you,' she replied. 'It was a terrible time.

He was a turbulent, dangerous man, and I was an innocent girl of fourteen. He took advantage of my naïvety.' She had been utterly infatuated with the handsome charmer, a rogue if ever there was one. She knew that now, but she had not had the wit to know it then. And he, Seymour, the new husband of her stepmother, Katherine Parr, had thought she was her mother's daughter and ripe for the plucking.

'What do you mean?' Robert asked, a trifle sharply.

'He would come to my room before I was up and tickle and slap me as I lay abed. Kat complained of it to Queen Katherine, but she made little of it. She had married the Admiral within weeks of my father's death. She threw propriety to the winds, for she was in love with him and blind to his failings. But her eyes were opened when she came upon us one day. I was in his arms and we were' – she paused – 'kissing. My innocence had been no proof against his determination. And she was so horrified, poor Queen Katherine, that she sent me away, for my own protection, as she told me. Then she died in childbirth. I have felt guilty ever since.' Of the disarray in which Katherine had found the pair of them, and the awareness that, had she burst in only moments later, matters would have advanced to a shameful conclusion, Elizabeth could not speak, even to her Eyes.

'But you were a child,' Robert said gently, kneeling by Elizabeth's chair and taking her hand. 'The Admiral took advantage of you. That was doubly wicked of him, for you were a princess also.' He was wondering how significant that pause had been, when she had told him about the Queen coming upon them.

'Aye, and it was high treason to marry me, let alone try to seduce me. I knew that. So did he – or he should have done. Later, as you remember, when he attempted to seize power from his brother, the Lord Protector, he was arrested. My servants were put in the Tower and I was interrogated. They tried to make me confess that I had agreed to marry him without the permission of my brother, King Edward. They were brutal and spared me nothing. They even locked up poor Kat in a dark cell. It went on for days, the questioning. But I had nothing to confess. In the end, they let me alone. By then, though, there was much gossip about me. The things people were saying! It horrified me, and I did not know what I could do to stop it. That was when I began wearing plain colours and sober attire, as became a virtuous Protestant girl, so that all who saw me would think that I could not possibly have stooped so low. I was fifteen then, and on the day the Admiral went to the block my interrogators were watching me, eager to see me betray by some sign or weakness that I had loved him.'

'And did you?'

'No.' Elizabeth shivered. 'I gave nothing away. It was ten years ago, but I can still feel the horror and fear I felt at the time.'

Robert put his arm around her shoulders and squeezed her tightly. 'My poor, poor Bess. I had no idea that the Admiral treated you so dishonourably, and you an innocent. I hope he did not take advantage of you.'

'Did he seduce me, you mean?'

'Aye, that too.' He was watching her closely. 'Your silence tells me all,' he said at length.

'I told you nothing,' Elizabeth retorted.

'You did not need to.'

'Oh, Robin, I cannot speak of it!' She was agitated now. She had revealed too much already. 'I was just fifteen!'

He kissed her then, long and deeply, his fingers tenderly tracing her back, then burrowing into her neck as he tilted her head to accommodate him. 'Tell me,' he said after he had let her go. 'I love you. You can trust me. Do you think it matters to me what happened ten years ago, apart from the fact that it distresses you still?'

Elizabeth relaxed. She took a deep breath. 'It happened once. That was all.'

'Did he force you?'

'Nay, but I did not intend that things should go so far. Before I knew it, they had.'

'And what was so terrible about it?'

'Nothing – at the time. It was only later, after he had died. Robert, I cannot explain. It felt as if a corpse had made love to me. In memory, the act became repulsive, horrible. And I thought that this must have been how my father felt after my mother was beheaded, and Katherine Howard. That someone you have held in your arms and known intimately is now a thing of horror.' She shuddered at the thought.

But this was not the only reason why she shrank from intimacy. She had heard, horrified, how her beloved stepmother Katherine Parr had suffered in childbed. She had been safely delivered, and yet she'd died. The same thing had happened to an earlier stepmother, Jane Seymour, to Elizabeth's grand-mother, Queen Elizabeth of York; and to several noble ladies she had known. She could not bring herself to tell Robert how much she feared it happening to her; the fear went too deep. Even if she found the courage to conquer it, she knew that giving herself to a man could lay her kingdom open to the loss of its Queen, with civil war likely to follow.

'*This* is why I do not wish to marry, why I play what Cecil is now calling "the marriage game",' she said aloud.

Robert had listened patiently, holding her close as she poured out her fears. Now he was quiet for a space. 'In time your fears may subside,' he said at last. 'I will not press you, I promise. There are other ways of giving and receiving pleasure. Let me help you. Let me show you how to relax.' He bent his lips to hers again, his hand straying up her stiff stomacher to the breast beneath. She tensed, and gently pushed it away.

'Give me time,' she murmured, hating herself for denying him.

Lying in bed wakeful that night, she regretted having said so much to Robert. She felt exposed, and somehow belittled by his knowing her closest secrets. Thank God she had not told him all.

She asked herself what she did want of him. His body, yes, so long as it should not possess her own. His hand in marriage – no. She might be jealous of his wife, but she liked the fact that he was safely married. She could enjoy his company, and more, without having to lose her independence or commit herself to him in any way. But what if Amy did die? Robert was not a man to take no for an answer. For him, it was all so straightforward. As he saw it, she had fears, he would conquer them. For Elizabeth, nothing had ever been that simple.

Without marriage, she was woefully aware, he was vulnerable, his position equivocal. He knew, as well as she, that the wolves at court were waiting to pounce and devour him. She, the Queen, was all that stood between them.

Why could she not be as other women? She loved to flirt, she loved the attentions of men. What was wrong with her then? Why could she not forget the horrors that had touched her life in childhood? Were they truly at the root of her fears? If that were so, she thought, with a sense of desperation, there was probably no hope of her ever overcoming them. They were rooted too deep.

She would not think about it any more. It was too distressing, dwelling on what she could not change. As sleep was eluding her, she fell to wondering if her mother had loved her father. God knew, he had pursued her passionately, by all accounts. He had even broken with the Church of Rome to have her. So how then – and Elizabeth had asked herself this many times before – could he have signed her death warrant and sent her to the scaffold? It could only have been because he was tricked into it by her enemies. That was what Kat and others had told her. Her father and her mother had been betrayed; both had been the victims of an evil plot.

It still grieved her that she could not clear her mother's name. Surely, if evidence could be found to show that Anne had not been guilty of adultery, incest and treason, she could now move her councillors to agree to the reversal of the judgement against her.

Then, as the first light of dawn was breaking over the silent palace, it came to her what she must do.

In the morning, as was her custom, she said her prayers, kneeling on the padded stool in her closet, surrounded by rich hangings of cloth of gold. Then, removing into her study, which was draped in similar splendour, she sent for Robert. Her manner was brisk and authoritative; there was no trace of the vulnerable Elizabeth who had unburdened her shameful secrets in the dark watches of the night.

'Robert, my Eyes, I have an important errand for you that I do not wish to entrust to anyone else,' she told him. He looked grateful for that, having at first appeared nonplussed at the change in her. 'I wish you to go to the Tower,' she went on, 'to the Records Tower, where they keep the documents relating to state trials. I want you to bring me the papers relating to Queen Anne, my mother.'

Robert frowned. 'Is this wise, Bess?' he asked. 'The charges against her and the witness depositions may distress you. Besides, your councillors have advised against raking them up, and with good cause.'

'Robert, if you had the opportunity of clearing your father's name, would you do it?'

'Of course. But I know I could not. His crimes were too public. None could deny that he did his best to overthrow Queen Mary.'

'No, and so *my* hands are tied,' Elizabeth said. 'I am sorry for it. But my mother's so-called crimes would of necessity have been committed in secret, and I have heard there was doubt about them at the time. I want to see what proofs were offered. I owe it to her memory to seek out the truth, if only for my own satisfaction and peace of mind.'

'Then I will go at once,' Robert capitulated. 'But don't say I didn't warn you.'

'Thank you, my Eyes,' Elizabeth smiled. 'Before you go, I thought I should tell you that I am turning down the Archduke

Charles. I will write to the Emperor to tell him that I prefer to remain single. If you see me being especially nice to Baron Breuner, it is only to sweeten the pill.'

And to lead the poor man on into thinking you may change your mind, thought Robin as he bowed himself out and went in search of a horse.

When he had gone, Elizabeth summoned Kat, and the two of them went walking in the gardens, the Queen striding ahead to keep out of earshot of the ladies trailing them at a discreet distance.

'Kat, my father courted my mother for many years before they could wed,' she began. 'I have often wondered how she kept his interest keen while fending him off – for that is what she did, surely?'

Kat gave her a speculative look. 'To what tends this, Bess?' she asked. 'Are you looking for advice on how to keep Lord Robert interested? It strikes me you don't need it!'

'Kat, you presume too much!' Elizabeth exclaimed, flushing.

'Aye, but you want frankness when it suits you, Bess.' Kat frowned. 'If I speak out of turn it is only for your good, my sweeting. No one else would dare to do so, so please take it in good part. And *please* be careful where Lord Robert is concerned.'

Elizabeth was on the verge of taking umbrage, but thought better of it. She slipped her arm through Kat's. 'It is I who should be begging your pardon, old friend,' she said. 'I know you mean well. But I would like to hear about my mother. It strikes me that I could take a page out of her book in the playing of this marriage game, and I am not talking about Robert Dudley.'

Mollified, Kat's face broke out in a broad grin. 'Well, most people believe that she held your father at bay for all those years, but it wasn't quite like that. A lady who had served her told me that she had done so at first, when he was bent on making her his mistress, but then he decided to marry her, and it was he who resolved to lay siege to her no more. The truth was, he could not have risked a scandal.'

'That makes sense,' Elizabeth observed. 'But how did they keep that flame between them burning?'

'Who knows what happens between a man and a woman in private?'

'Mayhap the very fact of holding off fed it,' Elizabeth suggested hopefully.

Kat gave her a curious look. So that's how it is, she thought.

Robert laid the bundle of yellowing papers before the Queen.

'These are from the Bag of Secrets, as they call it,' he said. 'It is the place where they keep all the documents relating to treason trials. The Records Tower is in much disorder, but they knew where to find these.'

'Thank you, my Eyes,' Elizabeth said, and waited. This was something she must do alone. Robert raised his eyebrows, read her mood, bowed and left.

She untied the tape. There were not as many papers as she had anticipated. Steeling herself, she opened out the top one. It was the indictment against her mother. She read it, knowing what to expect, but horrified all the same. Charge after charge of adultery with different men, and of incest with her own brother. How her mother had seduced him with her tongue in his mouth. How could they have known that? And then the charge of plotting the King's death. As if her mother, who had not – it had to be acknowledged – been popular, would have contemplated killing the only man with the power to protect her from her enemies! But it was all there, in revolting detail, and it would have been laughable had it not had such tragic consequences. Cromwell had gone to a lot of trouble to make a case against her mother and blacken her character.

She drew out the next document. It was the findings of the grand jury of Kent, who had decided – unanimously – that there was a case against Queen Anne. A similar document detailed the same findings from the grand jury of Middlesex.

Next she found a list of the peers who had given judgement at the trial. Among them was her grandfather, the Earl of Wiltshire. The verdict had again been unanimous. He had condemned his own daughter.

There was little else. No witness depositions, no summary of the evidence. Nothing to prove her mother guilty – or innocent.

She felt her anger and frustration mounting. There must have been *something*. The blood of a queen could not have been shed without good cause. Surely her father had been shown sufficient evidence to convince him that Anne should be committed to the Tower and beheaded? There *must* have been statements on which the charges were based, proof enough to persuade both those grand juries and the peers at the trial. Unless all the evidence had been lost – or destroyed.

She did not want to think that there had been deliberate destruction – that those dreadful charges had been based on lies, and that her father had colluded with his advisers in a shocking miscarriage of justice. Yet – and she had to face it – the evidence could have been so scandalous that it had been thought best to erase it from the records, as disparaging to the King's honour.

She summoned Kat Astley, and laid the papers before her.

'Kat, you told me years ago that my mother was innocent. But there are no proofs here either way.'

'Bless me, Bess, why are you raking this up now?' Kat was shaking her head as her eyes scanned the documents. 'Why do you question what I told you? Your mother was innocent.'

'But how do you know? And how can I prove it?'

'Some of the charges were clearly false. There was talk about it – furtive, of course – and some said that they were just an occasion to get rid of her. She was supposed to have committed adultery when she was barely out of childbed, which is the last thing a woman who has just been delivered wants to think about; but of course, it was a man who dreamed this up, and he was in a hurry. If Cromwell hadn't brought her down, she'd have done the same to him – or so it was whispered. I also heard that she had not been where they said she was when some of the acts were committed. What's more, no woman was accused with her. She could not have had all those lovers in secret without the help of at least one of her ladies. She was a proud woman, too clever to risk that kind of exposure.'

Elizabeth had tears in her eyes. 'Thank you, Kat, for setting my mind at rest on that score,' she breathed. 'And my father? Did he collude in bringing her down?'

'It was Thomas Cromwell, first and foremost. Katherine Parr, God rest her soul, once told me that she had spoken with Chapuys, the Spanish ambassador. He told her that Cromwell had admitted to him, face to face, that he had thought up and plotted the affair of Queen Anne. Cromwell feared your mother. He was a clever man, a very devil. He could have persuaded the King that black was white. Whatever proofs he showed your father would have been convincing ones, you may be sure of that. And if they are missing now, well, he probably anticipated that someone in the future would spot the flaws.'

Elizabeth was suffused with relief – and other, mixed, emotions. Her mother was clear of all the charges, she knew it for certain now, but it grieved her that she would never be able to prove it. And Anne, God rest her, had died in vain, innocent of the crimes of which she was accused. How must it have felt, knowing you were to suffer a terrible death for something you had not done?

Now her tears did flow as she sat staring at the blur of those fatal papers on her desk, and Kat, relapsing into her old way, drew her to her bosom and soothed her.

Seated beneath her gorgeous canopy of estate in the presence chamber, with the River Thames flowing majestically past beyond the impressive expanse of latticed windows to her left, and a warm summer breeze caressing her from the open window, Elizabeth laughed as Robert bent forward and murmured something outrageous in her ear. They were openly warm together now, much to the delight of the gossips at court – and the fury of Cecil. But Elizabeth cared nothing for that. Let Cecil stew. She was too busy enjoying Robert's courtship; it was the breath of life to her, a glorious game in which she had the mastery and this magnificent man was her supplicant. Of course there was more to it than that, but for the present she would think only of each precious moment and the thrill it brought. The future could take care of itself.

Her face changed when she saw a man in black being ushered into her presence chamber. She straightened in her throne as he approached and bowed low. What now?

'Your Majesty,' he said, with an elegant French accent, 'I bring heavy news. My master, King Henri, is dead. He was terribly injured in a tournament when a lance pierced his eye, and the doctors could not save him, for all our prayers.'

'God rest his soul,' Elizabeth said piously, appalled to hear of Henri's terrible end, but relieved that the lecherous, aggravating man would challenge her title no more. 'His sufferings must have been dreadful. I will write without delay to Queen Catherine to condole with her in her sad loss.' By all accounts Henri had been constantly unfaithful while his dowdy, dumpy Italian wife was continually pregnant. No doubt she was relishing her widowhood.

'I thank your Majesty.' The ambassador bowed again. 'I am come also to announce the accession of the most Christian King, Francis II.' A sickly, spotty, sullen teenager, Elizabeth had heard, who was too young and feeble as yet to exercise sovereign power. Catherine de' Medici would be seizing her advantage, make no bones about it!

'We shall write also to congratulate his Majesty on his accession,' she said graciously.

That afternoon, in council, she was less composed.

'The Queen of Scots is now queen of France also,' she fumed, 'and would be queen of England if she had her way. No, you needn't remind me, my lords, I know that the Catholics think she should be. But King Henri, though he proclaimed her thus, was ever a realist; *he* would not break the terms of the peace treaty. Queen Catherine is more of a threat. She has no love for me, and she is the power now at the French court. If she allies with the powerful Guises, Mary's uncles, they may do their best to overthrow me.'

'That is not the only danger,' Cecil continued. 'Mary's mother, as regent in Scotland, is aware that the Protestant lords there detest her because she is a Catholic. Naturally we support them in their desire to rule Scotland themselves and overthrow the old religion. But what if these two queens of Scotland and France unite against us with the aim of placing Mary on our throne, which they may very well do? That would make England a satellite of France and put paid to the ambitions of the Protestants in Scotland.'

'The answer is to make mischief for the French,' Elizabeth declared, thinking fast. 'And for me to take a husband who will give their King some trouble!'

Twenty pairs of male eyes turned on her in astonishment. Cecil sat up eagerly, like a dog waiting to be given a juicy bone.

'Does your Majesty have someone in mind?' he asked, not quite concealing the fervency behind his question.

'A Scotsman, the Earl of Arran,' Elizabeth said. 'He is Queen Mary's heir until she bears a child, and he is a Protestant. His name has been mentioned before as a possible suitor, and there can be no doubt that the Scottish lords who rule there would favour the match. We are all upholders of the true religion, and a marriage between Arran and me would unite England and Scotland as never before.'

'And if anything should befall the Queen of Scots, *which God forbid*,' Cecil said, struggling to keep his face impassive, 'then your Majesty would succeed to the throne of Scotland.'

'Exactly,' Elizabeth beamed. 'We are one in spirit, William. And with my backing, the Scottish lords could triumph over the Queen Regent. I have been told again and again that Queen Mary is content to leave others to govern her kingdom for her. She has been in France since childhood and has been raised to be its Queen. I hear she likes fine clothing and music; she will play her part gracefully.'

'I agree, Madam. A ruler she is not,' Bacon said. 'She can have hardly any memory of Scotland. A barbaric land, I have heard, and not to be compared with France, where she has grown up.'

'What she wants is to be queen of England,' Cecil said. 'That is her chief aim in life, by all accounts. Scotland seems not to be important to her.'

'Indeed, my Spirit,' Elizabeth agreed, smiling at her new name for Cecil. 'But we will show her that my crown is not hers for the taking. I will invite Arran to England.'

She knew that Robert would react like a child deprived of a treat. She must make him realise that this projected marriage was but an arrow to pierce the heart of her enemies. But she would enjoy flirting with Arran, if only to spite her empty-headed rival, Queen Mary.

A clerk entered the room and passed Elizabeth a letter. She read it and smiled, for more flirting was now in order. 'I should tell you, my lords, that Prince Erik of Sweden will not take no for an answer. He is coming in person to woo me!'

'That will put the cat inside the dovecote,' Sussex observed.

'He is a Protestant, and therefore a most welcome suitor,' Elizabeth said, thinking that Robert would now be even more jealous. 'I look forward to raising his hopes.' (If nothing else, she added to herself.) 'But what we really need is an alliance with the Emperor and King Philip against the French. My lords, I will charm Arran to keep the Scots sweet and unsettle the Italian woman in France, and I will play the adoring virgin with the Swede, but first I intend to see Baron Breuner and tell him that I am reconsidering my decision about marriage with the Archduke Charles.'

*

Elizabeth hunted, banqueted and danced her way through her first summer progress, an extended journey through her kingdom during which she could see and be seen by her subjects, and save money by accommodating herself and her court in the houses of her nobles and foremost citizens. During the months of July and August she was in high spirits as her great procession made its unwieldy way along the road from Eltham Palace to Dartford, Cobham and Nonsuch, and the people came flocking to greet her, calling out blessings upon her and bringing humble, touching gifts.

Her Master of Horse, Lord Robert, rode right behind her, and sometimes alongside, much to the ill-concealed chagrin of Cecil and the other councillors. Robert was with the Queen almost constantly, or never very far from her side – rather as if he were king already. He appeared in ever more lavish and dashing suits of clothing, dripping with jewels and puffed up as a turkey cock, his patrician nose held high with pride. Elizabeth could barely draw her gaze away from him. He was a prince among men, bold, comely and exciting. She thought of the Admiral less and less these days; that hurt seemed to be healing fast. She was in love with Robin – and she cared not who knew it. If she wanted to hold hands with him under the table, or caress his cheek, or steal a kiss, it was no one's affair but her own. She was the Queen, and none had the power to gainsay her.

At night, she would often summon him to her closet, or even her bedchamber if her temporary lodgings were less spacious. On these occasions she would close the door firmly on her women, telling them she had state secrets to discuss. Then she and Robert would fall upon each other – and state secrets be damned! Usually they ended up on her bed, tangled in a hot and heady embrace and lost to the world.

By and by Elizabeth had permitted what Kat would assuredly have called liberties. She had let Robert touch her breasts – which appeared to send him delirious – or her long, slender legs, his eager fingers caressing her over the new-fangled silk stockings she loved to wear. She even – sometimes – allowed him to guide her hand where he wanted it, but only over his codpiece; further she would not go. It was all exciting and wondrous, and the very secrecy surrounding it added spice – indeed, all the flavours of the Orient – to their loving. She enjoyed nothing more than watching Robin lose control. It pleased – and aroused – her to be in command of a man in that way.

'You are killing me,' he groaned one especially impassioned night, as he rolled on his back, panting as if he was *in extremis*. Moonlight streamed through the open lattice window, illuminating his noble profile. 'Why can I not have you?'

'You know very well,' Elizabeth teased, propping herself up on one elbow and planting delicate kisses on his cheek.

'Listen to me, Bess!' he growled, grasping her hand. 'I would be your husband. You have nothing to fear from me. You must see that.'

'Only scandal, as you have a wife,' she said, tart.

'But it will not be for long, and then I will be free.'

Elizabeth was suddenly chilled. 'Can you so easily contemplate the death of someone you once loved?' she whispered.

'No – of course not. I may not love Amy as I did, but I feel sorry for her. I do not wish her dead. Seeing her so ill and frightened is a torment to me, for I cannot help her. But a man must have some comfort in his life. I never loved Amy as I love you, Bess. We are two of a kind, you and I, and there will come a day when I am free to wed again.'

'I cannot be seen to be contemplating marriage with a married man.'

'Then give me cause to hope.'

Elizabeth was silent.

'At least give me some high office of state,' Robert urged once again. 'Your councillors hate me. They are envious and resentful. The court is full of talk about my being descended from traitors fleshed in conspiracy – I, who am utterly loyal, as *you* well know. Cecil is working hard to marry you to the Archduke, but mainly to spite me.'

Elizabeth flared. 'Robin, are you never satisfied? You control a great network of patronage. If people want to see me, they approach you – and I know it is at a price. Cecil tells me you do everything in your power to sabotage or undermine any marriage negotiations.'

'Do you blame me?' Robert smouldered. 'I loathe the idea of your marrying a Catholic, as should all true Englishmen! And if you take one of those pretty princes, I am finished.'

'But I have not said I will take one of them.'

'Nor have you said you will have me! Bess, you *love* me. You have said it, many times. You want me – despite what you say. And you need me.'

'I need no man!' Elizabeth retorted angrily, getting up and smoothing down her gown. 'And right now I need to sleep. *Alone*. Good night, Robin!'

At Nonsuch, an exquisite fantasy of a hunting box built by Elizabeth's father in the Italian style, Arundel welcomed his Queen with a flourish. The tapestries and furnishings she had insisted on having brought over from Hampton Court were already in place in the sumptuous rooms he had made ready for her, and he laid on a banquet with so many courses that it was three in the morning before she departed, yawning, to bed. There were masques, dances and hunts for her pleasure, and, prominent in every one, Arundel himself, pompous, dazzling and ridiculous in his expensive finery, paying her clumsy compliments and making excruciating declarations of his love. Elizabeth bore it all with good humour, but she reckoned that the magnificent set of silver plate he gave her as a farewell had been dearly bought.

Evidently Pickering, strutting before her at every opportunity, thought so too, for he now seized every opportunity of disparaging Arundel, while paying Elizabeth the most extravagant attentions. Elizabeth caught Robert watching them, his face like thunder. She smiled at him sweetly as she sailed past on Pickering's arm.

But there was Kat, darkly disapproving. So far Elizabeth had managed to avoid any confrontations with her – she was the Queen, after all, and above admonition now, surely – but one morning, as she was about to leave her bedchamber, she was astonished to see her old nurse fall creakily to her knees before her.

'Madam, my sweet Bess, I implore you in God's name to marry and put an end to these distressing rumours about you and Lord Robert,' the old woman pleaded, and there could be no doubting her sincerity. 'I must tell you, in your own interests, that your behaviour has occasioned much evil talk.'

Elizabeth's eyes flashed. She would not brook such presumption, even from one who was dear to her. 'If I have showed myself gracious to Lord Robert, he has deserved it for his honourable nature and dealings. It is beyond me how anyone – you especially – could object to our friendship. I am always surrounded by my ladies . . .' She faltered as she saw her old nurse pursing her lips.

'But you are not,' Kat challenged gently.

'They are within earshot,' Elizabeth insisted, flushing, for she would have it her way, 'and it would be obvious to them, and indeed to all, if there was ever anything dishonourable going on between us. But let me tell you this, Kat.' She was really cross now. 'If I had ever had the will or inclination, or had found pleasure in a dishonourable life, I do not know of anyone who could forbid me, even you. But I trust in God that no one will ever see me stoop so low.'

Kat's distress was painfully evident. She wrung her hands, almost weeping. 'But the rumours are so damaging to you, Bess. If I speak out of turn it is only because of the love I bear you. You surely do not want to alienate your people, after making such a good beginning and receiving such demonstrations of their affection. There are factions forming here at court: those who hope for much by supporting Lord Robert; and those who work against him. Will you see your court, and mayhap your kingdom, so much divided?'

Elizabeth shrugged, barely containing her impatience. 'I commend you for your devotion, Kat. As for marrying, I cannot take a husband without weighing all the advantages and disadvantages. I would be a fool otherwise!'

'In that case, should you not distance yourself from Lord Robert, and give these negotiations a chance to flourish?'

'Kat, you are bold to speak thus, and you are not my mother to say me yea or nay,' Elizabeth burst out, finding to her horror that she was near to tears. Mentioning her mother had made her think how wonderful it would be if Anne was alive and able to counsel and comfort her; and the thought of distancing herself from Robin had all but finished her. He was her joy, her comfort, her one fixed point in a maelstrom of shifting alliances. 'Oh Kat, dear Kat, that was unfair. You have been as a mother to me, and seen me through my darkest hours. Just understand that I need to see Robin constantly, because in this world I have so much sorrow and tribulation, and so little joy.'

'Hush, my lamb,' Kat soothed, rising and hastening to embrace her. 'Forgive me if I spoke out of turn. What is all this sorrow and tribulation you speak of?'

Elizabeth shuddered. There were times — and this was one of them — when she felt overwhelmed and isolated. She burst out, 'Alas, to be a king and wear a crown is more glorious to them that see it than it is a pleasure to them that bear it! My enemies are many, and some wear a smiling face. I feel so insecure, so alone sometimes. My crown is a burden as well as an honour. I know there are many who would topple me if they could, and many who would rule me. That is one reason why I dare not marry, why I deny myself the solace of marriage. I am not as other women. I am the Queen. I intend to remain the Queen.' The outburst had been cathartic. She was composed now, sure again in her chosen course, aware that only in moments of weakness did she waver and begin to believe there might be another way.

'Just be careful, sweeting,' Kat urged. 'Only yesterday Baron Breuner was quizzing your ladies as to how often you were alone with Lord Robert. Of course they swore by all that is holy that you have never been forgetful of your honour, but it is clear that the Baron sees Lord Robert as a threat to the Archduke's chances of success. And you and I, Bess, know well how many times you have been private with him.'

Elizabeth met her eyes. 'As I have been closeted with Cecil, with Bacon, with Sussex and others, yet no one accuses me of dalliance with them.' She giggled at the thought of solemn, virtuously married Cecil rolling on the bed with her. 'You need not worry about Baron Breuner, Kat. He has already raised the matter of Lord Robert with me; he asked me outright if I loved him. I told him I was so beset with my royal duties that I had not had time to think of love.'

In fact, she reflected after Kat had gone, reassured, into the outer chamber, she had of late thought of little else.

Word came that Prince Erik had set off for England, all afire to woo the Queen, but had been driven back to Sweden by storms.

'God is protecting me,' Elizabeth declared thankfully to her council. 'He does not intend for me to marry.'

Cecil bridled. 'Madam, my head is spinning from counting your suitors. Might I venture to suggest that you think of the needs of your kingdom and choose one of them?'

'God has given me a sign, good Spirit,' Elizabeth said loftily. 'And never fear, I always look to the needs of my kingdom, unfailingly.'

Erik appeared undaunted by God's disapproval. He put to sea again, only to be embroiled in a terrible storm that saw him once more washed up, battered but not defeated, on his native shore. Soon afterwards a letter came from him for Elizabeth, having bested its scribe and crossed the waves. It made her mouth twitch.

'Prince Erik writes that, although cruel Fortune has prevented him from coming by sea to claim me, he intends at the first opportunity to hasten through armies of foes to be by my side, as he is bound by an eternal love towards me.' She looked up at her councillors. 'It seems, though, that matters of state are more of an obstacle than armies of foes. He cannot come just now, so he is sending his brother here in the hope of obtaining a favourable answer.'

Just hours later Cecil came to inform Elizabeth that the Earl of Arran had arrived secretly in London. 'I have privily lodged him in my house at Westminster,' he said. 'We cannot have him getting caught up in the crush of suitors and hopeful ambassadors at court. That would never do, when you are supposed to be entertaining him only.' It was true, Elizabeth thought, things were getting rather crowded at court. She might start a harem, like the Sultan!

Two days later Arran was brought privately to see the Queen. She saw before her a mild-faced man of no special beauty and a somewhat awkward manner. It was hard to believe that the French regarded this vacuous specimen as a threat to Queen Mary, and certainly he was no great catch for the Queen of England. Even so, she would keep him dangling, for there was much she wanted of him.

They talked – if it could be described thus – of the threats from Scotland and France. Arran was only half listening. He seemed to be intrigued by a bee that was buzzing at the window.

'My lord,' Elizabeth tried again, 'it is not just a threat to England. It is a threat to Protestants everywhere, and we must deal with it.'

Buzz, buzz. Arran started and nodded. 'I am at your lady-ship's disposal,' he said. *Your ladyship?* She bristled but let it go.

'I want you to return to Scotland and lead the Protestant lords against the rule of the Queen Regent,' she told him, hoping to focus his attention. 'They are eager for your coming. Together we can overthrow the Catholics in Scotland and trounce their alliance with the French. I have arranged for Thomas Randolph, our agent, to accompany you.' That was as well, for the Earl might not find his way out of London otherwise.

Arran bent and kissed her hand.

'Madam, about my proposal,' he began, as if he had not heard a word of what she had said.

'We will talk about it later,' said Elizabeth firmly, but with a dazzling smile. The poor fool was not quite right in the head. She would get Randolph to pinion him in a corner and explain in words of one syllable what she wanted him to do, then she would pray that Arran's concentration span was sufficient for him to understand and actually put the plan into action; but she did not hold out much hope of that. Marry him she would not. Five minutes in his company had been enough to convince her of that.

'You are out of tune!' Elizabeth complained.

'No, it is your ears that are out of tune!' Robert countered.

She snatched the gittern from him and began strumming a melody on it, admiring the fine carving on its wooden panel and the elegantly fashioned sound holes. It sounded divine. Robert admitted defeat; like all her family, she had a gift for music.

'Bravo!' he applauded. They were sitting close together on a window seat in the gallery of Windsor Castle, replete after a good day's hunting in the August sunshine and a hearty repast in the banqueting pavilion. Everyone else was keeping a discreet distance.

Elizabeth struck up a merry *coranto*, but suddenly stopped, aware that Cecil was approaching, a sober presence amid the peacock colours of her courtiers.

'Madam, I must speak with you,' he said, with the briefest of nods at Robert.

'Is it urgent, William?' she asked testily.

'I think so, Madam.'

'Very well.' She rose and preceded him towards the deserted council chamber. 'Well, my Spirit?'

Cecil cleared his throat. 'Madam, I *must* speak. These rumours about you and Lord Robert have gone too far. I received this report today. It is being said around the court that you are with child by him.' He handed her a paper.

Elizabeth burst out laughing. 'William, this is a nonsense and you know it! You also know I mean to die a maid.'

'I know only what your Majesty tells me,' Cecil said stiffly, 'and that you have a habit of frequently changing your mind. Madam, I beg of you, use more discretion in your dealings with Lord Robert. There are no fewer than twelve envoys now at court, all urgently pressing the suits of their hopeful masters. You are in a strong position. The princes of Europe are queuing up for your hand, and while they live in hope, they remain friendly towards us. But how they will actually fare, God knows, and certainly not I.'

'You know my mind, William. Keep them waiting, keep them sweet.'

'Madam, their heads are spinning as fast as mine is. One day you are for the Archduke, the next you affect to be indifferent to his proposal. It is the same with all your suitors, even those fools Arundel and Pickering.'

'I have turned them both down,' Elizabeth said. 'I could not bear their prancing around me any more.'

'Well, Heaven be thanked for small mercies,' Cecil sighed. 'But what is this I hear from Bishop de Quadra? Apparently you have told him more than once that you yearn to be a nun and pass all your time in a cell praying.'

'I was teasing him,' Elizabeth confessed, giving Cecil an arch look.

'I fear he did not like your flippancy in such a matter. And yearning to be a nun does not ride well with the attention you pay Lord Robert. Madam, I fear these new rumours will be your undoing. I pray you, do not give your enemies cause for gossip.'

'Ah, my careful Spirit, there is no cause for gossip,' Elizabeth reassured him. 'Do you take me for such a fool?'

'No, Madam, but others think you abandon caution. Quadra believes that all is falsehood and vanity with you, and that you but toy with the Archduke.'

'God's blood!' Elizabeth exploded. 'I will teach him that he must not say such things! I will show him that I am honest in my dealings.'

Cecil concealed a smile. 'And Lord Robert? You will be more circumspect?'

She smiled innocently in turn.

Elizabeth fumed and fretted. How dare Bishop de Quadra speak of her like that! She must somehow show him that she was not trifling with him – and pay him back for his rude words.

Robert's sister, Mary Sidney, was the lady-in-waiting she loved the most after Kate Knollys. Mary and her husband Harry were especially dear to her – Elizabeth's brother, King Edward, had died in Harry's arms – and both were utterly loyal. Mary was raven-haired and exquisitely beautiful, a flower grafted from a noble tree; what was more, she had a good heart and a playful sense of humour. A true Dudley, she also had a penchant for intrigue. She was just the person to assist her mistress.

Elizabeth sent for Mary and told her that she wished her to visit Bishop de Quadra in secret. Mary's eyebrows shot up in surprise.

'You wish me to compromise his reputation, Madam?' she asked, incredulous.

'Nothing like that,' Elizabeth chuckled, 'although I should dearly love to see the good Bishop's face if it were! No, Mary, it is a ploy to revive the negotiations for my marriage to the Archduke. It is not something I can broach myself.'

Mary was trying but failing to conceal her dismay. Obviously she had been hoping that the Queen would marry her brother.

Elizabeth ignored her discomfiture. 'You will tell his Excellency that a plot was uncovered at Nonsuch Palace – a plot to poison me and Robert.'

'Oh, Madam!' Mary cried, a look of horror on her face. 'I did not know of this.'

'That is because there *was* no plot!' Elizabeth said, laughing. 'But you will tell him that there was, and that you are now so afraid for my safety that you desire to see me married to a great prince who can protect me from my enemies. You will beg him to reopen negotiations on behalf of the Archduke. That you, a Dudley, are beseeching it will carry conviction.'

'Your Majesty thinks he will heed *me*?'

'Yes, indeed.' Elizabeth was enjoying herself hugely. 'And you will say to him that he must ignore my apparent reluctance to discuss the marriage, as it is the custom for ladies in England not to give their consent in such matters until they are teased into it.'

Disconcerted though she was, Mary Sidney had to smile at the thought of the dignified, portly Bishop de Quadra striving to tease the Queen.

'Just tell him,' Elizabeth went on, 'that the time is ripe, and I might now be prevailed upon to give my answer, and also that my Council will urge me to do so as they are tired of all the delays. Assure the Bishop that you would not say such things to him if they were untrue. If it comes to it, you may even say that you are acting with my consent. Tell him I would never raise the subject myself, but that I should be glad if the Archduke would visit England.'

'Very well, Madam, I will try to see him tonight.' And Mary sped from the room on soft-slippered feet.

Later, towards midnight, she returned with Robert, who gave Elizabeth a challenging look. Of course he wanted to know why she had changed her mind about the Archduke – and involved his sister, of all people, in this covert intrigue with Quadra.

'Well?' Elizabeth asked, avoiding his gaze.

'The Bishop did not believe me at first,' Mary said, 'so he sought out Robert.'

'Fortunately, Madam, Mary had spoken to me beforehand and explained the situation,' Robert explained, a touch stiffly. 'I assured him that she wasn't lying. I think, coming from me, that carried some weight. And now, Madam, may I have your leave to depart?'

'Robin, calm down,' Elizabeth said. 'You know I am playing games.'

'I know nothing with you!' he retorted.

Elizabeth frowned. 'Mary, could you leave us, please?' she said, and when Mary had gone, she turned to Robert and put her arms around him. 'I will show you what I mean very shortly, my Eyes,' she smiled. 'This little charade is but a ploy to put Bishop de Quadra in his place, and teach him not to accuse me of being false and vain and fickle!'

'Ah,' Robert replied, his face relaxing into a grin. 'So you do not mean to marry the Archduke, then?'

'Not at the moment,' Elizabeth replied.

The September days were warm when the Queen removed to Hampton Court. Every day she was out in its spacious gardens, walking along broad paths lined with railed flower beds and heraldic beasts on striped poles in green and white, the royal Tudor colours.

'My father loved this place,' she told Robert, indicating the monumental red-brick complex of buildings behind her. 'He took it from Cardinal Wolsey and converted it into a pleasure palace for my mother. Alas, she was dead before it was completed.'

'It is a magnificent memorial to them both,' Robert observed, 'and your father did right to take it. No cardinal, or indeed any man of God, should own such a great house.'

'I have never liked it,' Elizabeth confessed. 'It is uncomfortable and unhealthy, for all it impresses people. I have miserable memories of being cooped up here when my sister, Queen Mary, believed herself to be with child. All was in readiness for the birth, and I, of course, was to be supplanted. It was a dismal prospect. But the days went by, then the weeks, and there was no sign of the babe's arrival. It was boiling hot that summer, and there were so many people crammed into the palace that the place stank. In the end, my poor sister had to accept what we had all long suspected: that she was not with child at all. I was never more glad to ride away from a place.'

'She was an unhappy woman,' Robert said.

'King Philip had much to answer for. And yet Cecil and the rest want me to marry a foreign prince? Pah! Baron Breuner has been seeking an audience, but I said no.'

Robert looked behind to check that Elizabeth's ladies were out of earshot. 'Far better, Bess, to marry one of your own,' he murmured.

She gave him a look. 'I have no wish to marry Arundel or Pickering.'

'That was not my meaning.'

'I know your meaning, Robin, and the answer is no!' And she turned and swept off in the direction of the palace.

He caught up with her and followed her through the wicket leading to her privy lodgings. 'Forgive me, Bess – if I spoke out of turn it is only because of my feelings for you.'

'I will say no more of it,' she shrugged. 'Come, I would have your opinion.' She led him through galleries and apartments brilliant with gold, silver and vibrant colours to the vast great hall, where her mother's initials – overlooked when they were supposed to be obliterated by Jane Seymour's – could still be seen if you knew where to find them. Above their heads soared the most magnificent hammerbeam roof in England; below, on the green and white tiled floor, some courtiers were rehearsing a masque. Gilded trees in great pots had been positioned along the walls in front of the tapestries, and a wheeled stage bearing a green hill strewn with paper marguer-ites completed the pastoral setting. At the Queen's approach, the players, several of them wearing what passed for classical costumes, fell to their knees.

'Rise, good people,' she said. 'I am but passing through. I

would not spoil the surprises you have in store for me later.'
Turning to Robert, she murmured, 'They are putting on the
tale of Endymion, as a compliment to both of us. Kate Knollys
told me, but I am not supposed to know it! The princely hunter
Endymion is yourself, and I am represented by Diana, the
goddess of the moon. Endymion is lured into an enchanted
sleep, but Diana wakes him with a kiss, purely out of pity,
charity and queenly goodness. She has never been kissed before,
nor will her lips ever again be sullied by such condescension.'
She looked at him slyly as she passed through the screens
passage to the processional stair that led down to the courtyard.
'You may make of that what you will, my Eyes!'

Some days later, after the court had returned to Whitehall,
Bishop de Quadra requested an audience. Elizabeth received
him, smiling.

'Your Majesty,' he began, beaming happily, 'I have come
about your proposed marriage to the Archduke Charles. It is
my understanding that your Majesty is now favourable to the
match and ready to give an answer.'

Elizabeth frowned. 'I have no idea where you obtained such
an understanding, Bishop, for I have no desire to marry the
Archduke or any other prince. Even if I had, I would only
consider marrying a man I have seen face to face.'

Quadra looked momentarily bewildered, but quickly recovered himself. 'Well, your Majesty, it is irregular, but I have
prevailed upon the Emperor to allow the Archduke to come
to England – incognito, perhaps.'

'No,' said Elizabeth robustly. 'It would be better if his
Highness did not come, because I cannot commit myself, even
indirectly, to marrying him.'

Quadra's patience snapped. 'We are wasting words, Madam.
Your Majesty must begin with the premise that you have to marry
someone, because that cannot now be avoided. Then you should
invite the Archduke to visit England. I assure you, you
would not be committing yourself in any way. The Emperor

is amenable to the idea. He is eager for the marriage to take place. All he asks is that his son be spared any public humiliation should your Majesty decide to turn him down.'

Elizabeth had been listening with mounting fury. Must? *Must? Should?* Who was the Bishop to say 'must' to a queen? But she kept her temper.

'I cannot invite the Archduke to England. It is not fitting for a queen and a maiden to summon anyone to be her husband. I would rather die a thousand deaths. The Emperor must take the initiative.'

Quadra was suddenly at his most avuncular. 'Of course, your Majesty. I understand such maidenly reluctance. There will be no difficulty in the Emperor making the request and putting arrangements in train.'

Elizabeth smiled graciously. 'Will there not? How very kind. In that case, I admit that I should be delighted to meet the Archduke.'

'Your Majesty will not be disappointed,' the Bishop declared, expansive in his moment of triumph, and foreseeing himself officiating at a royal wedding. 'Would you prefer the Archduke's visit to be a public or a private one?'

'I will think on it,' Elizabeth said. 'Do not press me further at this time. The Archduke must do as he thinks fit. I do not wish to become involved, and he must understand that I have not invited him. Remember, I am not committing myself to marrying him. I am not. I have not decided whether to marry at all.'

Quadra looked exasperated again. His dream of a royal wedding was fading fast. 'I will ask the Emperor to send his son without delay, Madam.'

'I trust your lodgings are to your liking, Robin,' Elizabeth said at table that evening. They were supping together in her privy chamber under the fierce glare of Henry VIII, with only the kneeling servitors and a few ladies in attendance. In the corner, Mary Sidney was plucking a lute. A great platter of the cakes Elizabeth so loved was on the table. She had eaten three so far.

'Since you kindly ask, Bess, I fear they are damp, being so near the river,' Robert admitted. *And*, his eyes accused, they are a long step from yours.

'Hmm. Then we must move you, my Eyes.' She rose suddenly. 'Come with me.'

She led him through a series of small chambers until she came to a fine suite of lodgings, well appointed and spacious – for Whitehall, the palace being old and rambling – and ushered him inside.

'You could not find better, Robin. These rooms are next to my own, which are through that door.' She flushed.

Robert caught his breath. 'Bess, do you mean . . .? At last . . .?' Desire was suddenly lively in him.

'You may come to my room later,' Elizabeth said, sending him a seductive look that nearly destroyed him.

He took her at her word. He could not have done otherwise, so badly did he want her. After midnight, when the palace was quiet and the only sounds were the regular cries of the watch and the occasional paddle of oars on the Thames, he rose from his bed, pulled on a nightshirt and a crimson velvet robe, and padded barefoot to the door in the corner. He lifted the latch and the door – miraculously – opened.

A celestial sight met his eyes. Elizabeth was sitting up in a bed ingeniously built of different-coloured woods and hung with Oriental curtains of painted silk. She lay propped up on pillows in a tumble of quilts of silk and velvet banded with gold and silver, with a book in her hands. Candles on the silver-topped table at her bedside and two finely chased cabinets threw flickering lights that caught the gilded fretwork on the ceiling. There was just one small window, open to the river. The maid-of-honour's pallet at the foot of the bed was unoccupied. They were quite alone.

Elizabeth raised her eyes from her book; there was no surprise in them, just the warmth of welcome. She was wearing a chemise of the finest lawn embroidered with silver thread, and her long red hair tumbled in waves over her shoulders, glinting like gold in the candlelight, which softened her angular features. She looked exquisite.

'I thought you would come,' she said softly, laying aside the book. Robert crossed swiftly to the bed and swept her into his arms, holding her long and tightly.

'I have dreamed of this moment,' he murmured, kissing her hair and her neck, then seeking her lips. For a short space she responded with equal fervour, but as his hands grew more adventurous, she stiffened.

'Oh, Robin,' she sighed, 'do not ask too much of me. What I want is to be close to you – and to take matters slowly. You know I dare not risk a scandal, but there are many pleasures that lovers can enjoy without that, are there not?'

'Let me show you!' he whispered, his need so urgent that he was happy to accept whatever satisfaction she was offering.

She had stopped him, of course, before things went too far. The next morning, luxuriating in her herb-scented bath, she was glad of that; she also knew that the memory of what had happened during those beautiful, stolen hours would live with her for ever. She realised that you could never fully know someone until you had lain with them and seen their innermost self. Now she fully knew Robert, knew she could trust him, and would have wagered her life that he was hers irrevocably. In revealing themselves to each other, they had forged a bond that no one could sunder.

They lay together secretly every night after that, unless the layout of her palaces made the risk of discovery too great. Sometimes Robert would moan that Elizabeth was killing him by withholding the final favour, but she was learning to bring him to ecstasy in other ways, and how to prolong the pleasure. She was discovering too how she could receive pleasure herself, and so they enjoyed a good semblance of lovemaking. Very soon all that was lacking was the ultimate consummation, which suited her very well. She did not think she could ever let herself go that far. If Robert pressed too near, all her old fears would come flooding back and she would tense and fend him off, provoking anguished gasps of protest. Then she would cozen him with kisses and sweet words and more daring things, as well she knew how these days, and soon he would spend himself and all would be well again. For her, at least.

Presently she became aware that tongues were wagging even more furiously than before. The gossips were now saying that Elizabeth's marriage to Robert was imminent. That brought her hot-headed cousin, Thomas Howard, Duke of Norfolk and premier Catholic peer in the realm, hurrying to court, where he made no secret of his loathing for Robert, or his disapproval of the Queen's behaviour.

'He told me to my face that he deplores your levity and bad government,' Robert seethed.

'God's blood, I will have him in the Tower!' Elizabeth erupted.

'And I will march him there, if you will let me. He had the effrontery to warn me that if I do not abandon my present pretensions and presumptions, I will not die in my bed.'

Elizabeth's eyes blazed. 'He is jealous, the varlet. He would be one of my close advisers, in your place, no doubt. But he is not worthy anyway, and now that he has shown himself so hostile, he has ruined what small chance he had. I will be watching him!' Let him put a foot out of place and she would summon her gentleman gaoler.

'He said something else, Bess. He had heard from Bishop de Quadra that there was talk of a marriage between us, but he said that he, Norfolk, and other lords would never put up with my being king. Even so, the Bishop had told him that I might be seeking a means to free myself from my wife so that I could marry you.'

Elizabeth suddenly felt chilled. 'What means?'

'He did not say, though his meaning was clear, damn him. But I am not seeking to free myself from my marriage, Bess

– in any way. God will soon do it for me. I'd not darken Amy's final days with talk of divorce, even if there were grounds.'

'And why should you?' Her tone was brisk. 'I will not have such idle speculation in my court. If you hear it, be sure to refute it as if it is a mere light calumny. But I warn you, my Eyes, do not protest too much, or people will believe it!'

Autumn lay golden on the land when Prince Erik's brother, Duke John of Finland, arrived in England, all but brandishing a pen with which to sign the marriage treaty. Elizabeth had sent a bullish Robert to receive him at Colchester, hoping that the sight of her favourite would convince him that his brother's cause was hopeless, but Duke John took Robert's smiling welcome to mean that the way was now clear for Erik and Elizabeth to marry.

The Duke sashayed into the court, jaunty bonnet a-quiver and fashionable cloak swirling, laden with gifts for the Queen. He bowed low every time she spoke to him, showered her with compliments in clumsy Latin, called her his dear sister and told her how beautiful and charming she was, and how vastly he was impressed by her wondrous realm of England. At first Elizabeth enjoyed herself immensely, playing up to his extravagant attentions, but the unsuspecting Baron Breuner was near moved to tears of frustration at the favour she bestowed upon Duke John, and before long she was hard put to it to keep the two men from each other's throats. It was all she could do to keep blowing first hot, then cold, then warm in each direction, dangling some hope of success but never committing herself. It was a game at which – God be praised – she was becoming more skilful with each day that passed.

'Madam,' complained Cecil, 'I am seeing nothing but wooing and controversy. I wish you would choose one and leave the others honourably satisfied.'

'Ah, my Spirit, but while they live in hope they remain my friends!' Elizabeth said sagely. And long might it continue! Although in truth she was a little frayed from the effort.

The King of Denmark now joined the melee. His envoy arrived at court with a proposal of marriage, and made a great show posturing in a crimson doublet embroidered with a heart pierced by an arrow.

Bishop de Quadra sought out the Queen as she sat conversing with Duke John in the gallery above the tiltyard. 'I see that your suitors are courting your Majesty at a marvellous rate,' he observed, the smile fixed on his face.

'Many are hopeful,' she answered dismissively, being in no mood to wrangle with him. Robert had just entered the lists and she could not take her eyes off him. As the contestants charged, she stood there, riveted.

'Maybe you are thinking of an alliance nearer home,' Quadra said softly.

'I am considering several options,' Elizabeth replied, clapping vigorously as Robert unhorsed her cousin, Lord Hunsdon. 'Bravo!' she cried. 'Bravo, my Eyes!'

Baron Breuner was watching jealously from his vantage point a little further along the gallery. As soon as he decently could, he requested an audience.

'Your Majesty, it seems there is no point my staying in England,' he said, his expression conveying that there was much point if she would only come to her senses. 'You do not want to marry my master the Archduke. Your heart is given to another.'

'I will be the judge of where my heart is bestowed,' Elizabeth said coolly, her good mood evaporating. If Breuner left England, Robert would be blamed for it. She was well aware that he was already viewed by everyone as the reason why she would not commit to any of her suitors. Cecil had warned her, more than once, that she was casting away her advantages because of him – and he was not the only one complaining.

When Robert came to her that night he was livid – but not with Breuner.

'Norfolk goes too far! He told me – he actually said to my face – that he would do all in his power to bring about your marriage to the Archduke. I answered that he is neither a good Englishman nor a loyal subject who advises the Queen to marry a foreigner.'

'Then I must be a traitor to my own throne, for I have contemplated it many times,' Elizabeth said wryly. 'But *contemplated* is all there is to it, and just now I do not want to think of importunate foreign princes, or their importunate ambassadors. God's blood, Robin, do not frown so! Norfolk is a fool. Leave me to deal with him. You and I have better things to do.'

She smiled and held out her hand.

Breuner was still at court, all smiles now, for some mysterious reason – and Bishop de Quadra was in a high good mood when next the Queen granted him an audience. He could barely wait to tell her his news.

'The Archduke Charles is shortly to set out for England, Madam.' He might have been informing her of the Second Coming. 'All your conditions have been met, and soon you will see him face to face.'

Elizabeth hardly needed to pretend to be disconcerted. 'But I understood that the Baron was leaving England, and that he would not press his master's suit further.'

'I must apologise for him, Madam. He gained the wrong impression, that your heart was set on another.'

She toyed with the rings on her elegant fingers, feeling as if she had been ambushed. 'Bishop, my heart is set on no one. I am not contemplating marriage at present. Of course, I *might* change my mind when I see the Archduke.' It was as unlikely as the Second Coming, but the Bishop might not appreciate such honesty – or the analogy.

She was pleased, though, to see that she had ruffled Quadra's feathers. It would serve him right for his presumption. 'Madam,' he said testily, 'you have all but invited him for your inspection.'

'No!' she snapped. 'I said only that I wished to meet him and get to know him, and that I could never marry a man I have not met. Others have put their own construction on my words.'

'Madam,' Quadra spluttered, 'I have it on good authority, from one of your own ladies, no less, that some reluctance to commit to marriage is expected of English ladies, and that you do but wait to be teased into an answer.' Steam might at any moment issue from the Bishop's ears, Elizabeth thought, suppressing a giggle. It was plainly beneath his dignity to have any truck with teasing.

'Members of my household often say such things, and with the best of intentions,' she countered, 'but they have never done so on my authority.' She was enjoying this immensely.

'Then I have been made to look a fool,' Quadra stuttered. 'I do not pretend to understand your Majesty.'

'Good Bishop, I hardly understand myself!' Elizabeth beamed.

One dark winter evening Elizabeth was sitting at a desk in her privy chamber, engrossed in translating a passage from Tacitus, when Cecil came to her, his face grave.

'Madam, before we go into council, I must warn you that my spies are reporting dangerous gossip about Lord Robert. It is being bruited, not just in England but also abroad, that he means to poison his wife so that he can marry you.'

'That is a wicked lie!' Elizabeth flared. 'Anyone who believes it is a fool, as Robert would be if he ever contemplated such villainy. But he is not, thank Heaven. He is too religious a man ever to think of such wickedness. Even so, were he to murder his wife, suspicion would immediately light upon him, and the hue and cry would be out. And I,' she cried, warming passionately to her theme, 'would I be so foolish as to marry him after that? They would say that I had been his accomplice, and it would cost me my throne. Who is spreading these stupid rumours?' She was almost tempted to commit murder herself.

'Bishop de Quadra for one,' Cecil said. 'He is the most inveterate gossip, and I suspect he reports every piece of idle chatter in his dispatches. That may be why this talk has spread beyond your Majesty's realm. Challoner, our man in Brussels, forbore to commit details of the rumours to paper, they are so foul. He hastened to assure me he knew they were false.'

'I should hope so!' Elizabeth fumed, then sighed deeply. This had all gone too far. 'What remedy is there, my Spirit?'

Cecil eyed her wearily. 'Marry, Madam – and soon. That would put an end to all the tales.'

Elizabeth threw him an exasperated look.

'I will deal with this my way,' she insisted.

She responded to the speculation by appointing Robert Lord Lieutenant and Constable of Windsor Castle. She took to praising his loyalty to herself and his zeal for the reformed faith. Let the world see that she had no cause to be ashamed of her Eyes! Her open favour would give the lie to the malice of her enemies. It had already enabled Robert to secure court posts and other offices for many of his friends. Now, in anticipation of his elevation to greater things – rumours or no rumours – people thronged more greedily than ever to obtain his patronage, and an eager faction formed around him in the expectation that he would soon be king.

Elizabeth knew that most people underestimated Robert. He might strut like a peacock in gorgeous plumage, but he had a fine mind, and he was hot for the Protestant cause. It had taken time, but many were beginning to see him as the champion of the new religion, and theological tracts were already being dedicated to him. It was known too that it was not mere jealousy that set him against the Archduke: he abhorred the prospect of England being tied to a Catholic power, or allied in any way to Spain, and many applauded him for that, even if they did not like him.

Elizabeth watched Cecil watching Robert. She knew her Spirit too well to suspect that he too was animated merely by personal jealousy. No, he saw Robert as a threat to her chances of making a good political marriage, and to the stability of the realm. He was so obviously taking care to be especially courteous and affable to Robert, but she knew that he was hand in glove with Norfolk and would bring the favourite down if he could. In December, however, Norfolk went too far, and publicly accused Robert of poking his nose into state affairs, where it most definitely was not wanted or appreciated. Elizabeth had had enough. She banished the Duke to the north to serve as Lord Lieutenant on the Scottish border. Let him simmer for a while in the wastes of Northumberland, and reflect where his arrogance had brought him!

1560

The Archduke Charles had not come after all. Someone had warned him that it might prove a humiliating exercise, and his father the Emperor would not allow him to expose himself to that. In December, a disgruntled Breuner had left England; and two months later, very reluctantly, Duke John went home, Elizabeth having most courteously turned down Erik of Sweden. Most people believed that the way was being cleared for the Queen's marriage to Lord Robert. Now there were not just rumours that he meant to poison his wife; there was also talk that he would divorce her. The consensus was that he would get rid of her by some means.

The truth was that Amy Dudley's health was deteriorating rapidly. Elizabeth found herself facing the fact that Robert might soon be a free man – and that he would waste no time in pressing his suit. She felt she ought to be exhilarated at the prospect, but in reality she saw herself cornered. Whatever Robert said or did, he could not purge her of her fears of what marriage would mean for her.

God be thanked, the trouble with the French and the Scots was at an end. The Queen Regent of Scotland had died, the Protestant lords had seized power, and the French had sued for peace.

'William, I want you to go to Edinburgh in person to negotiate a treaty with the Scottish lords,' Elizabeth instructed Cecil. Her other councillors looked dubious. What was the matter with them? Were they wondering what she would get up to without her Spirit's restraining influence? Things had certainly come to a pretty pass!

Cecil seemed to be entertaining the same concerns. In fact he looked alarmed. 'Is it really necessary that I go?' he asked. 'Randolph is a good agent. He can deal with this.'

'There is no more skilled negotiator than you,' Elizabeth insisted. Cecil did not argue, but when the meeting ended he waited until the others had left.

'Madam, I must ask. The banishment of my lord of Norfolk is preying on my mind. Does the idea of my going to Scotland proceed from Lord Robert?'

Elizabeth bridled. 'God's death, William, it is my idea, and you know it is a sound one.'

'You will not make any decision over your marriage while I am away?'

'You mean, am I going to do away with Lady Dudley and hasten Robin to the altar?'

Cecil was perturbed by her levity.

'It is no light matter, Madam. You know what people are saying, and you do nothing to discourage it.'

'What, that Robin and I have had five children in secret? I read that report. I hope the woman is behind bars now.'

'Madam, we can lock up as many offenders as we can catch – and we might as well lock up the whole court in the process – but that will not stop the rumours. Only your Majesty can give the lie to them.'

'God's blood, are you saying I am not circumspect? Or that I set a lewd example?'

'Madam, *I* know that you are without reproach. But others see what they want to see. You associate with Lord Robert, a man fouled with rumour. He could bring the realm to speedy ruin were you to marry him.'

Elizabeth lost patience. 'You fear only for your influence, William, and that colours your opinions. Now get ye gone to Scotland and stop fretting. I am the one who rules here, and I can manage without you for a few weeks.' She was being unfair to Cecil, she knew, for he had never put his own concerns before the needs of the realm, but she was sick to the teeth of his constant vilification of Robert. She couldn't wait to see the back of him.

Cecil went, unhappily, to Edinburgh. There, setting his worries aside, he negotiated a masterful treaty that gave Elizabeth everything she wanted and more. The Scots and the French had agreed peace terms. Most importantly, they would recognise Elizabeth as queen of England. Mary Stuart would stop quartering the arms of England with her own, and – God be praised – had undertaken to cease calling herself by Elizabeth's title.

The threat of war had receded. Elizabeth now stood triumphant in the eyes of Christendom.

Robert was peevish.

'Cecil has not secured the return of Calais,' he grumbled, 'or made the French reimburse you for all the money you have outlaid fighting them in Scotland – money England can ill afford.'

'By God, he has not!' Elizabeth concurred. Cecil's criticism of Robert still rankled. 'I will write and remind him of his duty.' Let Cecil feel the draught of her displeasure. He would soon stop complaining.

That was the only blot on the landscape of that glorious summer, her second as queen. Elizabeth basked in the golden sunshine, giving herself over to pleasure and love, and Robert was never far from her side. By day they rode and hunted through countryside baked brown in the heat, Robert stripped of his doublet and Elizabeth wearing a wide-brimmed straw hat to protect her fair skin; in the evenings they danced galliards, laughing as they leapt high in the air, or made music together, strumming ballads on lute or gittern; and at night they lay rapt in each other's arms. Ambassadors from politically amorous foreign princes still crowded the court, but it was plain to all that the Queen had eyes only for one man. And now the whispers were louder than ever: 'Wanton! Adulteress! Harlot!' But Elizabeth stoutly ignored them. She did not blench when Bacon, earnest to protect her reputation in Cecil's absence, ventured to protest that Lord Robert was ruining the realm with his vanity.

'Even the mean folk in the villages cry out against him, Madam,' Bacon persisted, 'and there is much grudging on the part of your nobles to see him held in such special favour, and – forgive me – the little regard in which your Majesty appears to hold marriage.'

'How dare they say such things!' Elizabeth exploded, incandescent with fury. 'I have *nothing* wherewith to reproach myself!'

'Madam,' replied Bacon, never faltering, 'I would be failing in my duty if I did not report what is being said. I know your Majesty will do what is best.'

'Oh, we will, we will, my Lord Keeper, never fear,' Elizabeth retorted, wishing all gossips at the bottom of the sea.

But there was no escaping the rumours. Cecil heard them, even in Edinburgh, and hastened to write to his Queen: 'It is my constant prayer that God will direct your heart to choose a worthy father for your children, so that the whole realm will have cause to rejoice and bless your seed.'

'Pah!' snorted Elizabeth when she read this, and when Cecil returned to court after his long, hot journey south, and all the councillors greeted him with effusive congratulations on his fine diplomacy, she showed herself cool and distant. She would not utter one word of thanks or praise.

'Madam,' murmured Sussex, appalled, 'he has negotiated a great peace. Will you not show him some mark of favour?'

'No,' said Elizabeth glacially. 'He has displeased us.'

Robert showed himself gleeful at Cecil's discomfiture. He was busily courting Bishop de Quadra, hoping to secure Spanish support for his own promotion in opposition to Cecil. Elizabeth had told him to say that she needed a swordsman to counter her scribes.

Cecil, painfully aware that he had been away too long, knew exactly what was going on. No longer did Elizabeth linger to talk with him after council meetings; she seemed to want to avoid him. Not only had she shown absolutely no gratitude for his hard bargaining in Edinburgh, she would not even defray his expenses! Worse still, she had actually boxed his ears when he complained. With a heavy heart he could only miserably conclude that Robert Dudley had made the most of his rival's absence, and that matters had moved on apace between Dudley and the Queen. He was sickened to find that gossip about them was livelier and more blatantly suggestive than ever. Talk of Dudley obtaining a divorce was rampant.

Elizabeth seemed to have been seized with a kind of madness that had addled her judgement. She made no attempt to preserve discretion. She visited Robert openly at the Dairy House at Kew, and it was being said that they spent long evenings there alone together. God only knew what they were getting up to.

Elizabeth loved the Dairy House; it was the one place where Robert had never lived with his wife. Elizabeth had made it clear to him, on bestowing the property, that it was out of bounds to Amy. She wanted to be able to call there unannounced, without running the risk of being confronted by Amy's woeful, sickly face.

One balmy summer evening, when Elizabeth returned from Kew late at night, her cheeks hectic and flushed, her eyes shining, Cecil was waiting for her. At that moment the Devil, complete with his pitchfork, would have been a more welcome sight.

'Madam,' Cecil said, bowing, and looking lugubriously unlike the Devil, 'a word, if I may.'

There was a time when she would have seen him immediately.

'Not now, William,' she answered, fanning herself, determined to put him in his place. 'I have just enjoyed a splendid evening at Kew. Do you not agree that Lord Robert has so many praiseworthy qualities? He has been most helpful in the matter of the Imperial alliance, and he has a good command of affairs in Europe. I am firmly of the opinion that he is deserving of further honours. That would be most fitting, would it not?'

Cecil gritted his teeth. Dudley had no business to be advising the Queen on politics. 'Praiseworthy qualities, loyalty and hard work in your service should indeed be rewarded, Madam,' he said pointedly. Inwardly he was alarmed. Such honours might be a preamble to making Dudley king – and then what would befall Cecil? And the Queen herself?

He sought out his fellow councillors. All, to a man, deplored the Queen's failure to take a husband.

'She will brook no master,' sighed Sussex, thinking how complicated things could become when women got above themselves.

'She means to use her marriage only as a bargaining tool,' said Bacon.

'It seems it is of little use to contemplate a foreign marriage alliance,' said Cecil gloomily, 'because I fear that she has already decided to marry Robert Dudley. Gentlemen, the situation is becoming desperate. Bishop de Quadra has warned me to expect a palace rebellion by Dudley.'

'Well he exaggerates everything,' Sussex observed, although the prospect of the Gypsy rampaging through the corridors of Whitehall was really rather worrying. 'But,' he added cheerfully, 'I have also heard it muttered that there are those who have had enough of queens and want to see her Majesty and Lord Robert clapped in prison.'

'Scaremongers,' Cecil sighed. 'I would that Lord Robert was there, though. His influence is too great, and it is pernicious. But what is the alternative to her Majesty? The next in line is also a woman, be she Katherine Grey or Mary Stuart. We have the prospect of petticoat rule *ad infinitum*! And I for one am weary of it. In truth, gentlemen, I am considering tendering my resignation. I may recall Sir Nicholas Throckmorton from Paris to replace me as Secretary.'

The others looked at him, horrified.

'How could Dudley possibly replace one such as you in the Queen's counsels?' Sussex asked. 'The Queen needs you. We need you. England needs you.'

'The Queen appears not to be aware of that,' Cecil said, his face drawn.

'There must be a remedy,' Bacon fumed. 'We must prevent the Queen from ruining herself.'

'I have written to our ambassadors abroad,' Cecil revealed. 'I have suggested that it would be helpful if they could convey in their reports how Dudley is disapproved of in foreign courts.'

'Ah, but will the Queen pay heed?' Bacon asked. 'She has ignored public opinion so far, and the advice of her ministers.'

'Perchance the threat of William's resignation will bring her to her senses,' Sussex said.

'Do not raise your hopes,' Cecil muttered gloomily.

When Elizabeth next visited Robert at the Dairy House, she found various items laid out on a table: some gold buttons, a silver mirror, sewing silks and some delicately embroidered stockings. Her eyes alighted on them in surprise.

'They are for my wife,' Robert said awkwardly.

She waited.

'They are gifts to cheer her,' Robert went on, sounding very much as if he was confessing to treason. 'I have not visited her often of late.' That, of course, was because the Queen had prevented it.

'How is she?' Elizabeth felt bound to ask, but her tone was cool.

'Not well, Bess. In truth, I am deeply worried about her. I have arranged for her to stay at Cumnor Place, the house of a friend of mine called Anthony Forster.' Elizabeth was aware that Robert had never set up a country seat, and that Amy had spent her married life moving from house to house. 'There are several ladies of quality lodging there, and she will have company. She is in very low spirits, and I hope that those ladies will help to restore her.'

Elizabeth felt oddly uncomfortable. A secret inner voice was whispering that it should be Amy Dudley's husband who was at her side to restore her. 'I am sure they will,' she said resolutely, putting all unpleasant thoughts firmly out of her head. Taking Robert's hand, she drew him away from the hateful things on the table into the pretty gardens. There was a shady arbour there where they could talk privily, and dally unseen, and she could make him forget about his wife's woes.

The court moved to Windsor Castle in good time for the Queen's birthday in September. She was twenty-seven, and she supposed her councillors would again take occasion to remind her that she ought to be married, so she took care to spend the day hunting with Robert at her side, shooting stags with a crossbow and not returning until late. Then it was to find a messenger waiting for Robert with a letter from Oxfordshire. She saw his face drain of colour as he opened it.

'She is dying,' he whispered. Elizabeth took the letter and read it.

'I am sorry for it,' she said. She wondered why he did not crave leave to go to Amy.

'It will be a merciful release,' Robert said, his face unreadable. She was unsure if he meant for Amy, or for himself – and she was not sure if she welcomed this news or not. Nor did she want to think of illness and death on this beautiful day, when one should feel happy just to be alive.

Bishop de Quadra came to see her that evening, to offer his master's congratulations on her natal day.

'I thank his Majesty,' she replied graciously, then decided, on an impulse, to ruffle Philip's feathers. 'Alas, I am in no mood to celebrate, for I have heavy matters on my mind. Lord Robert's wife is dead – or nearly so.'

Quadra's eyebrows shot up. 'Dead?' He collected himself. 'Well, Madam, from what I hear, it has been expected.'

It was Elizabeth's turn to look startled. What *was* the Bishop implying?

'It is well known that she is ill,' he said, as if he was reading her mind. No doubt her consternation had been plain to see.

'Please convey my condolences to Lord Robert,' Quadra went on, smooth as ever.

'I will,' she said. 'And Bishop, I beg of you, say nothing about this. You know how people will talk.'

Walking through the castle precincts the next day, and puffing a bit because the incline was steep, Quadra met Cecil. He felt sorry for the Secretary, who, for all that he was a heretic, was a clever, worthy man who should not now be in such disfavour. Alas, it was all the fault of that adventurer, Robert Dudley, who was blatantly doing his utmost to replace Cecil in the Queen's counsels.

Cecil seemed disposed to talk; indeed, it soon became clear that he was eager to unburden himself. That was a little surprising, because usually he was not exactly forthcoming, save when it served him well to be so; nor was he one to gossip or touch on sensitive matters.

'Bishop, may I tell you something in confidence?' he asked now, glancing around to check that no one was nearby.

Surprised, Quadra hastened to assure him that he was the soul of discretion. (He would report whatever was said to King Philip, of course, and perhaps to various interested persons at court, if it served his purpose, but otherwise he would be discreet.)

'This must be kept secret,' Cecil emphasised.

'You may rely on me to keep it so, Master Secretary,' Quadra declared.

'Then I may tell you that the Queen is conducting herself in such a way that I am about to withdraw from her service.'

Quadra was agog. This was momentous! He could not wait to pass it on to his master, and his friends too.

Cecil's face was grave. 'It is a bad sailor who does not make for port when he sees a storm coming,' he observed, 'and I foresee ruin impending through the Queen's intimacy with Lord Robert. Lord Robert has made himself master of all the business of the state, and of the person of the Queen—'

'The *person*? You mean they have proceeded to the ultimate conjunction?' the Bishop interrupted, astonished to be hearing such a thing from Elizabeth's chief minister.

'It would not surprise me,' Cecil sighed, 'but whatever the truth of that, the way her Majesty conducts herself with Lord Robert can only be to the extreme injury of her realm. He, for his part, has every intention of marrying her.'

'I cannot believe that she would be so foolish,' Quadra said, shaking his head. Wait till King Philip heard this!

'I do not believe that the realm will tolerate the marriage,' Cecil went on, 'and I do not intend to be here to find out. I am determined to retire to the country, although I suppose she will have me in the Tower before she will let me go.' He looked like a dog anticipating a blow from a cruel master.

'Is there anything I can do?' Quadra asked.

'I beg of you,' Cecil urged, 'remonstrate with the Queen! You have the might of Spain behind you. Persuade her not utterly to throw herself away as she is doing. Urge her to remember what she owes to herself and to her subjects.'

The Bishop promised he would do that as soon as the opportunity presented itself, and Cecil thanked him profusely. But there was an angry gleam in his eyes.

'Lord Robert would be better in Paradise than here!' he muttered.

'I believe he thinks himself there already,' Quadra observed drily.

'Nay, Bishop, I mean he would be better off if he were in Heaven. And so would we! I must be honest with you. I despair of the Queen seeing sense! It is all down to Lord Robert, of course. He will be the ruin of this realm, and of me. You do not know the half of it.' Cecil looked around him, bent his head closer and spoke in a low voice. 'They are thinking of destroying his wife. They have given out that she is ill.'

Quadra stiffened in silent amazement, remembering what Elizabeth had told him the day before.

'She is not ill at all,' Cecil went on. 'She is very well, and taking good care not to be poisoned. I trust that God would never permit such a crime to be accomplished, or so wretched a conspiracy to prosper.' He gave the Bishop a weighty look.

Quadra was stunned. Was Cecil actually telling him that Dudley and the Queen herself were conspiring to murder Lady Dudley? He had definitely said *they*, so who else could be involved but Elizabeth? If Cecil was so concerned for his mistress's reputation, he was going the right way about thoroughly wrecking it for good and all. Yet would the Queen, an intelligent woman, really be so rash as to risk her crown by abetting murder? Quadra found it inconceivable. There was no mistaking it, however: Cecil was distraught. His career was at an end and he faced ignominy and ruin, and all because of the upstart Dudley. Small wonder that he had thrown his customary caution to the winds, and perhaps even exaggerated! For even now, with disaster facing him, the man's thoughts were for the well-being of the Queen he had served and her godforsaken kingdom. It was beyond belief that he had meant to implicate her in a vile crime.

'Rest assured, Sir William, I will speak with the Queen,' Quadra promised, 'although I am not sure that it will help, as she has never taken my advice in the past.'

'She will pay more heed to you than to me, assuredly,' Cecil grunted.

Elizabeth watched Bishop de Quadra, who was standing in the crowded gallery, trying to ignore Lady Katherine Grey's efforts to make him notice her. She knew that the Bishop was waiting to catch her own eye, but on this glorious morning she could not be bothered with him. She was enjoying sitting close to Robert on this comfortable cushioned window seat, gazing into the eyes of her lover and laughing at some private joke he had made. Her ladies were waiting with her plumed bonnet and her embroidered kid gloves. Soon, with the sun rising high in the sky, she and Robert would be off hawking for the day.

A page approached and announced that a Master Bowes had arrived and was asking to see Lord Robert.

'Who is this?' she murmured.

'My man at Cumnor,' Robert said, his face darkening. 'I think I know what it betokens.' His voice had lost its usual bombast.

'Show him in,' the Queen said.

Bowes came hastening and knelt. His clothing bore the evidence of hard riding, and he appeared to be in some distress. His words tumbled out in a rush. 'Your Majesty, my lord, I bring grave tidings. My good mistress is dead. She was found at the foot of the stairs with her neck broken.'

Robert stared at him, clearly shocked. Elizabeth's mouth fell open. She was speechless, chilled to her soul.

It had happened again. Love had ended in violent death. Not so long ago, before matters had soured between them, Robert had held Amy in his arms and been as one flesh with her – and now Amy was a cold corpse, her neck broken. Just as Elizabeth's mother's neck had been broken, even more bloodily, for all that she had been loved passionately by a king. The two horrible images – imagined, because of course mercifully she had seen neither reality – were superimposed in Elizabeth's head: Amy sprawled with her neck twisted at the foot of the stairs; Anne lying on the bloodied straw of the scaffold, her neck severed.

'Tell me what happened,' Robert said, his voice hoarse.

'It was yesterday, my lord. Our Lady's Fair was being held in Abingdon, and my lady gave us all permission to go. Some protested, not feeling it fitting to go jaunting on a Sunday, but she insisted. It was almost as if she wanted us out of the house.'

'What of the other ladies, her companions?' Robert asked. Elizabeth had so far said nothing, but her hands were shaking. Quadra was staring at her.

'One of them said she did not see why she should go and rub shoulders with mean persons, at which my lady grew very heated, but the lady insisted she stay behind, and by the time we left she had retired to her rooms. My lady was going to dine with another, then spend a quiet afternoon resting. She was not looking well at all.'

'Did any servants remain behind?' Robert enquired.

'A few, but they had been given the afternoon off, and were in their own quarters. None of them saw or heard anything amiss, so they say. But when we got back late yesterday afternoon, and went into the hall, we found my lady lying at the foot of the stairs.'

'She was dead?'

'Yes, my lord. Her neck was at an impossible angle and there was blood in her hair from two head wounds.'

Elizabeth found her voice. 'Master Bowes, could those wounds have resulted from an accidental fall?'

Bowes was clearly overawed by the dread person of his sovereign looming above him. 'Yes, your Majesty,' he faltered, considering, then he turned gratefully back to Robert. 'I believe they could. The poor lady was very frail. Maybe she fainted on the stairs, or tripped. Mr Forster said I was to take horse at once to tell you the news. On the road, my lord, I met your man, Thomas Blount, riding towards Cumnor. He said he had gifts from you for Lady Dudley. I told him what had befallen her and he bade me ride on in haste to Windsor. He said he would continue his journey to Cumnor to see if he could find out more about this great misfortune, and discover what people were saying about it.'

'That is what worries me,' Robert said. 'What people will say. Madam, may we talk in private?'

'No, Lord Robert,' Elizabeth said, in a loud voice that could be heard by all those standing around. 'There is nothing to talk about. Your wife must have had a fall. I will have the news of this terrible accident announced in the court. Then it is my will and pleasure that an inquest be held. While that is taking place, we require you to go to Kew and remain there until you are recalled.' So saying, she rose and walked majestically past Robert, and away along the gallery.

Robert was plainly stunned. Those watching would later relate that his jaw actually dropped. He was realising that he must have sounded less concerned about his wife's death than about the consequences for himself. Was that what had angered Elizabeth? He looked around desperately, as if seeking some support, but the faces he saw were hostile. Now that the Queen had so publicly withdrawn her favour, the wolves were waiting to pounce. He got up and hastened after her.

He caught up with her in the presence chamber as she was about to go through the privy chamber door. Her two ladies fell back in astonishment at the sight of Dudley, wild-eyed and agitated, bearing down on her, and the usher guarding the door shot him a warning look.

'No, Robin!' she growled, her father to the very life. 'Importune me not!'

'Bess!' he pleaded. 'Hear me out. I have done nothing wrong! The greatness and suddenness of this misfortune perplexes me as much as it does you. Think what the malicious world will say! And I have no means of purging myself of the evil rumours that wicked people will put about. All I care about is that the plain truth be known. I did not murder my wife! I will employ every device and means in my power for discovering the truth, without respect to any person. I want a full inquiry, carried out by the most discreet and substantial men who can search and probe thoroughly until they get to the bottom of the matter. I would be sorry in my heart if they found that evil was committed, but it *must* appear to the world that I am innocent! Madam, you must believe that!'

Elizabeth had heard him out with an impassive expression on her face, but now she turned to go. 'Lord Robert, you know as well as I what people will think. There have been rumours that you intended Amy's destruction, or sought to be rid of her. It matters not what I believe. The coroner must decide in the matter, and until your innocence can be proclaimed to the world, you must leave court. If you stay and I show you favour, people will believe that I too am guilty. So go, now.'

She could not look him in the eye. If she did, she would be lost. This changed everything. The long, glorious summer was over, perhaps for ever. She made herself walk on and close the door. She must be a queen first – and a woman second.

While the coroner was busy about his business, Elizabeth kept mostly to her apartments. She did not feel like seeing anyone, and on the few occasions she came forth she appeared pale and agitated. She missed Robert unbearably, and of the implications – and the horror – of Amy Dudley's death she did not dare to think.

As soon as Robert had left court, Cecil had been back at her side, his talk of resignation forgotten. Effortlessly restored to his old supremacy in her counsels, he was her Spirit once more, supportive as ever, and unobtrusively shouldering the burdens of government that she did not feel she could face. She was like a broken thing, cast from daylight into nightmare, hardly able to think ahead.

Cecil was kind. He even showed some sympathy for Robert and visited him at Kew. It was easy for him to be sympathetic, Elizabeth thought, now that his rival was out of the way. Even so, she appreciated his strength and wisdom at this time.

They spoke often of Amy Dudley's death. It was the only topic of conversation at court, and speculation was rampant.

'Most people suspect foul play,' Cecil said, his face impassive.

'They think Robert did it,' Elizabeth said dully.

'He is hot to protest his innocence. He writes daily urging that the truth be uncovered. He too believes that his wife was murdered. He is zealous to seek out the truth and see justice done. Of course, he wants to clear his name. A man without friends at court is like a hop without a pole.'

'Do you believe him innocent?'

'Madam, it is no secret that I have little love for Lord Robert. But I find it hard to believe him capable of such cruelty. His wife was dying. He had only to wait a little longer. Do *you* believe it, Madam?'

Elizabeth looked him square in the eye. 'No, William, I do not. But I am of two minds about the matter. Either someone loyal to Robert murdered Lady Dudley in the belief that it would clear the way for him to marry me; or one of his enemies did away with her, knowing that calumny would fasten upon him. You know as well as I, my Spirit, that whatever the outcome I can never marry him now. People would always point the finger and say we plotted her death together. I have wondered if someone who was against our marrying decided to scupper any possibility of it.'

Cecil frowned. 'Have you discounted the likelihood that it was an accident?'

'If it was, it was a timely one,' Elizabeth said. 'And something struck me as very strange: the fact that Lady Dudley was so earnest to have her servants go to the fair, and became angry with those who insisted on staying. It was as if she wanted everyone out of the house for some secret purpose of her own.'

Cecil was silent for a few moments. 'I have heard tales about her that make me think she was strange in her mind. What of the testimony of her maid, who said that Lady Dudley was on her knees every day, begging God to deliver her from desperation?'

'You think she took her own life?' Elizabeth was amazed.

'Imagine, Madam, that you are ill, in much pain, and expecting death daily. You are alone and forsaken, your lord being continually away at court.' Elizabeth stirred at the implied criticism, but let it go. Cecil went on: 'You are deeply disturbed in your mind. You might take an easy way out, and make sure that no one is there to stop you.'

'But it is not an easy way!' she cried. 'It means eternal damnation. Who would willingly be cast out for ever from the sight of God for the sake of a few more days' suffering on Earth? Nay, William, there is more to this – there has to be. Mayhap Lady Dudley wanted people out of the way because she was expecting a visitor – the man who murdered her.'

'Madam, this is pure speculation,' Cecil answered, a trifle testily. 'There is no evidence for it.'

'William, by all reports she was intent on being left alone on that fatal afternoon. She was insistent that her people went to the fair, and angry when some wanted to stay behind. Why? She might well have planned a secret meeting with the person who killed her. The house was mostly deserted that afternoon. The murderer could have come, done his work and departed, unseen by anyone else.'

Cecil was adamant. 'Again, this is supposition, Madam. The evidence strongly suggests that Lady Dudley killed herself.'

'We cannot rule out any possibility,' Elizabeth insisted. 'God grant that the coroner reaches his verdict soon. Then the truth will be known.'

The coroner had spoken: Amy Dudley's death had been an accident.

'His ruling leaves no room for doubt,' Elizabeth declared to Cecil, considerably lighter in spirits.

'It certainly does not,' Cecil agreed, looking – much to her gratification – agreeably relieved. 'But still Lord Robert is not satisfied. He is adamant that his wife was murdered, and he has pressed for a second jury to be empanelled, to determine who was responsible.'

'No,' Elizabeth said firmly. 'One inquest is sufficient. If the death was accidental, no one was responsible, so there is no need for further investigation. The matter is closed.'

She ordered court mourning for Amy – one had to observe the formalities – and commanded Robert back to court at once. He came as fast as a falcon in full flight, but she saw before her a man chastened and much tried, struggling to recover his equanimity.

'God be praised that your name has been cleared!' she cried, as they embraced in the privacy of her chamber.

'All I care about is that I am restored to your favour,' Robert said huskily, holding her close as if he would never let her go.

'You are, you are, my sweet Eyes,' she breathed, 'and thankfully the matter is now closed.'

'Alas, Bess, I fear it never will be,' Robert murmured. 'Until Amy's murderer is found, I will not be exonerated. As I came through the court I was aware of people watching me, whispering behind their hands.'

Elizabeth stiffened. She was all too aware that he spoke the truth. Only this morning the Council had received a letter from a Puritan minister urging them to order an earnest searching and trying of the truth, since his part of the country was alive with dangerous and grievous suspicions about Lady Dudley's death. His was not a lone voice. The courtiers had tried and condemned Robert with themselves as jury and judge.

She drew away. Her greatest fear was that she herself would be seen as complicit in the murder of one who was perceived to be her rival, and that she would thereby lose the love of her subjects – the most precious jewel in her crown, as she was fond of putting it. It occurred to her that monarchs had lost their thrones for less, and she was a female ruler in a precarious, insecure position. Merely associating with Robert now could catapult her on a headlong course to ruin.

But Robert had other ideas. 'Marry me, Bess,' he said urgently. 'Proclaim to the world that you believe in my innocence!'

'And put my crown in jeopardy?' she flung back, distress making her vehement. 'If you think our marrying will stop the rumours, you are more stupid than ever I took you for. Robin, it will fuel them! People are saying that you murdered your wife so that you could have me.'

'We could wait a decent interval,' he replied.

'I assure you that will make no difference.'

'Then what future is there for us?'

'What future can there be?' Elizabeth burst out, angry now. 'How many times have I told you that I have no wish to marry? When will you believe it?'

Robert laid hold of her and crushed her to his chest. 'It is your womanly fears that speak, is it not? Think you I cannot help you overcome them?' His voice was urgent.

'Robin,' Elizabeth protested, struggling free, 'don't you think I would overcome them if I could? It is no joy to me, living with such terrors.'

'Methinks you will only conquer them by facing them. Then they will lose their power to frighten you.'

'Ah, Robin, you are become a philosopher. But you think only of one difficulty. I have other objections against marriage, remember, aside from this latest tangle.'

'Excuses, excuses! You are all excuses!' he erupted. 'You enjoy playing games, admit it. You want men fawning over you, competing for your hand. It suits your vanity to have it so!'

'How dare you!' Elizabeth snarled.

'I dare because you have permitted me to dare much else!' Robert flung back. 'I am a man, Bess, with a man's needs. How much longer do you think I will be prepared to play your games? I want you, and I will have you!'

'You presume too much!' she spat.

'Like Admiral Seymour?' he countered, and she felt herself flush with anger and – it had to be admitted – shame.

'That was ungallant of you,' she hissed, turning away from him.

Robert took her hand, instantly contrite. 'Forgive me, Bess, that was unworthy of me – but it rankles that you gave yourself to him, and will not give yourself to me.'

Elizabeth felt the familiar fears encroaching, threatening to consume her. 'I was young and inexperienced. I was not a queen with a reputation to protect. Robin, if I fall from grace, my enemies will pounce. I do not fear pregnancy just because it could kill me; I fear the scandal and ruin it would bring me.'

'Then marry me!'

'Have you not listened?' Elizabeth roared. 'God's blood, am I surrounded by fools? I – do – not – want – to – marry!'

'Then sleep alone in future,' Robert retorted, furious, and turned on his heel to go.

Elizabeth saw red. He had pre-empted her; in her fit of pique, she had been about to forbid him her bed. But instead he had rejected her! Not to be borne!

'Oh, I intend to!' she shouted. But when the door banged behind him, she fell into a storm of weeping.

Elizabeth sat at the head of the council board. She knew she looked unwell and heavy-eyed. Small wonder, as she had not slept much these past few weeks. The situation was worse than she had feared. All over the kingdom, irate clerics were thundering from their pulpits that the death of Lady Dudley was prejudicial to the honour of the Queen, and that something must be done to bring the culprit to justice. The scandal was the talk of Europe, with the most unfavourable conclusions being drawn and chewed over in every court, tavern and hovel. It was disturbingly clear that most people thought that Elizabeth had colluded with Lady Dudley's husband in her murder. Even Kat's husband, John Astley, had been banished the court for speaking his mind about Dudley, and of course the Queen of Scots had weighed in, cattily announcing that the Queen of England was to marry her horse-keeper, who had killed his wife to make room for her. Cecil had blushed when he read Elizabeth *that* report.

Once again he had been extraordinarily sympathetic, yet he had not shied from his duty.

'Our Protestant allies abroad are appalled at the rumours,' he told her. 'They fear you are hell-bent on self-destruction.' That had alarmed her, as had Bishop de Quadra's icy mien. Clearly the Bishop thought her guilty. Well, he would. She was a heretic in his eyes, and therefore capable of anything.

Robert had come begging forgiveness, his expression as appealing as a dog in disgrace, and she had graciously granted it, but she was finding it hard to forget what he had said to her. Even so, she wanted him near her. The sight of him still made her catch her breath. He was the very fabric of life to her, and she knew, as surely as she had faith in God, that she could not live without him. But although she kept him with her as often as she dared by day, at night she insisted on sleeping alone. What it cost her – all those fretful, wakeful hours, the books she had tried and failed to read, the times she had barely stopped herself from knocking on his door – he would never know, but she dared not risk any further scandal. She had enough to deal with as it was.

Throckmorton had sent his secretary, Robert Jones, over from Paris to ask the Council how he should counter the gossip; it was rife there also. Elizabeth sharply told Jones he had had no need to come.

'Madam,' he replied, 'there is every necessity for my being here. If your Majesty marries Lord Robert it would be folly.'

'Enough!' she exploded, outraged at such presumption. Clearly the man had more courage than sense. How dare he! She glowered at him. 'I have heard this before, and it does not behove you, a subject, to say it to me.'

Faltering, but undeterred, Jones persisted. 'But Madam, may I remind you that Lord Robert was involved in the plot to set Lady Jane Grey on the throne? That was treason. If he was capable of that, think what else he might be capable of.'

Elizabeth suddenly burst out laughing, but there was no real mirth in it. Jones was shocked. In his experience monarchs did not behave with such levity. It must be something to do with the Queen being a woman. Probably the wrong time of the month.

'Madam,' he ventured, more cautiously now, 'I hesitate to repeat to you what is being said in France about your Majesty and Lord Robert.'

'There is no need,' Elizabeth replied, composing herself. 'The matter has been tried and found to be contrary to what has been reported. You shall say that to anyone who repeats these vile calumnies. May I remind you that Lord Robert was at court when his wife died? None of his people were present at the attempt at her house, and things have fallen out in a way that should touch neither my lord's honesty nor my honour.'

Jones swooped. 'So your Majesty believes that there *was* an attempt on her life?' he persisted.

'I meant, if attempt there was,' Elizabeth said hastily. If she was honest with herself, she thought, there probably had been. Amy's death had been all too timely. Not for herself – she had never had any intention of marrying Robert – and not for Robert, for the rumours had effectively crushed his hopes. But *someone* had probably thought he was doing them both a service. Notwithstanding, none of the inquiries made by the coroner, Amy's family and Robert's friends had unearthed any clues. If there had been an assassin, he had left no trace. Maybe Amy's death had been accidental after all. It was conceivable that she had just tripped and fallen – a simple accident as the coroner had concluded. So why did Elizabeth have trouble believing that?

'Madam, it is not too late to revive negotiations for a match with the Archduke or the Earl of Arran,' Cecil said hopefully, clearly itching to draw up a marriage treaty. They were alone in the council chamber, the other councillors having dispersed with the obnoxious Jones. 'It would be a sure way of giving the lie to rumour.' And it would put paid to Dudley swaggering pridefully around the court, over-confident as ever and seemingly impervious to the gossip.

'I will think on it,' Elizabeth replied, a glint of tetchiness in her eyes.

'I trust that your Majesty has given up all thought of wedding Lord Robert,' Cecil said gently. He needed her to say it, for his own peace of mind.

'My judgement is not that addled, William,' she retorted. 'I am sensible of my duties and obligations.'

'Madam, might I venture to ask that you make that clear to Lord Robert?' Cecil suggested. That would put an end to the man's posturing.

'I have already done so,' she told him. Cecil looked doubtful, and he had even more cause to be when, only weeks later,

Elizabeth announced that she intended to elevate Robert to the peerage. *The peerage?* What had the man done to deserve that? He was a proven traitor who might or might not have murdered his wife. Was that now a qualification for nobility? Cecil shook his head, and kept on shaking it.

Predictably, as Robert, in the wake of the Queen's announcement, was seen to preen and wax ever more conceited, there was a fresh wave of rumours. Her Majesty would give him a dukedom. No, it was a barony. Was she paying him off or paving the way for greater things? More likely she did really mean to marry him after all. The two of them thought they had got away with it, did they?

The day set for the ceremony of investiture arrived. As the councillors and courtiers gathered, curiosity getting the better of disdain, Robert entered the presence chamber, resplendent in a dazzling new suit of clothes, and knelt before the throne.

'The coronet today, the crown tomorrow,' Bacon murmured in Cecil's ear.

'I think not,' Cecil smiled.

Bacon gave him a quizzical look. Did Cecil know something he didn't?

Elizabeth rose from her throne. A page brought her the Letters Patent of nobility. A second stood by bearing the scarlet robes of estate furred with ermine; a third carried the coronet on a velvet cushion.

Elizabeth took the patent and studied it for a while. The courtiers grew restive. Robert shifted his weight from knee to knee, for he was becoming numb. Suddenly the Queen drew her small jewelled knife from its sheath on her girdle and, to the astonishment of all present, sliced the parchment across. Slash, slash. The courtiers gaped. Robert stared at her in horror. How in God's name could she humiliate him thus, in the presence of many of his enemies?

'I have decided,' she said, looking up, but not at Robert, 'that I will not have another Dudley in the House of Lords, bearing in mind that this family have been traitors to the Crown for three generations. I thank you all for your attendance here today. You have my leave to depart.'

There was an excited explosion of whispering before the company began to file reluctantly away. It was only the Queen's presence, and her gimlet eyes boring into their backs, that kept the courtiers from breaking out in frenzied chatter. Only Robert stood his ground, glowering, furious.

'Good God, Bess! How could you do this?' he exploded.

'I have to make it clear to the world that I have no intention of advancing and marrying you,' Elizabeth said, her voice steady. Still she would not meet his eyes.

'I beg you not to abuse me thus in front of your courtiers, Madam. I do not deserve it. I cannot allow you to do this.'

She did look at him then. In fact, to his utter confusion, she stepped down from the dais and patted him playfully on the cheek.

'No, I should have remembered, the Dudleys are not so easily overthrown. But there is no "cannot allow" about it, Robin. I am the Queen, and people must see that I am in control. This is a sure way of putting an end to the gossip.'

'Then is it worth my hoping that things will change in the future?' His voice was taut with anger, hurt and frustration.

'Anything is possible,' she said lightly, and swept out of the room, surprising her clustering courtiers, who were huddling and whispering just outside the door. She sailed on, a smile playing on her lips.

Her ploy worked. Within a month the gossip had died down, even though Robert remained at her side, ardent and attentive. She had exactly what she wanted now: his company, his love, the mere heart-melting sight of him, and the promise of his arms around her at night if she so pleased (which she did not, or not yet). He was her consort in all but name. She wondered if she had ever really desired more.

Bishop de Quadra had finally thawed somewhat. She enjoyed baiting him, leading him to believe she was still interested in taking the Archduke, then hinting that she might marry Robert after all.

'It *might* please me to advance him,' she declared, a twinkle in her eye. 'I must confess to you, Bishop, that I am no angel, and I do not deny that I have an affection for him, for the many good qualities he possesses. I do see daily more clearly the necessity for marriage, and to satisfy the English humour it seems I must marry an Englishman. Tell me, what would King Philip think if I married one of my servants?'

Quadra answered stiffly, 'My master would be pleased to hear of your marriage, whoever your Majesty chooses, as it is important for the welfare of your kingdom. His Majesty, I feel sure, would be happy to hear of Lord Robert's good fortune.' Happy too, no doubt, at the prospect of the heretic Elizabeth's reign not long surviving her wedding.

The Queen inclined her head graciously.

'But is Your Majesty truly satisfied that Lord Robert's wife's death was an accident?' the Bishop ventured. There was much more that he could have said, and would have liked to have said, but the rules of diplomacy prevented him.

'There is no question of it,' Elizabeth said, her voice suddenly sharp as steel. 'And had the poor lady not fallen, she would have died anyway. She was mortally ill with a malady in her breast.'

'I find it strange,' said the Bishop, frowning, 'that Master Secretary told me she was perfectly well, only the day before she died.'

'What? Sir William said that?' Elizabeth was stunned. It did not make sense.

'Forgive me, Madam, he told me it was not true that she was ill, that she was very well, and taking good care not to be poisoned, for certain parties were plotting to kill her.'

Elizabeth paled. '*That* is not true,' she averred. 'She had been ill for months. Lord Robert was very concerned about her. We knew she was dying – and Sir William knew it too. Why should he say that?'

123

'I have no idea, Madam,' Quadra replied, starting to look perplexed. The Queen's reaction had seemed genuine enough.

But Elizabeth was beginning to have a very good idea. And after she had dismissed the Bishop, she fell to some hard thinking. Cecil hated Dudley – and always had. That master of political intrigue would have done much to prevent her marrying Robert, and had made no secret of his fears that it might cost her the throne, and England its Protestant saviour, whom men now called the new Judith or Deborah. She had known that Cecil had been thinking of retiring on account of Robert, for others had told her. She'd known too that she had upset him by her lack of gratitude for the advantageous treaty he had negotiated. Yet, with her eyes dazzled by Robin through those long, spacious, enchanted summer days, she had been blind to Cecil's misery.

Now she was not so blind. The events of the past months had opened her eyes. She knew that few princes had ever had such a counsellor, and that William, her Spirit, was that rare being, one that put the needs of his royal mistress and his country before his own ambitions and desire for advancement. And yet she had almost cast him away.

There was no talk of retirement now. From the moment Amy's death had been announced, Cecil had been back where he was before, effortlessly in control of affairs. It was Robert whose star had been eclipsed, Robert who had ended up cast into the wilderness – and Robert who had returned a chastened man, his wings clipped.

What game had Cecil been playing? He had known that Amy Dudley was dying; Elizabeth herself had told him, several times, and had kept him informed of the progress of Amy's disease. And he himself had told her of rumours that Robert was plotting to kill his wife so that he could marry the Queen. Had Cecil lied to Quadra, that inveterate gossip, so that when the end came the finger of suspicion would point at Robert and so wreck his chances of ever becoming king? It might even have destroyed him, although Cecil would surely have seen his own deception merely as a means of protecting the Queen from herself and ensuring the future security of her realm.

But there was something even more disturbing about what Cecil had told Quadra. The Bishop had definitely repeated that *certain parties* were plotting to kill Amy. Surely, surely Cecil had not meant to imply that she herself was involved? But what other accomplice would Robert have had? And if Cecil had wanted to protect her from the consequences of a marriage he deemed disastrous for her and her kingdom, why would he have as good as implicated her in the plot? No, she would not believe it of him. Quadra, that arch-intriguer, was stirring things up and putting his own construction on what Cecil had said.

But then, unbidden, came another thought that chilled her to the very marrow. What if Cecil, seeing it as his sacred duty to protect his Queen from making what he most certainly would have regarded as a disastrous mistake, had made sure that Amy Dudley died before God claimed her, with the inevitable result that her husband was blamed for her murder? Was Cecil capable of such villainy? In truth, she would have thought not, for he had always been an upright and God-fearing man, but there remained a glimmer of uncertainty. In this case, would he not have been convinced that the end justified the means? Who knew what went on in that clever, complicated mind? And if he *had* done such a thing, it had all turned out as planned, and Robert's chances of becoming king had been adroitly scuppered.

She chewed and agonised over the mystery as she lay abed that night. Would Cecil have dared? Robert was, after all, the Queen's favourite, and therefore should have been untouchable. But Cecil was a man who went about things in subtle ways. Long ago another subtle politician, Thomas Cromwell, had brought down Elizabeth's mother. *He* had dared – and he had taken the most calculated risk, for her father, King Henry, had been a fearsome man, terrible to those who offended him.

The next day she found herself looking at Cecil with new eyes, watching for signs that might betray his capacity for dark deeds, or his guilt and complicity in Amy's death. Should she confront him with what Quadra had told her? She fretted about it for days, not sure that she wanted her worst fears confirmed, for she shrank from facing the possibility that her most trusted minister was capable of murder. But in the end she could contain herself no longer.

'Stay awhile, William,' she said, as the councillors were preparing to depart. There was nothing unusual in such a request, and when they had gone he sat down, waiting for her to open her mind to him, as she so often did.

'Bishop de Quadra said an odd thing,' Elizabeth began, and she repeated the conversation. Cecil's face did not change. There was nothing in it that could be read as dismay or guilt. He seemed not the least bit perturbed.

'I fear the good Bishop has given your Majesty a somewhat garbled version of what I actually said,' he answered. 'I was being sarcastic, for one thing. And I was telling him of rumours that worried me. He has misconstrued it all. What on earth did you think I intended?'

'Forgive me, kind Spirit, I was merely puzzled,' Elizabeth assured him, feeling immense relief. 'It seemed a strange thing for you to say. But you have resolved it now.' She smiled at him. 'So you do think that Lady Dudley's death was accidental?'

'Indisputably, Madam,' Cecil replied. There was no hint of dissimulation in his eyes or his voice.

In the spring the court buzzed with fresh rumours about Robert Dudley. It was bruited that King Philip had promised to support his marriage to the Queen in return for England's return to Rome. The result, predictably, was a fierce wave of anti-Catholic feeling. Again, Elizabeth suspected Cecil of fomenting a ploy to discredit Dudley, and this time, she told herself, she was probably right, for he knew that Robert had been intriguing with Bishop de Quadra to enlist Spanish backing in his campaign to win her hand.

Robert was so dismayed at the rumours and backbiting that he began to speak of going abroad to live.

'There is nothing for me here,' he said dejectedly.

'What of me?' Elizabeth demanded, hurt at his easy rejection of all that they were to each other. Was she not sufficient compensation for everything he was obliged to endure?

'You know I love you, Bess,' he answered, his hand on his heart. 'But you keep me at arm's length. It is a ceaseless cruelty to me, for you have no idea how much I want you.'

'Me, or my crown?' she challenged. It was, by now, an old joke between them.

'You,' Robert said, his dark gypsy's eyes glittering as he took her in his arms and closed his lips on hers, hungry, insistent. She gave herself up to the moment, then, remembering what he had said, pulled away.

'But you are deserting me to go abroad.'

'You do not want me, Bess – not in the way I want you.'

'Give me a little more time,' she pleaded.

'I've heard that before,' Robert sighed. 'Bess, I am thirty next year. It is an age at which a man should be married and raising sons to carry on his name. But I am little better than your lap-dog, well groomed for your pleasure, always at your beck and call and offering unstinted devotion – but only when it pleases you. I want more than that. I want you as a man wants a woman. I want you as my wife.'

Elizabeth gently touched his cheek. 'I would not hurt you for the world, sweet, bonny Robin. Be patient with me, just for a little longer.'

Robert grasped her hand. 'How can I refuse you? But you know my life here is becoming unendurable. Cecil is out to ruin me.'

'I would never let him do that,' she assured him.

She knew what she would do. Robert had languished in the wilderness for too long. She would tip the scales once more. She would put an end to this alarming talk of going abroad.

When, soon afterwards, the court moved to Greenwich Palace, Robert – to his delight and, it must be said, bewilderment – was assigned a sumptuous apartment next to the Queen's. Gilded battens adorned the ceiling and tapestries in the antique style covered the walls; the fireplace and overmantel were of carved stone studded with painted Tudor roses, and on the floor there lay a costly Turkey carpet. It was a lodging fit for a king!

'This is my reward for your patience,' Elizabeth told him, when she joined him there moments after his arrival; he realised that she must have been waiting to hear that he had come. His servants, unpacking his gear, fell to their knees at her appearance. 'I hope you like it,' she said gaily.

'Madam, I am overwhelmed,' he replied, kneeling too, and kissing her hands.

'Do not kneel to me,' she commanded, raising him and dismissing his attendants. Then she drew him to the window, which overlooked the wide Thames. Below them there was a queue of barges waiting to unload a gaggle of well-dressed lords and ladies at the landing stage.

Elizabeth smiled. 'Do you know what room this is, my Eyes?'

'No. I have not been in it before,' Robert said, lightly brushing back a tendril of hair that had escaped from her black velvet cap.

'It is the Virgins' Chamber, and I was born here,' she told him. 'These were my mother's lodgings.'

'I fail to see why it is called the Virgins' Chamber,' he grinned, wishing to divert her from the sad subject of her mother.

'Look closer at the tapestries. They tell the story of St Ursula and her eleven thousand virgins.'

'Is there a message I am supposed to be getting?' Robert asked. 'Bess, you assign me these rich chambers next to your own; you say they are a reward for my patience. You raise all my hopes, then you talk of virgins!'

Elizabeth had to laugh. 'I assure you it was not deliberate! Now Robin,' and suddenly she was all coyness, 'I have gone so far, but I am a woman and will go no further. The rest is rather up to you.' She looked at him. Her eyes were impenetrable – as was the rest of her, he thought, irritated.

'Are you playing games with me again, Bess?' he demanded to know. 'And if I ask to bed with you, will you deny me at the last moment?'

'I never deny you willingly,' Elizabeth answered, and he almost believed it. Oh, she was maddening, infuriating – but, great God, he wanted her!

He pulled her to him, enfolding her against his breast. She could feel his body stirring against her, and excitement rose in her too. He bent his face to kiss her.

'Sweet Robin,' she whispered against the roughness of his beard, 'if I were a country maid, I would be yours. Nothing could please me more. But I am the Queen.'

'But you have just intimated that what happens next is down to me!' Robert complained. 'I have asked you to bed with me. I have asked you to marry me. You will not agree to either. What do you *want* from me, Bess?'

She felt him stiffen against her, and not with desire now. His whole body was taut with longing and fury. She knew what she was doing to him, and hated herself for it, but there was no remedy at hand. Except one.

'Come to me tonight,' she murmured impulsively, thinking that later could take care of itself. 'There, I have said it. I was waiting for you to ask, but you harangued me instead.'

'Dear God, I don't believe it,' Robert breathed, his mouth in her hair. 'Do you really mean it this time, Bess?'

'Do you doubt me?' she countered, gazing up at him.

'Would that I did not. You have tied me in knots. I never know which way to take with you. I had hoped that was your meaning when you said things were up to me – but you are the mistress of ambiguity at times!'

'Once it is out that you have these rooms, people will talk,' Elizabeth said. 'We may as well do something to deserve it!'

'And what will that something be?' he asked, relenting and kissing her.

'Now that would be telling!' Elizabeth giggled.

They lay abed, naked, in her chamber, the soft candlelight casting a golden haze on their skin. It was wonderful to feel Robin's beloved flesh against hers. Ardently, their clothes discarded, he had swept her into his arms and tumbled her on the bed, covering her face with kisses; and she had twined herself around him. This time, after months of denying herself, she wanted him with her whole being; never before had she experienced such a sense of intimacy and freedom. She felt herself opening up like a flower, the need for completion urgent in her. She could do this, she knew it; she would not be afraid any more. And the consequences be damned!

Robert slid his leg over hers, rough skin against smooth. He shifted closer, kissing her mouth, her eyes and her neck, murmuring unintelligible words of desire, his hands caressing, roving where they would all over her body. Excited beyond endurance, he mounted her and she felt him pressing against her, hard, urgent, insistent. In a moment, a little moment, he would breach all her defences.

In a flash there came to mind the corpse-white dead faces of those who had loved and died for it: her mother, Katherine Howard and Thomas Seymour, their necks all bloody, their headless bodies crumpled below them; Jane Seymour and Katherine Parr, faces twisted out of recognition with the pain of fatal childbirth; and Amy Dudley, who had known this very same flesh that was now assailing hers, lying broken and lifeless on the floor of Cumnor Place – Amy, whose lips were rotting in the rictus of decay, whose only caress now was from worms.

'No!' she cried, and with all her strength pushed Robert from her.

'Oh, aah, Bess, what are you doing?' he groaned, panting furiously as he slid away unsatisfied. 'Never do that to me!' The words came out as a gasp.

'I could not help it,' she wailed. 'I was frightened. I felt you against me, and I saw – oh, God help me, I saw death in all its horrible guises. Oh my Eyes, tell me I am not mad!'

'Not mad, but cruel,' he flung at her, struggling into a sitting position and reaching for his clothes.

'No, never, I could not be cruel to you. They came unbidden, those terrible faces with their dead eyes and all the blood . . .' She was weeping bitterly now.

Robert took a deep breath, then another. He laid a hand on her shoulder. Plainly this was no game.

He felt helpless. He had no idea how to help this woman who was sobbing so heart-wrenchingly beside him on the bed. This woman whom he wanted so fiercely, for so many reasons. Love, he knew, was only a part of it, albeit a substantial one. But there was in him a driving need to confound his enemies, to show them that there was more to him than a queen's pretty boy, and to emerge ascendant over them. The crown was now surely within his reach. He had been patient long enough, trusting that everything came to those who waited. Yet there remained just this one obstacle to be overcome, and he was suddenly no longer so sure that he could conquer it. Like a shoot creeping out from a seed in the soil, it began to dawn on him that he might never do so, and that Elizabeth's fears were so deep-rooted that no man would ever vanquish them.

He had never doubted that she would marry him in the end. There was that between them that could not be replaced by anyone else, however advantageous the match. But now, for the first time since Amy's death, he began to wonder if his future might lie elsewhere, especially if he wanted to breed heirs of his body, for it was dawning on him that he might never get them from Elizabeth. And if he could not sire princes, then at least he wanted sons to carry on his name and inherit his wealth. But how, loving Elizabeth as he did, was he ever going to do that? He knew how jealous she could be. Were he even to flirt with another lady, he would risk his power, his property and everything he held dear.

Feeling overwhelmed by it all, he let his hand fall from her shoulder. Elizabeth gave no sign that she had noticed, but she had, she had. She could not stem the tide of her tears; they kept rising as if from a bottomless well. She was racked with pain and guilt. It was bad enough that she herself had to bear these fears; but far worse that another, one so beloved, should suffer because of them. She did not think she could feel any more wretched than she did at this moment.

Making a tremendous effort she fought to regain mastery of herself.

'I am so sorry, Robin,' she whispered, lying there looking very forlorn.

He took her hand. 'What *can* I do to help you?' he asked.

'I wish I knew!' she blurted, and the tears welled again.

'Have you consulted your physicians?' he ventured.

'No!'

'You need to talk to someone. I am always here to listen, Bess, but I am no doctor.'

She clasped both his hands. 'Ah, Robin, you are more of a remedy for me than any physician could prescribe. If anyone can help me, it is you. Be patient with me. I will conquer myself, never fear. I just need time. And I could not bear it if you held tonight against me!'

He took her in his arms at that. 'Never, never,' he soothed, trying not to betray his concern. 'I will wait for ever, while there is hope that you will be mine one day.'

'I am yours already,' Elizabeth said. 'And may yet be more to you. I do wish it.'

He crushed her tightly to him at that, hope welling again in his heart.

Robert sought out Bishop de Quadra. He had a deal to propose, and a bargain that he had no intention of keeping. It was not to his liking, but he was ready to do whatever was needful – anything at all – to marry Elizabeth.

'My lord Bishop, you are known for a wise man,' he said, hoping that flattery would smooth his path.

The Bishop eyed him warily. 'If I can be of service to your lordship . . .' he murmured.

'Certainly you can, if you would do your best to persuade King Philip to support my suit to the Queen. I am sure you both appreciate the advantages it will bring.'

'Indeed – but to whom?' Quadra smiled.

'To our two kingdoms,' Robert said, reining in the urge to shake the man.

'And how, may I ask, would this marriage you propose benefit my master?'

'It would win him, its broker, the undying friendship of England, and of your servant here,' Robert declared. 'Tell him also that I fear I have been in error in regard to religion. I have even considered converting to the Catholic faith.'

The gleam in the Bishop's eye was unmistakable, but calculating too. The man was clearly asking himself if Robert was sincere – or if his possible conversion was just a means to an end.

'I will tell King Philip what you have said,' Quadra said at length.

Later, alone in his chamber, Robert felt disgusted at how low he had stooped. How could he even be seen to be thinking of forsaking the faith he held dear? That was not the right way to go about things. It went against his Protestant soul to inveigle favours from the Catholics. Moreover, the ploy was too transparent, and the Bishop had surely guessed his game.

Then it came to him – like a revelation – that he must show the world that he was a personage of moral fibre with deeply held convictions. Some that had heard him speak and looked into his heart knew it already, but there were not enough of them. He must be seen by all as a man of gravity, indeed, the most steadfast champion of the Anglican religion. To Quadra's bewilderment he abandoned their cosy chats and went about staunchly proclaiming his devotion to the reformed faith. None could deny that this in particular, and his many other accomplishments, eminently qualified him to be king; he doubted that any prince in Europe was so befitted.

His tactics worked. It was not long before he noticed, slowly but surely, a change in people's attitudes towards him. Cautiously, as if he was a snake who might bite or a sorcerer who might bewitch them with his magic, they were becoming more courteous, less dismissive of his opinions, and beginning to treat him at last as a man of gravitas. Elizabeth noticed this too, and was much gratified by it. Cecil noticed it, and was alarmed. God forbid that a Dudley should ever ascend the throne!

But that summer many believed it would not be long before that happened.

On a warm June night Elizabeth, bravely attired in a beautiful gown of cloth of silver, boarded her state barge to watch a pageant on the Thames. Robert was close behind her as she stepped nimbly along the narrow deck between the livery-clad oarsmen to the larger of the two cabins, which was sumptuously appointed with gilded paintwork, rich velvet cushions, curtains of cloth of gold, and a crimson velvet rug strewn with petals, which gave off a heady scent. The curtains were tied back, and through the expensively glazed window Elizabeth espied Bishop de Quadra among the press of courtiers crowding the landing stage, awaiting their own barges. It was chaos out there, and if they were not careful someone would end up in the river.

'My lord!' she called. 'Pray join us!'

Robert scowled. 'You do not need to flirt with the Catholics,' he muttered, but the Bishop, a delighted smile on his broad face, was now boarding the barge and there was no more time for grumbling. Lady Katherine Grey came, whey-faced as ever, with a platter of seed cakes and goblets of wine, and Quadra was made welcome as Elizabeth invited him to be seated with her and Robert on the opulent cushions. Now the barge was pulling away to the centre of the Thames in the torchlight, and a myriad other craft came gliding to form a flotilla around the royal barge, each boat having its own gaudy display, put on for the delight of the Queen and the crowds that lined the banks. There were dragons and unicorns, nymphs and gods, knights and damsels, all accompanied by music, verses and fireworks. It was a magical scene and Elizabeth revelled in it. She sat happily between Robert and Quadra, gaily pointing out the sights, devouring the cakes and clapping her hands. When the Bishop ventured to talk about politics, she hushed him with a raised finger and a wink, and went on swapping witticisms and jokes with Robert.

For all that he was a churchman sworn to celibacy, Quadra could see that this was a couple very happy in each other's company. If you could forget that they were two heretics, and that Lord Robert had very likely murdered his wife, they were perfect for each other. Mellow and expansive with good wine, cake and the undeniable honour of being invited to share this special evening with the Queen and her favourite, he felt moved to make an observation. 'Your Majesty seems very happy tonight,' he said, looking first at her and then at Lord Robert.

Elizabeth smiled. 'It is because I am,' she said.

'So the rumours are true, that you will marry Lord Robert here?'

'That would be telling!' Elizabeth laughed. 'But we do speak of it, do we not, Robin?'

Robert knew that she was enjoying teasing Quadra — and him too. 'If you like, Madam,' he said, playing along, 'the worthy Bishop here could marry us.'

The Queen giggled. 'I am not sure he knows enough English!'

Quadra's good mood evaporated. He disliked this banter about what was, after all, a weighty, nay, a sacred matter. Matrimony was a holy estate and a sacrament of the Church, and not to be spoken of lightly. But all was falsehood and vanity with this woman. She had a hundred thousand devils in her body, and he did not pretend to understand her.

'Madam,' he said, a touch stiffly, 'if your Majesty were to extricate yourself from the tyranny of Sir William Cecil and your other advisers, and restore the true religion in England, then you could marry Lord Robert as soon as you please, because King Philip would give you his full support, and with that behind you no one would dare to oppose your union. And I myself would gladly officiate at the nuptials.'

Elizabeth could see that the good humour had fled from Robert's face, but before he could say anything compromising, she beamed at the Bishop and thanked him for his advice and his good care for her affairs. She even went so far as to say that she would consider what he had said, and ignored Robert's angry gesturing behind Quadra's back. Later, though, when they were alone, and he had the presumption to take her to task for dissembling over such an important issue, she lost her temper.

'I am queen of this realm! Do not question my wisdom, Robin. I was invested with it at my coronation, and it is not seemly for mere mortals to disparage me. You would not have spoken to my father thus!'

'I did not bed with your father!' he flung back. 'You're very willing to come down from your cloud and consort with a mere mortal at such times.'

'Pah! Don't count on it, Robin. And you should know that it is in England's interests to have Spain's friendship at this time.'

'Even if it means compromising your principles over religion?'

Elizabeth snorted. 'You know me better than that. Come, dear Eyes, let's not quarrel. It was a lovely evening until you spoilt it.'

He came to her then; he could never resist her, and again he felt that her hand, the ultimate prize, was within his reach. But that night, as on the other nights that had passed since she had pushed him away, she seemed distracted and tense, and he had cause, lying there wakeful in the small hours, to wonder what his future held.

It seemed that Elizabeth was again playing games. Word had come that Erik of Sweden, ardent as ever, was on his way to England to renew his courtship.

'I don't know why he bothers,' Robert growled, and was heartened to be told by his friends that it was all over the court that the Queen had eyes for no one but him, and that people were laying bets as to when, not if, they would marry. But then a new portrait of Erik arrived, in advance of his person. Elizabeth had it set up in her presence chamber, and stood admiring it as her courtiers clustered around. She smiled archly at Robert, then turned her head to the painted face on the panel.

'If the King is as handsome as his picture, no woman could resist him,' she declared wickedly, and as she chatted to all and sundry her eyes kept straying in its direction, ignoring Robert standing simmering beside her.

He had cause to simmer even more when she received the ambassador of Charles IX, the new King of France. Mary Stuart's sickly young husband, Francis II, had recently died, and his brother now reigned. The Queen Mother, Catherine de' Medici, had made it plain that Mary was no longer welcome in France, and so she had returned home to Scotland, which was now in the grip of its Protestant lords. It pleased Elizabeth to think of the inexperienced Catholic Mary, who had dared to lay claim to her own crown, having to deal with these hardened, unforgiving men: barbarians, the lot of them, as Bacon had said. They would keep her well occupied and stop her making mischief!

But at least the Scottish lords were friendly to Protestant England, which would curb Mary's pretensions; and now King Charles was offering his friendship.

'Madame,' his ambassador said, 'my master not only sends his good wishes, but he has instructed me to say that he thinks you should marry Lord Robert Dudley. Indeed, he desires to meet Lord Robert.'

Robert's face brightened beatifically at that, and he looked at Elizabeth as if to say, *There! Not only Spain desires our marriage, but France too. The way has been smoothed for us* . . .

He was taking too much for granted! Turning to the French ambassador, the Queen smiled sweetly. 'It would scarcely be honourable to send a groom to see so great a king.'

A groom? How dare she refer to her Master of Horse, one of the proud Dudleys, thus! Robert burned with shame and fury, inflamed by the furtive smiles of the watching courtiers. Reptiles, all of them!

'Ah, but I cannot do without my Lord Robert,' the Queen was saying, 'for he is like my little dog, and whenever he comes into a room, people know that I am near.'

How Robert kept his temper he never knew, but anger was hot within him. What drove her to humiliate him publicly in this way? Did he mean so little to her? This was not the woman who had lain in his arms night after night. How could she be so two-faced, a female Janus? He thought of locking his door against her, but when it came to it he could not bring himself to do so. And in the end he was glad of that, because when he was lying there spent but unsatisfied after a stormy row that ended in passionate embraces, Elizabeth reached over to her bedside table, handed him a document granting him a pension of a thousand pounds a year – a staggeringly generous sum – and hope sprang anew.

After that his star was in the ascendant. He and she were as close as ever. Wherever she went he was just one step behind. Occasionally, cloaked and masked, she accompanied him to taverns, shooting matches, bear pits and other places a queen could never go. He would marvel at her, downing a flagon of ale with her coarsest subjects, or yelling out encouragement to the dog on whom she had wagered or the archer she favoured. She revelled in the freedom of it, enjoying the chatter and opinions of ordinary people, honest plain folk who would not cozen her with flattery and tell her what she wanted to hear. It was instructive, to say the least.

One evening in late spring he took her to the Mitre Inn in Holborn.

'Queen Elizabeth,' drawled an elderly fellow in his cups, 'now there's a woman, I say. King Harry to the life, God save her. But she's a fool to tangle herself with that whoreson Dudley.'

'He murdered his wife,' a woman said, and there were several murmurs of assent. *Aye, aye. That he did.* Under the table Elizabeth laid a restraining hand on a bullish Robert's hand.

'So I say the Queen should let him alone,' the old man continued, warming to his theme. 'What do you think, mistress?' He leered at Elizabeth.

'I think we should ignore malicious rumours,' she replied, smiling beneath her heavily painted face. 'But it is heartening to hear you speak lovingly of the Queen.'

'They bain't rumours,' put in a girl in dishabille, who was plainly a whore.

'And you are intimately acquainted with the whoreson Dudley?' Elizabeth rounded on her, enjoying herself immensely. The company roared with laughter. Only Robert was stony-faced.

'But the Queen should get herself married soon,' the innkeeper chimed in. 'Stands to reason, country needs an heir. And it ain't natural, a woman wanting to stay a virgin.'

Elizabeth stiffened. 'What *ain't natural* about that? It strikes me that a lot of women would be much happier without the ties of marriage.'

'Gawd, if they all said that the world'd grind to a halt,' the old man commented.

'Aye, but it's a man's world, and there's no denying that!' Elizabeth countered.

'You tell him, girl!' the whore said, and the other women chorused their approval.

'She still has to wed,' the innkeeper persisted.

'But not that bastard Dudley,' growled the old man. Robert's hand moved instinctively to where his sword was normally belted to his waist. He had, of course, left it behind, but still carried in its place a small dagger. London was not a safe city at night. Elizabeth nudged him. It was time to leave.

'Well, my masters, you have been good company!' she declared. 'I pray that we will meet again.'

One of the women was eyeing her closely.

'I've seen you before,' she said. 'Was it here?'

'Very likely,' Elizabeth said briskly, and rose to her feet, downing the rest of her drink in one go and gathering her cloak around her. 'God give you good night!' she cried.

When they left the inn, both she and Robert were slightly unsteady due to the strength of the ale. There was a cherry tree outside, and he drew her into his arms beneath its concealing branches. He was very drunk and seemed to have forgotten about the way he had been insulted. He kissed her deeply, holding her close, then drew away and swept her a wobbly bow.

'Dance with me, my lady!' he demanded.

Elizabeth giggled. 'Here?' she asked.

'Yes!' And he grabbed her hands, humming a tune and swinging her about, capering wildly around the tree. She was laughing so much when they had spun to a halt that she could barely catch her breath.

'Oh to have the freedom to do this every night!' she cried to the stars. 'I do envy my subjects!'

As they strolled along by the river towards Whitehall and the night air had its effect, Robert stopped laughing and grew morose.

'How can you let them get away with such talk, Bess?' he protested.

'You forget, I was not the Queen tonight,' she said, 'and they are ignorant folk, but loyal. Do not let their rude talk discomfit you. We have better things to think of.' And she drew close to him, slipping her arm inside his cloak.

At night she and Robin were lovers in all but the final consummation, sleeping spent in each other's arms after increasingly inventive acts of passion. With a little imagination, there was no end to the things one could do to give and receive pleasure, and she often wondered why, for him, all this was not enough. By day, people paid court to Robert as if he were king already; he looked, carried himself and behaved like a great prince.

Elizabeth, notwithstanding her growing reputation for parsimony – unfair, she thought, especially as she had inherited a bankrupt kingdom; she was only being careful – proved herself a generous lover. She restored the earldom of Warwick, confiscated after the execution of Robert's father, to his brother Ambrose, and with it vast swathes of land. But she continued to evade the subject of marriage whenever Robert raised it, and he was no nearer to calming her fears about sex, although God knew he had tried. Each time he had done so she had seized the initiative for some other kind of love-play, or the tears had welled – and he had not had the heart to press her. It occurred to him that, even if she did consent to marry him, it might be a marriage in name only.

It was well over a year since he had been cleared of culpability in Amy's death – surely a decent enough interval for mourning. There was no reason now why he and the Queen should wait. But it was proving impossible to pin Elizabeth down on the matter, and she was still insisting that she might marry one of her many foreign suitors. It was increasingly hard to stay optimistic. Despair engulfed him.

That summer the court departed on a great progress to the eastern shires. At Ipswich, lodged in Christchurch Mansion, the magnificent house of Sir Edmund Withipoll – a monastery before King Harry dissolved it, although there was little left from the monks' days, for now costly oak panelling clad the walls, the chambers were appointed with richly carved beds and chairs and tables, and supper had been served on silver-gilt plates – Robert was allocated a bedchamber next to the Queen's. It was a big house, but not *that* big, and given the close proximity of everyone else, Elizabeth deemed it unsafe for him to visit her at night, so he was sleeping alone when he was awoken by the most plaintive voice. He sat up quickly, dazed, rubbing his eyes, and was astounded to find Lady Katherine Grey kneeling right by his bedside, weeping pitifully.

'My lord, I beg of you to help me,' she sobbed, her thin shoulders shaking.

'For God's sake,' he hissed, 'hush! The Queen sleeps next door. What would she say if she caught you here?'

'Oh, *please*,' sniffed Katherine, even more pathetically. She was a pale, slight girl, certainly not worth being discovered with him in what would look like an alarmingly compromising situation. And to make matters worse, he thought, envisaging a majestic presence looming in the doorway, Elizabeth loathed her, not only because Katherine was, by law, her heir – although she would never, *ever* acknowledge her as such – but also because the young woman had foolishly made it her business to court Spain, hoping that King Philip would persuade the Queen to declare Katherine her successor – her *Catholic* successor. But what the blazes was Katherine doing here, crying her heart out, in the middle of the night? More to the point, what *would* Elizabeth think if she heard her and found them here together? Robert was utterly mortified at the thought.

Visions of the Tower took shape in his brain. He was desperate to get Katherine out of the room.

'Calm down and tell me what ails you,' he whispered, suddenly, horribly, aware that beneath the bedclothes he was naked. Oh God!

Katherine Grey swallowed and made an effort to stop crying. 'My lord, you have influence with the Queen. Tell her – *please* tell her – that I beg her forgiveness. I have married the Earl of Hertford in secret, without her permission, for I did love him and she had said no – and now I am with child. My lord is abroad on an embassy, and I am alone and do not know what to do. I fear her Majesty's wrath so much I wish myself in a far land . . .'

Robert wished her in a far land too – in fact, anywhere, so long as it was not this bedchamber. Fear made him cruel. 'Her *righteous* wrath,' he muttered, furious with the girl. 'You stupid little fool. How do you think her Majesty will react when she knows that the person next in line to her throne has married without her consent and is carrying an heir? Have you thought of the implications for the Queen – and the succession?'

Katherine crumpled in misery, crying harder than ever.

'Get out!' Robert commanded. 'I cannot help you, nor would I if I could.'

She rose, a pathetic picture of woe, and left the room without another word. As soon as he heard the quiet click of the latch, Robert began to breathe more easily.

He realised that he would have to tell Elizabeth what Katherine had revealed to him. The matter was too weighty and dangerous, and if he concealed it he would be guilty, probably, of misprision of treason. But when the next morning he approached the Queen, who was wearing a loose gown edged with fur, and eating her breakfast of manchet bread, pottage and light ale in the room that had been appointed her privy chamber, he found her frowning and distant.

'Have I offended your Majesty?' he asked, panic seizing him at the thought of what she might have overheard.

143

'Leave us,' she commanded her women. When they had gone she wiped her mouth and laid down her napkin. 'Who was in your room last night?' she asked, her eyes blazing. 'I swear I heard a woman's voice.'

'You did, Bess, and it was not what you think,' Robert declared, mustering a wounded expression, as if to say, *how could you think such ill of me?* 'There *was* a woman in my room, and I have come to tell you about her. It was Lady Katherine Grey.'

'*Lady Katherine Grey?* Elizabeth echoed, astounded.

'Yes, Bess. She woke me up, begging me to tell you that she is with child, having married the Earl of Hertford in secret.'

Elizabeth erupted, calling her cousin names not usually heard on the lips of a well-bred, well-educated lady. She shouted and raged, threatening all kinds of punishments. The rack and the thumbscrews were mentioned. But Robert knew that her fury proceeded from fear. Should Katherine bear a son, that child might live to challenge Elizabeth's title; moreover, he would be a dangerous lure for any who felt that England should be governed by a king instead of a queen.

There was no moving her. She was adamant. She summoned those councillors who were with her on progress and commanded that Lady Katherine and her husband must go to the Tower, and stay there while she decided what was to be done with them.

'Seek out witnesses to this pretended marriage,' she instructed. 'You will not find them, I'll wager. Then we will have it declared invalid, and Lady Katherine will be shown to be no better than she should be.' And no one, of course, would want her to be queen after that.

'That would suit her Majesty,' Cecil observed to Robert afterwards. 'She hates and fears any who might be perceived as a rival. Mark my words, no proofs of this marriage will be found. The Queen wills it, whether they exist or not.'

It proved to be the case. The Council ruled that there had never been a valid wedding ceremony and that the issue of

Lady Katherine's union with Lord Hertford was illegitimate and unfit to inherit. The punishment for the couple's defiance was imprisonment.

Robert wondered if Elizabeth's jealous vengeance proceeded in part from her awareness that Lady Katherine had been alone with him in his room that night.

1562

In the dark days of January, Robert again sought out Bishop de Quadra. This time there were no hints about converting back to the old faith.

'The French,' he said, 'are offering me substantial bribes to use my influence with the Queen on their behalf. But I will refuse them if King Philip backs my suit to her Majesty. A word from him carries great weight with her. Would you write on my behalf to his Majesty?'

Quadra sniffed. 'Her Majesty is already aware that my master is anxious to see her wed. She knows also that he has high hopes of you, Lord Robert. Therefore a letter such as your lordship suggests would be quite unnecessary. As I see it, the real stumbling block is her Majesty's inability to reach a decision about her marriage. I will raise the matter with her again, if you wish it.'

'Oh, I do indeed, and I am most grateful to your Excellency,' Robert said. He hoped fervently that someone other than himself could make Elizabeth see sense.

Elizabeth drew Quadra into a window embrasure, out of earshot of her courtiers, when he asked to speak to her privately. Out of the corner of her eye she could see Robert watching them. Aha, she thought.

'Madam,' the Bishop began, 'I have not liked to press you on this matter, but I am come to ask whether you have made up your mind to marry.'

'Is this about the Archduke?' she asked, guessing that it wasn't.

'Not specifically, Madam,' he replied. 'The word is that you have committed yourself elsewhere.'

Elizabeth smiled. 'Bishop, you should know that I am as free from any engagement as the day I was born; and I have resolved never to accept any suitor I have not met. I have realised that, as I cannot in all honesty ask great princes to come here for my inspection, I will have to marry an Englishman. And that being so, I can find no person more fitting than Lord Robert.' She paused, noting gleefully the surprise on the Bishop's face at her candour. 'What I need,' she went on, 'are letters from friendly princes, including my dearest brother, King Philip, recommending that I marry Lord Robert. Then my subjects can never accuse me of choosing him in order to satisfy my own desires. And Lord Robert himself would very much like such recommendations.'

Quadra was asking himself what game it could possibly be that she was playing now. Why didn't she just marry the man and put them all out of their misery?

'If I were you, Madam,' he advised, 'I would not hesitate any longer, but satisfy Lord Robert without delay. I know that King Philip would be glad to hear of your marriage.' Yes, thought Elizabeth, and he and the rest of Europe would see it as demeaning, which is why he would be glad of it! Marry Robert, and she would undermine her status and her authority, and leave the way open for a strong Catholic claimant to make a bid for her throne – such as the envious Queen of Scots, who was skulking north of the border and eating her heart out for the English crown.

Yet she could not go on expecting Robert to live on false hopes. She was aware that her relentless procrastination and evasion hurt him deeply, not only in his heart but in his pride also. She had seen him watching her talking to Quadra, his emotions naked in his face.

'I will think on it,' she told the Bishop.

Later, when Robert pumped her to find out what she had said to Quadra, she airily told him they had been discussing political relations with Spain. Then, hating herself, she gave herself up to her Robin with all the fervour of which she was

147

capable, cozening him to forgetfulness with her eager kisses and roving hands. But as ever, she drew back before he lost control.

'Will you always leave me so unsatisfied,' he groaned.

'You know why I must,' Elizabeth reminded him. 'Even if I were willing, I dare not court scandal. But I do love you, my Eyes!'

She made it up to him. She restored to him many of the lands once held by his father; she granted him a lucrative licence to export goods free of duty. When word of this got out, there was a fresh wave of rumours that their marriage was imminent. Some even said they were man and wife already.

'Very amusing!' Elizabeth giggled when recounting it to Bishop de Quadra. 'Do you know, my ladies even asked me if they were now to kiss Lord Robert's hand as well as mine!'

The Bishop smiled. Robert forced a laugh. But when they were alone, his fury burst forth.

'You are playing with me again, torturing me!' he shouted.

'Hush, people will hear!' Elizabeth hissed.

'I care not! Let them hear. Let them know that you and I bed together, that you at least accord me that privilege!'

'Well, *I* care!' Elizabeth hissed. 'I have a reputation to protect.'

'You know the solution to that!' Robert flung back.

'Is that the way to propose marriage?' she challenged him. That made him pause. Anger visibly draining out of him, he stared at her.

'You don't mean . . .?'

Elizabeth was not so certain that she did, but she had to placate him somehow. If she did not, she feared that she would lose him, and that she could not bear.

'Ask me and find out,' she said lightly, telling herself that she was not committed until the ring was on her finger.

Robert did not hesitate. Seize the day, he told himself exultantly, citing her own motto; falling to his knees before her, he grasped her hands.

'I never thought to see this moment,' he breathed, raising

them to his lips and kissing them with feeling. 'That you, my Queen, have at last condescended to accept your humble suitor.'

'You haven't asked me yet,' Elizabeth reminded him, a nervous smile playing on her lips.

'Then marry me, Bess! I pray you!'

She looked at him for a long moment, savouring what might be her last opportunity for stalling. 'Very well, my sweet Robin. I give you my promise. I will marry you. But not this year. There is much to be discussed beforehand.'

'I can wait,' Robert said fervently, and, standing up, he folded her to his breast and kissed her. 'A year will seem a little time.'

Even as she gave herself up to his joyful caresses, Elizabeth feared it would be barely enough.

What had she done? Robert was going about loudly proclaiming that she had promised to marry him next year, and people were offering him their hearty and – it must be said – often insincere congratulations. He found himself accorded a new respect and being treated with greater deference than ever, now that he was expected to be king. He was happier – and more proud – than Elizabeth had ever seen him.

She knew already that she could not go ahead with this marriage. She was still firmly resolved not to give place to any man. She could not face the thought of what marriage entailed. More importantly, her hand was the best political bargaining tool she had at her disposal – get wed, and what would she have left?

She could not hide her reluctance. When Robert spoke, as he often did now, of their forthcoming marriage and how he meant to support her in her role, especially while she was bearing the heirs that would assure the succession, she found herself shrinking inside and wanting to run away. She had an excuse now for fending him off at night: they would be married soon, and must wait. But he sensed the relief that lay behind her words, and soon it began to dawn on him that she, who prided herself on keeping the word of a prince, might default on this most crucial of promises.

Elizabeth was walking with Robert in the privy garden at Hampton Court, enjoying the autumnal sunshine, when she felt a headache threatening. Trying to ignore it, she led the way down to the riverside, where they watched the boats sailing past on the Thames, but within an hour she was feeling shivery and her stomach began to hurt.

Robert gave her his arm to lean on and took her back to the palace, where she instructed her women to prepare a hot bath scented with sweet herbs. That, she told them, should cure her. Having immersed herself in it until the water cooled, she bade them dress her again, then strode out into the gardens once more for a bracing walk. When she returned, she gave an audience in the sumptuous Paradise Chamber, seated on a golden throne upholstered in brown velvet and studded with three great diamonds. But as she welcomed envoys and petitioners, she began to feel faint; her head was swimming and she could not focus properly, and the Persian tapestries winking with gold, pearls and gems, which surrounded her on all four walls, became an alarming blur. By the time the last visitor bowed himself out, she was near to collapse, and had to lean against the table near the door to stop herself falling, upsetting a silver backgammon set as she did so. By the next morning she was coughing harshly and running a high fever. Her doctors looked at each other in dismay. There was no doubt about it: the Queen had smallpox.

Robert was distraught lest he lose her. And he feared for his sister Mary too. Elizabeth was now more devoted than ever to Mary Sidney, and Mary, Kat Astley and Kate Knollys were all with her at this distressing time. She called for them endlessly. In her delirium, she did not realise what she was asking of them, for she was unaware of what ailed her and had not been told. But smallpox was contagious, it could be disfiguring, and it was deadly. Robert knew it; Mary's husband knew it; both, loving her as they did, had warned Mary to stay away, but she was adamant. Her place was at Elizabeth's side. A part of Robert secretly rejoiced that she was there.

'It usually attacks only aged folks and ladies of a frail disposition,' he told Mary, more confidently than he felt. 'You are young and strong, so you have no need to worry. And the Queen is strong too. She will come through this, especially with you here to help her.'

'Fret not, dear brother,' Mary said gently, patting his arm. 'We are in the hands of God, and He will not fail us.'

Robert, of course, was forbidden the Queen's bedchamber, although he would have defied the contagion for her sake; after all, her physicians and her women were with her unceasingly, trying every remedy in their power to save her.

Elizabeth lay there uncaring, shivering violently, sweat pouring from her, the cough racking her raw chest. She inhabited a strange hinterland between fantasy and reality, which she left only when sleep fitfully claimed her. All she knew was that Kat and Kate were at her side, ministering to her, and that Mary Sidney's soft voice was sibilant in the background, a sweet, reassuring presence. That made a change from the doctors pulling and prodding her, applying those ghastly leeches, endlessly testing her urine, and bleating on about an imbalance of the humours and murmuring vague reassurances and admonitions to rest. When they left her alone she just drifted, too exhausted and detached even to worry about the seriousness of her condition.

Then suddenly there was a new doctor with a strange, guttural accent, a frowning face and an irascible voice.

'This is smallpox,' he told her.

Elizabeth was sufficiently herself to glance down in terror at her bare arms and hands and call croakingly for her silver-gilt mirror. Her beauty! What would become of it? What man would marry her if she was marred by the scars of this dreadful disease. No, it could not be! *Please God!*

'There are *no spots*,' she retorted, glaring at this new doctor, who had the temerity to glare back.

'It is still smallpox,' he insisted. 'The spots will appear very soon.'

'You are a fool. Get out!' And with a weak but imperious wave of her hand she dismissed him.

The spots did not appear, and her ladies and physicians were inclined to believe – indeed, they prayed – that the doctor had been wrong. But Elizabeth's fever worsened. Six days after her sickness had begun, she was beyond speech, delirious, and very ill indeed. Soon afterwards she lapsed into unconsciousness, and remained in that state for a night and a day.

'She is dying,' whispered the terrified doctors, and Kat burst into tears. An exhausted and tearful Mary hastened to warn Robert, who had kept an anxious vigil in the outer chamber throughout, snatching sleep on cushions on the floor and barely eating.

'We must summon the Council,' he said, his voice unsteady. He could not think beyond that, could not bear to contemplate a world without Elizabeth. But when Cecil and his colleagues arrived, their frantic talk was all of the succession. When the Queen died – there seemed to be no 'if' about it – who should succeed her?

They argued and argued, and for once they did not exclude Robert from their counsels. Some favoured Lady Katherine Grey, who had now – predictably and helpfully – converted back to the Protestant faith and was the next heir under Henry VIII's Act of Succession. Others wanted a man to rule, and nominated the Earl of Huntingdon, whose claim was rather too distant for credibility. The rest thought that the judges should rule on the matter. No one, it seemed, was ready to declare for the Queen of Scots. Her name was not mentioned. But what was clear was that opinion was divided and that the situation might just escalate into civil war, with factions already forming around the rival claimants.

Robert was horrified to see that the courtiers were already preparing to go into mourning; some had even ordered black material.

'The Queen is not dead yet!' he protested to Cecil. Cecil looked at him and saw a distraught soul, and in that moment he warmed for the first time to this man who had been the bane of his life. Who could but feel sorry for him? Yes, Robert Dudley was ambitious and bombastic, but right now there was no doubting his devotion to his Queen. 'We cannot give up on her!' he said wildly.

Lord Hunsdon, Elizabeth's bluff, soldierly cousin, the brother of Kate Knollys, agreed. 'Where's that German doctor fellow?' he roared. 'Get him back here.'

Dr Burcot came reluctantly. The Queen had not heeded him before, so he was not prepared to treat her now. 'No,' he declared firmly, 'I will not attend her.'

Hunsdon was not a man to take no for an answer. Drawing his dagger, he gripped the recalcitrant doctor by the throat and held it to his breast. 'Get in there!' he ordered. Burcot went, muttering curses.

Taking one look at the unconscious, fevered figure on the bed and her exhausted attendants, he took control of the situation.

'Build up the fire and bring me as much red flannel as you can find,' he commanded. Then he rapped out the ingredients for a potion he had himself devised. Within a very short time Elizabeth was lying swathed in flannel on a mattress before the fire, being fed Burcot's remedy in sips.

Many hours later the doctor emerged. Robert and Cecil, who had been waiting for news, looked at him fearfully.

'The Queen is now conscious and speaking,' Burcot announced, looking about warily to see if that thug Lord Hunsdon was lurking somewhere, and thanking God that he wasn't.

'Oh, God be praised!' Robert breathed, tears in his eyes.

'Amen to that,' Cecil declared, relief flooding him.

'But she is still very ill and might yet die,' the doctor warned. 'She knows it, and is asking to see her Council.'

What of me? Robert thought desperately, watching the lords file behind Cecil into the royal bedchamber. After all we have meant to each other, has she forgotten me?

But there was Cecil again, framed in the doorway, beckoning him in. 'You are called too,' he said, 'and it is fitting that you should be here.'

'Robin!' came a weak voice from the bed. 'Come here.'

Robert was shocked to see Elizabeth. Her long red hair, spread out over the high pillows, was dark and stringy with sweat, and her face looked white and drained, the hooked nose jutting out in gaunt relief, the heavy-lidded eyes sunken. But to him she still looked beautiful. He hastened to her bedside and knelt, clasping her limp hand and kissing it.

'My Eyes!' she smiled weakly, then her face turned to Cecil, who had taken up his position on the opposite side of the bed. The lords of the Council gathered around respectfully, trying not to wrinkle their noses at the foetid smell in the hot, airless room.

'I have been dangerously ill,' Elizabeth murmured, so quietly that they all had to strain to hear her. 'Death possessed every joint of me, and I know that he may still be waiting to claim me.'

'No, sweet lady,' Robert protested, still holding her hand and trying to infuse it with his strength.

'Hush, Robin. This is important. I must make provision for the governance of my realm in the event of my being called hence by God. And so, my lords, I command you to appoint Lord Robert here as Lord Protector of England, and to pay him a salary of twenty thousand pounds.'

There were gasps of surprise as Robert's jaw dropped. She was entrusting her kingdom to him? Then, God knew, she had meant to marry him after all. This proved it, and it proved also the extent of her trust in him. Exultation swept through him – until he remembered that she might yet be snatched from him, and became aware that the councillors were muttering amongst themselves and casting baleful or speculative glances in his direction. Let them! He would show them how he fulfilled Elizabeth's trust. He turned to her to express his thanks, but she gave a faint squeeze of his hand and went on speaking.

'I ask you also to ensure that Tamworth, Lord Robert's servant, be assigned a pension of five hundred pounds per annum.' Robert knew why she had ordered this. Tamworth, who slept on a pallet bed near his master, had been privy to his secret meetings with Elizabeth; he knew – or had guessed – about their nights together. Such a generous pension would buy his silence. One glance at the privy councillors told Robert that they were thinking much the same thing, but Elizabeth had seen their reaction and was ready for them.

'My lords, I may shortly be facing divine judgement,' she said, her voice a little stronger now, 'and I want to declare to you that although I love, and always have loved, Lord Robert dearly, as God is my witness, nothing unseemly has ever passed between us.'

Well, thought Robert, it depended on what you termed unseemly. Others might take a different view, as was apparent in the faces of the lords grouped around the bed, although some – Cecil among them – were nodding sagely, as if they had known the truth all along. After all, why would Elizabeth risk meeting her Maker with a lie on her lips?

At least there were no protests. To a man, the councillors promised to do all that she asked, although it was undeniable that some gave answer reluctantly. As they left the room, Robert heard Sussex say something about not wanting to distress the Queen as she was all but gone, and later that day Bishop de Quadra, ever abreast of events, warned him that those promises would not be fulfilled. He realised that, if Elizabeth did die, he would face weighty opposition.

When Dr Burcot returned with more of his efficacious potion, he found his august patient staring in horror at her hands.

'The spots! I am coming out in spots!' she wailed.

'God's pestilence,' he swore at her, having no time or patience for courtesies. 'Which is better? To have the pox in your hands or face – or in your heart, so that it kills you?' Then he marched out to inform the waiting lords and councillors that the spots were a good sign. 'They indicate that the worst is over,' he told them. 'Soon the pustules will dry out, scabs will form, and later they will fall off. We must stop the Queen from scratching!'

'Has he ever tried to stop the Queen from doing anything?' Bacon muttered in Cecil's ear. But Elizabeth, terrified lest her beauty be destroyed, proved an obedient patient, and thenceforward, to the profound relief of Robert, her councillors and her courtiers, she improved rapidly. Within a very short time she was up and about again, and a special coin was minted to mark her recovery. But, as everyone knew, God had been extraordinarily merciful.

When she at last resumed her seat at the head of the Council, Cecil, with the consent of the rest (or most of them, for there *had* been dissenting voices) had prepared what he was going to – indeed, must – say to her.

'Madam,' he declared, 'we, your loyal and loving lords and subjects, wish to express our great gratitude to Almighty God that you have warded off Death, that blind fury with his abhorred shears, who cuts us off at his whim.'

Elizabeth inclined her head graciously. It was gratifying to hear such expressions of devotion, and her heart was full of thanks for her recovery and her strong constitution. For the thousandth time she looked down at her hands. God had been merciful there too. Her scars were rapidly fading. In a few weeks there would be nothing to see.

'But, Madam,' Cecil went on (she had guessed that there was more to come), 'this illness has brought home to us all, as nothing else, that only your Majesty's most precious life stands between peaceful, stable government and the miseries and wars likely to follow upon a disputed succession. Madam, we, your councillors, and Parliament, are resolved to urge your Majesty to marry Lord Robert without delay and provide us with an heir of your body.'

It was as bad as Elizabeth had feared, and of course they had every reason to urge her. 'I have said that I will wed Lord Robert next year,' she said.

'Why wait so long?' Cecil asked. 'Madam, let us be done with delays, negotiations and fruitless prolongings. We beg of you, for the security of your realm, marry now!'

Elizabeth bristled. 'My lords, this is unworthy of you. I am barely risen from my sick bed. I am not well enough to think of marrying at this time. Allow me to make a full recovery, and then I will attend to your request.'

Before anyone could protest – and Cecil already had his mouth open to do so – she stood up and made her way to the door, taking care to maintain an invalid's tentative gait. And the councillors had no choice but to get to their feet and bow.

When she reached her privy chamber she did feel drained, and sat down gratefully by the fire, telling herself vehemently that this was certainly not the time for her councillors to be bullying her into marriage. And then – as if she had not enough to contend with – she saw Kat hurrying towards her, weeping, and knew that some new mischance had come to pass, and all thoughts of marriage flew out of her head.

'Bess, I hardly know how to tell you,' Kat cried, wringing her hands. 'Mary Sidney has the smallpox.'

'No!' Elizabeth burst out. 'No, please God! If she dies, it will be on my conscience. I asked her to stay with me when I was ill, and she nursed me devotedly, putting herself at risk – as you did too, dear Kat. And now she has caught the pox from me. What can I do?' Burying her face in her hands, she gave in to her unaccustomed weakness, and fear, and collapsed in tears. And that was how Robert, summoned by Kat, found her some minutes later.

'Hush, hush, my sweet,' he soothed, cradling her in his arms. 'Do not blame yourself. You knew not what you were saying. We all warned Mary, but she insisted on staying with you. She loves you as a sister.'

'Where is she, Robin?' Elizabeth asked, resting her head on his shoulder, which at that moment represented a refuge from a cruel world. This terrible news must be hitting him hard too; his love for Mary was probably the most unselfish emotion he had ever experienced. And her husband, loyal Sir Henry Sidney, in whose arms Elizabeth's brother King Edward had died – he must be distraught.

'She is at Penshurst. She was needed there because Harry is abroad. My God, I pray she will weather this. As for my brother-in-law, I do not know if the news has reached him. I dare not think how he must feel.'

'Robin, we must put our trust in God.' Elizabeth sat up, setting her pearled cap to rights and trying to be positive. 'We must pray that He will recompense you all for your wonderful service to me, and when Mary recovers, as I trust she will, I will reward her as amply as she deserves. As for you, sweet Robin, a reward is long overdue. I have decided to promote you to my Privy Council.'

Robert fell to his knees, seized her hands and kissed them fervently. 'Bess, I will be worthy of this honour, I swear it! And yes, we must have faith: Mary will get well.'

'I will pray for her. But I must tell you one thing, my Eyes. In order to silence your critics, I am preferring Norfolk to the Privy Council also. I know there is no love lost between you, but I have to be seen to be fair.'

Robert grimaced at her mention of Norfolk, but Elizabeth ran her fingers through his hair. 'Would another pension of a thousand pounds make up for it?'

'For that, I will go out of my way to be friendly to his lordship,' he replied, kissing her. 'Even though it will nearly kill me to do so!'

Good news came in a series of messages from Penshurst. Mary Sidney was recovering. She hoped to return to court soon. Expansive with relief, Elizabeth sent for her jeweller and ordered lavish gifts for her dearest friend, then sent Robert down to Kent to take them to his sister.

When he returned some days later, Elizabeth took one look at his face and her hand flew to her mouth in dismay.

'She has died?' she whispered.

'No, Bess.' He was struggling to stay in command of himself. 'But she will not be returning to court. Not ever.'

'What do you mean? Tell me, for God's sake!'

'The smallpox has left her hideously scarred. The physicians say there is no hope of improvement. Harry is in great grief.'

Elizabeth closed her eyes in horror. This was truly terrible, and she herself was responsible. Poor Harry Sidney – and poor, poor disfigured Mary. Elizabeth could not bear to imagine what she looked like now. All that beauty destroyed in a trice. It was horrible, too horrible to contemplate.

Robert was shaking his head sadly. 'Harry told me that when he left to go abroad, he had said farewell to the fairest lady in his sight. But when he returned he found her as foul as the smallpox could make her. The wife he knew is lost to him.'

'I am suffering with him,' Elizabeth declared, shivering at the thought that this could so easily have been her, and swamped with guilt. 'And she, my sweet Mary, how is she taking it?'

'She says little. She keeps to a darkened room and will not come forth. She does not want anyone but her maids to look upon her.'

'Oh dear God, why?' Elizabeth cried. 'I must go to her.'

'Not yet, I beg of you,' Robert pleaded. 'She would not want to receive you.'

'But she has been as a sister to me! Surely she does not think that a few pockmarks will alter my love for her?'

'Give her time, Bess. She knows that we who love her will not be swayed by that.'

But Elizabeth could not let it rest. As soon as she was fully herself again, she made Robert saddle her fastest horse, and with him, and a handful of attendants following behind, she cantered at speed down to Penshurst. There her arrival was hastily announced, and as she strode through the soaring great hall and ascended the curving staircase to the private apartments above, Sir Henry Sidney came down to greet her, surprised in his hunting gear and not at all fittingly dressed to receive his Queen. But it did not matter. Ceremony was set aside as Elizabeth drew him into her embrace and they wept together for the tragedy that had befallen them.

Elizabeth insisted on seeing Mary, and would not take no for an answer.

'Do not announce me,' she commanded. 'I know that she will refuse to admit me if you do.'

Harry led Elizabeth and Robert through the long gallery to a bedchamber cast in gloom. Heavy curtains shrouded the windows and the only light came from a single candle and the flickering firelight. Mary was seated on a chair, her back to them. She wore a black veil. At the sound of the door opening, she turned her head slightly.

'Harry?'

'Mary,' he said, stepping to her side and kissing her hand. 'I bring our good friend.'

'Robert?' her voice was full of hope.

'Yes, good sister,' Robert answered, moving into the firelight. 'And Bess is here.'

'Do not get up,' Elizabeth said from behind him. 'Forgive me, Mary, I had to come.'

'No! No! I do not want your Majesty to see me like this,' Mary protested weakly. Her head was still turned away, her face hidden by the veil.

'Do you think that matters?' Elizabeth asked her. 'It means everything to me that you are restored to us.'

'I am not the woman you knew,' Mary faltered.

'You are still *you*!' Elizabeth countered. 'Take off that veil and let me see your dear face.'

'No, not even for your Majesty can I do that.' Mary was becoming agitated now. 'I can never reveal myself in public again. I am become deformed and hideous, and people will shrink from me.'

Harry Sidney made a gesture of abject despair. Tears were streaming down his cheeks.

'Even Harry cannot bear to look upon me!' Mary burst out. 'My life is over.'

'Not so, sweetheart!' he protested.

'Nonsense,' declared Elizabeth, and with a swift movement she pulled the veil from Mary's head – and stepped back in horror. For the once smooth and beautiful face she had exposed was now rutted with deep, pitted lesions like a stony landscape, and the scarred eyelids were nearly closed. Mary screamed, snatching the veil back, and Elizabeth drew in her breath.

'Oh, my dear friend,' she said, 'I am so deeply sorry. I can never forgive myself.'

'Well, I can,' Mary answered spiritedly. 'It was no one's fault but my own.'

'Sweet wife,' Harry appealed to her, 'we none of us care what you look like. It is the soul within that we love. Will you not join us for the supper that we must, in all courtesy, serve to her Majesty? You will be among friends.'

'And I myself will act as our servitor,' Elizabeth declared.

Mary paused in the act of pulling her veil over her head.

'Mary, you must learn to live again,' Harry urged.

'Very well,' she said, and they all breathed out in relief.

But she was adamant that she would not return to court, which meant that Elizabeth could see her only when she visited the Sidneys, which was not as often as she would have liked. Again and again she begged her friend to come back to serve her, and at length, becoming as used as she ever would to her disfigurement, and worn down by her mistress's pleas, Mary agreed. But she was a mournful, wraith-like figure in her black veil, and both women were relieved – Mary openly, Elizabeth secretly – when Henry Sidney was sent to Ireland, as Lord Lieutenant, and Mary was able to go with him.

Judging the mood of her councillors and people in the wake of her brush with death, Elizabeth was reluctant to summon Parliament.

'Not yet!' she insisted. She had no intention of being bullied into marrying. She had no peace from Robert on the subject, let alone Cecil, and her Lords and Commons could be demanding and stubborn.

'Madam, the business of the kingdom cannot wait,' her Spirit persisted.

'After Christmas,' she said firmly.

'There are pressing matters to be discussed,' Robert weighed in. Since his preferment to the Council her Eyes had made himself cognisant of all, and conscientious in making his voice heard, and on this issue he, Norfolk and Cecil were in accord.

Arundel spoke up. 'Madam, it is the succession of which we speak.'

'It is not seemly for you, a subject, to interfere in such a matter,' Elizabeth reproved him, very angry now.

'With respect, Madam, it is the right of your Lords and Commons to interfere in a matter that touches the whole realm,' Arundel answered.

She rounded on him furiously. 'You would not have dared say that to my father!'

'Your father, Madam, made continuous efforts to secure the succession, as I remember,' Arundel countered.

'And he would have had your head for such insolence!' she shouted, hot tears of temper welling.

'Let us calm down,' Cecil intervened; never mind the succession: war was threatening here in the council chamber. 'Madam, leaving aside the question of your successor, which it is your Majesty's prerogative to decide, may I remind you that Parliament has the power to vote for the revenues that the Crown badly needs at this time?'

He had her there, damn him! The treasury was all but empty. She gritted her teeth and summoned Parliament.

1563

Even before Parliament convened, Westminster was abuzz with talk of the succession. Members coming up from the shires had but one aim in mind, which they shared with the Lords donning their fur-trimmed robes in readiness for the opening ceremonies. After the previous autumn's smallpox scare, the matter must be settled once and for all.

Robert was bursting with anticipation. It was now 'next year', Elizabeth had given him her promise, and the whole country, miraculously, was on his side.

The Queen was seated defiantly in state on her throne in the House of Lords as Dean Nowell of St Paul's delivered the opening address. And, predictably, he did not waste time in raising the subject that was on everyone's mind.

'Just as Queen Mary's marriage was a terrible plague to all England, so now the want of Queen Elizabeth's marriage and royal issue is like to prove as great a plague,' he declaimed. Elizabeth glowered at him, but he faced her boldly. 'Madam, if your parents had been of like mind, where would you have been then?' *You* would have been in the Tower had you spoken thus to my father, Elizabeth thought, simmering with wrath. But the Dean ploughed on, ignoring her icy gaze. 'Alack!' he cried. 'What shall become of us?'

I know what will become of *you*, she thought viciously. How she contained her fury she did not know, and she was mightily relieved to depart soon afterwards (inwardly vowing never again to show favour to Dean Nowell), leaving both houses to their furious debating. She knew she had not heard the last of them and, sure as the Dreadful Day of Judgement, a lovingly worded petition signed by all the Lords and Commons arrived at Whitehall soon afterwards. Before she knew it, Elizabeth found herself standing once more in her presence chamber, facing her Commons.

The Speaker, looking suitably intractable and kneeling at the head of a deputation of his equally intractable fellows, read it out to her. 'Your Majesty, we, your loyal and loving subjects, so rejoice in the bounty and fruits of your Majesty's rule that we earnestly desire to see its glorious continuance, and to this end we urge you most humbly to marry as soon as it may please you, or to designate a successor; for in so doing you will strike terror into your enemies and replenish your subjects with immortal joy.' He went on relentlessly to remind her of the terror felt by her people during her illness, and warned her that unspeakably awful civil wars might result if she died without naming her successor. A very long list of calamities would ensue: the meddlings of foreign princes, the warring of ambitious factions, seditions, slaughter, the destruction of noble houses, the subversion of towns, the stealing of men's possessions, attainders, treasons . . . Elizabeth wondered if bad weather might even be on the list.

The Speaker droned on, clearly uncomfortable to be delivering such a lengthy petition that laid its message on rather heavily. 'We fear the heretics in your realm, the malicious Papists. From the Conquest to the present day, the kingdom was never left as it is now without a certain heir. If your Highness could conceive or imagine the comfort, surety and delight that should come to you by beholding an imp of your own, it would sufficiently remove all your scruples.' Elizabeth was not particularly fond of any imps, even royal ones, so this particular argument left her singularly unmoved, and it did not even begin to address what must happen before the said imp could be beheld.

Having finished at last, the Speaker looked up nervously and held out the petition. Elizabeth nodded and took it from him as if it had been contaminated by poison.

'I thank you all,' she said, summoning up far more graciousness than she actually felt. 'I will read over your petition, and make my answer as soon as is convenient.' Then she made her escape in as stately a fashion as possible.

Robert hastened out after her.

'No!' she said when he caught up. 'Not now, Robin. I have heard enough about marriage for today.' But there was Cecil, ready to waylay her at the door to the privy chamber. She groaned inwardly.

'You heard what Parliament wants?' she growled.

'Yes, Madam.'

'And no doubt *you* want to give me your advice!'

'Madam, the matter is so deep that I cannot reach into it. But I will say, God send it – and you – a good issue!'

'Amen!' said Robert. Elizabeth sailed past them, not deigning to reply.

She would not, could not, give in. She was the Queen, by God! How dare they manoeuvre her into a corner on a matter that touched her so closely? If she married, she would do it in her own time and no one else's.

She summoned the Speaker back, and received him and other members in the gallery at Whitehall. Standing deliberately in front of a magnificent portrait of a menacing Henry VIII, she welcomed them as they knelt before her.

'I thank you all for your petition,' she said, smiling as benignly as was humanly possible. 'I assure you that I am as worried about the succession as you are, especially since my illness. The matter occupied my mind constantly as I recuperated. And when I thought myself on my deathbed, I desired to live not so much for my own safety as for yours.' She was watching their faces closely. She knew she had won their sympathy.

'I labour under an intolerable burden,' she went on. 'You ask me to name a successor, but I cannot wade into so deep a matter without weighty deliberation, and I am concerned about choosing the right heir. If my choice were to lead to civil war, you, my loving subjects, might lose your lives – but *I* hazard to lose both body and soul, for I am answerable to God for my actions.'

A few heads were nodding sagely. Many faces showed understanding. But now Elizabeth frowned. 'It is not your place to petition me on this matter. But I know the difference between men who act out of love and those who make mischief. I have no wish to hear you speak of my death, for I do know that I am mortal, but I appreciate your concerns. I promise you, I will take further advice, and then I will give you an answer. And I assure you all,' she added, her smile radiant again, 'that though, after my death, you may have many step-dames, you will never have a more natural mother than I mean to be to you all.'

It was a touch of genius, she felt. Her words had clearly left the deputation feeling comforted, and they departed happily with hearty words of thanks and much praise for the Queen's wisdom and her care for them. But two days later Elizabeth had to face a contingent from the House of Lords, who were not so easily quelled. They urged her, nay, demanded of her, to marry whomsoever she pleased, and as soon as she pleased. Then they had the nerve – the overweening audacity – to say that even Lord Robert would be a better choice than no husband at all. The look on Robert's face would have stopped an army in full charge, and it was well that he had to control his anger, being in the Queen's presence.

'Name your successor,' the Lords begged, 'since law and order dies upon the death of princes.'

Elizabeth froze, and there was an awkward silence until Norfolk, unsubtle as usual, broke it. 'The Queen of Scots has a claim to your Majesty's throne.'

'She is barred by the Act of Succession, and by virtue of being born out of the realm,' Elizabeth said coldly.

'Even so, Madam, she takes her claim seriously, as do the Catholics in England and abroad. We, your faithful lords, are anxious to have it disposed of, for as mere natural Englishmen, we do not wish to be subject to a foreign prince, and Queen

Mary is a stranger. The very stones in the streets would rebel at the prospect of her ruling this realm!' As would I, Elizabeth thought. Mary queening it in her pretty gowns in France, with her pretty head unbothered by state matters, was one thing; Mary queening it in Scotland, just on England's doorstep, and scheming to get Elizabeth's throne, was quite another.

She stood there fuming, waiting for them to finish haranguing her. She did not bother to conceal her irritation. 'My lords, I made allowances for the Commons, but I expect *you* to know better than to press me on such weighty matters. It is not impossible that I will marry.' She looked at Robert and was gratified to see that his rage had subsided and that he was regarding her with an expectant smile on his face. 'I am not old,' she went on. 'I am not yet thirty. The marks you see on my face are not wrinkles, they are the fading scars of smallpox; and although I might be old to start bearing children, God may send them to me if He wishes, as He did to St Elisabeth. So you had better consider well what you are asking, for if I were to declare a successor from among my kinsfolk, it would cost England much blood.'

That silenced them! They left meekly as lambs, and as the days passed and it became clear that a chastened Parliament – obediently awaiting a response to its petitions – was deliberately refraining from debating the succession, Elizabeth began to believe that she had quelled the Lords and Commons into silence. But Robert was not prepared to be silent. One night, as they lay abed and she expected him to claim her as usual, he did not. Instead, he raised himself up on one elbow and looked down at her, and he was not teasing or amorous.

'Bess, with all this talk of marriage going on, you have not said a word of it to me, and yet you have promised to marry me this year. Why will you not satisfy Parliament and tell them that that is your intention?'

Elizabeth's tired mind fumbled for words. 'Sweet Robin, I have not forgotten my promise. But I shall say to you what I intend to say to Parliament when I can face responding to those two great scrolls they had the nerve to force upon me. If you think that I have vowed or determined never to trade the single life for marriage, put that out of your mind, for your belief is awry.' She reached up and traced his cheek and beard with her finger. 'I love you, Robin. And though I think the single life would be possible for a private woman, I do strive to tell myself that it is not meet for a prince. Be patient with me a short while longer, for if I can bend my liking to your need, I will not fail you.'

'But you have *promised*,' Robert persisted. 'Is this a woman's promise?' He was irate now.

'Anger makes dull men witty, but it keeps them poor,' she riposted. 'I *have* promised, on the word of a prince!'

'Then why the ifs and the striving? Surely you knew your mind when you gave that promise?'

Elizabeth flared. 'Of course I did! But there is far more to the matter than two lovers plighting their troth. If I have given you an answer answerless, it is because you, like Parliament, have forced me to it!'

'Why can you never be straightforward?' Robert flung back. 'With you, all is obfuscation and delay! What is an answer answerless if it is not another of your stalling tactics? Elizabeth, the country needs an heir. I need an heir. I need a wife too, and the only woman I want is you. But if you keep me waiting much longer, I swear I will look elsewhere.'

They both drew back, appalled – he at having blurted out what had sometimes, disturbingly, crept into his mind lately, and she at the notion that he might abandon her and find love with a lesser mortal.

'Get out,' she snarled, picking up a pillow and hurling it at him, then kicking him for good measure.

'Don't worry, I'm going!' Robert shouted, not caring who heard. And, ducking as the next pillow came hurtling through the air, he grabbed his nightgown, pulled it on furiously, and stamped back to his own room.

*

For ten days after that he did not attend Elizabeth in the court or attempt to come to her chamber at night. At first anger tided her along, and jealousy. Had he – the traitor – dared to carry out his threat? Was he at this very moment paying court to some bejewelled hussy with a rich father and fat manors? She almost howled at the thought. By God, she'd have both their heads! But as the days went by with no sight of Robert, and whispers proliferating at court about a rift, she grew concerned. Where was he? How dare he take leave of absence without permission? She needed him here, on the Council, where his duty lay – not to mention by her side and in her bed.

She sat sulking through council meetings, snapping at everyone. The item highest on the agenda was the Queen of Scots' marriage. At least, Elizabeth reflected crossly, it was not hers. Almost she could feel some sisterly affinity with her rival, for it seemed that queens were the particular prey of marriage-making male advisers. That might just account for Mary having recently made overtures of friendship. There had even been talk of a meeting between the two queens. Elizabeth wasn't sure that she wanted to come face to face with the cousin whose beauty was lauded throughout Christendom; Heaven forbid, she herself, nine years the senior, might be found wanting! And there were so many contentious matters that lay between them, not the least of which was Mary's disquieting plan to marry King Philip's son, Don Carlos.

Mary's motives were deplorably transparent. She was obviously aiming for a strong Catholic alliance that would overthrow Cecil's carefully negotiated Treaty of Edinburgh and put pressure on Elizabeth to acknowledge her as her heir – at the very least! And if Mary married Don Carlos the might of Spain could end up camping right on Elizabeth's doorstep, threatening invasion. Not to be tolerated!

But Mary had been duped. She had got it into her pretty, brainless head that Don Carlos was a brave and gallant prince who would champion all her dangerous causes. But Elizabeth knew, through her rather better diplomatic channels, that he was not only deformed but mad. He liked to torture animals. He was sadistic and violent towards servants and the girls he pursued with evil intent. There was even a tale that, misliking a new pair of shoes, he had forced the hapless cobbler to eat them. A fine husband for the Queen of Scots he would make!

'But she is determined to have him,' Cecil said, having discussed all this with Elizabeth.

'I have warned her that, if she marries Don Carlos, I would consider her my enemy for ever afterwards,' Elizabeth told him. 'I wrote to her; I said, consider well your steps. I also offered England's firm friendship if she would be guided by me in her choice of husband.'

'I doubt she will agree to that,' Sussex observed, shaking his head.

'I recall your Majesty suggesting that Queen Mary might wed an English lord,' Cecil remembered. 'That might be a way of keeping Scotland friendly.'

An idea occurred to Elizabeth then; an idea that was so perfect in most ways that it almost took her breath away. Here was her opportunity to neutralise the threat posed by Mary Stuart – and to be revenged on the treacherous Robert.

She would offer him as a husband for the Queen of Scots.

That would pay him back for putting unkind pressure on her – and no doubt on Parliament – and for his monstrous threat to look elsewhere for a wife. Well, she would give him one, served up on a platter with red hair and a crown, just as he liked them!

'We will offer her Lord Robert,' she announced, beaming.

'Lord Robert?' echoed her astonished councillors, to a man.

'Lord Robert,' she affirmed, looking very pleased with herself.

'Madam,' Cecil said, 'should we not wait until his lordship returns from Warwick before discussing this?'

'Warwick?' It was now Elizabeth's turn to be astonished. What the devil was he up to there? Visions of him secretly plighting his troth to some well-dowered milksop country bumpkin came to mind, followed by a highly satisfying fantasy of his being dragged in chains to the Tower, the headsman plodding vengefully at his heels.

'Did you not know, Madam? He is visiting his brother.'

She recovered herself hastily, and took refuge in a lie. 'Of course, yes. But it will do no harm if we discuss my proposal in his absence. You may persuade me it is a foolish idea, and then there will be no need to bother him with it. But gentlemen,' and she looked at them with gimlet eyes, thinking rapidly, 'there could be many good reasons for such a marriage. Lord Robert's loyalty has never been in doubt. He is indebted to me for his advancement, and he is not the man to forget it. He would work tirelessly to represent our interests in Scotland. Once wed to him, Queen Mary would be out of the marriage market, and the threat from Spain would recede. Moreover, he is a staunch Protestant, and as such would be far more acceptable to the Lords of the Congregation than Don Carlos, who is not only Catholic but insane.' The more she considered it, the more pleased she was with herself for thinking up such a marriage.

Her councillors heard her out patiently, but when she fell silent Cecil spoke. 'These are strong justifications for the match, Madam, but there is one matter that I must raise, and I'm sure I speak for us all. It was everyone's understanding that your Majesty had promised to marry Lord Robert yourself, and very soon.'

'It is what we have all hoped and prayed for,' Bacon put in. Norfolk's face said plainly that he was neither hoping nor praying for any such thing, but he nodded and said 'aye' along with the rest.

'My lords, I am willing to make this sacrifice for the future security of my realm,' Elizabeth said, determined to argue her corner but suddenly beginning to realise what the sacrifice would actually entail. Never to see Robert again, or but rarely; never more to enjoy his stimulating companionship, lie in his arms or feast her eyes on the manly charms that so delighted her. Already she was jealous of pretty, brainless Mary enjoying that which Elizabeth had denied herself. In fact, she could not bear the thought. Of course it might be too late – Robert might already be wed to the country bumpkin, which prospect she could not bear either. Oh, why, *why* had she quarrelled with him? Now look what he had made her do! She would either have to give him up to the Queen of Scots or suffer the humiliation of seeing him married to another. God's blood, what a mess!

She swallowed. She must be a queen first, a woman second. That was the only way to retain the respect of the men who served her. 'I want to see England and Scotland draw close in friendship,' she declared bravely. 'It will be hard for me to renounce Lord Robert, but I will do it willingly so it be for the advantage of my people.' She consoled herself with the thought that royal marriage negotiations were usually so prolonged that it would be months, if not years – or not at all – before she had to part with her Eyes. She was surprised to find herself thinking of him as hers once more, when only minutes before she had been prepared to consign him to oblivion – or the Scottish court. It amounted to the same thing.

Cecil was beaming at her approvingly. Oh, she knew his game. Nothing would please him more than to see Robert exiled to Scotland and swaggering about in his gallant finery among the thistles and the sheep. Once he was safely on his way north, her court would once more be open house to the ambassadors of princes hopeful to win her hand – and her kingdom. 'An excellent plan, Madam,' Cecil said.

But the others looked dubious.

'With respect, it is unlikely that the Queen of Scots will agree,' Sussex warned.

'She may surprise us,' Elizabeth said, with more conviction than she felt. 'After all, Lord Robert is a very proper man, and she has known only a weak, sickly boy for a husband. Let her once set eyes on his lordship and her opinions may rapidly change!' She cleared her throat, feeling murderous towards both of them at the thought. 'Gentlemen, I will see Queen Mary's ambassador, and raise the matter with him.'

And I will do it now, she thought, rising from her chair, before I lose my nerve.

She summoned the ambassador, Sir William Maitland, as suave and crafty a diplomat as one could hope (or not) to meet. He was a dark, personable fellow whose lean, inoffensive features concealed one of the most clever and devious minds in Scotland. Naturally he wore the plain black attire favoured by the Calvinist Scottish lords, but he wore it with elegance, and it was of good cloth. Elizabeth received him in private, smiling munificently, then took a deep breath.

'Sir William, as a fellow sovereign, we are conscious of the problems facing your good mistress Queen Mary in finding a suitable husband,' she said.

'Your Majesty is most kind to concern yourself with Queen Mary's affairs,' Maitland said smoothly, anticipating a tirade against the appalling Don Carlos.

'I will do more than that for her,' Elizabeth continued. 'I am prepared to offer her a husband in whom Nature has planted so many graces that she will prefer him to all the princes in the world.'

'And who might that be, Madam?' Maitland asked.

'Lord Robert Dudley,' Elizabeth replied, as if a fanfare was sounding in the background. To her fury, Maitland chuckled.

'A merry jest, Madam! Ha! Ha!'

'I was not jesting,' she barked.

He had the grace to look embarrassed. 'Ah. Of course. A thousand pardons, Madam.' He was actually stuttering. 'I had understood that you were to marry Lord Robert yourself. Well, ahem, indeed, this is great proof of the love you bear my Queen, that you are willing to give her something – I should say someone – so dearly prized by yourself.'

Elizabeth was all serene graciousness once more.

'However,' Maitland continued, 'I feel certain that Queen

Mary would not wish to deprive your Majesty of all the joy and solace that you receive from the company of Lord Robert.'

The smile froze on Elizabeth's face. Joy and solace? she thought. There had not been much of that lately. But not so long ago there had, oh, there had . . .

She was not unmindful of the implication in Maitland's words, and was determined to refute it by showing him that giving up Robert would not hurt as much as he thought. She said lightly, 'Unfortunately Lord Robert's brother, the Earl of Warwick, is not as handsome as he, for had this been so Queen Mary could have married him and I myself could have become the wife of Lord Robert.'

'Your Majesty ought to marry him anyway,' Maitland replied, 'and then when it shall please God to call you to Himself, you could leave the Queen of Scots heiress to both your kingdom and your husband; that way, Lord Robert could hardly fail to have children by one or other of you.'

Elizabeth smiled again, but tightly. Not the tedious matter of her death again! Did Maitland expect her to die so soon? If she had anything to do with it, she would long outlive that simpering, empty-headed she-cat now queening it in Edinburgh.

She realised that she had gone too far now in what had begun as a malicious game of revenge. There was Cecil, praising Robert to the skies whenever Maitland hove into view. 'Sir William, a better Protestant you could not find! And a man of many parts, talented in warfare, in learning, in statecraft.' Elizabeth had never thought to hear the like from Cecil's lips, and eyed him suspiciously.

But there was Maitland playing along! 'A more proper and fit husband for my good mistress could not be found. This will indeed be a marriage made in Heaven!' Yet it was writ plain on his face that the proposition of Robert as a husband for his Queen was nothing short of an insult. Those raised aristocratic eyebrows said in no uncertain terms that it was beyond belief that anyone would *think* that Mary would stoop to wed a commoner still under a cloud of suspicion on account of the death of his wife. Elizabeth wouldn't have minded wagering that Maitland would say nothing to the Queen of Scots of how he had praised Robert. But Mary would hear of it, she did not doubt! Bishop de Quadra, that inveterate gossip, knew about it, and he would certainly tell King Philip, who was bound to mention it . . .

But wait a minute, she told herself, with a sense of abject relief – there was another contender for Mary's hand, another English nobleman who would certainly be far more acceptable to her: Lord Darnley. He was just seventeen, a great, gangling lad with a supremely good opinion of himself and looks that could slay a maiden at fifty paces. What was more, he was Elizabeth's own cousin on the Scottish side – his ambitious mother, the Countess of Lennox, was the daughter of her aunt, Margaret Tudor – and the royal blood of England ran in his veins. Henry VIII, in his wisdom, had excluded the Scottish descendants of his sister Margaret from the Act of Succession, believing that he was about to conquer Scotland and marry the infant Queen Mary to his son, Prince Edward; but the Scots had not unnaturally resisted his rough wooing, which consisted mainly of a vicious swathe of slaughter throughout the Scottish lowlands and the burning of Edinburgh. Yet there were those, even now, who held that Lord Darnley – whose legitimacy had never been in question – had a better claim to the succession than Mary Stuart; at least he had been born in England!

That, in fact, was the chief drawback to Mary marrying Darnley. Let them unite their two claims and they could prove very dangerous adversaries indeed. Another was that Darnley was a nasty piece of work and spoiled rotten – which led to the third drawback, his scheming, doting lady mother, who was even now in the Tower for having plotted in secret to send him north and wed him to Queen Mary.

Hmm, thought Elizabeth. And hmm again. Darnley's very nastiness could be used to her advantage. Give Mary enough rope, and she might hang herself. Elizabeth pondered. She doubted that Darnley had the brains to carry through any treasonable plan successfully, but even so, would it be wise to let him loose north of the border?

The matter needed much thought and delicate handling. For now, it was best to act as if there could be no question of Darnley marrying Mary. And in mooting Robert as a husband for her, Elizabeth had hit on the perfect way of showing the gangling boy and his adoring, meddling mother that she meant business. But she had now seen a way of rescuing both herself and Robert from the impossible situation she had created.

Pleased with herself, and feeling magnanimous as a result, she gave the order for Lady Lennox to be released from the Tower, on the strict understanding that there must be no more plotting to marry her spoiled boy to the Queen of Scots – ever.

Then, in June, Robert returned from Warwick, to find a court abuzz with gossip about his impending departure for Scotland and the nuptial couch of Mary Stuart.

'You *said* that you would look elsewhere,' Elizabeth said sweetly, biting into a great slice of tart. 'I have but done your looking for you, and found you a great prize. You have my leave to go and claim it.' She was affecting nonchalance, but her heart was thudding disconcertingly.

Robert gave her a withering, desperate look. 'I cannot believe that you have opened these negotiations without once consulting me,' he said, shaking his head. 'Did it never occur to you that, my feelings for you aside, I might not want to leave England, this land that I love, and all whom I hold dear?'

'Robert, you and I must be above such considerations. It is because you love England that I know you will serve her well and faithfully in Scotland.'

'Bess, you know that I would serve you anywhere, and my country. But is it all over between us, that you would send me from you?'

'It is far from certain that these negotiations will come to a happy conclusion,' she said, trying to still her raging thoughts.

'Is this another of your games?' Robert suddenly roared, his patience driven beyond endurance.

'I am above such things!' Elizabeth snarled. 'How dare you question me, your Queen, on policy!'

'Madam, I crave your pardon,' Robert said icily, executing an exaggerated bow. 'And I also crave your leave to withdraw. You shall not find me importuning you again. With you, all is policy.'

'Wait, Robin!' she cried, as he turned to go. 'You cannot leave me thus.' Tears welled, to her immense chagrin.

'Why not?' His eyes were cold. 'You promised to marry me; you led me on, then you offered me to another. What more have we to say to each other?'

'Robin, this business of the Queen of Scots . . .' She was really weeping now. 'I admit it, I was jealous. But there is more to it than that. It is a cover for something else, which I cannot discuss, the matter is so secret. Believe me, Robin, I do not want to send you to Scotland. But I need to be seen to be pressing for this marriage.'

Robert paused. 'And what of your promise – *the word of a prince*?' She did not like the way he said that, but she supposed she could hardly blame him.

'I have not forgotten it, on my honour. Give me time,' she pleaded. 'I will make it up to you, I swear. Trust me.'

He was not to be easily mollified. 'How, Bess? What have you left to give but your hand in marriage? Or will you at last let me enjoy the one treasure you have withheld from me these past years? You know how I have longed for it. How do you think a man can live, drawing back at the last moment?'

'Robin, you think of one thing only!' Elizabeth sniffed, calmer now. 'What would happen if you got me with child?'

'Then you would *have* to marry me, and stop playing games with the Queen of Scots,' he retorted.

'Oh, I see what you are about! No, Robin, it was not of the

flesh that I spoke when I said that I would make it up to you. It suits my policy, and my inclinations, to make you rich, a veritable prince!'

She had him there. She could tell by the gleam in his eye. She relaxed a little and moved towards him. 'Would the lease of Kenilworth Castle make up to you for the things of which, for the present, you are denied?' she asked, knowing that he had wanted that magnificent stronghold for a long time.

There was a long pause as Robert gave her a look which said plainly that he thought she was buying him off. Then, to her relief, he smiled. With men it was all property and ambition.

'So, a castle instead of a crown,' he said at length. 'But which crown? One I would willingly forsake for a castle; the other would be worth more to me than all the castles in the world. I think you take my meaning.'

'It is a token of my good intent,' Elizabeth told him. 'It must satisfy you for now.'

He swallowed. 'Do not think that I am not grateful for it. But when one has been promised the sun, one can only be dismayed to be given a star.'

'The sun is already shining on you,' Elizabeth chided him. 'There would be many to agree with that. And who knows, sweet Robin, one day you may have sun, moon and stars – and Kenilworth!'

He laughed at that. 'You have not been impervious to my hints, Bess! By God, it is a castle fit for a king! And it is near my brother at Warwick.'

'You want it, then, my Eyes?' she teased him.

'Of course, sweet fool. You know I do!' And he drew her into his arms at last and kissed her soundly.

Robert had been pacified – for now. He was happily drawing up plans for grandiose improvements at Kenilworth, which sounded as if it would rival even Whitehall when it was completed. There would surely never be a castle in the world to touch it. He could not resist proclaiming to the world how bountifully the Queen had enriched him. All was well again. God was in His Heaven, and Robert Dudley was back in favour.

It was, of course, common knowledge now that he occupied sumptuous apartments next to Elizabeth's in all the royal palaces. He acted as her co-host at many court entertainments and kept state like a prince, with his vast train of servants. His following grew, as more and more of those who perceived that his star was flying high sought his patronage.

Elizabeth spoke no more of his marrying the Queen of Scots; she was careful to keep her plans secret from him. When Thomas Randolph prepared to return to Scotland in that plague-ridden summer, which carried off her old adversary, Bishop de Quadra – towards whom she had actually come to feel rather affectionate – she instructed him to urge Mary to allow her good sister of England to choose a husband for her.

'If she consents, tell her I shall be as a mother to her, and will look into her right and title to be my next heir,' she promised, feeling anything but maternal towards her cousinly rival. 'And then, Thomas, you will offer her Lord Robert Dudley.'

Randolph thought he understood. So this was why Dudley had been so publicly advanced lately. He was being groomed for the crown matrimonial of Scotland, for which, in Randolph's humble opinion, he was in no way qualified. Good God, the man was born of a long line of traitors, he had probably done away with his wife, and he was – it had to be said, although not out loud, of course – Queen Elizabeth's leavings. Heaven only knew what he and she had got up to together! The things he had heard . . . Randolph did not know how he would summon the courage to face Queen Mary and offer her Dudley. What an insult!

'It is asking too much of her,' he confided to Cecil. 'It will debase such a noble lady to marry someone so inferior to herself.'

'Our good mistress does not view him in that light,' Cecil observed drily.

But now that good mistress, playing for time in her

accustomed fashion, had summoned Randolph again. 'I have changed my mind,' she told him. 'You shall keep the Queen of Scots guessing whom I have in mind for her until I instruct you otherwise. That way she will be so busy wondering what we will offer that she will not pursue any foreign marriage.' Randolph's shoulders sagged with relief. He could have kissed the Queen's feet, only he feared a prickly response to such an uncharacteristically extravagant gesture.

Fate played into Elizabeth's hands. That autumn the appalling Don Carlos fell ill.

'I hear that his condition is quite serious,' she told her Council. 'Certainly it will put an end to this present talk of a marriage between him and Queen Mary.' She picked up a letter. 'And Randolph reports that her Majesty is most intrigued by our offer to find her a husband.' Elizabeth had been gratified to read that pretty, brainless Mary had frequent crying fits and bouts of melancholy, which Randolph had attributed – but not in so many words – to her need for a man in her lonely bed. 'It seems that she is most eager to wed,' she went on. 'Of course she wants an heir of her body' – her glacial glance swept the table in case any dared to say that she herself should too – 'and she says that she is unsuited to the single life. Give her a few months of wondering, and she will fall into our lap like a ripe plum.'

But Cecil now had his eyes on other ripe plums. The Queen's mention of heirs had spurred him to venture once more into dangerous territory. The very next day, he raised the matter of her own marriage – and just after she thought she had got away with avoiding all discussion of Parliament's petitions.

'Madam, you have given your word to your Lords and Commons,' he reminded her, as Robert sat there looking for all the world like a cat that was about to plunge its whiskers into a great bowl of cream. Clearly he thought that this was his moment. And in all fairness it really ought to have been, but Elizabeth just could not say the words.

'We are mindful of our promise,' she declared with an effort, not looking at Robert, 'and we mean to look into the possibility of reviving negotiations for our marriage with the Archduke Charles.'

'God's blood!' Robert roared, banging his fist on the table, as the other councillors stared at him, and then looked nervously at the Queen, wondering how she would react to this unacceptable loss of temper in her presence. But Robert was past caring about deference. 'England does not want or need a Catholic king, or a foreigner,' he stormed. 'Not when you have a zealous Protestant far nearer at hand. Why revive this marriage now?' His withering look said what, even in his fury, he dared not say aloud, which was that he knew Elizabeth's promises to be worthless.

'The Emperor's friendship would be more advantageous to the realm than my marriage with a subject,' she said, her voice cold.

'What matters,' intervened Cecil, 'is that there are no further delays, and that your Majesty marries soon. The negotiations with the Archduke dragged on an unconscionably long time before.' And no doubt you intend for them to do so again. He did not need to say it – and nor, by his expression, did Robert.

'Good Spirit,' Elizabeth reassured him, 'should the Archduke prove willing, I will be content to accept him.' Robert sat there shaking his angry head and biting his lip to stop himself from snarling at her. She was grateful that they were not alone.

'Very well, Madam, I will make another approach to the Emperor,' Cecil said, briskly in a tone that boded well for the speedy concluding of negotiations, and he hurried away to compose the letter before she could change her mind.

Robert did not come to Elizabeth's bed that night. His fury was palpable, even through the dividing wall, and – which was hardly surprising – she did not sleep. The next morning, without asking her permission, he was away at dawn, galloping huffily north to inspect – and no doubt criticise – the works he had put in hand at Kenilworth. And there he stayed, sulking, for a week. Elizabeth refused to admit to herself how much she missed him.

He was back, glowering at the council board, by the time the Emperor's response arrived. Cecil's face was equally gloomy.

'It appears that his Imperial Majesty has not forgotten that your Majesty formerly rejected his son,' he told Elizabeth. 'He has also heard rumours that you mean to marry my Lord Robert here.'

The tension in the room was umistakable. Robert looked smug and Elizabeth went rigid in her chair.

'Maybe your Majesty would like to make an approach to the Archduke yourself,' Cecil suggested helpfully.

'No I would not!' Elizabeth snapped. 'It is the Archduke's place to make the approach. It is unthinkable that I, a maiden queen, should take the initiative.' She dared not look at Robert.

'Then I will approach my diplomatic contacts and see if the Emperor can be persuaded to agree to this,' Cecil offered. He did not feel confident of success. Indeed, he thought he should warn the Archduke to proceed slowly, given that the Queen was much inclined to celibacy and would – as ever – take some persuading. Cecil, like Robert, was beginning to wonder if Elizabeth really would ever marry; and he was almost alone in surmising that she had never given herself to Dudley.

Maiden queen indeed! Robert thought, not quite knowing how to express his fury. How long would Elizabeth go on making a public fool of him? There was only so much a man could stand, and he was damned if he was going to sleep with her while she trifled with his heart and his pride, and provoked and belittled him with her talk of marrying other men.

1564

The Emperor Ferdinand's envoy, Herr Allinga, stood before the Queen, all obsequiousness and courtesy. Only Cecil and two of her ladies were in attendance. She sat on her throne inwardly fuming as both men praised to the skies the advantages of her marrying the Archduke, declaring all the good reasons for it – as if she had not heard them before. In truth, she was thinking of Robert, uncomfortably aware that she had gone too far this time.

She glared at Cecil and Allinga. 'Gentlemen, you may as well save your breath, for I will never be induced by appeals to reason, but only by stern necessity. I have inwardly resolved that, if I ever marry, it will be as the Queen, not as Elizabeth.'

'I understood that your Majesty was eager for the match,' Allinga said, looking completely bewildered, and clearly wondering what he was doing in England.

'I have always been eager for it,' she lied, 'and it was the fault of your master, the Emperor, that the earlier negotiations broke down.' Cecil almost gaped at her in dismay. Was she trying to wreck all his stressfully negotiated diplomacy by offending his Imperial Majesty? It seemed, God help them all, that she was.

'The Emperor behaved like an old woman,' she went on, as if injury was not sufficient on its own without insult added to it. 'He refused to let his son come to England. It is unreasonable of anyone to expect me to accept a suitor without seeing him first, and it is proper for the Archduke to make the first move towards reviving his courtship, since I myself cannot do so without covering myself in ignominy. For my part, I would far rather be a beggar woman and single than a queen and married.'

Cecil, feeling uncharacteristically savage, hurriedly steered

Herr Allinga out of the room, and he was not surprised when the envoy sympathetically (in the circumstances) told him there was no point in pursuing the matter further.

'You must be patient with her Majesty,' Cecil hastened to reassure him. 'Knowing her of old, I believe that she is by no means averse to the marriage.' But Allinga went home all the same, and who could blame him?

Matters remained decidedly cool between Elizabeth and Robert. Even the departure of the Emperor's envoy had not thawed Robert's frigid manner towards her. When she attempted to cozen him with her ready wit and a warm, repentant-looking (she hoped) smile, he responded only with chilly courtesy.

Have it your own way! she fumed. She would show the world that she needed no man in her life! And she would show Robert who was mistress here.

Randolph was now back in London, having left Queen Mary none the wiser as to whom her English suitor might be – and, as Elizabeth had anticipated, desperate to know.

'You are to return to Scotland,' Elizabeth commanded him. 'You may now tell the Queen of Scots that we are offering her Lord Robert Dudley as a husband.' Randolph hid his trepidation by bowing low.

When he had gone, with dragging steps, to start packing, Elizabeth summoned Robert. She could put off the evil moment no longer.

He came, stiff and unrelenting, his face cold. One glance and she feared that she might falter in her resolve. Given how things stood between them, he would think that she really meant to do this. And really, it would be better for him to believe it – for now, at least.

'I have made up my mind,' she said firmly. 'I want you to marry the Queen of Scots, if she will have you.'

Robert erupted. 'No!' he raged. 'No, and no again! I will not leave England and everything I hold dear, not even for you, especially to go and live in a land of barbarians.'

'Robert, I am not asking you. I command it, as your Queen!'

That broke him. She had never seen him weep, and she was stunned to see tears in his eyes now. 'God,' he said helplessly, trying to compose himself. 'God help me . . . Bess . . . Damn you, I am distraught at the thought of leaving you. We were so close. You promised to marry me. What the devil has gone wrong? How could you do this to me – to us?'

She nearly gave way. But it would be better for the successful outcome of her scheming that Robert believed her sincere. That way, none would guess what she really intended.

'Robert, I insist – no, I ask – for your co-operation in this important matter. This is how you can serve me best.'

Robert was struggling to control himself. Anger, pain and bitterness suffused his handsome face. He knew he had no choice but to obey, but he knew too that he would never, ever understand how this woman, whom he had so faithfully loved – and still did love, God help him – could treat him so cruelly.

Elizabeth looked up from her desk and laid down her pen. Cecil stood before her holding a letter with a broken seal.

'From Thomas Randolph, Madam,' he said, passing it to her. She read it and smiled. Mary's feathers had been ruffled. She had shown no enthusiasm for marrying Robert; indeed, she had asked incredulously if it would stand with her honour to wed a mere subject.

'You had best go and put him out of his misery, William,' Elizabeth said.

Cecil found Robert in the tennis court, whacking a ball against the penthouse above the wall with grim fervour. He was utterly relieved to hear that the Queen of Scots did not want him for a husband, and joyfully welcomed the implied slur. Aversion to the match was, at least, one thing they had in common.

But that was not the end of it. Even though she knew there was no chance of Mary's agreeing, Elizabeth continued to press the matter. She had Cecil write a sixteen-page justification for the marriage, to be sent to Randolph in Edinburgh. She smiled at the thought of Mary's response, not sparing a thought for poor Randolph, who would have to read it out to her. Brainless Mary might well fall asleep, not having much head for politics. But she would wake up, of course, when he got to the part where Elizabeth promised her that with Dudley would come the English succession – subject, of course, to the consent of Parliament. A small clause to which Mary might not give much credence, but a crucial one.

Mary not only woke up, she sent an ambassador, Sir James Melville, to Elizabeth's court to foster goodwill with her dear sister of England. Elizabeth took to the cultivated, charming and urbane Melville at once, and even Robert, withdrawn and resentful under his assumed patina of courtesy and princeliness, began to wonder if it were true that the Scots were actually barbarians after all.

Elizabeth enjoyed flirting with Melville. It was important to her that he found her more beautiful, more accomplished and much, much cleverer than his own Queen. She was determined that every word he wrote in his reports home would show up Mary as wanting in every respect.

She was delighted to find that Melville was as proficient as she at languages, and enjoyed besting him in conversation. Responding to his compliments, she took care to appear in different stylish outfits, all dripping with jewels: one in the English fashion, one in the French, and a third in the Italian.

'Which do you prefer, Sir James?' she asked, twirling in her heavy silk skirts, her low-cut pleated Venetian bodice almost falling off her shoulders.

'I like you in this one, Madam,' Melville told her. 'But they are all beautiful, as is their wearer.'

'And do you like this headdress?' she persisted, making a minuscule adjustment to the jewelled caul and bonnet that crowned her long red curls.

'Assuredly, Madam,' he smiled. 'It suits you charmingly well.'

'Tell me, Sir James, what colour hair is considered best in

your country?' Elizabeth trilled, tossing her long locks over her shoulder for effect.

'In Scotland, Madam, we like a bonny lady whatever colour her hair is,' Melville replied, sensing that all his diplomatic skills were about to be brought into play.

'How does my hair compare with your Queen's?' Elizabeth enquired. 'Which of us is the fairest?'

It seemed to Melville that any political rapprochement between England and Scotland might hang on his answer. He thought rapidly. 'Madam, it would be impossible to decide. You are both faultlessly fair.'

Elizabeth tapped him playfully with her fan. 'That is no answer!' she chid him.

'Then, Madam, I can only say that you are the fairest Queen in England and Mary is the fairest Queen in Scotland.'

'A diplomat's answer, but it tells me nothing!' she reproved him, with an arch smile. 'Each is the only queen in her realm, so each must of necessity be the fairest. You must choose!'

Melville was sweating in his velvet suit and cloak. 'Then, Madam, I can only say that you are both the fairest ladies in your courts, and that your Majesty is very white in complexion, but her Majesty is very lovely.'

Elizabeth was not letting him off so easily. 'Which of us is the tallest?'

'Queen Mary,' he replied. It was well known that Mary was six feet tall.

'Then she is over-high,' Elizabeth observed happily. 'I am neither over-high nor over-low. Does your Queen play well on the lute and virginals?'

'Reasonably, for a queen,' Melville told her, then realised – too late – that his words could be taken the wrong way. That evening Elizabeth's cousin, Lord Hunsdon, sought Melville out after supper, and he found himself being very firmly steered along a gallery above a chamber in which someone was playing the virginals in a most accomplished manner. Hunsdon paused to listen, nodding appreciatively, so Melville followed suit, peering over the gallery to see – to his amazement – the Queen herself at a keyboard bearing the famous Boleyn arms.

'Her Majesty has excellent talent,' he murmured.

'Reasonable, for a queen,' smiled Hunsdon. Melville winced.

Just then the music stopped, and Elizabeth rose and left the room. Seconds later she was advancing along the gallery towards them. When she raised her left hand, Melville thought she was about to strike him for his earlier *faux pas*, but she merely cuffed him gently. 'Well, Sir James, how naughty of you to enter my chamber without leave!' she said. 'How did you come to be here?'

Melville realised that he had a part to play in this little charade, which had obviously been staged to teach him a lesson. 'Madam, forgive me,' he pleaded. 'I heard such melody as ravished me and drew me to this chamber, I know not how.'

Elizabeth sank down on a cushioned chair, clearly pleased. 'I do not usually play before men,' she told him. 'I play when I am solitary, to shun melancholy. But now you can tell me, who is the better musician, myself or Queen Mary?'

'It is yourself, Madam,' Melville conceded, without flattery.

'I thank you,' Elizabeth smiled. 'I hope you will be at court tomorrow night to watch me dance.'

'Madam, for that privilege I will gladly delay my departure,' Melville assured her. And when he had seen her twirling and leaping in *branles* and galliards, and she asked if Mary danced as well as she, he was ready with his answer. 'Not so high or energetically, Madam,' he said. In truth, he had never met a woman as vain, and he thanked God that his Queen, who had every cause to be proud of her looks and accomplishments, had only a proper pride – and a becoming modesty.

The next day he found Elizabeth in a more businesslike mood. She brought up the matter of Queen Mary's marriage, and insisted that Lord Robert would make her an excellent consort.

'It seems selfless of your Majesty to offer my Queen one for whom you clearly cherish great affection,' he ventured.

'If I had ever wanted to take a husband, I would have chosen Lord Robert,' Elizabeth declared, 'but it is my own resolution at this moment to remain a virgin queen until my death, and nothing will compel me to change my mind save any undutiful behaviour on the part of the Queen my sister.'

'Madam, you need not tell me that,' Melville answered, thinking that, from what he had heard, there were more ways than one to be a virgin. 'I know your stately stomach. You think that if you were married, you would only be a queen of England. But now you are king and queen both. You will not endure a commander.'

'You are perceptive, Sir James.' Elizabeth's eyes twinkled. She wished her councillors – and Robert – were as intuitive.

'As for my mistress, she loves your Majesty so much that she could never contemplate being undutiful in any way.'

'We hope and trust that will always be the case,' Elizabeth said, not forgetting for a moment how Mary had claimed to be queen of England, and dismissed him.

Robert had simmered in the background throughout Melville's visit. He had been desperate to know what was being discussed – apart from hair and gowns – behind closed doors when Elizabeth conversed with Melville alone. As he lay restless in his great empty bed, he wondered what new strategy she was cooking up to make the Queen of Scots take him, Robert, for her lawful wedded husband. God's blood, it was *his* marriage that was under discussion, and it looked as if he would be the last to know whether it was going ahead, or even if a date had been set!

It was now months since he and Elizabeth had slept together, and he was damned if he was going to make any move towards her. He had even thought of secretly taking a mistress, because a man was a man, after all. But even there she had him. The truth was he did not want any other woman; it seemed to be his fate to want the one he could not have. And while there was the remotest chance that Elizabeth's ever-changing mind might once more focus upon him in the way it had once done, he was determined not to jeopardise his prospects. In the meantime, though, he felt that wearing his displeasure on his sleeve might bring her to heel. It worried him that so far such tactics had got him nowhere.

Did she really mean to wed him to the Queen of Scots? How could she seriously contemplate it, after all they had been to each other? Or was the whole farce a devious ploy to test his loyalty and prove that it was not just a crown he lusted after? One never knew with Elizabeth. Her opinions were mercurial, her intent often masked by obfuscation. It might be that all this talk of the Scottish marriage was yet another delaying tactic, since speculation that Elizabeth would marry him had lately all but ceased. He wished he could be certain. It occurred to him that he had endured nearly six years of uncertainty, yea, and of celibacy too! By God, he was now thirty-two, and these four years a widower – and he still lacked heirs to inherit the wealth that had been bestowed on him. A man needed a wife and sons. This life he was leading was not natural – and it was all Elizabeth's fault. Rage – no stranger to him these days – again consumed him.

It was at that precise moment that the door opened and Elizabeth, alluring in the candlelight in a black velvet night-gown, her burnished hair loose about her shoulders, walked softly in. He sat up with a jolt, unable to believe his eyes.

'We need to talk, Robin,' she said in her usual forthright way, and sat down on the bed, her face unreadable.

'I don't think I want to hear what you have to say,' he replied sullenly, wishing that he didn't find her so enchanting.

'It pains me to see us like strangers,' Elizabeth said, 'and I have not been fair to you. I see now that I should have been plain from the first, but I thought my plan would only work if you believed that I really meant to marry you to Mary.'

'And you do not?' he asked, hardly daring to hope.

'No.' She smiled at him, a touch shamefaced. 'It's complicated, as it always is with me. I know full well that Mary will not

190

marry you, and that I am safe in pursuing these negotiations. No, Robin, I have another husband in mind for her, one who will suit her – and me – well, but I do not want to be seen to be putting him forward.'

'So I am the decoy!' Robert said, understanding dawning.

'Yes, my Eyes, you are the decoy. You will never know what it has cost me to pursue this policy.' Elizabeth met his gaze. Her eyes were brimming. 'I cannot bear us being estranged.'

Robert shook his head despairingly. 'I wish you had told me, Bess. I thought you were testing my loyalty. You could have relied on me to play your game. Another of your games! And you could have spared us both much hurt. I cannot begin to tell you—'

'Don't!' she interrupted. 'It is in the past now. I just want us to be as we were before. I need you, Robin.'

'And I need you, Bess.' He bent forward and drew her into his arms. It felt sublime after their long abstinence. 'But I need you in a different way. Be mine *now*! And when all this play-acting is over, marry me!'

Elizabeth responded hungrily. Her urgent lips and fingers told him more than any words could convey. Soon they were riding the storm, oblivious to everything but their passion for each other. Instinct told Robert that this was the moment when he would gain mastery over his Queen. Consumed and gasping with long-suppressed desire, he pulled off her gown and rolled her on to her back amidst the disordered bedclothes. Then he mounted her, hard and insistent, and was about to enter her when he sensed her going rigid beneath him – just as she always had.

'Not now,' he rasped. 'I can't stop. I must have you!'

'No!' Elizabeth squealed. 'Please, Robin! *Please!*'

Shuddering, he drew back, his breath coming in jagged spurts. She lay there sobbing quietly beside him.

'I cannot go on like this,' he sighed at length. 'Bess, you must trust me. I love you more than I have loved any woman. I will never betray you, or hurt you. If you are worried about my getting you with child, I have come by a device that will prevent it.' He clambered to his knees and reached down into the chest at the foot of the bed. From it he drew a short linen sheath with ribbons attached, and deftly he tied it on.

'Now you may be sure that no child will ensue,' he declared, lying down beside her once more and taking her again into his embrace.

Elizabeth had watched the whole performance in dubious silence.

'It is known to be effective,' Robert promised. 'And as we both know, the act of love can hold no terrors for you. It is not as if it would be the first time.' He bent forward and kissed her neck, his hands moving purposefully but gently over her body. He could feel her relaxing. 'Come now!' he said, his voice tender.

Elizabeth knew that denying him at this moment would be the worst thing she could do. She owed him something precious to make up for the suffering he had endured on her account these past months. She had already given him everything else of herself. Could she now give this ultimate gift?

He was moving against her, desire lively in him. She tried to relax, to tell herself that her fears were as insubstantial as cobwebs and could be blown away as easily. It would be all right. This was the man she loved. It would not be as it had been with the Admiral, nor would it end as it had done for her father and mother. The heavens would not fall; the executioner was not about to hone his axe, and there would be no blood shed on account of this night. But still she shrank from giving herself. That flimsy bit of linen might yet be the cause of her downfall.

'Not now, Robin!' she cried. 'Wait until we are wed.'

With an immense effort, Robert drew back once more, his face contorted like that of a man in pain. 'I hope you mean it this time,' he gasped.

Later, after she had willingly pleasured him, and he had paid his debt to her in return, they lay together at peace, exchanging gentle words and light, replete caresses. Lying curled up in the crook of Robert's arm, her head on his shoulder, Elizabeth was glad that she had not succumbed to his pleas, and thoroughly relieved that there could be no risk of her being with child. What was more, to her great surprise, she had enjoyed tonight's love-play more than ever before, had felt a deep physical pleasure and a release that had had her clinging to Robert as a drowning man clings to a rock.

He was gazing down at her, his eyes warm and appreciative.

'Well, my lady? When is the wedding?'

Elizabeth let him wait for a heartbeat. 'As soon as I can extricate you from the negotiations with the Queen of Scots,' she told him.

'And when will that be?'

'Sweet Robin, I am not playing games this time,' Elizabeth assured him. 'This is high politics and I must await the opportune moment.'

Robert shifted on to his back, staring up at the carved canopy of the tester bed. 'More waiting! I trust it will not be for long this time.' There was an edge of impatience to his voice. 'Who is it that you mean the Queen of Scots to wed?'

Elizabeth sat up, clasping her arms about her knees. She knew that this was a time for honesty. 'If I tell you, it must go no further. It would jeopardise everything.'

'You know you can trust me,' he assured her.

'It is Lord Darnley.' She threw him a wicked smile.

'Darnley? Good God!' Robert exclaimed.

'Yes, Darnley. And Randolph reports that smitten, brainless Mary wants to marry him. She instructed Melville to approach his mother, Lady Lennox. Cecil says that Melville is all for it.'

'Has Mary ever met Lord Darnley?'

'No, but she likes the fact that he is of the royal blood of England *and* the noble blood of Scotland, and she has heard reports of how pretty he is, and what nice manners he has.'

'The fellow can't even grow a beard,' Robert sneered.

'But by all the accounts she has heard, he is a lusty youth, and his scheming mother has long been in good hope that Mary will condescend to marry him.'

'She has been in and out of the Tower enough times on that account,' Robert said. 'My head spins just thinking about it.'

'Lady Lennox is a great intriguer,' Elizabeth growled, 'and a troublemaker to her soul. The Earl her husband persuaded me to ask Queen Mary to restore his estates in Scotland, but now I fear that if he goes north to treat with her he will intrigue for the marriage, and I don't want that happening just yet, so I have written again to Mary, demanding that she refuse him entry to her kingdom. That should make her all the more determined to favour the Lennoxes. In the meantime, my Eyes, you are the cover for my true intentions.'

'But – *Darnley*!' Robert said again. 'I pity the woman who marries that vicious boy.'

'Only a fool would do so,' Elizabeth observed, looking at him slyly.

'I know your game,' he told her. 'Give Mary Darnley, and he will destroy her.'

'That's exactly what I thought,' she replied. 'But it is a dangerous matter and I must needs keep a cool head. A marriage between Mary and Darnley would unite two claims to my throne. Some would say that I am mad to consider it. But I believe that neither of them has the brains – or the means – to pursue their claims to a satisfactory conclusion. And Darnley is trouble, and weak with it. Mark my words, if those two wed, disaster will ensue and distract Mary from coveting my throne. Trust my judgement, dear Eyes.'

'Very well, then, I will be patient a little longer,' Robert sighed.

'The best things in life are worth waiting for,' Elizabeth pronounced, already regretting having mentioned marriage. But what else, at such a moment, could she have done? She was running out of favours!

'You will not be disappointed, my Queen. I have been told that I couch a lance well,' Robert grinned.

'And who has told you that?' Elizabeth demanded in mock anger.

'Legions of fair ladies,' he teased her, and got a pillow thrown at him for his bragging. 'Help!' he cried, pulling it over his head. 'Mercy!'

Elizabeth laughed. 'You are a rogue, my Eyes!'

Suddenly Robert grew serious. 'I never thought we would be like this again, or that you would finally consent to wed me,' he said. 'This has been the happiest night of my life.'

'I was to have bestowed on you a slightly different honour,' Elizabeth said. 'That was why I came. That, and to put things right.'

'A different honour?' he murmured. 'I don't understand.'

'I came to tell you that I have decided to raise you to the nobility as earl of Leicester,' she smiled. 'And I am not trifling with you this time.'

Robert whooped with elation. 'My God, I thought you would never do it!' he cried.

'Shhh, you'll have the whole palace awake!' Elizabeth reproved him, giggling.

'Thank you, Bess. Thank you!' He took her hand and kissed it avidly. 'This means so very much to me. Especially after my father lost his title and all his honours, and people have pointed the finger, saying that I am unworthy of your love and favour. This − and what you have confided to me this night − sets all to rights. I do declare that I am the luckiest man on Earth.'

She was beginning to wonder if, this time, she had gone too far to turn back. 'Yes, but Robin, you must understand why I have come to this decision. On the face of it, it is to make Queen Mary think the more of you, and make you a husband fit for a queen. *Which* queen we will not say!'

'I care not why you have done it, Bess, save it renders me more worthy of you. Tell me truly: will that day surely come when we two can be wed? Do you mean it this time?'

Elizabeth kissed him, not even daring to contemplate the future. 'After tonight, who could mistake my meaning?'

*

The presence chamber in St James's Palace – that noble residence which King Harry had built for Anne Boleyn, who never lived to see it completed – was thronged with courtiers and dignitaries. There stood Melville, delaying his departure once more at Elizabeth's request, so that he could report to his Queen how gallantly her ardent suitor had borne himself at his ennoblement, and how fine a husband he would make for her.

Elizabeth's gown, encrusted with jewels, sparkled in the candlelight and dazzled everyone. Glittering like an icon, she rose from her throne as Robert, attired in robes that did sufficient justice to a future king, knelt on the dais before her. He was playing his part well, conducting himself with the greatest dignity and gravity, but she could not help remembering him naked on the bed with her the night before, and she was smiling when they handed her the ermine-trimmed mantle. As she lifted it onto his shoulders and tied the golden cords, she could not resist tickling his neck. He looked up at her, startled, and their eyes met for a second, yet hers were now impassive as she arranged the gold collar of his earldom on the mantle. But she had seen Melville raise his eyebrows, and knew he had observed the caress.

After the ceremony, as Robert received the congratulations of his fellow peers, several of whom could hardly wait to see him packed off to Scotland, Elizabeth beckoned Melville.

'How like you my new creation?' she asked.

'A fine lord, Madam,' Melville replied. 'But methinks you would prefer to marry him yourself.'

'Not at all,' she said. 'I look upon him merely as a brother and a friend. An old friend – we were children together. It is for his loyalty and his princely demeanour that I offer him to Queen Mary. And yet I think you like yonder long lad better!'

Her gaze rested on young Lord Darnley, glowering in a corner. That sulky youth had burning aspirations to be king of Scots; he hated Robert, and he certainly hated watching his rival being groomed to supplant him. If looks could have killed, Robert would now be lying dead on the floor.

Melville looked at Darnley with distaste. 'No woman of spirit would choose such a man,' he muttered. 'He is more like a woman with his beardless lady face.'

And would suit your Queen very well, Elizabeth thought. They would make such a pretty pair. Brainless, both of them! Aloud, she said to Melville, 'Attend me in my chamber. I would show you my treasures. And you, my lord of Leicester, and you, Sir William, come with us.' Robert and Cecil followed them into her lodgings and even through to her bedchamber. This invitation into the holy of holies was a signal honour for Melville.

Elizabeth took from a cabinet a miniature of Queen Mary and kissed it affectionately. 'See how I love your Queen, my cousin,' she said, placing it back in the cabinet beside a small package inscribed in her familiar hand *My Lord's picture.*

'May I see that one?' Melville asked.

'It is a private thing,' Elizabeth declared, wishing that she had thought to remove it earlier.

'It would be a great honour to see something that is clearly very precious to your Majesty.'

Reluctantly Elizabeth unwrapped the package to reveal an exquisite miniature of Robert looking exceptionally debonair. It was the best likeness of him ever made, and she treasured it.

'This would be the perfect gift for my Queen,' Melville declared.

'Ah, Sir James, I would that I could let her have it, but alas, I have no copy,' Elizabeth demurred.

'But your Majesty has the original,' he pointed out. Robert was smirking behind his back. Cecil looked as if he had swallowed gall.

'All the same,' insisted Elizabeth, 'I do not wish to part with it. You may tell Queen Mary that, in the process of time, she will get all that I have, and I will send her a beautiful diamond in token of my love for her.'

She would not meet Robert's eyes for fear that she might laugh aloud.

*

Before Melville left for Scotland, he was surprised to find the new Earl of Leicester bearing down on him determinedly.

'Sir James, I must say this to you.' Robert glanced over his shoulder to see that no one was within earshot. 'I am not worthy to wipe the shoes of the Queen of Scots.'

Aye, thought Melville, but you are worthy of doing as much – and more, if gossip could be believed – for the Queen of England.

'You do not want this match, my lord?' he asked.

Robert shrugged. 'It is my belief that my secret enemy, Sir William Cecil, thought up and plotted it, to get me out of the way.'

'I think your Queen too is a great dissembler,' Melville confided, 'but I must tell you that she has agreed that commissioners from both kingdoms should meet at Berwick to discuss the marriage.'

'Then it seems I must cultivate a taste for haggis,' Robert said lightly. 'But tell me, Sir James – is it true that you have been paying visits to the Spanish embassy?'

It was true, and for a moment the normally urbane Melville was nonplussed. 'A courtesy visit, nothing of importance,' he said after the slightest pause.

'It could not have been to try to revive negotiations for Queen Mary's marriage to Don Carlos?' Robert persisted.

'I should have thought that your lordship would have been pleased to hear that it had.'

'And so I would have been,' Robert said, 'save that it is never going to happen. Don Carlos is now so far gone in madness that there can be no question of his marrying anyone.'

'So I was informed when I enquired after his health,' Melville fenced. 'But if your lordship can keep a secret, I can tell you something that may be of great advantage to you.'

Robert's eyes lit up. 'I can keep a secret,' he said.

'Queen Mary has her eyes on another suitor,' Melville told him. 'But I am not at liberty to say who it is. I tell you only to set your mind at rest. She will not have you. That I can promise.'

Soon afterwards Mary gave the Earl of Lennox leave to enter Scotland.

The commissioners had met at Berwick. The Earl of Moray, bastard half-brother of Queen Mary and leader of the Protestant Lords of the Congregation, had demanded assurances that Queen Elizabeth would settle the succession on her dear sister if Mary agreed to marry the Earl of Leicester. The English deputation refused to confirm that she would do so – or more likely did not know. Moray lost his temper, and the meeting ended in acrimony.

Back in England, Robert was doing his best covertly to whip up support for the Darnley marriage. He knew that Elizabeth was given to changing her mind, and was determined to pre-empt her.

Some weeks later a letter arrived from the Scottish lords, informing the Queen that Mary would not agree to marry the Earl of Leicester unless Elizabeth promised to name her her heir.

'What in Heaven do we reply, Madam?' Cecil asked.

'We say nothing,' Elizabeth answered. 'Mary will never accept Robert, even if he comes with a crown. No, she wants to marry Lord Darnley, and as he is my subject she must be a suitor to me for my consent.' She smiled at the prospect of Mary in a suppliant role. It would compensate for the Scottish Queen's insulting rejection of Robert.

'May I suggest that Darnley be permitted to join his father in Scotland, to whet the Queen of Scots' appetite?' Cecil proposed, a gleam in his eye.

'That is a capital idea!' Robert enthused, clearly delighted to be out of the running – and no doubt plotting another royal wedding closer to home, Cecil thought.

'Certainly a marriage with Lord Darnley would pose less of a threat to us than one to a great Catholic prince,' Elizabeth said thoughtfully. 'But for the present he must remain here. Absence, they say, makes the heart grow fonder. Let Mary ponder on what she is missing!'

*

The air was crisp and cold but invigorating as Elizabeth and Robert galloped out in the early-morning dark for their usual ride. Christmas was approaching. The baked meats were even now being prepared in the royal kitchens. Men had gone to the woods to fell the Yule log. The choristers and children of the Chapel Royal were busily rehearsing carols and a new motet written by Thomas Tallis, one of the gentlemen of the Chapel Royal, and making a divine sound in the process. But only the servants had been stirring as the two cloaked figures left the palace by a wicket gate.

They raced across the park, on ground that was hard with frost, and made for the chase beyond.

'I love being out at this time, when few souls are abroad,' Elizabeth said, as they slowed to a trot by a stream.

'I love being alone with you,' Robert said, extending a hand and squeezing hers.

They trotted on for a mile or so in companionable silence, enjoying the beauty of the winter dawn. But then . . .

'I don't feel well,' Elizabeth said suddenly. 'Robin, I have to get to a privy, soon.' She wheeled her horse and cantered back towards the palace, barely making it in time to avoid disgracing herself in public.

By now she was very ill indeed. Repeatedly she vomited, or suffered a looseness of the bowels, and when she was not in the privy she was lying shivering in her bed, complaining that she was freezing to death. But her forehead was burning up. The doctors, having prescribed an infusion of blackberry leaves, stood around looking worried and helpless until she shouted at them to go away. It was Kat and Kate Knollys who soothed her, making her take sips of the revolting brew, chafing her hands and mopping her brow. And mercifully, just in time for the twelve days of merrymaking, Elizabeth was soon back on her feet.

'For a time, Madam, you had us sore afraid,' Cecil confessed.

'Don't say it, William!' she warned, but there was no deterring him now.

'Madam, I would be failing in my duty if I did not pray God to send some man whom it will content you to wed. Otherwise, I assure you, I have no comfort in living.'

The Bishop of Salisbury, standing nearby, added his voice. 'Your Grace, I must tell you how wretched we have been, not knowing under which sovereign we would live, should something evil befall your precious person. I trust that God will long preserve you to us in life and safety!'

Elizabeth was about to say something tart in response – this was all a bit dramatic, she felt – but there was no mistaking the relief and sincerity in both men's faces. 'I thank you, my lords,' she replied. 'I promise I will give due thought to the matter in this coming year. But for now, let us make merry, for Christmas is upon us!'

1565

Paul de Foix, the new ambassador sent by the Queen Mother of France, made an extremely elegant bow. The French were very good at these things, if not at much else. As she extended her hand to be kissed, Elizabeth noted that Cecil was hovering hopefully nearby, and that Robert was frowning, doubtless feeling beleaguered by all the recent talk of the Archduke Charles renewing his suit. She suspected that he would not be pleased when he heard what Paul de Foix had come to say, because her spies had told her that Queen Catherine was determined to thwart the ambitions of the Habsburg Emperor, France's great enemy.

She smiled at the ambassador's elaborate courtesies, and the smile stayed fixed on her face as he proposed his young master, King Charles IX of France, as a suitor for her hand, impressing on her the very great honour his Majesty was bestowing by offering her his most sacred person – a king, no less! Which would have been all very well had Elizabeth not heard that Charles's most sacred person was a pimply fourteen-year-old dwarf with knobbly knees.

'Do not marry him, Bess!' cried her woman fool – engagingly called Ippolita the Tartarian – capering across the floor on her short legs. 'He is a boy and a babe!'

Robert laughed out loud.

'Be off with you,' Elizabeth snapped at the fool, but with a twinkle in her eye as she turned to the bristling Foix. 'Take no offence, Monsieur, she is a scamp who should know her place! But she has a point. Sensible as I am of the honour done me by his Majesty, I fear I am too old to marry him. I think not of now, for I am only thirty-one, but of the future. I would rather die than be despised and abandoned by a younger husband, as my sister was. Why, the age gap between us is so wide that people will say that your master has married his mother!'

'Then, Madam, there is no more to say,' Foix sniffed, mightily offended.

Had this idiot *no* idea of how to play the game? Elizabeth flared. 'Does the King of France have so little regard for me that he would drop his suit so precipitately?' she cried. 'I but wished to draw his attention to the difficulties that might have to be faced, so that he will understand why I cannot give him an answer at once!'

Foix was suddenly all smiles again, and went on his way imagining the credit he would have in store with his terrifying mistress, Queen Catherine. Meanwhile, Robert was pounding after Elizabeth.

'What are you playing at now?' he growled, manoeuvring her into a closet where they could be private.

'My usual game,' she replied, wrenching herself free. 'And you have no right to be angry with me, Robin. I need to keep the French friendly. I do not want them making an alliance with the Scots. Surely even you can see what would happen if Charles were to marry Mary.'

'*Even me?* That was uncalled for,' Robert protested.

'Well I do wonder sometimes! It might have occurred to you that I do not want the Emperor thinking that his son is the only contender for my hand.'

'Yes, yes, I see your reasoning,' Robert replied testily. 'But if you were to marry me – *as you promised* – there would be an end to all this diplomatic posturing, and it would not matter what the Emperor, or anyone else, thought.'

'Oh, but it would – and I would lose my trump card, which may prove to be my only means of keeping other princes friendly.'

Robert's face fell as he took in the full implication of Elizabeth's words. God's blood, she was not reneging on her promise? She *could* not, not now, after all that she had said.

'There are surely other means,' he said hoarsely.

'Yes, but not ones I wish to deploy just now,' she said gently. 'At present the advantage is mine. I would keep it a while longer. That is all.'

'So you have no intention of considering this latest proposal?'

'What do you take me for? A cradle-snatcher? Come, Robin, it's a man I need. On the word of a prince, I will not marry the French King.' And with that she danced out of the room.

'I have told Monsieur de Foix that I must consult with my lords on the matter,' Elizabeth told her councillors. Most of them were openly hostile to the French proposal. Only Robert, curiously they thought, seemed in favour. There really was no accounting for the man's reasoning.

'The Habsburg match is more feasible,' Cecil pronounced.

'The French one is more prestigious – a king as opposed to an archduke,' Robert countered.

The others raised their voices in protest, but Cecil said nothing.

'Madam, saving your presence, King Charles will follow the usage of his forebears and spend himself consorting with pretty girls, rendering useless all hopes of an heir,' Sussex pointed out. Robert gave him a look that said plainly that he would have quite liked to render Sussex useless for opposing him.

Elizabeth quelled them all with a rap on the table. 'Enough, my lords. We must pretend to entertain the proposal – for now.'

Robert groaned, but she ignored him and sent for Foix to attend her in her privy chamber, where they remained closeted until late in the evening. Robert was seething when she joined him in bed that night.

'What in Heaven did you find to talk about all that time?'

'Oh, he was very charming,' Elizabeth related, secretly enjoying his discomfiture. 'Of course I had to sit there listening to lengthy eulogies on his master's precociousness and his most unusual maturity! King Charles has declared himself to be in love with me – primed by his mother, no doubt. I have agreed to an exchange of portraits, and even hinted that I might permit King Charles to visit me secretly . . .' She smiled at the thought. 'You do realise I might have to keep this up for months?'

Robert lay back, barely containing his frustration. She was stalling again, he was convinced of it. He felt like weeping – or throwing something at her, preferably something she held precious.

Elizabeth snuggled down beside him. 'It will all be an act, my Eyes. I'll not have him – ever! And in the meantime I will spin things along with the Archduke, and keep the Emperor warm. With France and the Empire competing for England's friendship, we can all relax for a while.'

Well, perhaps *you* can, thought Robert.

Darnley had finally been granted permission to go to Scotland, with the caveat that he was not even to think of proposing marriage to the Queen of Scots. He had hastened north at the speed of lightning, not giving a second thought to Elizabeth's command when the Scottish crown hovered glittering within his reach.

The Queen laughed aloud when Cecil showed her the latest reports from Edinburgh. 'By God, Mary is besotted! *She thinks him the lustiest man she has ever seen*. Her nobles are spitting fire!'

'They do not want a Catholic king,' Cecil observed, which was putting it mildly. 'A Catholic queen is bad enough.'

'Ah, but this Catholic king comes with a claim to my crown,' Elizabeth said. 'How can she resist him?'

'He is a liability, Madam,' Bacon reminded her. 'He is spoilt, unstable and ambitious.'

'An ideal match for my dear sister,' Elizabeth beamed. 'You will see!'

But then Cecil showed her a new letter from Mary, demanding that Elizabeth recognise her claim to the English succession.

'No,' Elizabeth declared stoutly. 'Tell our good sister that, if she consents to marry my lord of Leicester, I will promote her claim behind the scenes here.'

Robert was staring at her. She quelled him with an imperceptible shake of her head. 'Say that I cannot allow her claim to be examined,' she went on, 'nor will I publish it until such time as I myself am married, or have made known my resolve to remain single – the one or the other I mean shortly to do.' She would not look at Robert.

Some days later there arrived a report from Thomas Randolph in Edinburgh. The Queen of Scots had wept to hear Queen Elizabeth's message. She had used evil speech of her. But it barely signified because in truth she was in love with Darnley. She had even nursed him through an attack of measles.

'Measles!' Elizabeth echoed, as her councillors smiled. 'How touching! And how foolish and unmaidenly.'

'There is more,' Cecil said. 'She wants to marry him. Her lords are against it; they think such a marriage would lead to their utter overthrow.'

'Then we must pray that my dear sister pays heed to them,' Elizabeth concluded piously. God grant that Mary did the very opposite!

On an early spring day in March the Queen heard the clatter of horseshoes on the path below her window at Windsor. Pushing aside the tapestry curtains, she rose from the great ornate bed where she had been luxuriating after a long night of love-play with Robert (who had departed an hour or more ago), and hastened to open the casement, leaning out to see who was there.

'Good morning, sweet Robin,' she called, seeing him below beneath a chestnut tree, mounted on a fine steed. Quickly he doffed his feathered hat and bowed in the saddle – and then she saw that he was not alone. There was the Spanish ambassador, Guzman de Silva, gaping at her open-mouthed, before he hastily uncovered and bent his head too. Too late she realised why he had looked so astounded, for she had not thought to put on her nightgown, and the sheer lawn chemise she had worn – briefly – in bed left very little to the imagination. In fact, one really needed *no* imagination . . .

She drew back, but it was too late. The damage had been done: she had revealed her intimacy with Robert, and much else, to the world – for that was what revealing it to the Spanish ambassador would effectively mean. It came to her that she had grown careless. Only yesterday, in a devil-may-care mood, she had summoned Robert to attend her as her ladies were engaged in the complicated business of robing her for the day – and she wearing only her nightgown. Under the shocked gaze of the speechless women, he had gallantly handed her the fine linen shift that she was to wear next to her skin, and she had kissed him. Soon, she knew, word of her indiscretions would be all around the court – as proved to be the case.

She braved it out – worse had been said of her – and playfully tapped de Silva on the head the next time she saw him, and told him she was ashamed that he had seen her undressed, to which he responded chivalrously. But gossip was again rampant, and public opinion running high. She knew that some were saying she had best marry Robert and be done with it, to avoid any more occasion for scandal. And then occurred that outrageous incident in the tennis court.

She was watching Robert playing against Norfolk, the two of them stripped to their shirts and breeches and looking – especially Robert – very pleasing indeed to the eye. Theirs, she knew, was only a surface friendship – they barely tolerated each other – and when, after the game, Robert drew a handkerchief out of his pocket and mopped his sweating brow, Norfolk's face darkened. He was glaring at the handkerchief, and she recognised it as one that she had given Robert in one of their most intimate moments; it was edged with gold and silver embroidery, done devotedly by Kat Astley, and her initials could clearly be seen.

'By God, you are too saucy, my lord!' Norfolk spat. 'How

dare you impugn the honour of our lady the Queen? You deserve my racquet in your face!' It was not impossible to imagine him carrying out his threat. The racquet was quivering in his hand.

Elizabeth stood up. 'Desist!' she bawled. 'My lord of Norfolk, you will not behave thus in my presence, or indeed at any other time when you are at my court. Touch my lord of Leicester in anger, and you will suffer for it, I promise.'

Norfolk, aware that right hands had been cut off for drawing blood at court, mumbled profuse apologies, his face red with suppressed fury, and bowed himself from the tennis court. Robert came to her, voicing his thanks – although his expression showed that he would have preferred to settle things as men were supposed to do – but Elizabeth cut him short.

'You were a fool to bring out that frippery and provoke him,' she scolded. Then, in a murmur, she added, 'We must be more circumspect in future.'

Robert had no intention of being circumspect. He was determined to be the winner in this marriage game she insisted on playing. He was going to proclaim his intentions to the world, and then Elizabeth would have to remember her promise and dispense with all the other nonsense.

To that end he gave a great feast, to which he invited many lords and ambassadors, and the Queen as guest of honour. Then he arranged a tournament for her entertainment, so that the whole court might see them together, presiding in the centre stand. Finally – the *pièce de résistance* – he invited a company of players to perform a comedy of manners in the Queen's presence chamber. Elizabeth was all smiles – until she realised that the comedy was a play about marriage. She bit her lip as the buxom goddess Juno sang the praises of matrimony at great length, drowning out a very slight and unenthusiastic Diana's advocation of chastity. She frowned ominously as great Jupiter, the arbiter of their dispute, gave his verdict in favour of marriage.

'Very novel,' Guzman de Silva said afterwards, as nymphs

and satyrs danced with wild abandon around the room, hinting rather blatantly at the more private joys of wedlock.

'Very!' Elizabeth snapped. 'But the theme is quite threadbare, I think.'

That night she did not come to Robert's chamber.

He was still sleeping alone – and not by choice – when Sir William Maitland arrived in April to inform Elizabeth that the Queen of Scots had resolved to marry Lord Darnley.

'Well, Sir William, I am astonished!' Elizabeth exclaimed. 'This is a strange proposal. I marvel at Lord Darnley's disobedience. He is my subject and requires my permission to marry. That has not, as yet, been given.'

'I am sorry that your Majesty is offended,' Maitland said, his usual suave manner somewhat ruffled. Elizabeth suspected that he was none too pleased about the Darnley marriage either.

'And I am sorry that my orders have been defied!' she retorted. 'And others will be too!'

In council she issued a formal warning to Mary, stating that if she went ahead with this marriage, it would be perilous to the amity between them. 'Tell her she can take her pick of my nobility,' she ordered.

And so it begins again, Robert thought resentfully, though he had to admire Elizabeth's acting skills. None would have guessed that she wanted this match she was so indignantly deploring. But when the formal warning to the Queen of Scots was drawn up, and Robert was asked to put his signature to it, he refused; if he signed it, Mary might think he was the nobleman she was supposed to pick. And he did not trust Elizabeth.

Cecil was looking remarkably complacent. Afterwards, when the Queen had withdrawn, Sussex confronted him.

'You know, don't you, that she has done this on purpose,' he said. 'All this display of outrage is a sham.'

'If I did not know better, I would be wondering if her Majesty had sent Darnley north to tempt Mary into making a disastrous choice,' Throckmorton said, his air of innocence not quite as convincing as he had intended.

'Why would you think that?' Robert asked, realising that diversionary tactics were called for. 'Mary has chosen him because he has a claim to the succession. It strengthens her own claim to the English crown. No wonder her Majesty is angry – and justifiably concerned.'

'The marriage also poses a new Catholic threat to England's security,' Cecil interposed. 'Think how our English Catholics will be encouraged by it!'

God, he had a cool head, Robert thought admiringly. He and Elizabeth both. They were taking a risk – but a finely calculated one. Firstly, the Scots lords would never allow any Catholic intriguing in their Calvinist fastness; and secondly, he doubted that Mary and Darnley had the wits between them to take on the might of England.

Throckmorton was dispatched north to command Darnley home and convey Elizabeth's disapproval in no uncertain terms to Mary. Lady Lenox was bundled off once more to the Tower. And now that he was more or less out of the running as far as the Queen of Scots was concerned, Robert put pressure on Elizabeth to set a date for their wedding. Even Cecil, his former enemy, was encouraging him. Negotiations with France and the Empire had dragged on to no purpose – anyone could see that. The prize, Robert believed, was at last within his grasp.

Elizabeth was looking strained as she took her seat at the head of the Council. While the French were demanding an immediate answer, Robert was manoeuvring her into a corner of her own fashioning, and she did not want to be there.

They were all watching her: Cecil, impatient after years of what he was pleased to call dithering; Norfolk, fearful lest she throw herself away – as he would see it – on Robert; Sussex and others, weary of these constant debates about this marriage and that, and impatient to see the matter settled; and Robert himself, willing her, badgering her in fact, to declare her intention of having him.

'Tell Monsieur de Foix that the answer is no,' she said, and burst into tears. 'It is *you*, my lord of Leicester, *you*, Sir William, and *all of you*, my lords, who have sought my ruin by scheming to get me married!' she raged, jabbing her finger at each of them. They stared at her, astounded.

'Madam, I would never force you to do anything against your will,' Cecil protested, his voice gentle.

'I beg of your Majesty, do not doubt my loyalty,' Sussex pleaded, and others echoed him. Robert said nothing. He knew he had pushed Elizabeth too far, and now he was seeing for himself what it had done to her. A part of him longed to take her in his arms and comfort her, but the rest of him was suffering the usual exasperation at her fear of commitment. Was this yet another example of her endless procrastination?

It did not help that his fellow councillors also took the Queen's outburst to mean that he had put too much pressure on her. To relieve her of his importuning, they began to pursue the match with the Archduke, who could surely never be as ardent a suitor. Soon afterwards, they even contrived the sending of a new envoy, Adam Zwetkovich, who came to England under cover of returning the late Emperor's Garter insignia, fearful – for he had spoken with his predecessor – lest he would find the Queen blowing cold when he arrived.

'You will support this match, my lord,' Norfolk hissed to Robert, as they waited for Elizabeth to arrive in the presence chamber. 'You must abandon your own suit.'

Robert would have liked to box Norfolk's ears, but, watching the Queen welcoming Zwetkovich with radiant smiles, he knew that he had no choice – for now – but to heed the insufferable man; and he knew it again later, when Elizabeth appointed him and Throckmorton joint commissioners to negotiate the Habsburg marriage. Inwardly he felt a sense of desperation, knowing that, if Elizabeth married the Archduke, he himself stood to lose everything: royal favour, precedence, influence and position. No husband would tolerate him near the Queen, and he would be abandoned to the not-so-tender mercies of his enemies.

Elizabeth, the woman he loved and longed for, had done this to him. With a little word she could have put all to rights, but she had not said it. Her unkindness was bitter gall to him – and after all her promises, everything she had said! He could not quite believe – although he, of all people, had cause to know – how quickly Fortune's wheel could turn.

'It is my belief that the Queen will never marry me,' he confided dejectedly later to Silva, the Spanish ambassador. 'She has made up her mind to wed some great prince, not one of her own subjects.'

'I think not, my lord,' the ambassador replied. 'Your affair is not off!'

'I wish I could believe it,' Robert sighed. He suspected that Silva too was working for the Habsburg match and was only being friendly in case a miracle happened and Elizabeth did decide to marry her favourite. It was wise to have a foot in each camp.

'Her Majesty told Meister Zwetkovich that she had never said to anybody that she would *not* marry the Earl of Leicester,' Silva revealed. 'But you must have been playing your part well, my lord, because he replied that you were the warmest advocate of the match with the Archduke.' (Silva did not add that Elizabeth had insisted to Zwetkovich that she had always acted with due decorum in regard to Leicester. He did not need to. It was no secret that the Imperial envoy had been closely questioning her maids and ladies.) No doubt, Robert thought, Bess had told the envoy that she loved him as a brother, damn her!

He was overjoyed when he learned that a stalemate had been reached. Once more Elizabeth requested that the Archduke come to England to be inspected; this time the Emperor would not hear of it. She had insisted that it would be the Emperor's responsibility to finance the Archduke's household; he was adamant that it was hers. She had declared that she could never marry anyone of another faith; the Emperor would not hear of any religious compromise.

And it was at this juncture that the news came winging into England that the Queen of Scots had married Lord Darnley.

'She has broken all her promises!' Elizabeth raved. 'She has subverted religion in her realm! The Scottish lords are in rebellion, to a man. What a stupid fool she is! Anyone with half a brain in their head would make peace with them without delay. Write to her and say so!'

Back came the furious reply: 'Her Majesty desires her good sister to meddle no further.' Worse still, Mary had had Throckmorton arrested for refusing to accept a safe conduct from Darnley as King of Scots.

'I have every cause to meddle, as she puts it!' Elizabeth shouted. 'Darnley is my subject, and I have the right to recall him to England to answer for his disobedience. Mary should have insisted that he obey me, then negotiated with me for the marriage. *That* would have been the proper way to go about things. Instead, she goes ahead and marries him without my permission!' Immediately she extended the hand of friendship to Mary's half-brother, the Earl of Moray, head of the Lords of the Congregation.

One July evening, as she was sitting alone in her chamber brooding on Mary's perfidy, Kate Knollys came to her.

'Madam, forgive my intrusion, but we are worried about Mrs Astley.'

Elizabeth rose. 'Worried? Why?'

'I think your Majesty should see her for yourself.'

Elizabeth hastened through the gallery to her privy chamber, where she found her ladies and maids clustered around Kat, who was slumped on a bench.

'What's wrong, Kat?' she barked, fear making her sharp. Kat moaned, and Elizabeth knelt before her and tilted her chin upwards. To her horror she saw at once that her old governess's face was distorted on one side, the eye and mouth looking as if they were sliding downwards.

She grabbed Kat's hand. 'Squeeze!' she commanded, but the hand lay limp in hers. 'Kat, speak to me!'

Kat tried to speak, but all she could make were unintelligible sounds.

'Blessed Jesus, send for the doctors!' cried Elizabeth. 'Hurry!' Two women sped away, as the rest waited anxiously. Still on her knees, the Queen rocked Kat in her arms, patting and stroking her back to soothe her. She could sense the fear imprisoned in the older woman's damaged body. And then she felt Kat quieten and hoped that she was comforted.

Dr Huicke arrived within minutes. He bent down and raised Kat from the Queen's embrace, but as he did so her heavy body slumped sideways, her head fell back and her hood dropped to the floor. Her eyes were open, staring.

Elizabeth was inconsolable. Kat had been her beloved friend and confidante; she had been as a mother to her since her childhood. It was no comfort that Kat had died in her arms; all she could feel was the horror of it. Those sightless eyes – eyes that would never again light up in joy at the sight of the motherless girl she had loved, that would never again dim in reproach because that girl had disappointed her. Her life had been devoted to Elizabeth's welfare; there would never be one such as her again. And it was for this that Elizabeth wept – and wept again.

Her grief was made all the worse because Robert was not there to assuage it. They had not shared a bed in weeks, and his pride, smarting because of her latest delaying manoeuvres, had made him keep a resentful distance. He was giving her the space she had said she wanted, and it was doing neither of them any good. Oh, how she missed his tenderness, the physical closeness of him! She was weary of the marriage game; she just wanted the masculine kindness that only her Eyes could give, especially now, when she was feeling so low.

But then, burdened by anger and grief and regret, she saw

him flirting with pretty Lettice Knollys, her own cousin (and, though no one said so openly, her niece). Lettice was the daughter of her beloved Kate Knollys; aged twenty-two and married to Walter Devereux, Viscount Hereford, these five years, she now served as lady-in-waiting alongside her mother in the Queen's household, and Elizabeth had become close to her. She had doted on the exquisite creature, who so much resembled herself with her flame-coloured hair and spirited character. But Lettice had a beauty that few could match, with her slanting green eyes and her air of seductive allure; even Elizabeth had to admit that this kinswoman, ten years younger than herself, was incomparable. And because Lettice was of her own blood, and dear Kate's child, she had felt little jealousy, only a sort of maternal protectiveness. But now Robert was flirting with the girl, and henceforth there could be no looking at Lettice without seeing her as a rival.

Kate Knollys had also seen what was going on. 'Madam, dear coz, do not take this seriously,' she urged. 'Gossip has it that my lord of Leicester was put up to it by Sir Nicholas Throckmorton, in order to discover whether or not you are serious about marrying him.'

'Pah!' Elizabeth snorted. 'Mary should have kept Throckmorton in prison! How dare they play with me!'

In retaliation she began to flirt outrageously with one of Robert's friends, handsome young Thomas Heneage, a member of her Privy Chamber, who was reasonably safe because he was married. Heneage, seeing preferment and riches winging his way, was suitably – and indeed flatteringly – gratified by his Queen's apparently amorous attentions, and repaid them ardently in kind, usually when Leicester was looking on, or so it seemed to the latter.

Robert had indeed intended to give Elizabeth a jolt, hoping that when she saw him paying court to another lady she would suddenly realise that she had been a fool to keep him waiting for an answer – or anything else, for that matter. But there was no denying the charms of Lettice Knollys, with her seductive eyes and pouting lips. He did not think it would take him long to wheedle her into his bed; by all accounts she had little love for her dull husband. It was comforting – even liberating – to know that he could desire another woman. It was also distancing; he realised that Lettice was now occupying part of the space in his mind that Elizabeth had filled. It felt as if he had been unfaithful. He was not sure if he liked the feeling.

He knew he still wanted Elizabeth – the woman he thought of as his, and who was indeed his, more than she was any man's – when he saw her flirting with that dolt Heneage, who was supposed to be his friend. He exchanged harsh, insulting words with Heneage; he warned him off, only to have the fool laugh in his face. The courtiers were smiling behind their hands to see them at loggerheads, two rampant dogs after a bitch on heat. Unendurable!

Robert stood before Elizabeth, looking wounded. She regarded him coolly. 'Yes, my lord?'

'I ask your Majesty's permission to go and stay at my own house, as other men do.'

'No,' she replied.

'I will not stay here to be your lap-dog,' he said.

'You will do as I command!' she snapped.

'But there is no place for me here. You love another.'

'You are a fine one to talk!' she screeched. 'Making eyes at that jade Lettice. Don't think I haven't seen you.'

'It is a flirtation, nothing worse than any of those you have enjoyed with your many suitors,' Robert flung back. 'Now you know how it hurts!'

'So you did it purely to hurt me?' Elizabeth blazed. 'You are despicable!'

'One who has a glass head should beware of stones!' Robert could not resist retorting. He knew he had gone too far, but it was too late now to retract.

'Go away!' she cried. 'I will not sully my eyes with the sight of you! Go!'

He went. He tried, twice, to make it up with her, only to be dismissed by her ladies, on her explicit orders. Three days later she was still sulking. After that she departed scowling to Windsor, where she finally summoned Robert to attend her in private. By then he was too incensed to guard his tongue, so his audience was brief.

'I am touched that you have condescended to see me, Madam!' His voice was heavy with sarcasm. 'I can only conclude that you have indeed cast me aside for another!'

'Remember that I could say the same about you!' she retorted. 'Indeed, seeing how little you care for me, I am sorry for all the time I have wasted on you. Get out!'

Their row had been overheard and was now the subject of common gossip. Even Cecil, on being told how Elizabeth had said she was sorry for the time she had wasted on Robert, commented, 'And so is every good subject!' The courtiers were laughing at him, Robert knew, and he took occasion to upbraid one or two for it, and had another run-in with Heneage just to make himself feel better. But he was soon to regret it.

When next he showed his face in the crowded presence chamber, Elizabeth glared at him. 'My lord of Leicester,' she cried, 'I hope you are here to make answer for yourself. It has come to my attention that you have been high-handed with one of my servants, Master Heneage. God's death, my lord, I have wished you well, but my favour is not so locked up in you that others shall not enjoy it! And if you think to rule here, remember this, that I will have but one mistress – and no master!'

The whole court was looking at him, gloating, enjoying his humiliation. He wished he had not come, and that he was elsewhere – anywhere; even the Tower would be a welcome refuge. What could he do? Matters had deteriorated so badly between himself and Elizabeth that they had incomprehensibly become queen and subject instead of lovers and friends. He knew, with a leaden heart, that his only chance of regaining her favour was to humble himself; and so, setting aside his pride, he fell to his knees and begged her pardon, as sincerely as he could. She grunted none too graciously, and would not look at him.

Humility was now the watchword of his days. He stayed skulking in his lodgings for the next week. He sent no message to an offended Lettice, having resolved not to pursue her any more. When he did finally venture forth into the court he took care to blend into the background, to dress elegantly but not showily, and to speak of the Queen with elaborate courtesy and deference. Then he learned that Heneage had been sent away from court, and his heart began to sing once again.

A day later, incredibly, miraculously, he received a summons from Elizabeth, conveyed by Cecil.

'This state of affairs cannot go on,' the Secretary said. 'My lord of Sussex and I put in a word for you. You see, you are our only hope.' He smiled ruefully. 'Things have come to an impasse with the Archduke. France is out of the running. Heneage, thank God, has gone home. If her Majesty is to marry, she *must* make a decision soon. We are all weary of the delays, and, most important of all, there is the succession to consider. She knows you, my lord – you do not have to pass inspection – and you are a good Protestant. I know we have had our differences, but I am prepared to back you if she will have you.'

'William, I am deeply humbled,' Robert said, surprised. He knew that Cecil had never had a high opinion of him, but it seemed that he had changed his mind, and that left him feeling immeasurably more cheerful.

'No need for thanks,' Cecil said. 'You face no easy task, as we both know. Now get yourself in there and make a beginning.'

Elizabeth was alone in her closet, working on one of her translations – Plutarch this time. She looked up as Robert entered, her face unreadable. Only her fingers, pleating the fabric of her skirt, betrayed her nervousness.

'You sent for me, Madam,' he said, rising from his bow, his face as impassive as he could make it.

'Yes, Robin.' Her use of her private name for him was encouraging. She sounded weary and dejected as she looked at him. 'I think we have both been fools.'

'I have been the greater fool,' he admitted. 'You were right, my Queen: I carried on that flirtation to test you.'

'So Cecil persuaded me. But Robin, it hurt me. I could not bear the thought of you with another.' Elizabeth's eyes filled with tears. 'After all we have been to each other . . .' Her voice tailed off. He could see that she was deeply distressed.

He knelt beside her, feeling unduly emotional himself. 'Can you forgive me, Bess? Is there any way that I can make it up to you?'

She laid her head on his doublet, trembling, her shoulders heaving. He clasped her tightly and held her until the storm subsided. The nearness of her, the feel of her in his arms brought home to him forcibly what he had so nearly lost. He realised that his own cheeks were wet.

'I have asked too much of you,' he murmured into her hair.

'And I of you,' Elizabeth whispered. 'It is not natural for a man to wait so long for a woman to make up her mind. But I am not as other women, Robin. The horrors in my past rise always before me. I do not think that I can truly give myself to any man. And I don't know what to do!' She burst into a fresh torrent of weeping.

Her cry was from the heart; there was no mistaking it. Robert swallowed. He was seeing his life stretching before him, one long frustration of waiting and endless delays, a future without the fulfilment of marriage and children, or even of sexual release – unless of course he risked all by indulging in covert affairs, which would be a betrayal of the woman he loved and might well lead to storms, as he had just experienced, or worse. He saw his hopes of a crown foundering on Elizabeth's uncertainties and fears; it came to him forcibly that she might never marry.

'You don't have to do anything,' he assured her gently. 'I will always love you, and I will always be ready to do you any service. If you want to marry me, I am here. If you do not, I am still here.' They were the most selfless words he had ever uttered, and he realised – with some surprise – that he meant them unreservedly.

Elizabeth wept anew at his words. 'I do not deserve such kindness,' she sobbed. 'I have been terrible to you.'

'True,' he agreed, trying to smile. 'I think that we have been terrible to each other. But now, my Bess, we will be kind, and show ourselves to the world in unison.'

She drew away and touched his cheek, a brave smile on her face. He had never seen her so vulnerable.

'Friends again, sweet Robin?' she asked.

'Friends for ever,' he replied, and kissed her hand.

Some days later they went hunting in the Great Park, accompanied by a select group of courtiers. Robert was none too pleased to see Heneage among them, or to see Elizabeth showing the young man marked favour, but he was mollified by her warm attentions to himself. She did truly seem determined to show the world that they were close once more, and he reciprocated in kind, gratified to be enjoying once more the deference and envy of his peers – and the discomfiture of his rival.

As dusk fell they dismounted. It was a balmy summer evening, perfect for a walk along the North Terrace with its spectacular views over Eton College and the valley of the Thames, followed by a stroll around the labyrinthine paths of the pretty garden below it, their attendants following at a discreet distance. Presently they encountered Silva and an Italian envoy taking the air with several other gentlemen. Silva hailed the Queen with a courtly bow.

'Good evening, your Excellency,' she said, smiling graciously.

'Your Majesty,' he smiled, 'this is a pleasure.'

'It is indeed,' Elizabeth beamed. 'I would know if you have

made progress with the Imperial ambassador. You said that you might put pressure on him and his master to have the Archduke come to England.' Silva had said no such thing, but Elizabeth was determined to play it her way. No archduke, no marriage. She knew that he would never come.

Silva looked at her mischievously. 'I wonder if your Majesty has noticed anyone you have not seen before among these gentlemen.' He indicated the men of his suite, waiting a respectful few feet away. 'Could you be entertaining more than you know at your court?'

Elizabeth was dumbfounded. Robert had rarely seen her so nonplussed. He caught the panic in her eyes. She was casting them from man to man, frantically trying to place them all, looking to see if any resembled the Archduke's portrait. He *could* not be here! she was telling herself. He dare not be here! It would flout every law of protocol.

Then she realised that Silva, that grave-faced Spaniard, was laughing. She was so hugely relieved that she took his little joke in good part and joined in.

'It might be no bad idea for the Archduke to visit me incognito,' she said lightly. 'Would his dignity allow it, do you think? I promise you, plenty of princes have come to see me in that manner.' She smiled archly.

Robert's ears pricked up. That was news to him. Then it dawned on him: she was bluffing, of course. It was the kind of provocative remark that she liked to make. Well, he *hoped* that she was bluffing!

'I do declare I am feeling well disposed towards marriage,' she was saying.

'Then, Madam, let us hope for a happy outcome,' Silva replied.

The Queen of Scots had spent her honeymoon raising an army and marching on her rebel lords, who had fled into England. Moray, Elizabeth learned, was on his way to her court.

'I cannot be seen to be succouring traitors who rebel against their lawful Prince,' she told her Council, in something of a panic.

'But these are good Protestants, Madam,' Cecil reminded her.

'Yes, and I am sympathetic to their objections to this ill-advised marriage,' Elizabeth said. 'But rebellion is treason. This is not the way to go about putting things right.'

'Will you receive Moray?' Robert asked.

'I will – but it will not be the kind of reception he is hoping for!' Elizabeth said grimly.

She was dressed dramatically from head to toe in black when Moray was announced, and she kept him on his knees for a long time, before the whole court.

'My lord, you have rebelled against your lawful sovereign,' she reproved him. 'You look to us for aid, that I know. But we will not maintain any subject in such disobedience against his Prince, for we know that Almighty God would recompense us with the like in our own realm.'

'Madam, we serve a common cause, that of the true religion,' Moray protested, his face dark with fury, his knees beginning to ache.

'We are aware of that,' Elizabeth told him, 'and for that reason we will permit you to remain in England. But as we love peace, we will not engage in a war with Scotland.'

Moray muttered his thanks and staggered to his feet as elegantly as he could. Soon he had cause to perceive the wisdom behind Elizabeth's refusal to become involved. Mary, it was clear, was digging her own grave.

'She might have won the battle, but she will not win the war,' Elizabeth told her councillors. 'Without Moray she cannot control her lords; they are an unruly, quarrelling bunch, by all accounts. Darnley, I am credibly informed, spends half his life drunk, and the rest of it conducting himself wilfully, haughtily and viciously. He complains already that he is never sufficiently honoured. The Queen is no longer infatuated with him, and there are constant jars between them.' She smiled in satisfaction. 'What did I predict, gentlemen, when Darnley took it upon himself to propose to Mary?'

They all knew, of course, who had manoeuvred him into that position.

'There is worse, Madam,' Cecil said, producing a letter. 'I had this today, from Thomas Randolph. It seems that Darnley has cause for jealousy. Queen Mary is turning increasingly for *advice* – he smiled as he stressed the word – 'to her secretary, one David Rizzio, an Italian. Apparently it is he who determines all at her court, much to Darnley's chagrin.'

'All?' Elizabeth enquired, her eyebrows raised.

'All and more, or so it is rumoured,' Cecil said, scanning the letter. 'This Rizzio has a fine singing voice, which seems to be his prime qualification for controlling access to the Queen and ruling all. Darnley, Randolph writes, is spitting fire!'

'And Mary thought herself too good for my lord of Leicester here!' Elizabeth observed. 'See to what depths she now descends. Her name will become a byword for scandal if she persists in her folly, and it will redound on others too. People will say that women are unfit to rule!' Her eyes flashed.

'No one could possibly say that of your Majesty,' Cecil responded, as he knew he was expected to do.

'Aye,' chorused the others, just as dutifully, and happily, in most cases, heartily. Robert's eyes were warm. Elizabeth looked at them all with affection. She was blessed in her lords – unlike Mary.

'I wonder what Moray and his fellows will do,' she mused.

The word was that Moray was preparing to go back to Scotland.

'Where he will raise an army against his Queen!' Robert said. He would dearly have loved to fight for the Protestant cause, but did not dare to suggest it. He could guess what Elizabeth's answer would be.

'We shall see,' Cecil said. 'So much is speculation. But I doubt that his return will portend well for Rizzio – or Darnley. By the way, my lord, the Queen is not pleased to hear complaints that your followers have been picking fights and brawling with Norfolk's.'

'I know. She told me herself.' Robert frowned. 'I explained that Norfolk is jealous; he puts them up to it. He will do anything to discredit me. But I ignore him; I depend only on her Majesty.'

'That, my lord, is the problem,' Cecil said drily, 'and her Majesty must deal with it.'

Elizabeth did, but not in the way Robert had hoped. Before all the court, in the guise of making a joke, she tapped him with her fan and said, 'You have been provoking jealousy, my lord! You must not display too much familiarity towards me. And you, my lord of Norfolk,' – another tap with the fan – 'have been immoderate in your conduct. You must set all quarrels aside, both of you!' Reluctantly the two men shook hands, unsmiling, Robert smarting at the reprimand.

The courtiers were still laying bets that the Queen would marry him. The French ambassador, no less, had expressed the belief that Robert remained the chief contender for her hand. Even his enemies – Norfolk excepted, obviously – clearly felt it expedient to be pleasant to him and seek his favour. He and Elizabeth were as friendly as two turtle doves these days, but she would not permit him her chamber, and they were lovers no more.

He found himself looking back on the days of their passion as a golden time, but he realised, with profound sadness, that it was now in the past. Unsatisfied, desire had raged – and then, inexplicably, dwindled. A fire needed feeding, or it would burn out, and there had been precious little to fan the flames in recent months. There had been a time, not so long ago, when the very touch of Elizabeth's hand had left him craving more. He could not recapture that feeling, try as he might, and he feared that she felt the same. If so, she had even less cause to marry him. Yet they remained close, and – when they were not fighting – she still treated him with the special favour that she had always shown him. If, by a miracle, she decided that he was the husband for her, he would not hesitate. And it would not be just the lure of a crown that would beckon him; what they had between them was more solid than many marriages, and maybe, if she summoned the courage to give herself to him, their passion would be rekindled. He devoutly hoped so.

On Christmas Eve Elizabeth was standing with her ladies in the great hall, watching the men bringing in the yule log, which would burn on the hearth throughout the twelve days of celebrations. Around her, servants were merrily decking the hall with holly, ivy and bay, and setting the tables for tomorrow's feast. She loved this season, and was enjoying herself hugely, so she was not pleased to see Norfolk bearing down on her.

'Yes, my lord?' Her voice rang out sharply. Her ladies scuttled away to a safe distance. She was wont to slap them when others aroused her ire.

'Your Majesty, as your premier peer, I feel it my duty to raise a delicate matter with you,' the Duke began, bravely venturing where few had gone before.

'Indeed!' she retorted. 'Then let us go where we will not be overheard. Come walk with me in the gallery.' She led him out of the hall and along to a window embrasure overlooking the river.

'Speak, my lord,' she commanded.

Norfolk plunged in fearlessly. 'It is the matter of your marriage. As a maiden queen, you have never experienced the joys of matrimony, and I feel it incumbent upon me – for the sake of the kingdom, you understand – to reassure you that it is a most pleasant and fulfilling state—'

'My lord of Norfolk!' Elizabeth roared. 'Only last year your poor wife died in childbed, and she only twenty-four. And I recall that your first wife suffered the same fate when she was just sixteen! I'm sure that matrimony was a pleasant and fulfilling state for both of them!'

'I but meant, Madam, that, so the couple be spared to each other, they may find great happiness together. Indeed, I am not daunted by my sad losses, but am about to make a third marriage, so highly do I value the institution.'

'And which lamb is it you are leading to the slaughter this time?'

'Elizabeth Dacre, you recall, Madam. You did give your permission.' He looked at her nervously.

'Fool that I was!' Elizabeth retorted. 'But think, my lord: what would have happened to England had I taken your advice and wed, and then suffered the same fate as your poor wives?'

'Many women bear healthy children and live to rear them,' Norfolk countered, feeling nevertheless as if he was sinking into a mire.

'And some do not! There are no guarantees!'

'We can all of us say that, Madam. Life itself is uncertain. We can each of us be cut down without warning.'

'Did you come to cheer me up this Christmas tide?' Elizabeth snarled. But Norfolk was on a one-man mission, and did not heed the warning note in her voice.

'Think of the succession, Madam! The matter must be settled soon. Most of your subjects want you to marry the Archduke Charles. If some have appeared to endorse a marriage with my lord of Leicester, it is because they believe that is where your heart lies, not because they think that the match would be beneficial to the realm or good for your own dignity.'

Elizabeth stood there seething. 'I have long been aware of your hatred for the Earl of Leicester,' she said. 'You must not let it colour your judgement. I, and I alone, will decide who, and when, I marry. And believe me, my lord, I have the succession ever in my thoughts! Now go. I have let you off lightly because of the season!'

Norfolk departed in high dudgeon, and sought out Leicester.

'You, my lord, should remember that you agreed to abandon your suit to the Queen!' he growled.

Robert regarded him evenly. 'Did I?' he said. 'I'm sure that your lordship is correct.' And he gave Norfolk a tight smile and went on his way. Later that day, as Norfolk rode home to his estates to celebrate Yuletide, he congratulated himself on having done his Queen and his country a great service.

Elizabeth stood in her privy chamber, shaking. Not on account of that prattling fool, Norfolk – although God knew she had wanted to box his ears, and perhaps even send him for a salutary spell in the Tower – but because of the letter she held in her hand: the letter that had just arrived from Scotland.

Mary was with child. Pretty, brainless, imprudent Mary had achieved – despite her marriage having fallen to ruin – the one important thing that Elizabeth had not. The knowledge was like bitter gall in her mouth.

'Leave me!' she commanded her women. As soon as she was alone, she gave way to tears, hot, jealous tears – and that was how Robert found her. He had heard the news and realised how deeply it would upset her.

'Sweet Bess,' he gentled her, gathering her in his arms. 'You are in a far happier condition than the Queen of Scots. Your subjects love you; your lords are loyal; *I* love you. Think how Mary's lot pales beside yours. Her lords, for the most part, are in rebellion against her. Who knows what they will do? Her husband is estranged from her; they avoid each other's company as much as possible, by all reports. She spends her days in the company of the upstart, Rizzio, and pays no heed to those who warn her of the scandal she is causing. There is even gossip that the child is not Darnley's. You would not want to change places with her.'

'True,' Elizabeth sniffed. 'But she has done something I cannot do!'

'Why can you not do it? Ask yourself. The past is behind you.'

'Ah, Robin,' Elizabeth said sadly, 'it is not just the past that deters me. Were I to have a son, there would be those who would clamour for me to stand aside so that a man could rule. I know the temper of my lords.'

'Not so, Bess!' Robert protested. 'It may have been so at the first, but you have proved your mettle now, and they love and respect you for yourself. And with a husband standing firmly beside you, supporting you, no one would dare try to take from you the crown that is rightfully yours.'

'Ah, Robin, you make it seem so simple!' Elizabeth cried, breaking free. 'And no doubt the husband you speak of would be yourself.'

'It *is* simple, Bess!' He went down on one knee and seized her hand. 'I pray you, marry me! I would be your strength and support; I would honour you and respect your position.'

Elizabeth looked down at him. Her tears had dried, and she was smiling. 'I will consider it,' she agreed. 'It is Christmas now. I will give you an answer by Candlemas!'

'But that is weeks away!' he cried.

'Then you must wait!' she told him. 'It is not so very long, and you can be sure that I will weigh very seriously what you have asked me.'

He was more confident of success this time, even though he had lost count of the other times he had been hopeful. He felt that he had presented Elizabeth with the most acceptable solution to her concerns. It would be enough for him to be her husband and wear the crown matrimonial; he would not pursue sovereign power. Instead he was resolved to use his influence much as he did now. But over the Christmas festivities he could not resist dropping hints about the imminent change in his prospects, and bearing himself like the king he hoped soon to be, while Elizabeth let him do it, and kept him constantly at her side.

The court buzzed with speculation. Robert's enemies girded their loins for protest. The French ambassador spread it around – without any truth – that the Queen and her lover had slept together on New Year's Night. Silva angrily denied it, fearing that if this got back to the Emperor – and the diplomatic grapevine was alive with gossip – it would scupper the match with the Archduke.

An ugly incident at the Twelfth Night feast did not help matters. To Robert's fury, Thomas Heneage drew the sought-after bean hidden in the traditional cake, and was chosen as King of the Bean for the evening, his ancient office being to preside over the revelry.

'We must do everything he commands!' Elizabeth cried, laughing at the prospect. Who knew what undignified and hilarious challenges, dares, forfeits or orders the King of the Bean would issue? No one had forgotten the Christmas that witnessed the stately Cecil crawling about on his knees under the high table looking for the Queen's slipper (which had, helpfully, been hidden beneath her skirts), or Elizabeth herself planting a kiss on the lips of her highly embarrassed Archbishop of Canterbury. Robert himself had been King of the Bean then.

Heneage was suddenly at Robert's ear. 'Ask her Majesty which is the more difficult to erase from the mind – jealousy, or an evil opinion implanted by a wicked tale-teller,' he ordered.

'What the hell are you implying?' Robert asked angrily. 'People will think that I have been unfaithful to the Queen.'

'Do it!' Heneage snarled. 'Or I will tell the company that you have refused to obey me.' People were already staring curiously at them.

Robert rose unwillingly to his feet. He posed the question to Elizabeth.

'Both are difficult to get rid of,' she answered, 'but in my opinion it is much harder to remove jealousy.' She gave him a strange look.

'I will castigate you with a stick!' he muttered to Heneage.

'That is not a punishment for an equal,' Heneage retorted, 'and if you come to insult me thus, you will discover whether my sword can cut and thrust.'

Others were avidly taking in every word of this heated exchange.

'This gentleman is not my equal,' Robert said stiffly, 'and I will postpone chastising him until an appropriate time.'

Soon afterwards he watched as Heneage approached the

Queen and whispered in her ear. She frowned and summoned Robert to her side. 'If, by my favour, you have become insolent, my lord, you should soon reform,' she reproved him. 'Remember, I could debase you just as I have raised you.' Heneage stood by, grinning smugly.

Robert was extremely hurt. The episode had depressed him, and he stayed in his lodgings for the next four days, not venturing to sally forth into a court that would be either hostile or laughing at him. He felt deeply humiliated, and wondered why Elizabeth had turned on him so unfairly.

Elizabeth too was upset. Heneage's insinuation that Robert had betrayed her had struck at her heart and she had lashed out accordingly. But on reflection – which did take several days – she concluded that the slur had been born of sheer malice and envy. No wonder Robin was hurt.

She summoned him, and there was yet another tearful reunion. Robert thought it augured well for the future. It was plain that she could not do without him.

1566

In the name of friendship, King Charles had graciously decided
to bestow the Order of St Michael – France's highest order
of chivalry – upon two of Elizabeth's subjects, the choice to
be hers. She named Leicester and Norfolk – Leicester because
she needed once more to placate him for her failure to name
the day, and Norfolk to pre-empt any jealousy. She need not
have bothered. Norfolk was so resentful of Leicester receiving
the honour that it took all her powers of persuasion to stop
him from boycotting the investiture.

Robert was – almost – certain that the ceremony was a
prelude to the announcement of his forthcoming marriage to
the Queen. But Candlemas came and departed without Elizabeth
mentioning marriage at all, let alone making a proclamation.

'How many more times will you break your word?' he raged.

Elizabeth sighed. 'Robin, be patient, just for a little longer.
This is a delicate time in regard to foreign negotiations. And
to please me, pretend to support the Habsburg marriage.'

'Very well,' he flung back. 'Marry the Archduke, for the sake
of your realm. Don't worry about *me*.'

'I commend you for your selflessness,' she said, deliberately
ignoring his sarcasm.

He could not believe it when, later that day, he saw her
brazenly flirting, in full sight of himself, with the gallant Earl
of Ormond. It was too much. After another violent quarrel,
heated sufficiently, it seemed, to make the very walls combust,
he left court.

He had had *enough*, he told himself, as he rode furiously to
his house at Kew. He was *weary* of strife and the intrigues of
the court, and Elizabeth's endless, tortuous games. He was *sick*

of being blamed for her failure to marry, even though he had urged her to do so countless times. Everyone marked his failings, *never* his better qualities.

Cecil wrote to him, as did Throckmorton. Feeling genuinely sorry for him, and concerned that the only really viable husband for the Queen was out of her sight, and possibly – this was even more worrying – out of her mind, they kept him updated on state affairs. Robert wrote to Cecil that he despaired of Elizabeth ever marrying, and was taken aback to read that she was still in a vile mood, and that, if he took Cecil's advice, he would stay away from court, lest he incur any more blame. When he thought about it, in truth he was glad to do so.

The trees were in bud, and a light March breeze was in the air when Cecil brought Elizabeth a letter bearing the Queen of Scots' seal. She read it with mounting horror.

'God's death!' she swore. 'Rizzio has been murdered.'

According to Mary, Darnley and many of the lords who had once opposed him had burst in upon her as she was having supper with Rizzio and a few friends. There had been an unseemly brawl, with Mary's very life being threatened. One conspirator had even rammed a chair into her belly – and she six months gone with child. Darnley had held her fast as the lords dragged a frantic Rizzio from her presence and stabbed him to death, fifty-six times. Mary had then found herself a prisoner, for the lords had got Darnley on their side by promising him that he could rule in her name, but she had persuaded him – with truth, no doubt, given what Elizabeth knew of these turncoats – that they had no intention of keeping their word. Together she and Darnley had escaped, and now, thanks to the support of the loyal and trusty Earl of Bothwell, she had reasserted her authority and the traitors were in flight. But it had been a close thing.

Elizabeth shuddered; in fact she could not stop trembling. That a queen, answerable only to God, should be disparaged and threatened thus was scandalous, and treason of the highest order. She too was a queen. What would it take to make her lords plot against her in such a way? Not that she could imagine it, for she ruled by their love, but it was a salutary warning. You did not take these things for granted. She had been right all along not to marry. Darnley's base example proved that. But he, arrogant fool that he was, had been a mere pawn in the conspirators' hands. What had happened proved that Mary was isolated and vulnerable – and that made Elizabeth feel vulnerable too.

Loudly she voiced her horror at the way that Mary had been treated. She attached her miniature of the Scottish Queen to a chain and wore it at her waist to proclaim her solidarity with her dearest sister. She told Silva, 'Had I been in her place, I would have taken my husband's dagger and stabbed him with it!' Seeing his aghast expression, which clearly told her that he believed her capable of it, she hastened to add, 'Of course, I would never do such a thing to the Archduke!'

She wrote to Mary; there was a new kindness between them. She wished her dear sister a happy hour (Heaven knew the poor woman had few enough of them), praying that God would send her only short pains when she bore her child. 'I too am big with desire for the good news,' she concluded – and meant it.

Still feeling vulnerable, she sent one of her ladies to summon Robert, with a message complaining of his unkindness. As she had hoped, he came to her, full of apologies, and they made up their quarrel, as they had the many that had preceded it, but during his absence there had grown a distance between them.

'Never again will I permit you to leave my side,' Elizabeth declared.

'I am yours to command,' Robert answered formally, still smarting from having had to apologise for what *she* had done – or, rather, not done.

'God's blood, Robin, must you be so stiff with me?' she exploded.

'I am your devoted servant, you know it,' he answered, with more warmth than he felt.

She sighed. 'I want more than that, and *you* know it.'

'All I ask is that you show the world that you hold me in some esteem,' he replied.

She promised that she would. She assured him that she would never humiliate him publicly again. She kept him once more at her side, showed him the same favour as of old, and did her best – not very successfully, for she was born to it – to cease flirting with her other admirers; all the same, they did not fall into their old easiness with each other.

In April, unable to bear the situation any longer, Robert craved leave to visit his estates in Norfolk.

'Is this how you repay me for my favour?' Elizabeth challenged him.

'Bess, I *must* go. Pressing business calls me, otherwise I would not leave you for the world.' But his words lacked conviction. She let him go.

No sooner had he arrived in Norfolk than a letter from her caught up with him. He read it, appalled. What had he done to deserve such a stinging, vicious rebuke? He had never meant to offend her. Surely the coolness between them was as painful for her as it was for him, and she, like he, welcomed the respite. Did his long service and his years of devotion and loyalty count for nothing? He had tried, God, he had tried, just to find his way back to how it had once been between them, and those heady days of love and glory. But he was beginning to think that it might be impossible to recapture that. If you had to try so hard, maybe the moment had gone. And maybe Elizabeth knew it too. He was so grieved that he wanted to crawl into a cave, or even a tomb – somewhere, anywhere, he could find oblivion.

Then a fresh summons came. The Queen commanded his return to court. He went with a leaden heart, not knowing what to expect, and not daring to hope. But hope, as it proverbially does, sprang anew when he was informed that she would receive him in private, and it leapt for joy when she stretched out her hands, her eyes full of tears. This time, he would not be the one doing the apologising.

*

'The Queen of Scots is lighter of a fair son,' Elizabeth announced. She had emerged from the council chamber, visibly trembling. 'Cecil told me.'

'An heir to Scotland,' Robert said. 'I am glad for Queen Mary, poor lady. She has suffered much.' And to think that the child could have been his! He could have been father to the future King of Scots. He felt the usual pang when he thought of his childlessness. He would give much to be the father of any child, king or not.

'Yes, I rejoice with her too, of course,' Elizabeth said, but her tone implied the opposite.

'What is wrong, Bess?' Robert asked, but of course he knew the answer.

'For all her troubles, Mary has triumphed,' she said. 'And she has done the one thing that it seems I cannot do, for I am of barren stock.'

'That's nonsense!' Robert retorted. 'Do you not think you are being a little dramatic and self-indulgent? As for your being barren, that has yet to be proved.'

Elizabeth opened her mouth to protest, but he silenced her by putting a finger on her lips. 'Hear me out,' he said, folding his arms around her. 'There is no reason why you should not bear a child, an heir to England – only your baseless fears, which you *can* overcome if you put your mind to it. You are a normal woman. Your courses come regularly, you know how to feel the pleasure that betokens conception.'

'Is this another ploy to get me to marry you?' Elizabeth asked, eyeing him warily. Such talk made her feel decidedly uncomfortable. It was not seemly for a man to say such things to her, even Robin.

'Nay, I but seek to reassure you, Bess,' he said tenderly. 'There is no ulterior motive, no agenda, just the kindness that has been between us of late, thank God.'

She kissed him back – a brisk, affectionate kiss, not a passionate one. 'Thank you, but leave it, Robin. I do not want to think about it.'

*

That August the Queen led the court on a progress through Northamptonshire and Oxfordshire. Robert pressed her to be his guest at Kenilworth, and plans were made for her visit.

'Madam, is this wise?' Cecil warned. 'People are saying that your arrival at Kenilworth will presage an announcement of your betrothal to my lord of Leicester.'

Elizabeth looked alarmed. 'Of course it does not.'

'But that is what people are saying.'

'That settles it. I will not go.'

Robert protested loudly when she told him of her decision. 'Just because you are visiting me does not mean that you are going to marry me,' he complained, with only a touch of wistfulness in his voice. 'You were planning to stay with Cecil, but no one suggests that you have designs on him.'

'That's a silly analogy,' she muttered.

'Do come!' he pleaded. 'Prove the world wrong! Besides, I want you to see the improvements I have made to the castle. I promise you, you will be lodged splendidly and well served. And the dreaded word "marriage" will not be mentioned once!'

Elizabeth thought about it for what seemed an endless minute. 'You've persuaded me!' She smiled. Let the world go hang itself. What did she care about what people were thinking?

The visit to Kenilworth was a great success, even if it did disappoint the ever-hopeful gossips, but when Elizabeth returned to London afterwards she found Parliament in a recalcitrant mood. She was in desperate need of money, but her treacherous Lords and Commons refused to approve any new taxes until she had heeded their petitions and resolved the weighty – and most urgent, they stressed – matter of the succession.

'How dare they dictate terms to me!' she stormed in council. But when she had recovered her aplomb she sent a message to Parliament to say that, on the word of a prince, she *would* marry. The Lords and Commons had heard this before, too often, and sat tight.

'I will never allow Parliament to meddle in such a matter,' Elizabeth fumed. 'I need those taxes for the good of my people, and these fools are obstructing me. They should vote them freely and graciously.'

'If your Majesty *were* to marry, you could spare yourself all this aggravation,' Cecil pointed out.

'Don't you think I am aware of that, my Spirit?' she retorted, then sighed, slumping in her chair in defeat. 'Very well. I will write to the Emperor, telling him that I will accept the suit of the Archduke.'

Cecil almost ran to fetch paper, pen and ink, before she changed her mind.

Parliament was duly informed of the Queen's resolve to marry; but until the Emperor responded to the Queen's letter, she could not reveal whom the fortunate suitor would be – or even that there was a specific fortunate suitor in view. When next she heard, the Commons wanted to send a deputation to wait upon her, to beg her to name her future husband, and her successor should she die childless.

'It is insupportable, what they ask!' Elizabeth said hotly.

'Madam, they want only the future security of the realm,' Cecil pacified her.

'That is a matter for me to determine. God's blood, they would never have been so rebellious in my father's day.'

'Your Majesty should at least consider receiving the deputation,' Robert urged.

'No,' she said mutinously.

'Madam, the Lords support them,' Cecil persisted.

'They would never dare!' she spat. But they did. They added their weight to this new petition.

'Norfolk, you and your kind are traitors!' Elizabeth declared, narrowing her eyes at the Duke as he sat stony-faced at the council board.

'Madam, they but have your good, and England's, at heart,' Robert declared. It was unheard of for him to defend Norfolk.

'Robert, you are as bad as the rest of them!' she cried. 'The whole world might have abandoned me, but I had thought that *you*, of all people, would not do so.'

'I would die at your feet!' he swore hotly.

'What has that to do with the matter?' she shouted, and stormed out of the council chamber straight – almost – into the willing arms of Silva, who was in the antechamber waiting to speak with Cecil. Elizabeth was beside herself, distraught that Robin had failed to support her stand. Villainy, pure and simple!

'I am so angry with my councillors,' she raged, 'and with my lord of Leicester most of all. What do you think, Ambassador, of such ingratitude in one to whom I have shown so much favour that my own honour has been compromised? I am determined to dismiss him and leave the way clear for the Archduke to come to England.'

Silva, to whom this was manna from Heaven, clucked soothingly.

'My nobility are all against me,' Elizabeth went on plaintively, 'and my Commons refuse to attend to any business until I agree to their demands. I do not know what these devils want!'

'It would be an affront to your Majesty's dignity to agree to any compromise,' Silva said, his tone oozing with sympathy.

'Yes, but I have no choice,' she rejoined bitterly. And that was the problem, of course. She could not do without Parliament.

At length she gave in. She summoned a delegation from Parliament to wait upon her, but, she insisted, the Speaker was not to be of their number. *She* would do all the talking; she had prepared one of her special speeches for the occasion. And once she had her Lords and Commons cowering on their knees before her, through the sheer force of her steely gaze, she erupted in righteous ire.

'Unbridled persons in the House of Commons have plotted a traitorous trick,' she said sternly. 'I am not used to demands being made on me to name my successor, and you, my lords, have acted rashly in supporting the Commons in this nonsense.

Was I not born in this realm? Were not my parents? Whom have I oppressed? How have I governed? I will be tried by envy itself. I need not use many words, for my deeds do try me. I have sent word that I will marry, and I will never break the word of a prince, for my honour's sake. And therefore I say again, I will marry as soon as I can, and I hope to have children, otherwise I would never marry.'

She paused. Having admonished them, she would appeal to their reason and understanding. 'None of you has been the second person in the realm, as I have, or tasted of the practices against my sister. There are some now in Parliament who tried to involve me in their conspiracies back then.' She paused to let that sink in, and was gratified to see a few looking nervously at each other. 'Were it not for my honour, their knavery would be known.' Several pairs of shoulders slumped in relief. 'I would never place my successor in that position. My Lords and Commons, the succession question is full of peril to the realm and myself. Kings were wont to honour philosophers, but I would honour as angels any that, when they were second in the realm, did not seek to be first!'

They looked chastened at that. Some were clearly sympathetic at the thought of their Queen being placed in such a difficult position – and all on their account too. Elizabeth glowered at them. 'You are impertinent to summon me thus; it is for me, your Prince, to decide who should follow me; it is monstrous that the feet should direct the head. I hope that the instigators of this trouble will repent and openly confess their guilt.'

Perceiving the ripple of consternation that trembled through the kneeling ranks of men before her, she decided that it was time to remind them what she was made of (she had not forgotten the recent experiences of the Queen of Scots). 'I care not for death,' she went on. 'All men are mortal, and though I be a woman, yet I have as good a courage as ever my father had. I am your anointed Queen. I will never be by violence constrained to do anything. I thank God I am endowed with such qualities that, if I were turned out of the realm in my petticoat, I were able to live in any place in Christendom.'

Her eyes scanned the faces of the Lords. She had scored a victory there, she thought. But the Commons looked mutinous still. They had heard her out in sullen silence. Sure enough, just days later, there were more calls in Parliament for her to accede to their petitions.

Elizabeth had had enough. 'Tell the House that it is my express command that they proceed no further in their suit, but satisfy themselves with our promise to marry.' That galvanised the Commons to uproar, and provoked accusations that the Queen was attacking the lawful liberties of her subjects. Still the members would not vote for a subsidy, and soon Elizabeth realised, to her consternation, that they had her well and truly cornered. What had started out as a plea for her to marry or name her successor had rapidly turned into a war of words over the rights and privileges of sovereign and Parliament.

'Madam, I *urge* you to give in,' Cecil pleaded.

'Very well.' Her lips were tight, but she knew when she was beaten, and had no wish for a showdown over the wider issue. 'Tell the Commons that they may have a free debate about the succession, and that I graciously remit one third of the tax I requested.'

The Commons were so gleeful at their victory that they approved the bill for the subsidy without even waiting to discuss the succession. But when the bill was laid before Elizabeth for signature, she was angered to see that her promise to marry had been enshrined in its text. Picking up her quill, she scrawled in the margin: 'I know no reason why my private answers to the realm should serve as a prologue to this bill; neither do I understand why such audacity should be used to make an Act of my words.' And when she dissolved Parliament, she glared at both Houses and said frostily, 'Beware how you prove your Prince's patience, as you have done mine! A more loving prince ye shall never have!'

'I won,' she said afterwards, beaming at Cecil.

'I think your Majesty is mistaken,' he replied. 'The succession is not settled, the marriage is not concluded, dangers may ensue, and there is general disquiet about the future. Parliament's concerns are real, as are mine.'

Elizabeth stared at him, poised to utter a tart retort, but she was not such a fool that she could not ingest the truth in his words, and the retort died on her lips. She had the grace to look chastened.

1567

It was a bitter February morning, the sky brooding and grey. Elizabeth ordered the fire made up and mulled wine to be brought, and was playing her virginals, with Robert accompanying her on the lute, when Cecil made an unexpected appearance.

'News from Scotland, Madam,' he announced in a grim voice, as Elizabeth looked up startled. 'Darnley is dead. The house he was staying at in Edinburgh has been blown up and destroyed to the very foundations.'

'God in Heaven!' exclaimed Robert.

Elizabeth was speechless. She had known that there was bad blood between Darnley and Mary, and between Darnley and the nobles whom he had betrayed after Rizzio's murder, but never had she dreamed that it would come to this.

'It is murder, no less,' she whispered. Then, in a stronger voice, 'Is it known who is responsible?'

'There are many rumours, Madam. Some say the Earl of Bothwell.' Elizabeth knew Bothwell as the only Scottish peer who had refused bribes from England. She had thought him an upright man; could she have been wrong? Power, or the hope of it, corrupted even the best. She had seen it happen with her own eyes.

Cecil's thoughts evidently ran the same way. 'Bothwell helped Mary and Darnley to escape after Rizzio was killed. He helped her regain power. Since then it has been bruited that they are lovers. It is all too believable. Darnley had the French pox; he was recovering in the house that was destroyed. The next day he was to have resumed married life with Queen Mary.'

If silences could be pregnant, then this one went to full term.

'By God, you are not implying that *Mary* had him murdered?'
Elizabeth burst out.

'Far be it from me to repeat evil of a queen, Madam, but
that is what people in Scotland are saying – and saying very
loudly.'

'I will not believe it,' Elizabeth declared. All the same, she
wrote to Mary, urging her to remember her honour and not
look through her fingers at those who were said to have done
her pleasure in the matter. She exhorted her, out of affection,
she protested, to take her counsel to heart, and not to fear to
proceed even against those nearest to her. *Even Bothwell*, was
the implication.

But Mary seemed frozen with an inexplicable inertia. When
obscene placards naming Bothwell as Darnley's assassin and
Mary's lover were plastered all over Edinburgh, she did
nothing. When Darnley's father brought a private prosecution
against Bothwell for the murder of his son, Bothwell posted
so many of his armed followers in Edinburgh that Lennox was
too intimidated to attend court; and in the absence of his sole
accuser, Bothwell was acquitted. Elizabeth was horrified. In
compassion, she released a distraught Lady Lennox from the
Tower, and asked herself for the umpteenth time why Mary
was lifting no finger to pursue her husband's killer.

Each post seemed to bring worse news. Bothwell had gone
so far as to abduct Mary and immure her in his castle at Dunbar
on the wild Scottish coast not thirty miles from Edinburgh.
Some said slyly that she had gone willingly. There were reports
that he had raped her, but other intelligence asserted that
she had colluded. The next news was as explosive as the
gunpowder that had blown up Darnley's house: Mary had
married Bothwell, not three months after the murder of her
husband, and – this was beyond belief – in a *Protestant* ceremony,
at his insistence.

'And he is still the chief suspect,' Elizabeth commented
grimly. 'God's teeth, what is Mary thinking of? I have sent
to tell her that I am deeply perplexed because she has failed to

bring Darnley's assassins to justice, and has showered favour upon the one man whom common fame insists is guilty. I do declare that she has taken leave of her senses.'

She remembered how she herself had reacted when Amy Dudley had died. She had been in a similar situation to Mary. But she had not immediately married Robert, the husband who was the chief suspect. Oh no, she had sent him from court until his name was cleared, and she had kept on resolutely refusing to marry him, at some cost to herself. But Mary – this was what she could not understand in a queen, and never would – had impulsively married the man widely reputed to have murdered her husband, and now (and could she blame them?) all the world was baying for her blood.

'I am ashamed of what she has done,' she fumed to Robert. 'Moreover, Bothwell hates the English – always has done. If a remedy is not found, we will have an enemy on our doorstep. What worse choice could Mary have made, from our point of view, let alone hers?'

The Scottish lords evidently agreed. Not a month had passed since the marriage when they took up arms against Bothwell, and after a brief skirmish Mary was taken prisoner and brought back to public humiliation in Edinburgh, where crowds had gathered to witness her paraded through the city. 'Burn the whore! Kill her! Kill her!' they cried out. Elizabeth shivered when she heard of it. It was unbelievable that the Queen of Scots had been brought so low.

Mary was imprisoned in a lonely castle in the middle of a lake, and there she miscarried of the twins conceived of rape. (Elizabeth persisted in calling it that, because she would not have it said that a princess would have stooped so low, but privately – and she would never have admitted this to anyone – she had her doubts). It was while Mary was lying abed, weak from loss of blood, that the Lords of the Congregation forced her to abdicate in favour of her infant son, who was now crowned as King James VI. Her dour half-brother, the Earl of Moray, was appointed regent.

'They have gone too far this time,' Elizabeth thundered, boiling with indignation. 'It is not for subjects to imprison their queen! Whatever Mary did – and I can only deplore her failure to act when she should have done – she is still an anointed monarch, to whom, by nature and all the laws of God and man, her people owe loyalty and obedience. It is unthinkable that a queen be divested of her authority.' Such treatment set a dangerous precedent, as she was all too aware.

Robert and Cecil exchanged glances across the council board. They could both see how distressed Elizabeth was by this turn of events. Cecil even ventured to lay a comforting hand on her shoulder. She rounded fiercely on him.

'You need not fear for me, good Spirit!' she declared. 'I will fight for her release.'

She did everything in her power. She sent Throckmorton to Edinburgh to work for a reconciliation between Queen Mary and her lords. She insisted on Mary's restoration. Throckmorton was to demand that Darnley's true killers be pursued and brought to justice. Above all, he was to make haste!

Bothwell, however, had fled abroad. In Edinburgh the fanatical preacher John Knox was stirring up more hatred against Mary with his inflammatory sermons. Worse still, the Scottish lords resented Throckmorton's interference. They would not let him see Mary. They even threatened to execute her, and warned that they would abandon the peace if England did not stop poking its nose into Scottish affairs.

Elizabeth, infuriated, dashed off another letter to Throckmorton. 'Ask them what warrant they have in Scripture to depose their Prince? Or what law find they written that subjects may arrest the person of their Prince, detain them captive and proceed to judge them? No such law is to be found.'

Robert tried to calm her. 'Bess, heed me. It is vital to go carefully. Throckmorton writes that any attempt to rescue Queen Mary may well lead to her being put to death. And remember, these men are Protestants; they should be our allies.'

'She would surely have been put to death if I had not

intervened,' Elizabeth said firmly. 'And allies or not, they are traitors to their Queen.'

'Then we must fight them, if need be,' he said stoutly, feeling profoundly grateful that it had not been his fate to marry the Queen of Scots. Even so, all his chivalrous instincts had been aroused by her plight.

'Fight them?' Cecil echoed. 'God grant it may not come to that. We should be coming to terms with them. A Protestant Scotland augurs well for peace in the future.'

'I will not recognise the Earl of Moray as the ruler of Scotland,' Elizabeth insisted. 'I will show him that I do not respect his authority by recalling Throckmorton.'

'Madam, it will be an empty gesture,' Cecil sighed. 'Moray is in power in Scotland whether we like it or not, and the Scottish people do not want Mary restored.'

'She is their anointed Queen!' she cried. 'We cannot just leave her there to languish in prison! You should have thought of a way to revenge her and deliver her! I mean it, William, I will declare war on the Scots, and you can warn Moray and his traitors that if they keep Mary locked up, or touch her person, I will not fail to avenge it to the uttermost.'

'Madam—'

'Hold your peace!' Elizabeth snarled. 'Any person who is content to see a neighbouring prince unlawfully deposed must be less than dutifully minded towards his own sovereign!'

Cecil recoiled, stung. It was the first time that she had ever accused him of disloyalty. But he collected himself and said evenly, 'Madam, Robert is right. If you threaten the Scots with war, they might indeed carry out their threat to execute Queen Mary.'

Elizabeth subsided at that. She sat there, her face puce, biting her thumb, a sure sign that she was distressed. Then she turned without another word to domestic matters, signalling that the subject was closed for the present.

After she had gone, the councillors looked at each other in sympathetic collusion.

'I would not take her displeasure too seriously,' Bacon said.
Cecil sighed. 'No, I thank you.'

'For all her Majesty's protests, I doubt not that in her heart she likes this new order well enough,' Bacon observed.

'Aye, she denounces Moray at every turn, yet she has no real intention of going to war,' Cecil concurred. 'Even so, her behaviour is wrecking years of successful diplomacy.'

Robert had been regarding them all darkly. Now he spoke out. 'She does not want people to think her prejudiced against Queen Mary. Above all, she fears that her own subjects might be emboldened by the example set in Scotland to do the same to her. She has not forgotten her quarrel with Parliament last year.'

'I understand her fears,' Cecil said. 'However, although she says she will never acknowledge Moray's rule or King James's title, she will in the end, mark my words. She knows she has not the power to change the situation in Scotland.'

When Elizabeth was calmer, she turned with relief to a report sent by Sussex, whom she had dispatched to Vienna to report on the Archduke. Sussex wrote glowingly of Charles of Habsburg: he was tall, well-proportioned, cheerful, dignified, rich, popular and well-educated. Like Elizabeth herself, he spoke four languages. In all, he was a paragon among men. There was nothing to mislike about him, Sussex enthused – except for the fact that he was refusing – absolutely, and very inconsiderately – to convert to the Protestant faith.

She asked her councillors for their advice. Should she permit Charles to hear Mass in private, even though it had been made illegal in England? He had, after all, expressed a willingness to accompany her publicly to Anglican services.

'It seems a fair compromise,' Cecil said.

'Aye, indeed,' agreed Norfolk.

'I am against it,' Robert declared, and was promptly seconded by several others.

'Well you would be,' Norfolk sneered.

The argument went on – and on – for weeks, while Elizabeth,

delighted at this opportunity of stalling yet again, insisted that she could not make up her mind. Meanwhile, Robert had been paying Protestant preachers to fulminate against the marriage from their pulpits. In private, he never let up cozening the Queen with sweet words and artful persuasion.

It all paid off. In the end she instructed Sussex to tell the Emperor that it was against her conscience and her policy of religious uniformity to allow the Archduke to practise his religion in private. Cecil, Norfolk and Sussex were furious with Robert; and the Emperor was appalled at how things had turned out. It was some time before he could give thanks for his son having escaped the clutches of that fickle, wilful, heretical usurper he had so nearly wed.

'But you were right to reject him,' Robert told Elizabeth. 'You have saved England from religious controversy and the threat of rebellion or even civil war. Remember how Thomas Wyatt rose against Queen Mary when she proposed to marry King Philip?'

Elizabeth shuddered at the memory. Her suspected, mercifully unproven involvement in that rebellion had landed her in the Tower. She knew for a certainty that she had done the right thing in regard to the Archduke, for in so doing she had shown her subjects that she would never forfeit their love and loyalty, or allow the laws of England to be subverted.

She smiled at Robin. There had been a subtle shift in their relationship of late. He had become more of a friend and supporter than a lover. Kindness had almost imperceptibly replaced passion. She knew he still longed to wed her, but she was aware also that he was more realistic about his prospects in that respect than he had once been. She loved him truly – he was all the world to her, and always would be – but she had to admit to herself that she was happier now that he did not ceaselessly pester her to surrender herself to him. It was some time since he had attempted to talk her through her fears of marriage. It was as if he had reconciled himself to the fact that she might never overcome them.

Yet sometimes she found herself on the verge of weeping at the remembrance of how things had once stood between them. That had gone for ever, she knew, and in its place there was a terrible sense of loss that sometimes threatened to overwhelm her.

1570

Cecil was looking strained. The past year had been the most nerve-racking of Elizabeth's reign. The trouble had begun when the Catholics of the north, who had stubbornly resisted the religious reforms of the past forty years, had risen in a revolt against her Protestant rule that had only been suppressed with great severity on the part of her generals. Norfolk, whose treachery had come as a lightning bolt from the sky, had allied with the northern Catholic earls – not so much on account of his faith as in determination to oust Cecil and Leicester from the Council.

King Philip, seizing the moment, had threatened war. Then Pope Pius V, outraged by reports of mass executions in the wake of the uprising, had published a bull excommunicating Elizabeth. Elizabeth herself was outraged when she heard that Pius had released her Catholic subjects from their obedience to her and pronounced that it would be no sin to assassinate her.

'It is, effectively, an incitement to the Catholic faithful to mount what they would see as a crusade against you,' Cecil had pronounced, 'and it is perhaps the most dangerous threat we now face.'

Elizabeth sat stony-faced. If she had thought herself insecure before, she realised that her position was now even more precarious, and that she might never know a moment's peace again in the wake of this new danger.

It did not help that Mary Stuart was now an unwelcome prisoner in England. Two years ago Mary had escaped from Scotland with only the clothes on her back, and come into England seeking Elizabeth's support, hoping that her dear sister would furnish her with an army to defeat her rebellious lords.

'What shall I do with her?' Elizabeth had demanded of her Council.

'Surely your Majesty will not do as she asks?' Cecil had said.

'I'm not a fool, William!' she'd snapped. 'She has claimed my crown; it has been her life's ambition to sit on my throne, and she still covets it, if I am any judge of character. God knows, she never ceased demanding to be named my successor. Do you think I would give her the wherewithal to press her claim?'

'A wise decision,' Cecil hastened to say. 'But we still have to decide what to do with her.'

'Whatever we do with her, she will make trouble for me,' Elizabeth said. 'She is tainted by scandal; the Scottish lords insist she is an adulteress and a murderess, and she has never been cleared of that charge. Do you think that I, a maiden queen, could receive such a person at my court? I have my reputation to protect. So she must not come to any place near where I am.'

'Send her back to Scotland,' Sussex said.

'But she is a sanctified queen who has been appallingly treated by her traitorous subjects and unjustly deposed and imprisoned,' Elizabeth declared, 'and if she has never been cleared of the charges laid against her, neither have they been proved.' Of course, Mary was a brainless fool, marrying Darnley, alienating her nobles, subsuming herself to Bothwell, then arriving in England penniless and expecting her dear sister to provide her with an army.

'If we keep the Queen of Scots in the north, as your Majesty suggests, we will be placing her at the heart of a region peopled by Catholic recusants,' Cecil warned. 'That could prove most dangerous.'

'As I said, William, she will make trouble for us whatever we do with her,' Elizabeth sighed. 'Therefore I dare not leave her at liberty.'

Well, she had done her best. She had arranged for Mary to

be held securely in the north pending a hearing of her case in England, and appointed the faithful Sir Francis Knollys as her gaoler, much – she knew – to his distress and that of his wife, her dear Kate, whom she had insisted on keeping with her at court, hating the idea of being apart from her beloved half-sister. Knollys had asked, again and again, to visit Kate, or had begged permission for her to visit him, and his pleas had grown even more frantic when Kate fell ill. But then Kate had died, at the Queen's side but far from her distraught husband – and all because of Elizabeth's selfishness. She saw that now, as she had not at the time, and found it hard to forgive herself. It was a grief she would have to live with always. The expensive funeral she had arranged in Westminster Abbey had borne witness to her remorse.

Before that catastrophe, the Scottish lords had produced a set of letters – 'Conveniently found in a casket in the possession of one of Bothwell's men,' Cecil told the Queen – claiming that Mary had written them to Bothwell in the weeks leading up to Darnley's death.

Elizabeth read the transcripts. They contained shocking, foul proofs of adultery and murder, and it was at that point that her sympathy for Mary evaporated. And once the English commissioners had read this damning evidence, Mary's fate was sealed. Again Elizabeth had been in an impossible position. The majority of her subjects hated and feared the Queen of Scots; the Scottish lords did not want her back in Scotland, and Elizabeth could not risk giving such a dangerous creature her freedom, for Mary would surely plot against her.

The English tribunal, set up in York to hear Mary's case, had its instructions. It found that nothing could be proved against her. The Scottish lords, who had attended with their helpful casket of letters, went home. Mary, to their relief, did not. She was to remain in honourable captivity as Elizabeth's guest. Naturally there were protests from King Philip and other Catholic rulers, most of whom wanted Mary on the throne of England, for they saw her as the rightful Catholic claimant. All the more reason, Elizabeth knew, not to set her free!

Yes, the realm had suffered turbulent upheavals, and Elizabeth had to face the sobering fact that she was alarmingly vulnerable to her enemies at home and abroad, and that her Catholic subjects might at any time rise against her, especially now that there was a Catholic claimant to the throne living in England. It was ironic that she, who had vowed many times never to make windows into men's souls, had now been forced to the point where she must consider all Catholics potential traitors. And now there were rumours that Norfolk, the premier Catholic peer, had been scheming to marry Mary, to God knew what end. Elizabeth had sent Norfolk to the Tower after the rebellion, then set him free at the urging of Cecil and Robert, on the grounds that the Duke had been more fool than traitor. He was her cousin too, and had confessed himself in error. Now, in the wake of her excommunication, she wished she had kept him under lock and key.

Cecil was bracing himself for yet another confrontation with his often difficult Queen, who was sitting at the head of the council board impatiently tapping her fan on the edge of the table.

She was looking as strained as he felt, and no wonder. She had aged a little, he thought. She was thirty-seven now, and the years of troubles and responsibility had not been kind to her. Normally she took great care with her appearance when she went abroad at court or in public, and it was obvious that she used cosmetics to prolong the semblance of youth and loveliness; but today she was wearing the same old black dress that she had worn to council meetings for the past three days. It did her few favours. It did not matter to Cecil, who cared little for outward display; but he knew that Elizabeth cared passionately that men saw her as ever-young and the embodiment of beauty.

What mattered to him was that her childbearing years were running out, and once again he was mentally girding his loins to enter battle with her on the subject of her marriage.

'Well, William? What's on your mind?' she asked sharply.

He sighed. 'Madam, these recent plots and conspiracies, and the late northern rebellion, have been trying for us all. They have shown us how insecure your realm is. But it would be less so if your Majesty had a husband at your side and sons to succeed you.' Warming to his argument, he went on, 'Without an heir, Madam, you stand alone. You are unguarded, at risk from traitors, invaders and assassins. And if you die without heirs, there will be no bar to Queen Mary succeeding here. Everything you have worked for will be overthrown.'

Once upon a time Elizabeth would have glared at him for venturing to bring up yet again the sore subject of her marrying, but she too had been shaken by the perils of the past months.

She turned to Cecil now. 'You speak truth, my Spirit,' she said at length. 'I agree, the matter is urgent. I should marry. The birth of a Protestant heir, especially a son, would put paid to Mary's aspirations.'

Cecil, Robert and the rest were looking at her in amazement. No resistance? No histrionics? Matters must indeed be desperate!

'I am relieved that your Majesty has come to this decision at last,' Robert said, as all eyes swivelled towards him.

'Yes,' she replied, glaring at him, 'even though I am as averse as ever to the idea of marriage.' She turned back to Cecil. 'Who shall it be?'

Robert suppressed his anger. She was playing with him again – with them all, for all he knew.

'Shall we try to revive the match with the Archduke?' Sussex asked.

'We can send an envoy, but the Emperor has made it clear that he is no longer interested,' Cecil said. 'His son was kept dangling for too long.'

'He is courting a fat Bavarian princess,' Elizabeth sneered. 'So much for his devotion to me!'

'He has been kept waiting for an answer for eleven years,' Robert observed. 'I understand how he feels.'

Elizabeth shot him a look aimed to pierce his presumption like an arrow.

'In fact, there is a new proposal from France,' Cecil announced. 'King Charles has suggested a match with his brother, Henri, Duke of Anjou. He sees it as the cornerstone to a new alliance between England and France against Spain. And Madam, we need the friendship of France at this time, given that Spain supported the rebellion.'

'You do not need to tell *me* that,' Elizabeth reminded him. 'How old is the Duke of Anjou?'

'Nineteen, Madam.' Cecil's face was impassive. Robert was trying not to laugh.

'Well I am too old for him,' Elizabeth declared.

'Not at all,' Cecil soothed her. 'Your Majesty's beauty is renowned; no man could resist you. You have the gift of eternal youth.'

Elizabeth ceased being tetchy and smiled. Such compliments, even from crusty Cecil, were the breath of life to her.

'Shall I send Sir Francis Walsingham to France to discuss the matter?'

Walsingham was Cecil's protégé. He had a brilliant mind, huge ability and a severe Puritan outlook. These were qualities that not only commanded the respect of the Queen, but could prove useful to her, and she liked Walsingham for himself, for they were well matched intellectually and she knew that he was devoted to her. She had taken to calling him her Moor, on account of his customary black clothes and swarthy looks. Sir Francis had been placed in charge of Cecil's spy network; he loathed Catholics, especially the Queen of Scots and the Spaniards. On that account alone, Elizabeth knew that she could trust him implicitly.

Walsingham went dutifully to Paris, with instructions to say that the Queen welcomed the idea of a marriage to the Duke of Anjou, but that she could not change her religion, and would expect any husband of hers to abide by the laws of England.

When he returned, some weeks later, one look at his lugubrious face told Elizabeth that negotiations had not gone well.

'The Duke is surrounded by priests, Madam,' he reported, distaste in his tone. 'He is adamant that he will never abandon his faith. But that is not the only reason why I would advise against pursuing this marriage.' He coughed, clearly – for his was a strictly moral soul – not relishing what he had to say. 'He is not a normal man. He is corrupt, like all the Valois. For one so young, he is notorious for his womanising, yet he also favours men. He is completely given to voluptuousness, and reeks of perfumes. If you had seen the way he dresses, the jewels, the rings . . . Well, delicacy prevents me from saying more.'

'You have said enough, my Moor,' Elizabeth reassured him, thinking that she could never take a husband whose vanity might lead him to see himself as her rival. As for his sexual proclivities . . .

'But where does this leave us with the French?' Cecil asked.

'I will deal with that, good Spirit!' Elizabeth smiled.

She summoned Fenelon, the French ambassador. She took care to dress in virginal white, and made a great play with her fan, so as to appear both coy and demure.

'Monsieur, you are most welcome,' she told the gallant Fenelon, whom she much liked. 'It is of marriage that I wish to speak.'

'By all means, your Majesty,' he answered eagerly. Was the plum to fall into his lap so easily? He was aware of how many had gone before him and failed.

'Few have any idea of how much I have regretted staying single for so long,' Elizabeth declared. Robert, standing nearby, drew in his breath.

'Madame, I can help with that state of affairs,' Fenelon hastened to assure her. 'I would deem it a great honour if I could bring about a marriage between your Majesty and the Duke of Anjou.'

'Ah, but I am too old for marriage,' Elizabeth said sadly, 'even though I have never received a proposal I liked better. The Duke is so much younger than me.'

'So much the better for you!' Robert joked. She laughed, but she had detected an edge to his voice. He was not getting any younger either.

The interview ended with Fenelon assuring the Queen that her hand would be the greatest prize to which Anjou could aspire, and that he would do everything in his power to bring the negotiations to a happy conclusion.

'We have France in our grasp,' Elizabeth murmured to Robert after the ambassador had bowed himself out. 'Pretend that you support the match.'

'You can rely on me,' he told her, resigning himself to yet another round of the game.

The recent threats from foreign aggressors – from the Queen of Scots, the Spaniards and the Pope – had made all loyal Englishmen even prouder and more protective of their Queen. They knew how much she loved and cherished her true subjects, and many of them would have laid down their lives for her. That November, this upsurge of national fervour and affection gave birth to a new celebration, that of Elizabeth's accession day. Bells pealed, thanks were rendered in every church for a queen who had delivered England from popery, and there were spectacular jousts at Whitehall, at which Elizabeth appeared garbed as Albion's shining sun, and Astraea, the virgin goddess of justice.

'This day should be observed every year!' Robert declared, overcome by loyal fervour. Let England's enemies see how much her Queen was loved!

'It shall be, so my people wish it,' Elizabeth said. Already she had heard people calling it the Golden Day, and her subjects' observance of it touched her heart like nothing else, stiffening her resolve to stay wedded to her kingdom rather than taking a husband, and to be the mother of her people instead of having children of her own.

Elizabeth's heart was bursting with pride and gratitude as she fastened the mantle of nobility across Cecil's chest. He was Baron Burghley now, as a reward for his manifold services to her. No prince, she kept telling everyone, had ever had such a counsellor. She was blessed in him, and in her other advisers. Cecil, Leicester, Sussex and Walsingham – these were the men who were now closest to her, especially now that Throckmorton had died and Bacon was ageing; and while they did not always see eye to eye among themselves, they were united in their loyalty to her.

The new Baron Burghley and the Earl of Sussex were in favour of the Anjou marriage; Leicester, predictably, was not, although he saw the need for England to have a strong ally. He knew that the others thought he was still hoping to marry the Queen himself, but he was aware that the likelihood of that was receding day by day. If they wed, he knew, it would be almost as brother and sister. They were no longer young, and their desire for each other had burnt itself out. Yet even now he hoped to fan the embers.

'You do not need to marry Anjou to obtain King Charles's friendship,' he told Elizabeth, as they rested by the fire one chill February evening. Elizabeth sat with a bandaged leg resting on a footstool. She had an ulcer that had been slow to heal, but it was much improved now.

'Ah, but I am more bent to this marriage than I have ever been,' she said. 'I am sending an envoy to Paris to inform King Charles that I am ready thankfully to accept their proposals and treat with them. It is to be a secret for now, my Eyes.'

And you will not go through with it, Robert thought. He

pitied Walsingham, now resident ambassador at the French court, and the man who would have the task of keeping the negotiations afloat while the Queen blew hot and cold.

He leaned forward impulsively and took her hand. 'You would not consider me, Bess?'

She smiled at him affectionately. 'You deserve the laurel for trying, but no, Robin. Not now, at any rate. I have to be seen to be eager to wed Anjou.'

Yet that did not stop her from openly flirting with the infuriating Heneage, and with a newcomer at court, the lawyer Christopher Hatton, whom rumour said had been advanced by the Queen after she had admired his accomplished performance – and his good looks – in a masque. He was strikingly, masculinely beautiful, a paragon in the tiltyard – and how he danced! Robert looked on in envy as Elizabeth twirled, dipped and jumped for Hatton's benefit before the whole court. She was as slender as ever, lithe and supple now that her ulcer had healed – whereas he, Robert, had put on weight and was less impressive on the dance floor than he had once been. His jealousy surged when he heard her calling Hatton her Lids, just as she had called himself her Eyes. He much preferred it when she called the interloper her Mutton – she affecting to be a shepherdess, with Hatton as her sheep – although of course he would have preferred her not to call him anything at all. Certainly he, Robert, could think of a few choice names for him!

Hatton bombarded the Queen with compliments and gifts. He made love to her with his dark, intent eyes. He wrote her eloquent love letters. He told her that to be absent from her was Hell's torment. His wits, he declared, were overwrought with thoughts of her. Love me, he begged her. She was in her element.

'Look at him jig!' she enthused to Robert, as they watched the debonair Hatton leaping about the floor, a chain of fair ladies in his wake. He had eyes for none of them, she noticed with approval.

'I can send you a dancing master who can do far better,' Robert retorted sourly, unable to resist a barb.

'Pish!' Elizabeth shrugged. 'I will not see your man. He does it only for a trade.' And her eyes remained firmly fixed on the tantalising muscular physique of Hatton.

'I am going to marry the Duke of Anjou,' Elizabeth announced to her Council.

'All things considered?' Burghley asked.

'All things considered, dear Spirit,' she said firmly. Robert gave a snort of disgust, but she ignored him.

'This will make the Pope's malice vanish in smoke,' Burghley observed. His voice was suffused with relief.

'Is the Duke not too young to be married to your Majesty?' one impudent councillor piped up.

'How dare you speak to your Queen like that!' Robert flared, as Elizabeth flushed in anger. 'Of course he is not too young for one so beautiful.'

'So you had best keep your silly opinions to yourself,' the Queen snapped.

'I do beg your Majesty's pardon,' stammered the councillor, seeing his hopes of preferment and a dazzling career at court rapidly sliding away.

'Do you think she will really go ahead with this marriage?' Sussex asked later, when Elizabeth had retired.

'Who knows?' Burghley shrugged. 'At least she is keeping the French friendly when we most need them.'

An envoy from Queen Catherine duly arrived with a portrait of her son, a formal proposal and a long list of demands, none of which Elizabeth was prepared to concede. She looked at the portrait and saw a dark man with heavy jowls and an earring resting on his wide ruff – Catherine de' Medici to the life (if you discounted the moustache), which was enough to deter any ardent bride. She was reluctant to proceed further, but the wearisome pretence must be kept up for as long as it served her purpose.

Anjou was reluctant too. A report reached Elizabeth that he had publicly declared that he would not marry an old creature with a sore leg. He could probably have heard the resultant explosion in Paris, and Queen Catherine felt obliged to send a profuse apology for her son's unforgivably rude words. Elizabeth, in turn, felt obliged to dance in front of Fenelon at every opportunity, just to prove that there was now nothing wrong with her leg.

'I hope,' she said to him, 'that the Duke of Anjou will not have cause to complain that he has been tricked into marrying a lame bride.' There was no question in her mind that she could ever marry Anjou now, the spoilt brat. Even so, his cruel remark had hurt.

'The age gap does concern me,' she was moved to confide to Lady Cobham, her close confidante since Kate Knollys's death two years earlier.

'Well, Madam, my advice would be not to press ahead with your plans,' Lady Cobham agreed. 'The great inequality in age concerns me too.'

'Pah!' cried Elizabeth, much affronted. 'There are but ten years between Anjou and myself!'

Lady Cobham – realising rapidly that while it was perfectly all right for the Queen to refer to such things, it was most certainly not all right for any lesser mortal to do so – did not dare to correct her.

Elizabeth was furious with Anjou for making his antipathy to the marriage so public. It was mortifying! She was the greatest catch in Europe, was she not? The best match in her parish, as Walsingham put it. Far greater princes than Anjou had vied for her hand. It was humiliating to have this young coxcomb wax unenthusiastic about the glorious prize that was being offered him. Well, she would make it clear that there was a price to be paid for such insulting behaviour.

'This marriage contract leaves much to be desired,' she declared, pushing it away from her. 'William, you can tell the French that the return of Calais is the price of my hand.'

'They will never agree to that!' Burghley protested.

'Tell them also,' she went on, ignoring him, 'that my

conscience will not allow me to permit the Duke to hear Mass in private. I do not see why he cannot worship as an Anglican.'

'All this talk of his being staunch in religion is just a ruse,' Robert said, unhelpfully in the circumstances, she felt. 'He is merely pretending, to wring more concessions out of us. Your Majesty is justified in taking a stand.'

'You just want to marry her yourself, don't you?' Burghley muttered in his ear.

'Not at all,' he muttered back. In fact, he had secretly advised the French to stay firm in the matter of the Mass. Elizabeth would give in in the end, he had told them. Now he was not so sure, and it was clear to everyone that she was up to her old tricks, stalling, procrastinating and stringing out negotiations. It was clear also that she had no real intention of marrying Anjou. And good riddance too, Robert thought savagely. The thought of that pervert doing with her what he himself had longed to do for years made him feel sick.

Another French envoy came and went without any progress being made. A stalemate had been reached. The negotiations skidded to a halt, then collapsed, gasping, in the dust.

Burghley came to the Queen, his face pained, barely able to keep the exasperation out of his voice. 'Madam, I see how it is with you in regard to the French marriage. I will instruct your Council to devise other means for your preservation, although how your Majesty shall obtain remedies for the perils that threaten you is, I think, only known to Almighty God.' And he took himself off, muttering in his distress, to commiserate with Walsingham and Leicester.

'We should have known at the outset,' Robert reflected. 'Her Majesty's heart is not inclined to marry at all. We did our best to smooth the way for her, but at each point she made the usual difficulties.' In fact, he himself had done his best to make difficulties, although mercifully the others were not to know that. 'Fear not,' he went on. 'We still have a good understanding with France that may yet lead to an alliance.'

*

Elizabeth's face was white with rage. In her hand she held incontrovertible evidence that Norfolk – whom, of her magnanimity, she had graciously freed and forgiven – had been plotting to marry the Queen of Scots, plainly to overthrow Elizabeth and reign jointly with Mary over England. But the Duke's letters had been intercepted. Dangerous plotter he might be, but an inept one at that. Worse still was his betrayal. Elizabeth was his cousin as well as his Queen.

'Draw up a warrant for his arrest,' she commanded, her voice icy, and within hours Norfolk was in the Tower.

'But had the common people had their way, he would have been liberated,' Burghley reported, frowning. 'He has ever been popular with them, and when word spread that he had been taken, there were crowds outside the Tower when he arrived, all protesting his innocence.'

'They will soon find out the truth!' Elizabeth seethed.

'Indeed they will, Madam, for he has already confessed to some of the charges, although he denies that he had ever meant to harm your Majesty. For all that, the evidence we have against him is enough to send both him and the Queen of Scots to the block.'

Elizabeth hesitated. Her face was drawn.

'Norfolk is a fool,' she said at length. 'He has been seduced into treason by his misguided devotion to Queen Mary.' God rot that brainless, aggravating woman! 'But must I send him to his death? It is a deed much against my stomach. And he is of my blood.'

'Madam, the Duke has committed treason. It is the most heinous of crimes, being against your sacred person. Was he thinking of ties of kinship when he plotted with the Scottish Queen? I think not.'

'Madam, to show weakness now would be to encourage others who would play traitor,' Robert said.

'Then I must consider what to do for the best,' Elizabeth said. 'As for Mary, she is an anointed queen, and not a subject. There can be no question of doing violence upon her person, treacherous though she is.'

'Madam,' Cecil bristled, 'we have proof that she will stop at nothing to gain her freedom and the English crown.'

'To execute her would set a dangerous – and doubtless illegal – precedent,' Elizabeth insisted, twisting her hands in agitation. Her cousin, she realised, was virtually untouchable, and therefore doubly menacing, for she could never be rid of her. 'From now on she must be held more securely and closely watched. And Burghley, have the Casket Letters published, so that the world might know what she really is. We cannot have scenes like those at the Tower repeated. I will not have traitors cheered or my justice derided.'

'The most effective remedy would be for your Majesty to recognise Queen Mary's son as king of Scots,' Burghley urged.

'We will do that too!' Elizabeth declared.

The uncovering of the plot had shaken Elizabeth to the core.

'An alliance with France is now absolutely essential,' she told her Council. 'We must seal it with a marriage. See if you can revive the negotiations, my Spirit. Let it be known that I will allow Anjou his Mass in private.'

But Walsingham now sent a timely warning: do not proceed! Anjou, he wrote, would utterly refuse the Queen, for he had his sights set on becoming king of Poland. If her Majesty persisted, she would invite a humiliating public rejection.

Her Majesty did not persist. She had looked in the mirror that very morning and seen the first strands of grey in her thinning hair. When she looked again she noticed new lines about her eyes, which had surely not been there the last time she checked. She was thirty-eight, and it dawned on her that she was beginning to look it.

Through the good and discreet offices of her women, a curly wig was made for her, of a red shade to match her own hair. Soon she ordered a long false tress that she could attach at the back of her head. Within days most ladies of the court were wearing something of the sort. Elizabeth then began using a paste made of powdered eggshell, borax and alum, to smooth and whiten her skin. When her painter, Nicholas Hilliard, came to take her portrait, she insisted that he did so outdoors, where there was no shadow, so that her face would appear luminous and ageless. It was vital, she knew, to preserve the mask of youth. Let her courtiers and ministers – yea, and foreign princes – perceive the signs of ageing, and they would begin to wonder if she was past marrying.

Robert noticed the change in her appearance. He said nothing, but felt melancholy at this evidence that youth was fleeting. Elizabeth should know that, however she looked, he would love her, and love her for herself. Beauty lay in the inner woman, not upon the skin.

Armoured in her wig and make-up, the Queen faced her Council, only to be told that Anjou had definitely lost interest in both her and the crown matrimonial of England. She snorted at that. 'Since my attempts to get a husband have caused me to be so ill used, I hope you can now understand why I prefer to remain single!' she declared.

But the French were not giving up so easily. Just two days later, Queen Catherine, as keen as Elizabeth for an alliance, offered her youngest son, Francis, Duke of Alençon, as a substitute for Anjou.

'He is a far less scrupulous fellow when it comes to religion!' Burghley said, clearly relieved, and in fact almost rubbing his hands in glee. 'This marriage is ten thousand times better than the other. Alençon is known to be friendly to the Protestants in France, and he is not so obstinate and restive a mule as his brother. He is more moderate, more flexible – and the better fellow.'

'He is also unlikely ever to become king, and therefore could live in England,' Sussex added.

'And he is more apt to get children,' Leicester observed, and was rewarded by seeing Elizabeth wince.

'But he is only seventeen!' she objected. 'He is reportedly very small for a man, and his skin is said to be badly scarred from smallpox.' Her eyes met Robert's; both were remembering his poor sister Mary. He thought it unkind in Elizabeth to use that for an excuse.

'Queen Catherine writes that his beard covers the worst of the scars,' Burghley reassured her. 'She also says that he is vigorous and lusty.'

'Then God help him,' Robert said sourly. Elizabeth banged the table.

'You will not say such things!' she rapped.

'I beg your pardon, Madam,' Robert said, sketching an ostentatious bow from the waist. 'It was but a joke.'

'And not a funny one. No, my lords, Alençon is too young and too small.'

'He is the same height as yourself, Madam,' Burghley protested.

'Say rather the height of your grandson!' she retorted. Cecil had to smile, for his namesake was just five. 'They called Alençon Hercules at birth, but he could not live up to it, so to save himself embarrassment he changed his name to Francis when he was confirmed.' They all laughed.

'Nevertheless, Madam,' Burghley persisted, 'Sir Francis Walsingham urges us to proceed with negotiations for the marriage. This is an opportunity not to be missed. Alençon would make the perfect husband for your Majesty.'

Robert glared at him.

1572

Elizabeth looked at the tiny timepiece set into her bejewelled bracelet. It had been Robert's New Year gift to her, and many had marvelled at it, never having seen the like. But she was not thinking of their delighted amazement now. She was wondering if Norfolk's trial was over, and what the verdict had been.

At long last Burghley came to her. His face said it all.

'Guilty,' she whispered.

'And condemned to a traitor's death,' he added.

Norfolk would not suffer it, of course. As a peer of the realm, he was entitled to be spared the full horrors of hanging, drawing and quartering, because monarchs customarily commuted the sentence for those of noble blood, but he would still lose his head. And Elizabeth, his cousin, must sign the death warrant. Suddenly she understood something of what her father must have felt when he signed the paper that would send her mother to a bloody death.

She could not do it. She shuddered away from the prospect. It was against her every instinct to condemn Norfolk to a fate that had haunted her dreams since childhood.

'He has asked that I be appointed guardian to his children,' Burghley said.

'Yes, yes, of course,' Elizabeth answered distractedly.

'The execution is set for the twenty-first.' Five days hence.

'No,' she said.

'No?' Cecil was bewildered. The law must take its course; there could be no question of that.

'He is the premier peer of the realm, and he is popular with the people.'

'Madam, he would have had you assassinated. Greater persons have died for much less.'

'Oh, dear Spirit, *I* know that well!'

Cecil stared at her, appalled at what he had said. 'Dear Madam, forgive me. It was thoughtless of me.'

'I know you intended no hurt, old friend,' she said, forcing a smile. 'But no, Norfolk shall not die.'

'I beg of you, Madam, to do your duty. Make an example of him, lest others mistake your mercy for weakness. His death must be a deterrent to other would-be traitors.'

'I will think on it,' Elizabeth promised. Cecil knew of old what that meant.

But she did think on it. She thought of little else. The matter overshadowed her every waking moment. She would steel herself to do her duty, then find herself shrinking from it at the last minute. Every time she came to put pen to paper, she saw before her Anne Boleyn kneeling in the straw on the scaffold, and imagined the terror that her mother must have felt in those final moments of her life. No, she could not do it.

They all put pressure on her, Burghley, Robert and her other councillors; they were relentless, but she resisted them. The days turned into weeks. In the Tower, Norfolk would be wondering why he had not been marched out to the block.

'Your Majesty has ever been a merciful lady,' Burghley cozened her, 'and in being so you have suffered more harm than justice. Do you think you will be more beloved by letting others get away with treason?'

Elizabeth gave in. She signed the warrant for Norfolk's execution. But that night, overcome by distress, she rescinded the order. The next morning a crowd turned up at Tower Hill to witness the spectacle of a great duke dying, and found that they had had a wasted journey.

The councillors could not understand the Queen's reluctance. They pressed her, again and again, to let the law take its course. She protested that she felt ill under the strain and retired to her bed.

Then she became ill indeed, disgustingly so.

'We fear for her life,' her physicians admitted. 'She can keep no food down, and she has a constant bloody flux.'

Robert was in terror lest Elizabeth die. Despite her protests that she did not want him to see her in such a state, he sat for three days by her bed, with a distraught Burghley on the opposite side, taking it in turns to feed her sips of boiled water, which was all that she could tolerate. Both of them feared what would happen if they lost her, and both knew that they would grieve immensely. When St George's Day came, the day Elizabeth had appointed for Burghley to be admitted to the Order of the Garter, it was Robert who deputised for her and conferred the honour on him, both of them grim-faced and heavy-hearted. They were friends now, despite themselves, their earlier rivalry forgotten. They corresponded frequently, visited each other's houses, and – although they did not always agree – enjoyed an amicable working relationship, united in their love for their royal mistress, their Protestant faith and their loyalty to the realm.

They both gave heartfelt thanks, therefore, when Elizabeth recovered, and both had tears in their eyes when she rose from her bed and sat once more in her usual place at the head of the council board.

'God's blood, my lords, what whey faces!' she chided them mischievously. 'I just ate some bad fish.'

'Madam,' Burghley protested, 'I know that I speak for us all when I say that the severity of your illness was very terrible to us, who love you. What if you had died? The succession is unresolved, and England would surely be lost to our enemies, who would force the Catholic religion on our people—'

'I have said that I will consider marrying Alençon,' Elizabeth interrupted, not wishing to hear more of the woes that would befall her kingdom should God call her hence. She had heard it oft-times enough.

'But in the meantime, Madam, will you please summon Parliament urgently, so that measures can be taken to prevent the Queen of Scots from plotting against you ever again. Public feeling is running high against her. So long as this devilish woman lives, you cannot rest in quiet possession of your crown, nor can your faithful subjects assure themselves of the safety of their lives.'

'Very well, I will call Parliament,' Elizabeth agreed. But she continued adamantly to refuse to sign Norfolk's death warrant.

'The Lord Treasurer has died,' Elizabeth informed Robert sadly, remembering William Paulet, Marquess of Winchester, the man who had shown her kindness when he escorted her to the Tower in her sister's reign.

'God rest his soul,' Robert said. 'He was an upright nobleman.'

'I would like you to fill his shoes, my Eyes,' she said.

'Me – as Lord Treasurer?' He was surprised and pleased. 'It is an honour, Bess, but I do not have sufficient learning and knowledge. It should properly go to Burghley, who deserves it.'

'Then I shall offer it to him,' she agreed. 'It will help relieve his gout!'

That was the only time she felt her spirits lighten during that ghastly spring. In May Parliament met to debate the catalogue of Queen Mary's crimes.

'Cut off her head and make no more ado about her!' both Lords and Commons clamoured.

'I will not do it!' Elizabeth cried, near to hysteria. The execution of a queen would set the most dangerous precedent of all, and the very thought of it raised the terrible spectres of her mother, Katherine Howard and Jane Grey, three other queens who had met that fate.

'Parliament must legislate to bar Mary from the succession,' she declared, 'and she must be warned that, if she plots against me again, she will suffer death.'

Back came Parliament's unequivocal answer: 'Warning has been given her. The axe must be the next warning!'

Elizabeth was equally adamant. 'Honour does not permit

me to attaint a foreign queen who is not subject to English law.'

Parliament did not care about such niceties. It was baying for blood. 'If her Majesty does not put to death this husband-murderer and arch-traitress, this Scottish Clytemnestra, she will offend not only her conscience but God Himself!' These brave words were followed by a petition voicing the call and cry of all good subjects against the merciful nature of her Majesty.

'I will not put to death the bird that, to escape the pursuit of the hawk, has fled to my feet for protection,' Elizabeth declared. 'Honour and conscience forbid! Nor do I have any desire to provoke armed retribution on the part of Queen Mary's Catholic allies.'

In the end, after much wrangling and bad feeling, her will prevailed, and Parliament contented itself with drawing up a bill depriving Mary of her pretended claim to the throne. From henceforth it was to be an offence for anyone to proclaim or assert it. But when the bill was laid before the Queen for her signature, she vetoed it.

'Effectively, Bess, Mary has escaped censure,' Robert protested. He had a high colour these days, and was well-nigh purple with fury.

'I despair!' Burghley groaned. 'Madam, how can you be so lenient when all our intelligence suggests that King Philip and the Pope are set upon overthrowing you and setting Queen Mary up in your place. And then what will become of us all?'

'I have no legal jurisdiction over her,' Elizabeth protested.

'Then her imprisonment is illegal.'

'It is necessary!' she retorted. 'But I will not harm a hair of her head.'

'Well then,' Burghley said slyly, 'if you will not proceed against her, at least make an example of Norfolk.'

Elizabeth was about to open her mouth to disagree, but realised that she dared not. She had forced her will upon them in sparing Mary, but now she would have to throw Norfolk to the wolves. They deserved no less.

'Bring me the warrant,' she commanded in a tight voice. They laid it before her, and with a shaking hand she signed it.

She did not sleep at all that night.

She had vowed never to go to the Tower again. It was a horrible place, redolent of terrible deeds that had touched her too nearly. But Norfolk was kin, and she felt she had a responsibility. She needed to do what she could for him, to make reparation for sending him to his death, and she was determined to ensure that her orders were carried out. The next day, brimming with guilt and dread, she summoned Robert to attend her in private.

'I want you to come with me to the Tower, now,' she said.

'Are you mad, Bess?' he erupted, astonishment making him forget the courtesy due to her. 'Besides, the execution takes place tomorrow.'

'I have no intention of witnessing it, or of seeing Norfolk,' Elizabeth said. 'I cannot explain why, but I want to make sure that the arrangements have been made in a seemly and proper manner.' There would be no arrow chest for Norfolk's mangled remains, as there had been for her mother, no provision having been made for a coffin.

'It will distress you,' Robert warned, concern in his gaze. 'Let me go for you.'

'No, my Eyes, I must do this,' Elizabeth insisted. 'I have sat on my throne for fourteen years now, and this is the first time in my reign that anyone has been sent to the block. I have a debt of conscience to pay.'

'Very well,' he said. 'I will stay by your side. But do not say I did not warn you.'

It was a warm June day, but both donned cloaks with hoods. The Queen was travelling incognito, and refused to take any attendants with her. She and Robert left Whitehall by the road going south, tethered their horses at a waterside inn near Chelsea, then hired a boat to the Tower. As the astonished boatman pulled in where he had been told, at the Queen's Stairs, the private royal entrance to the fortress, and Elizabeth sat rigid in the cabin remembering how it had been for her when she had been brought here a prisoner in Mary's reign, the Constable and a detachment of yeomen warders – who had been sent word ahead by a trusted messenger – came saluting to receive their mistress.

'No fuss or ceremony, good sirs,' Elizabeth said briskly, mounting the steps where once she had sat in the pouring rain, refusing to enter the fortress for fear of never leaving it. And now she had condemned Norfolk to the very fate she had herself dreaded. 'Where is the Duke being held?'

'In the Bell Tower, Madam,' the Constable informed her.

'Has he been well fed and looked after?'

'Aye, Madam.' The officer's face was impassive, not betraying whether he thought this visitation strange or otherwise.

'See that he is given a hearty last meal, and that a minister be brought to attend to his spiritual needs,' Elizabeth commanded. 'Has provision been made for a coffin?'

'Aye, Madam, of stout oak.'

'Good. He shall be buried in the chapel.' She nodded in the direction of St Peter ad Vincula, where lay her mother and many others who had suffered execution in or near this place. 'Lay him to rest next to his cousins, my late mother Queen Anne, and Katherine Howard, before the altar.'

'It shall be done, Madam.'

'The axe – is it sharp?'

'The hangman was honing it this morning.'

'Bid him do his task well, and cleanly. Let it be quick.'

'I will ensure that, Madam.'

'Do it, as you love me,' Elizabeth said fervently. 'I do not want the Duke's suffering on my conscience. Leave us now. Tell the boatman to wait.'

She walked on a little with Robert, past the Watergate, through which so many prisoners had entered the Tower under Tudor rule – but not so many in recent years, she reminded herself. 'God, I hate this place,' she said.

'So do I,' he muttered. So wrapped up had she been in thoughts of her mother and Norfolk that she had forgotten entirely that Robert's father and his youngest brother Guilford had been imprisoned here and died by the axe on Tower Hill. Robert and his brothers had been incarcerated here for months afterwards, and his older brother John had been so weakened by the experience that he died immediately after their release.

'If you go into the Beauchamp Tower you will see the carving I made with my brothers,' he said, his voice hoarse. 'It is our family crest. And somewhere there is the name Jane, carved by Guilford.'

'Poor Jane Grey,' Elizabeth murmured, shuddering. 'Come, let us go. At least we can leave at will, unlike when we were held here in Mary's reign. This place gave me the horrors then, and it still does now.'

'You should not have come,' Robert reproved her.

'I had to,' she told him. 'Norfolk will be the first person I have ordered to be beheaded here – and pray God he will be the last.'

The next morning she was looking at her timepiece again, chewing her lip and pacing up and down in her bedchamber, when suddenly there came the sound of cannon fire – the guns on Tower Wharf announcing Norfolk's execution, as they had done her mother's, thirty-six years before. She fell to her knees, overcome with regret and remorse, and that was how Robert found her. He had heard the guns too, and knew how she must be feeling. He knelt and held her close as she huddled against him weeping, her shoulders juddering. He raised his hand to stroke her hair – and felt only the coarse weave of her wig. His own eyes were moist as he laid his cheek against her head, and not just on Norfolk's account.

Negotiations for the French marriage proceeded – and dragged on. The chief stumbling blocks for Elizabeth – or the ones she was prepared to discuss with her ministers – were Alençon's youth and her fear that France was trying to draw her into a war with the Spanish Duke of Alva, whom King Philip had sent into the Netherlands with a vast army to rout out heresy. France had no sympathy for Protestants, whether Dutch or French – they called the latter Huguenots – but Queen Catherine was as nervous as Elizabeth about having a Spanish army entrenched on her doorstep. And so Elizabeth blew hot and then cold, and her councillors fretted lest these marriage plans go the way of all the others.

That summer she departed on her usual progress and presently came to Kenilworth, where Robert had promised her a feast of princely sports. They were out every day hunting deer (and Robert was exerting all his charms to pursue a rather different quarry), and were closing in on their prey one afternoon when a messenger on a lathered horse caught up with them.

'Your Majesty, there is terrible news from France!' he shouted, and Elizabeth abruptly reined in her steed, with Robert following close behind her.

'Tell me!' she commanded, turning the animal back in the direction of the castle, and signalling to the messenger and the rest of her party to accompany her.

'There has been great slaughter of the Huguenots,' the man panted, clearly having ridden hard. 'During the marriage celebrations of the Princess Marguerite to the King of Navarre, the Queen Mother and her Catholic friends tried to murder the leader of the Huguenots, Admiral de Coligny, because – it is said – they resented his influence on the King. They did not succeed, but the attempt provoked riots in Paris, where the people panicked. Then the Queen Mother gave the order for all the Huguenots to be turned out of the city, but before they could leave, the Catholics rose and massacred them in cold blood. They say that four thousand souls have perished. All over France the slaughter has been repeated, and we have heard that ten thousand are dead.' Tears were pouring down the messenger's cheeks. 'Your Majesty, I have seen the atrocities that were committed . . .' His voice tailed away. He had no words or stomach to describe the rivers of blood in the streets, the streams choked with mangled bodies, the little children . . .

Elizabeth found herself weeping too. 'This is monstrous!' she cried, horrified. 'They are devils. I cannot believe what I am hearing. Tell me, is my Moor safe?' A known Puritan, Walsingham would have been a marked man; the blood-crazy mob would not have bothered with the niceties of diplomatic immunity.

'Madam, he hid while the killings were going on, and was spared, but he is much shaken. I bear a letter from him for your Majesty.'

'Thanks be to God,' Elizabeth breathed, but it was only a small mercy in the wider scale of events.

They had now reached the castle. Having sent the messenger to the kitchens for some much-needed refreshment, Elizabeth, still deeply distressed, called for Burghley and Robert to attend her. Together they read Walsingham's letter, which divulged more details of the dreadful bloodbath in Paris, and then they debated what was to be done.

'I must leave for London immediately,' Elizabeth said. 'Cancel the entertainments and send the musicians home. And tell the French ambassador that he must go back to Paris without delay. I will hear no more talk of marriage.'

There was a great outcry against King Charles, Queen Catherine and all Catholics when tidings of the massacre of St Bartholemew's Eve, as it was now being called, became known and spread across England. Elizabeth joined in the outraged chorus of disapproval, but that was all she could do.

'I dare not seek to avenge the Huguenots,' she told her councillors, her eyes haunted by guilt. 'We need the French alliance. Believe me, it goes against my stomach, my faith and my humanity to do nothing. I am forced to be a hypocrite, for the sake of policy. Tell me, what can I do to ease my troubled conscience?'

'Might I suggest that your Majesty secretly sends arms to those Protestants who remain in France?' Burghley advised.

'Yes, I will do that,' Elizabeth agreed, trying not to weep. 'And before God, I will do everything else in my power to protect them. Often diplomacy can be more effective than military action. But I would that I could do more.'

Elizabeth was at Oxford when Fenelon begged for an audience so that he could offer her an official explanation for the accident – as he had the gall to call it – that had occurred in his country. She kept him waiting for three days, then received him in a darkened chamber hung with black, with herself and all her courtiers wearing the deepest mourning. Everyone was silent as he walked forward between the stony-faced, hostile Stygian ranks to kiss the Queen's hand. Her face loomed pale in the gloom, and her expression was grim.

'I cannot say welcome, your Excellency, for I am not sure if that would be proper,' she said coldly, loud enough for the entire room to hear. 'It is my dearest hope that King Charles will clear his name in the eyes of the world.'

'Madam,' Fenelon hastened to explain, 'his Majesty had uncovered a Protestant plot against himself and his family, and he had to act quickly to avoid assassination. I assure you, it is not his Majesty's intention to persecute the Huguenots.'

No, it was his mother's, Elizabeth thought. And there was no plot. You do not fool me.

'Such provocation does not excuse widespread violence,' she said sternly. 'I wept when I read the reports of the killings. So did all good Christians. However, because his Majesty is a king and a gentleman, I am bound to accept your master's explanation.'

'Madam, you are most gracious to say so,' Fenelon declared. '*Nothing* is more important to his Majesty than his alliance with England.'

'I am comforted by that,' Elizabeth said, relenting only very slightly. 'I hope that, in the weeks to come, he will do *everything* in his power to make amends for so much blood so horribly shed, if only for his own honour, which is now blemished in the eyes of the world.'

'I have *every* confidence that he will, Madam,' Fenelon said, knowing that King Charles was unlikely to do any such thing. 'And now, let us proceed to happier matters, such as your Majesty's marriage to—'

'I do not wish to discuss my marriage when I am overcome with grief for the poor murdered Huguenots,' Elizabeth barked.

'Madam, the Duke of Alençon took no part in the massacre. He spoke out against it.'

'I am *very* gratified to hear it. And now, Ambassador, you have our leave to depart.'

Fenelon went dejectedly. The English alliance was important to France too, with Spain so hostile. God knew he had worked for its happy conclusion long enough. But he feared that it would be some time before Elizabeth thawed sufficiently even to discuss it.

1573

The rumours about the Queen and the Earl of Leicester had never subsided completely. Tales that they were secretly married (bad enough), or had children (worse), or were fornicating shamelessly (shocking, but so enjoyable in the telling) were still in circulation. Reports of these came through with dismal regularity to the Council, and offenders were dealt with increasingly severely. Some were sentenced to the pillory, some to a spell in gaol, others to have their ears cut off.

Often Robert found himself wishing that there was truth in the rumours. He was forty and still single; he had no children to carry on his line or inherit his fortune and his great houses; and as for fornication (he sighed very deeply when he read those particular calumnies), it was years since he and Elizabeth had shared a bed, and for most of those years he had not – fool that he probably was – been able to bring himself to betray her with another woman.

The truth was, he loved her, and a part of him still believed that she would relent and marry him after all. The more rational part of him was coming to terms with the fact that it might never happen. But while there was hope, he could live with the frustrations imposed by his invidious position.

In truth, he never had been able to understand why Elizabeth would not marry him. Her fears seemed to be trifles, or excuses, more like. If she had permitted Seymour to penetrate her defences, why should she not allow him, Robert, the same joy? For joy it would be, for them both, he had absolutely no doubt. There were deep bonds between them that would never be severed, bonds of love, loyalty and devotion. In many respects they were like a long-married couple, looking to each other's interests, tolerating each other's foibles (although he, it had to be said, was obliged to be far more tolerant than Elizabeth), sharing likes and dislikes, and giving affection and support.

But it wasn't enough! And Elizabeth was still egging Hatton on, flirting openly with him. If you believed Hatton, she had led him to think that she loved him above all others. There had even been talk that Hatton had enjoyed what he, Leicester, had been denied for thirteen years now. At the very least she had permitted him some liberties – possibly the same liberties she had permitted Robert. Not to be borne!

Yet Elizabeth still wanted Robert near her all the time. He was almost permanently at her side when she sat enthroned in her presence chamber; he attended her often when she ate, standing by the table or (when they were alone) sitting down with her; he was her constant daily companion, and she did not trouble to hide her affection for him. Much of her flirting with Hatton was done in his presence, greatly to his chagrin, but he reasoned that she probably did it to make him jealous. Maybe he should not be jealous; maybe he should be content with his lot. He was king in all but name: the court deferred to him as if he wore the crown matrimonial, Elizabeth sought his confidential advice in matters of state, much as she would a husband's, and he enjoyed great riches and privileges. But the very thought of them begged the question: who would inherit them when he was gone? And so he would come around again to the vexing question of marriage and children. Soon Elizabeth would be too old for motherhood – she was forty next year – and he himself was older. He was weary to his bones of waiting for his future to be decided.

Recently, jealous because of Elizabeth's intrigues with Hatton, Robert had indulged in a flirtation with two young ladies of the Queen's household, Douglass Howard, Lady Sheffield, and her sister Frances. Douglass was twenty-five and very beautiful, with a high forehead and luxuriant raven hair piled high on her head – a true Howard. Widowed at twenty, she was ripe for an affair, and Robert seized his advantage, much to the fury of her sister, who fancied him too.

It began as a flirtation, a game that was never intended to be serious. What Robert did not expect was to experience more than desire for Douglass, and for his feelings for Elizabeth to change. Imperceptibly he found himself longing for Douglass's presence, the vital warmth of her, her come-to-bed eyes; and he also found himself regarding Elizabeth as past history. That shocked him. How could he possibly feel that way about the woman whom he had been desperate for so long to marry? But, he had to admit, it was true: Elizabeth no longer ignited passion in him; friendship and devotion, yes, and had she been willing he would still have wed her, for ambition was lively in him. Yet the fact was – and he must face it – that she was not willing, and never had been. Could it be – dare he think – that his future lay with Douglass?

While seeking to quell the confusion in his heart, he knew that he had to be extremely careful. Elizabeth had already remarked upon the catfights between Douglass and Frances.

'They keep squabbling over some fool who had the poor sense to come after them both,' she'd said. 'Well, I'll not put up with it. If they can't behave as young ladies should, I will send them home.'

Robert looked at her furtively. There was no hint that she was baiting him. He thought that she had not guessed who the fool in question was, and that pursuing Douglass would prove to be a risky enterprise.

He made it his business to warn first Douglass, then Frances, to cease their spatting, but he could not stop the rumours that were somehow now proliferating the court. The favourite was having an affair! People were agog. It was bruited that he and Douglass had been lovers for years, had in fact committed adultery during the lifetime of her husband. One tale even had it that Robert had poisoned Lord Sheffield after the latter had discovered them *in flagrante* and ridden post-haste to London to demand a divorce. Robert sighed when he heard that one. It was so obviously untrue – *and* it was not the first time that his enemies had accused him of poisoning someone. Where did such tales originate? How did people know that he was sleeping with Douglass? They had taken such care to be discreet. Did the very walls have ears?

He took to arranging secret trysts in his own house, or away from London, at inns far beyond the eyes and ears of the court. Never did he contemplate smuggling Douglass into his lodging, which was close to Elizabeth's. He trusted no one; he dared not think of the consequences if word of their liaison ever reached the ears of the Queen. Of course, he could have called a halt to the whole thing, save for the fact that he was so smitten – led by his codpiece, he ruefully told himself. It was unutterably good to feel intense desire for a woman again.

But Douglass wanted marriage, not just an affair.

'I cannot, sweeting,' Robert kept telling her. 'My devotion to her Majesty precludes my making any other commitment.'

Douglass pouted. Her lips really were most delectable. He found himself fantasising about them, and the swell of her firm, full breasts above the pearl-encrusted border of her bodice. Elizabeth's breasts were small, not much for a man to cup. It worried him that he was making such comparisons.

'Do you *really* think the Queen will marry you?' Douglass asked doubtfully.

'I live in hope,' he admitted.

A slight frown furrowed her perfect brow. 'It is unkind of her, and unfair, to make you wait. A man like you should be married with a brace of sons at his knee. The words "dog in a manger" spring to mind.'

'You should not speak of the Queen like that,' Robert reproved gently.

'Pardon me!' Douglass said, tossing her hair. 'She does not like me, and I would give her more cause not to!' She leaned into him, revealing a little more of her bosom than was decent.

'Darling, I have told you, I am committed to the Queen,' he protested, feeling himself grow hard. 'There are two ways open to us: you could continue as my mistress, which I should like more than anything in the world; or I will help you to find a husband.'

'Neither is acceptable to me,' Douglass said, her mouth a little *moue*.

'Sweetheart,' he pleaded, 'as you know, I cherish you. I want you to be mine. I am a man, with a man's frailties, but even so, one with a conscience, and I mean to act honestly in this matter.'

'How can you be acting honestly when my reputation is being dragged in the mire?' Douglass pouted. 'Today I heard servants gossiping that I had borne you a child. I told them never to repeat any such thing, as it was not true, but I could see by their smirking that they did not believe me.'

A chill shivered down Robert's spine. If the palace servants were repeating gossip like that, it would not be long before the Queen heard it; in fact it was as inevitable as death. Truly, it was becoming impossible to keep this love affair a secret, and Douglass was right: her reputation would soon be irrevocably ruined.

'I have done everything in my power to protect us,' he said, knowing that it sounded lame and promised her nothing.

'Except the one thing that would silence the gossips!' she retorted. 'My lord, when my family placed me with the Queen, it was to guard my reputation and help me to another good marriage. My honour is very dear to me, as I am sure it is to her Majesty. What would she say if she heard that I am your mistress?' She smiled sweetly at him.

Robert dropped his head in his hands and groaned. The threat had been implicit.

'Very well, I will marry you,' he said, knowing that it was not what he wanted, but that lust and honour had to be satisfied. 'But it must remain our secret. There would be serious consequences if word of it got out.' He refrained – just in time – from adding that Douglass might as well remain his mistress, for all the good marriage would do her.

She kissed him lasciviously, her little tongue toying with his, and permitted his hands to rove over her bodice; her dancing eyes said that he might go much further later. She had got what she wanted.

But she rejoiced too soon. When Robert arrived one day at the pretty house he had rented for Douglass at Esher, and saw it filled with spring flowers in preparation for their wedding, he knew a terrible doubt. And when Douglass told him that she was with child, a child that – ironically – he wanted but dared not own, he knew that he would not marry her after all. She could not threaten him now. One word of her illicit pregnancy and she would never be received at court again – and neither, he feared, would he. He told her – God forgive him the lie – that he had new hopes of the Queen, and that his first duty naturally must be to her. Douglass ranted at him and even screamed, but to no avail. He would support her and her child, he promised, and visit her when he could. She was weeping as copiously as Niobe when he left, and it was a long time before she rose miserably to her feet and laid away the beautiful cream satin wedding gown embroidered with gold forget-me-nots, thinking that she would never trust a man again.

1574

Robert had a son. Elizabeth was appalled to hear it. The mother
was that trollop Douglass Sheffield, whom she had rightly
guessed was no better than she should be. The child had been
christened with little fuss, but sufficient to warrant word of
the event being bruited around the court, and the Queen had
overheard Frances Howard prattling about it. They had even
had the effrontery to name the brat after Robert, proclaiming
his paternity to the world.

How *could* he have betrayed her so – and with such a one?
She spent many a sleepless night weeping into her pillow,
devising numerous ways of being revenged on them both. The
torturers in the Tower had nothing in their repertoire compared
to what Elizabeth was planning to do to Robert and his dirty
little whore. She was mortified to realise that their affair had
probably been going on last year, on her birthday even, when
Robert had come to her, all smiles and adoration, and presented
her with a gorgeous fan of white feathers with a handle of
gold engraved with his emblem, the bear, and hers, the lion
of England – entwined, if you please! And this when he was
actually entwined – and certainly not in the heraldic sense –
with another woman. What an empty conceit – and deceit, yea
– his gift had turned out to be! And now, she supposed, he was
celebrating the birth of his bastard.

Indeed he was. True to his word, he was maintaining the
establishment for Douglass at Esher, and visited her there
when he could get away from court, although his visits were
never tranquil. How could they be after he had jilted her? Even
so, he took delight in the lusty son she had borne him, but
bitterly regretted the fact that this fine boy, his namesake, was

of necessity baseborn, the child of his sin. For, great lord such as he was, it seemed a cruel irony that the only son he had sired could not inherit his lands and property. It was at times like these that he found himself filled with resentment against Elizabeth. Other men married at their pleasure. Why couldn't he? It wasn't as if she wanted to marry him herself!

But, if he was strictly honest with himself, he knew that his desire for a son had not been strong enough to spur him into risking all by marrying Douglass. His passion for her was dying an easy death, for she was neither his soul mate nor his intellectual equal, as – he must concede – Elizabeth undoubtedly was. And Douglass, who had once seemed to be invested with all that was becoming in a woman, was fast turning into a shrew. It shamed her that the world knew she was Leicester's cast-off leman, hidden away so that she should not offend the Queen, and that her son was a bastard. Her reputation was ruined.

'I shall go to the Queen and ask her to *make* you wed me,' she had threatened during one particularly heated quarrel. 'We shall ride her displeasure and then you will *have* to do the right thing by me and Robin!'

'You little fool!' Robert shouted. 'She'd have us both in the Tower, and then what would happen to our son?'

'She would not go so far. It is no crime to marry.'

'Do you understand nothing? When the Queen is jealous, she is vengeful. Remember what happened to Katherine Grey?' A poignant memory of a pale wet face came to mind; poor girl, she had died in captivity at just twenty-eight, still separated from the man she loved – a salutary example to anyone who was contemplating defying Elizabeth and marrying for love.

Douglass fell silent. She just stood there in her fine parlour, glaring balefully at him.

'So are you never going to make an honest woman of me, even for the sake of our child?'

'No.' He was adamant. He did not love Douglass, he did not particularly desire her any more, and their marriage would bring him ignominy rather than advantages. Nevertheless he hated himself for what he was about to do. He had thought about it with increasing frequency. 'We must part, and put an end to this charade. Let's not pretend that we are happy together. You want your freedom as much as I do. I will continue to make generous provision for our son, and cherish him as a father should. He will lack for nothing – and neither will you.'

He saw by her face that she would capitulate. Loving him – if that was the right word – had not brought her what she had hoped for, but money compensated for that, no doubt. It often did, he reflected.

'Very well,' she agreed. 'You need not fear that I will make a scene. I mean to get married, if any man will have me, and then you can take Robin into your household, as is fitting.'

'Then we are both well suited,' Robert declared. 'Come, let us drink to our bargain.' As he raised his goblet, he knew what he would do. He would make one final, extravagant, determined bid for Elizabeth's hand.

1575

It was a hot July day when Elizabeth arrived at Kenilworth. Robert had ridden out to meet her at Long Itchington, seven miles away, and entertained her there to a lavish dinner in a sumptuous pavilion he had had erected especially for the occasion. By the time they sat down to a table laden with meats and fowl with sauces of every description, he had ceased worrying about how much all this was costing him. It would be a worthwhile investment if everything went to plan.

In the afternoon he and Elizabeth enjoyed some good hunting before making their way to the castle. By then it was dusk, and a thousand torches flickered in the balmy evening air as the Queen, followed by a great procession of courtiers and attendants, rode up to the drawbridge. She saw that it had been decorated with cornucopias of fruit and vines, the symbols of earthly bounty; one cornucopia was hung with musical instruments, another with armour.

'They are here to show that all that I own proceeds from your Majesty, and that I would lay down my life for you,' Robert said, sitting tall and elegant in the saddle beside her. She noticed that he was filling out his pointed doublets these days, but he still cut a dash with his manly bearing and his dark gypsy's eyes. There really was no man to touch him, she thought, even now. She was very near to forgiving him.

She had never told him that she knew about his bastard son. The next she had heard, he had abandoned his trollop, and not before time too. His behaviour had not been honourable, but Elizabeth was no fool. She could easily guess why Robert had not married the mother of his child. He had something – or rather someone – far greater in his sights, and this was why he had invited her to stay at Kenilworth. She did not doubt that his lavish welcome was symbolic of something of much greater magnitude than mere entertainment.

The castle was surrounded by a vast lake on three sides, and as she approached the outer gatehouse Elizabeth saw rising from the water a magical island illuminated by torches, and upon it a silken-clad Lady of the Lake attended by nymphs. The Lady recited Kenilworth's history to the Queen, naming all its illustrious owners − many of them Elizabeth's own ancestors − before offering up the castle to her as a gift.

'I was under the impression that it was mine already,' she muttered under her breath.

There then followed much fussing and ceremony as players dressed as sibyls and porters presented the Queen with the keys to the castle, and trumpets heralded her arrival in the inner court. In front of her, majestic and beautiful, rose the enormous hall built by her great-, great- (she forgot how many greats) grandfather, John of Gaunt, Duke of Lancaster; to her right was the massive ancient keep; and to her left the magnificent new lodging built by Robert to receive her. He himself escorted her to the sumptuous chambers prepared with every thought for her comfort, then dismissed their attendants. They were alone for the first time in months. Beyond the great oriel windows fireworks were sparkling, fizzing and cracking in the velvety sky. The noise was deafening.

'We brought in an Italian skilled in pyrotechnics.' Robert, standing behind her, had to shout to be heard. 'Fortunately we were able to dissuade him from his plan to shoot cats and dogs into the air!'

She giggled at that, suddenly the young girl he had once known. Could they be lovers again? Would all that he had done here to show his devotion convince her that they really should marry?

'I have had a glorious garden planted for you,' he told her when the display was over. He was like a child, eager to show off its treasures and craving approval.

'I cannot see any garden from here,' she said.

'You will see it tomorrow,' he promised, looking a little crestfallen. 'It lies beyond the keep. I am sorry that you do not have a view of it.'

'No matter, dear Eyes,' Elizabeth said, moving to the opposite window. It overlooked the lake, and in the torchlight she could see at the edge of the water a fountain with statues of naked nymphs. They really were quite voluptuous – and they were directly under her window. Had that been deliberate? she wondered, feeling the first thrill of excitement she had experienced in what seemed like a very long time.

Robert came up behind her again and stood as close as he dared without actually touching her.

'They are very life-like, those statues,' he observed. 'What do you think of them?'

'They are very naughty,' Elizabeth chuckled, 'and would inflame any mind with too long looking!'

'As you have inflamed mine!' he declared. 'Their beauty – wondrous as it is – cannot compete with yours. It is the sun compared to the moon, and I am dazzled by it, mere mortal that I am.'

It was the kind of compliment she loved, especially as it came from Robert, for he had known her in former years when she had not looked for such extravagance, and lavish flattery had not been part of their accustomed love-play. Nevertheless he had said these words to please her, and he was clearly gratified to see her break into a smile.

'You wax lyrical tonight, Robin!'

'It is your nearness that makes me so bold.' He slid his arms around her slim waist. It was a long time since they had been so close. She did not resist, but neither did she react.

'I have missed our intimacy, Bess,' he murmured in her ear.

'You made up for it elsewhere, I hear,' she said, tart.

'A man cannot live by bread alone,' Robert said, pulling her closer to him. 'It was for lack of you that it happened. I am sorry if I hurt you.'

'I thought of making you sorrier!' Elizabeth taunted him, remembering those tortuous nights spent plotting revenge. 'Is all this an apology?' Her delicate hands indicated the luxurious room and the lake beyond the window.

'That – and, I hope, more,' he murmured. 'A new beginning, if it pleases you.'

'We shall see!' she smiled, extricating herself from his embrace. He was not getting off so lightly. She clapped her hands to summon her maids from the bedchamber.

Robert bowed. 'Then I bid you good night, my sweet Bess,' he said, satisfied. It had been a good start. He would win her around; he was practised in it, after all. As to his ultimate purpose, he trusted to the joy of their reunion to accomplish that.

As he left the great chamber, Robert surprised a young woman dozing on a chair outside the door. Her expensive silk gown proclaimed her to be one of the Queen's ladies-in-waiting, and when she looked up he recognised her at once. It was Lettice, the former Lady Hereford, now Countess of Essex, whom he had once pursued. She had been away from court for some months, running her absent husband's estates while he was busy subduing a rebellion in Ireland. Robert was struck anew by her beauty, which was even more powerful in maturity than it had been in youth. Her flame-red hair framed a perfect oval face from which sloe eyes looked out sleepily in the most seductive of expressions.

'My lord,' this vision said, rising languorously and smiling. 'This is an unexpected pleasure.'

'The pleasure is all mine,' he said, enchanted. Desire was still unsatisfied in him.

'Is the Queen abed?' Lettice asked.

'She will be soon. You do not need to attend her. Others are on duty.'

'Then I am free for the night after all.' It was more of an invitation than an observation.

He drew in his breath. 'Is your good lord here?'

'No,' she replied dismissively, 'he is at Chartley, making ready for her Majesty's visit. Afterwards he goes back to Ireland.' Essex had been much applauded for his firm rule in that wild land, but now, suddenly, to Robert, he seemed as great and troublesome an enemy as the rebel Irish were.

'Do you go with him?'

'No. I prefer to remain at Chartley.' She looked up at him with those strange slanting eyes in which he could see flecks of gold reflected from the torchlight. They drew him in. He bent and kissed her lightly on the lips. Then he left her, much to her bewilderment. He dared risk nothing that might compromise this last and most costly bid for Elizabeth's hand.

When Elizabeth woke and looked out of her window, she gasped in astonishment. Below, in the crook of the walls, there was an exquisite little garden, with stone vases full of flowers and new-scythed turf.

Robert had done this for her! He must have arrayed a small army of gardeners, who in turn must have worked silently through the night, for she had heard not a whisper. Her heart leapt.

'I thank you for the garden, dear Eyes,' she said, as he escorted her to the nearby parish church for Sunday service. 'It is a pretty conceit.'

'You know you have only to express a wish for something, and I will do all in my power to give it to you,' Robert assured her, nodding at the congregation, who were all craning their necks to see the Queen. Elizabeth smiled graciously at them before taking her seat in the front pew. Behind her, seated with the ladies-in-waiting, Lettice stole a sleepy look at Robert, and smiled.

After church, there was a lavish feast in old Gaunt's soaring great hall, with music to follow, and in the evening there was another firework display. The weather continued hot and sultry, and the next day it was so sweltering that Elizabeth begged leave to rest in her room. Only late in the afternoon did she emerge, demanding to go hunting, at which Robert leapt into action – as speedily as he had leapt out of Lettice's bed as soon as word came that the Queen was astir – and ordered horses to be saddled.

When they returned that evening, torches again lighting their way, a wild man sprang from the bushes, wearing a costume of moss green with leaves attached.

'I know that face,' Elizabeth said to Robert. 'I have seen the fellow at court.'

'George Gascoigne, the poet. He has assisted me with the entertainments.'

Gascoigne – the so-called wild man – recited some verses in company with his sidekick, Echo, then enthusiastically broke a branch over his bare knee to show that he was willing to be tamed and submit to the Queen's authority. The broken branch unfortunately ricocheted, causing Elizabeth's mount to rear in terror, almost throwing her, and there were gasps of dismay from the watching throng. An expert rider, she managed to stay in the saddle and calm the horse, and almost burst out laughing when she saw Robert's mortified face.

'No hurt! No hurt!' she cried, and everyone cheered, the terrified Gascoigne more enthusiastically than anyone else.

The programme over the next few days was packed with marvels. Robert had laid on more hunting, bear-baiting, masques, water pageants, breathtaking acrobatics, and spectacular fireworks over the lake. There were feasts, banquets and picnics. It was all designed to show Elizabeth how delightful her life would be if she wed him. He had even arranged for a rustic wedding to be celebrated in the castle courtyard, so that the Queen could share in the joys of her subjects and reflect on the bliss of the married state.

It did not quite have that effect. The bridegroom, in his tan jerkin, was limping; he had injured himself playing football, but that did not stop him from jesting bawdily with his sixteen groomsmen, who all subsided into awkward silence when they saw the Queen sitting on her flower-bedecked chair on the castle greensward, and made fools of themselves showing off at tossing the quintain, which made her laugh uproariously.

A troupe of Morris dancers then danced before her, after which her favourite spiced cakes were served, to which she helped herself amply, and the bride-cup was passed around, so that the guests could drink the health of the newly married pair. The high point of the proceedings was the arrival of the bride, an ugly wench long past her first youth, who stank a bit in her homely finery. Revelling in her moment of glory, she carried herself as if she were far superior in beauty to her bridesmaids, who were drawing lewd comments from the men.

The wedding party went off to the church for the nuptials, and when they returned, there was dancing before the Queen. Elizabeth nodded at Robert, and the two of them rose, linked hands and bade the minstrels strike up 'Sellenger's Round', to which they danced with gusto, everyone cheering them on and clapping. Elizabeth then went indoors to rest, while the company settled down in high good humour to watch a pageant performed on the grass by players from Coventry. When Robert looked up, there Elizabeth was, leaning out of her window, clearly enjoying the performance.

'Again!' she called down, when it had finished. 'Ask them to come back and repeat it.' And so he did.

The next day had been appointed for the climax of the entertainments, a masque written by George Gascoigne, on which Robert had outlaid a fortune. It was to be sumptuously presented and richly dressed, with ambitious, awe-inspiring scenery, and performed in a silken pavilion that had been set up in a suitably pastoral setting three miles from the castle.

The masque was loaded with meaning, having been devised to convey an unmistakable message. It told of one of his favourite themes, of two goddesses – Diana, the virgin huntress, and Juno, the goddess of marriage – and how each tried to persuade a nymph called Zabeta – there was no mistaking the near anagram of the Queen's name – to follow her example.

Inevitably, as Robert had instructed, it ended with Juno warning Zabeta that she should not heed Diana, but should follow her own example and pursue the delights of matrimony. As a finale, the lion of England was to be shown entwined with the bear of the Dudleys, so that none should be in doubt as to whom Zabeta was meant to share those delights with – or what they might be!

Unfortunately the gods were not disposed to smile upon this celestial contest. It rained that day and the masque – to Robert's desperation – had to be abandoned. That night he made his way to Elizabeth's apartments, determined to convey its message in person. She was leaving on the morrow, and so far he had not managed to pierce her defences or revive their former closeness. She had eluded him at every turn, and there had been many of them during the past fortnight. He was acutely aware that he was making a desperate gamble.

She had gone to bed, her women told him. She had a long journey the next day.

'Bid her sleep well,' he made himself say, his heart plummeting like a stone.

In despair he hastened to find Gascoigne, whom he came upon slumped on a bench in the courtyard, replete with good wine.

'Wake up, man!' Robert cried, shaking the fellow. 'I need you to do something for me.'

'W–what?' slurred the poet. 'Oh, my lord! Sorry, I was ashleep.'

'Never mind that,' Robert said. 'You're awake now. I want you to sluice cold water over your head and write me some verses.'

'Verses?' blinked Gascoigne. He was not even sure if he could determine whether it was night or day, let alone write verses. Holding the pen might be beyond him . . .

'Yes. I want you to adapt the poetry in the masque to something that can be read out to the Queen before her departure in the morning. Go to, hurry! Much depends on this.' Robert was almost dancing in agitation.

Gascoigne yawned. There was no accounting for the whims of the great. 'Yes, my lord. I will do it now.' He got up unsteadily and ambled off, remembering how impressed Lady Essex had been when he divulged to her – which he supposed he ought really not to have done – the plot of the masque.

'I have never known anything to equal the princely pleasures you have laid on for me, my lord,' Elizabeth declared, as Robert bowed low before her. This was goodbye, and he had only one card left to play. He knew that it was his last chance, and did not hold out much hope of success. He watched the Queen, shrouded against the downpour in a blue cloak embroidered with flowers, mount her palfrey, raise her gloved hand in fare-well, bend her hooded head against the rain and ride off at a stately pace for Chartley; then he gave Gascoigne a nod.

Elizabeth started as an apparition dressed in golden leaves emerged from a clump of trees at the far end of the drawbridge, announced himself as Sylvanus, the god of woodlands, and began declaiming his verses, improvising to describe the heavy rain as the tears of the gods at Elizabeth's departure, and begging her in appalling, hastily cobbled doggerel to stay. She pulled up her horse out of courtesy, hoping that this would be short, but the apparition cried that she had no need, as he would run with her for twenty miles to complete his tale. Then he resumed his recital. When she heard the name Juno – thank God Lettice had warned her – she decided to take him at his word, and dug in her spurs. His rain-soaked leaves weighing him down, the god Sylvanus hastened after her as best he could, capering beside her mount and reciting his verses faster and faster until he was running and spouting them between harsh breaths, but very quickly the Queen outpaced him, and he realised that he could not keep to his boast for one mile, let alone twenty. He watched, crestfallen and panting, as his quarry disappeared into the distance, thankfully out of earshot. His voice halted, dwindled and died.

As soon as he saw Gascoigne's face, Robert knew that his

hopes were buried in the mud, along with all the burnt-out fireworks and gaudy rubbish that his servants were clearing up. Everyone was congratulating him and telling him how successful her Majesty's visit had been, but for him it had proved an abject failure. Such an opportunity might never come again. All that outlay . . . He doubted that his finances would ever recover. It was galling to have been defeated by, of all things, the weather!

He put on a brave face. He saw his steward, to give instructions for the re-ordering of Kenilworth, then took horse, as arranged, to rejoin the progress at Chartley, where Lettice, thank God, would be waiting for him . . .

The Earl of Essex was dead, struck down in Dublin Castle by an attack of dysentery. Even on his deathbed he had had his revenge on the wife he believed faithless, and sent a dying request to the Queen that *she* would be as a mother to his children, which was a slap in the face for Lettice. It was not unusual for the heirs to earldoms to be made royal wards, and Elizabeth readily acceded to Essex's plea, granting the wardship of his young son Robert to Lord Burghley.

Soon it was being whispered that, *in extremis*, Essex had not asked for his wife. Rumour had it that he had heard scurrilous talk about her and the Earl of Leicester. Certainly there was bad blood between Essex and Leicester, and no wonder! For a knight to seduce the wife of another knight was a grave breach of chivalry, and it was no doubt on account of this betrayal that Essex had altered his will to prevent Lettice having the care of their children. As for Leicester, had Essex lived, they would surely have become violent enemies, for it was said that they had quarrelled savagely not two months before Essex's death. It was even being whispered that Essex had believed himself to have been poisoned with some evil in his drink. Well, it was not far to see who might have been responsible for that!

Elizabeth did not hear the rumours. She was too heavily preoccupied with state affairs, maintaining the ever-delicate balance of power between France and Spain, and keeping up the pretence that she was hankering to marry the Duke of Alençon. Robert was pressing her to let him go and fight with the Dutch rebels who had united under a new leader, William of Orange, against the occupying Spanish, but she would not hear of it. It was too costly a venture, and she feared to provoke King Philip too far.

'I marvel that you should suggest it,' she said to Robert. 'You have not fought a campaign for — what is it? — twenty-five years. And look at you, old man! Look at your red face and portly belly. Soft living has done for you.'

Robert winced, bitterly disappointed. Elizabeth could be cruel when it pleased her. Yes, he felt himself slowing down, but he was still able to please a lady, and he knew he had the skills to command an army. He longed to show his mettle in the field once more, all the more so as the champion of the Protestant faith. He stayed silent, however, not wishing to provoke any more nasty remarks. God, Elizabeth had a barbed tongue! He felt a great melancholy wash over him.

Maybe, he reflected as the months went by, she had been right. His health was not what it was, and it seemed that his strength was gradually sapping away. The feeling had crept up on him, barely perceptible at first, and then inexorable.

'You should get yourself cured!' Elizabeth pronounced. Her brisk manner did not quite conceal her concern.

'Aye, Bess. I am going to Buxton to take the waters.'

'You need to lose weight,' she commanded, brutally candid as ever. 'Look at me: I am as I was when I became queen. My coronation gown still fits me.'

'Your Majesty is blessed with the gift of eternal youth,' he replied, resolutely ignoring the horrible red wig, the white make-up and the lines it could not conceal.

'That is because I eat sparingly,' she retorted. 'They offer me twenty dishes at every meal, but I take only five, and they are usually chicken or game. I have seen you guzzling at table, Robin. The remedy is in your own hands!'

He bore her reprimand patiently, forbearing to mention the many cakes and sweetmeats she consumed, which ruined her teeth even if they did not ruin her figure; she was right, he knew, and she did have his interests at heart. In June he travelled north in slow stages, wishing he felt better. While staying as a guest of the Earl and Countess of Shrewsbury at Chatsworth he received a letter from Elizabeth in which she mischievously prescribed him a diet of two ounces of meat a day and a twentieth of a pint of wine, adding that on feast days he might have also the shoulder of a wren at dinner and a leg of wren at supper. It made him smile; in fact it was a tonic to him.

During his visit the redoubtable Lady Shrewsbury presented to him her husband's charge, the Queen of Scots, and so he found himself for the first time face to face with the notorious Mary, the author of so much havoc. He saw before him a tall, large-boned woman, dressed in black, with wiry brown hair, dark eyes, a long face and an uneven nose. No beauty, he thought, and wondered why men thought her so, and why she inspired such devotion among Elizabeth's enemies. She held no charisma for him, although he knew that Elizabeth was desperately curious about her and would pump him for information – and to see if she had cause for jealousy – on his return.

Mary was pleasant enough; he admired her exquisite embroideries, and found himself thinking that she had a pretty lilt to her voice, although he grew weary of hearing it raised plaintively in complaint about her continuing confinement. He tried to show himself sympathetic without being overly so, or committing himself in any way, but he was relieved when she said she was tired and their meeting ended.

Burghley, reading Robert's account of the interview back at Whitehall, was intrigued.

'I should like to meet her myself,' he declared.

Elizabeth snorted. 'No, my envious Spirit!' she chided. 'I have heard too often how her beauty and wiles can make the wisest men act foolishly.'

'But Madam—'

'No, William!' she repeated, and then collapsed into giggles. Imagine her stately, morally upright Lord Treasurer being seduced by the Queen of Scots!

1578

Elizabeth and her ministers were dismayed to hear that King Philip was building an *armada*, a great fleet of ships, especially when her spies informed her that this was in readiness for what was being called 'the Enterprise of England'.

Since her excommunication by the Pope, she had anticipated a war with Spain, and it now seemed that she was surrounded by enemies, with her only hope of friendship vested in an unstable France. It did not help that Alva's great Spanish army was lurking just across the Channel in the Netherlands, which made her very jittery; nor was she pleased to hear that the former Duke of Alençon – who had been created Duke of Anjou on the accession of his brother, Henri III, to the French throne – had taken it upon himself to interfere in the affairs of the Dutch.

'He is acting without the backing of the French government, Madam,' Burghley informed her.

'That's one mercy, but he could easily upset the situation in the Netherlands,' Elizabeth said, frowning. 'I think a distraction is called for. We must revive the marriage negotiations.'

Her councillors stared at her. She was nearly forty-five, and highly unlikely to bear children now, yet still she was the greatest matrimonial prize in Europe, and still she behaved as if she really was the goddess of beauty, as the poets called her. They wondered how Anjou, a young man twenty-two years her junior, would react to new overtures from England and the reality of marriage to this ageing Hebe, a goddess of youth with an ambrosial cup well past its best.

To their surprise he pre-empted them, for what he lacked in height he more than made up for in ambition, and the crown of England was a compelling lure, especially now that fame and glory in the Netherlands were eluding him. With the backing of Elizabeth, he might yet emerge victorious and win the renown he so craved. No sooner had the matter been debated in council, it seemed, than Anjou had dashed off a letter to the Queen, assuring her of his entire devotion and his willingness to be guided by her in all his doings. He professed to be astonished that, after two years of silence, he should wake up to the wonder of her existence, and pleaded most touchingly with her to revive their courtship.

And so it begins again, Elizabeth mused, smiling as she read his ingratiating missive. She felt rejuvenated to be playing the old marriage game once more. It proved that she was not so long in the tooth as some might think. In high good humour she ordered three new gowns with very low necklines – and let Robert dare say a word about that! – and six ropes of fine pearls.

But now there was Walsingham, recalled from France to be principal secretary, frowning and muttering about Anjou deceiving her.

'He is like all his race, Madam, devious and corrupt. Think who his mother is! He means to cozen you, so that when he marches at the head of an army into the Netherlands, you will not raise a squeak in protest.'

Elizabeth was furious. Squeaking was the least of it. 'God's death!' she exploded. Pointedly ignoring Walsingham, she turned to Robert. 'My lord of Leicester, please inform Mr Secretary that it is not in the least surprising that the Duke should have fallen in love with me. He is only going to the Netherlands to give himself better means to step over hither.'

'You heard that, Francis,' Robert said, trying not to laugh.

Elizabeth was walking in the gardens of Whitehall with Mendoza, the Spanish ambassador, assuring him, convincingly she thought, that she was the friend of Spain, and that she was deeply sympathetic towards the plight of the Queen of Scots, whom Philip had naturally championed – well, short of invading England and rescuing her. They were just returning to the palace when a piece of paper came fluttering through the privy door to the garden, as though someone unseen had deliberately thrown it at the Queen's approach.

Elizabeth froze. She lived in fear of being attacked or assassinated, and she knew that there were many subtle means of killing someone. She had heard tales that the Borgias used poisoned gloves or letters to get rid of an enemy, who had then died an agonising death as the venom seeped into the skin . . .

Before she could stop him, Mendoza swooped to pick up the paper, which turned out to be a letter bearing the Earl of Leicester's seal. He handed it to her with a bow, and she summarily dismissed him, puzzled. Why would Robin send a letter in this manner? He was at Leicester House, and not well at all, she knew. Oh God, was he dying? Was this an urgent summons?

With trembling fingers she broke the seal and opened the letter. Yes, it was his writing. *Forgive my sending to you like this,* he had written, *but I know not how to break this news to you otherwise. You know, none better, that I am in failing health, and that it is therefore a matter of urgency that I look to the future and get myself an heir. I crave your pardon, but the truth is that I have married Lady Essex, who is with child by me.*

It was the cruellest blow, and it came as an utter shock. She could not believe it. After all these years, and all the love between them, to forsake her, the Queen, if you please, for that hussy – and to *marry* her! It was the most unforgivable betrayal. And to write such news in a letter – it was the act of a coward. A true man would have come and told her face to face, and explained his treachery. But now he was asking to see her, begging her to visit him, as he was in his sickbed – his *marriage* bed, more like! Oh, she knew her Eyes of old: he knew how illness won her sympathy. Well, he should not have it this time. He would never have it again. She would have them both in the Tower. *With child!* How *could* he?

How she made it up the stair to her rooms she did not know. Once there, she dismissed her ladies and paced up and down, rereading the letter, scarce knowing what she was doing. It was hard to take in, that she had lost him to another. She still could not believe it. Did he not know how much she had loved him, and still did love him, God help her? As for that bitch Lettice, she wanted to claw her eyes out and mar that perfect beauty, so that Robert would never have any more pleasure in her. That conjured up the thought of them lying together, sharing that pleasure, which made her cry out in agony. Weeping torrents, she sank to the floor, beating her breast.

It was an hour before she managed to compose herself. By then the white heat of her anger had cooled a little, but she was still spitting fire at the enormity of what Robin had done, and she would tell him so, yes, she would go *right now* and do that, and let him know how deeply he had hurt and displeased her, and that nothing would be the same again, ever.

She pulled on her cloak, taking care to draw its voluminous hood down over her ravaged, reddened eyes. Then she hastened down the stair and out through the gardens to the private landing stage. Here she commandeered her barge and had herself rowed to Leicester House on the Strand, where she alighted at the jetty. Ahead stood the large, imposing mansion that Robert had recently built for himself, complete with an Italianate *campanile* – and all by royal favour, the ungrateful traitor. No doubt he had built it for *her*, Elizabeth thought viciously as she made her solitary way up the path through the lawns.

She had been seen. His servants came running, and when they saw who it was, come alone to see the master, they gaped and subsided into hasty bows. Then they escorted her indoors and led her up the massive oak staircase to the great chamber. And there was Robert, regarding her as a mouse looks when cornered by a particularly menacing cat, before remembering to make an elegant obeisance. Of *that woman* there was no sign.

As soon as the door had closed and they were alone, Elizabeth sprinted across the room in three strides and slapped Robert across the face. '*How could you?* she cried, all her pent-up anguish bursting forth.

Clapping his hand to his inflamed cheek, he looked at her, stupefied. 'Because there was no hope for us,' he said sadly. 'These twenty years I have loved you, Bess, and cherished the constant hope that you would do me the honour of becoming my wife. But you made it plain, again and again, that you did not want me, and that your fears of marriage were such that you hated to contemplate it.' His tone grew more urgent. 'Bess, I have given up my youth and my prime waiting for you, and you, in turn, have seen fit to reward my humble service amply.' He waved his hand to encompass the richly appointed room. 'But a man needs a wife in his bed and he needs an heir – and those things you could not give me. I do not blame you, but I think you now owe it to me to let me snatch some happiness while I can, for I am not as young as I was.'

'I thought you loved me,' Elizabeth said, tears starting from her eyes at hearing him confirm in words that he was lost to her.

'And so I do!' Robert protested. 'My marriage has not diminished my love for you. But you and I know that for years we have been more like brother and sister than lovers. You know too that I will always be utterly devoted to you.'

Elizabeth could not answer. She was too distressed. She was remembering all the times he had begged and importuned her to marry him, and all the times she had refused, or kept him waiting for one of her answers answerless. Regret and remorse flooded her heart. If only the clock could be put back . . . And yet, if she had it all to do again, would she do it differently? Would not her answer be the same? She was not like other women; she was a damaged thing, and she was the Queen. And remembering that, she knew she must retrieve her composure before she made a fool of herself. This man before her was a subject; he had merely married a wife, as noblemen did. It was no crime, and nothing to get worked up about. She should bravely have smiled her approval and retained her pride. Well, she would play her part properly now. Besides, it was late; the sky was growing dark, and she had to get back to Whitehall.

'Nothing has changed,' Robert said, looking at her with great compassion. She bridled. She did not want his sympathy, not when he was about to bed his trollop – his pregnant trollop. No doubt *that* had been the reason for this furtive marriage.

She glared at him. 'No, nothing has changed, my lord. You will attend me at court as before. Where is your – wife?' She had not wanted to say the word, lest it make what had happened more true.

'She is at Wanstead,' Robert said.

'Wanstead?'

'Aye, I have bought Wanstead Hall from Lord Rich.' It was a former royal residence, and very fine, as she recalled. Elizabeth hated to think of *that woman*, her victorious rival – and all the more deadly for securing her victory in secret – living in such state. Well, the battle might be won, but the war was by no means over!

'That is as well for her, then,' she said. 'You may tell her that she has incurred my severe displeasure, since she has married without my permission, which, as the widow of an earl, she was bound to seek. You can tell her also that she will not be welcome at court again.'

Robert opened his mouth to protest, but quickly closed it. If he was hoping that she would change her mind when she had had time to calm down and reflect, he had best think again!

'I understand why you feel as you do,' he said, holding out his hands to her. She ignored them.

'You understand nothing!' she snapped. 'I shall look for you at court when you are *recovered*.' She laid heavy emphasis on the last word, hoping to shame him for lying to her. 'I bid you good evening, my lord.' And she left without a backward glance.

When she got back to Whitehall, she sent a message of

apology to Mendoza, telling him that she could not see him to resume their conversation because she was unwell. Then she crawled into bed and gave herself up to grief.

The next day, in council, Elizabeth ordered that an envoy be sent immediately to France to reopen negotiations for her marriage to the Duke of Anjou. Robert was not present. He had sent a message begging to be excused, saying that his illness obliged him to travel north to Buxton again to take the waters. Elizabeth thought it was more likely that he had gone to Wanstead to be with *that woman*. She had never felt such hatred towards one of her sex – not even the Queen of Scots – as she now felt for that viper Lettice.

'You should know, gentlemen, that my lord of Leicester has married Lady Essex,' she announced, her face a mask of disapproval. Twenty faces turned to stare at her.

'He had your permission, Madam?' Burghley asked gently.

'Yes, of course,' Elizabeth lied. No one should know how he had deceived and hurt her.

Robert stayed away for two months. Probably, she reasoned, he was giving her time to acclimatise herself to the situation. More likely he was enjoying his honeymoon, the bastard. But old habits died hard – or not at all. Despite herself, she worried that he really was ill, and that the waters were not proving of any benefit. Then she would torture herself with thoughts of him romping in bed with *that woman* at Wanstead, as he had romped with her in happier times, only going further . . . *all the way, with no one to say nay to him.* She bit her lip. She could not bear to think of it.

Hatton saw how miserable she was and attempted to cheer her by flirting outrageously. As he steered her into the dance one evening, he murmured in her ear, 'There is only one woman that *I* would ever marry, and it is yourself, fair Eliza.'

'You are very presumptuous, my Lids,' she chided him, trying to smile all the same.

'You know you have my undying adoration,' Hatton vowed,

his dark eyes full of intent. 'To serve you is Heaven; to lack you is more than Hell's torment.'

Such devotion! Suddenly tears filled Elizabeth's eyes and she gripped his hand tightly. 'I could not bear it if you ever betrayed me as my lord of Leicester has by marrying someone else, especially as he too swore undying loyalty to me.'

'Is that the reason for this great and continual melancholy?' Hatton drew her into a window embrasure to give them a little privacy and allow her time to compose herself. 'Great Queen, marry me, and learn what true devotion is! I swear I will make you happy again. I worship at your feet! Let me worship at the altar of Hymen!'

'Christopher, I do not want to marry!' Elizabeth burst out, punching him in the ribs. 'Marriage can only be injurious to me, and you, dear Lids, are like the rest. You want me for my crown.'

Hatton was taken aback by such brutal candour. 'I protest, Madam, that my love for you overrides all else. It is unnatural for a man not to marry, and indeed it is against the law of God. Were you to have me, I would be the happiest soul alive!'

'Alas, faithful Lids,' she said, smiling weakly, 'I am done with men.'

She perked up considerably whenever letters arrived from Robert. She had missed him unbearably during his absence, and deeply regretted their quarrel. So what if he had married? *That woman* was never coming to court, so he was right – nothing need change. She would have as much of him as before, and more, if she had anything to do with it. She would keep him at her side for as long as it pleased her, and be damned to *that other*, whom she refused to name, even to herself.

'Write and tell him,' she commanded Hatton, 'that his absence has been too long-drawn-out. I would that he does as his physician says, but if the waters of Buxton do not cure him now, he is not to encumber himself and me with such long journeys in the future.' That should re-establish who was in command, and what was expected of Robert. It was his Queen's wishes that counted, not his wife's. And it should be clear to him that he was to behave towards her as if nothing had changed. That way she could permit him to remain her favourite, as before. She doubted that the pain of his betrayal would ever go away, but this way it was manageable – and she might even find that, one day, she could forgive him. For now, however, she would make life difficult for him, and give him cause to rue his ill-considered marriage.

Her bad mood persisted. She snapped and grouched at her councillors all that summer, and lashed out in temper at her hapless maids. Everyone knew why, and that did not improve her humour, because she liked to be seen as being in command of herself. Robert, back at court and finding it virtually impossible to obtain leave to go home and support Lettice through a difficult pregnancy, felt as if he was treading on eggshells. He had made a decision never to mention his marriage in Elizabeth's hearing, but still it lay between them like a dividing sword. Gone was the intimacy of their past friendship; rarely now did they share jokes or correspond when apart, unless it was on official business. Instead Elizabeth found herself losing her temper over silly things, berating Robert with her sharp tongue, and waxing obstinate when he came asking for favours.

It did not help that she was suffering from excruciating toothache, the result of eating too many sweet delicacies. Her poor face was inflamed, and she would sit in council rocking with the pain, biting on a clove and pressing a hot, damp cloth to her cheek. Often she would not attend meetings at all, which sometimes brought the business of the realm to a standstill.

Her councillors clucked soothingly, but they had a kingdom to run and some matters were pressing.

'Madam, about the French marriage . . .' Walsingham began.

'Not now!' Elizabeth rapped.

'Then maybe we should discuss our shipbuilding programme,' Burghley said quickly. 'Philip's fleet grows by the day.'

'The marriage is the more pressing matter,' Walsingham persisted. 'It could be years before the *armada* is ready to sail.'

'Did you hear what I said?' Elizabeth screeched, bending down swift as quicksilver and throwing her pointed slipper at him. 'By God, you wearisome Moor, you deserve to be hanged for your impertinence!'

Walsingham had ducked and escaped injury. He straightened himself and regarded her evenly. 'Then, Madam, I ask only that I be tried by a Middlesex jury. They are notoriously lenient these days.'

Even Elizabeth, in agony as she was, had to smile at that. But the pain persisted, preventing her from sleeping. Finding her moaning in misery in her privy chamber, Robert – who had come in response to a peremptory summons to discuss the threat from the Netherlands – knelt beside her, as of old, and soothed her, rubbing her angry-looking cheek and fetching more cloves and wet compresses.

'Bess,' he said, reverting without thinking to his familiar name for her, 'you will have to have this tooth pulled. You have been suffering for months.'

'Yes, I *have* been suffering for months,' she retorted. She was not talking about toothache.

Resolutely he ignored that. 'It must be taken out,' he repeated. 'Shall I send for the barber-surgeon?'

'No!' she cried.

'Bess, it will be over in seconds, and that is surely much better than the terrible pain you are experiencing.'

'No!' she repeated. 'I do not want to lose my teeth. King Philip has had most of his out, I hear, and now he has to live on slops!'

He let it rest there. He stayed with her through the night, trying to distract her by reading to her and comforting her when the pangs became too hard to bear. It seemed, miraculously, that they had slipped effortlessly into their former companionship, and he was glad of that, although his thoughts kept straying to Lettice at Wanstead. He missed her so much, and he was tired, unutterably tired, and craving his bed. But he was so deeply relieved to be restored to a better footing with Elizabeth that he was happy to put up with that.

In the morning, groggy from lack of sleep, he left Elizabeth slumbering at last. As he passed out of her apartments he met the Bishop of London, come to take morning service in the Chapel Royal. He liked Bishop Aylmer, a stout Protestant like himself, and mentioned that the Queen was unwell and might not be able to attend.

'What ails her Majesty?' the Bishop asked, all concern.

'Toothache,' Robert told him. 'She has had it for months, but will not suffer the tooth to be pulled.'

'I sympathise,' Aylmer said. 'I too have been suffering. Hmm. Listen, I have a suggestion.'

That afternoon, as Elizabeth sat listlessly cradling her cheek in her presence chamber, where her musicians were doing their best to distract her with the sublime melodies of Phalèse and Mainerio, and her courtiers were standing around impatiently waiting for her to rouse herself and notice them, Bishop Aylmer was announced.

'You are welcome, Bishop,' she said, rousing herself. 'My lord of Leicester informed me of your coming.' Leicester and Aylmer exchanged complicit glances.

'Your Majesty, I come to express my sympathy for the trouble with your tooth,' the Bishop began. Elizabeth looked at him wrathfully. 'I too have toothache,' he persevered, 'and I am told that your Majesty fears to have your tooth extracted. Well, fear not. I have brought with me a barber-surgeon, who has agreed to take out my tooth in your Majesty's presence, so that you may see that there is nothing dreadful about it.'

'He is a brave man,' Robert murmured to Sussex.

'Rather him than me,' Sussex muttered. 'I'm not sure what I'd fear more – her Majesty's countenance, or the pincers!'

Elizabeth was biting her lip and frowning. 'Very well, Bishop,' she said at length. 'Show me.'

The waiting barber-surgeon was fetched from the ante-chamber, and a chair was set on the floor. The barber-surgeon placed a cushion over its back, and the Bishop laid his head on it and opened his mouth wide. As Elizabeth looked on with morbid fascination, the barber-surgeon produced an alarmingly large pair of iron pliers, which he used to grip the offending molar. There was an excruciating crack, and the Bishop's hands tightened on the arms of the chair, but not a sound did he make, even though the surgeon had to use some force to pull out the tooth before holding it aloft in triumph. His patient stood up rather shakily, wiped the blood from his mouth, and bowed to the Queen.

'And now, Madam, will you let this fellow take out your own tooth?' Robert asked.

Elizabeth was about to refuse, but a vicious shaft of pain made her change her mind.

'We will,' she capitulated, and signalled to her ladies to follow with the barber-surgeon into her privy chamber, where the operation was finally performed with very little fuss.

The tooth had gone, but the bad mood persisted. Even the best efforts of Ippolita the Tartarian and her fellow fools could not rouse Elizabeth, nor could the little black boy whom she kept in her privy chamber, dressed in wide breeches and a jacket of black taffeta and gold tinsel; he tried capering about in his usual comic fashion, and juggling balls in the air, but she regarded him listlessly.

She had no excuse now to refuse to see her councillors, but when next she took her seat at the head of the board it was to find that they had united against her.

'Madam, you must act to prevent the Duke of Anjou from leading a French army into the Netherlands,' Burghley insisted. 'I urge you to marry him now. We are of one mind on this.'

Robert took it upon himself to speak for them all, as he did increasingly these days. 'Your Majesty cannot afford any delays,' he said bluntly. 'I speak as a faithful and true subject when I say that there must be no dithering, no procrastination and no stalling. This marriage must go ahead. Our very security depends on it.'

'Be silent,' Elizabeth snapped, furious at his presuming to tell her what she must and must not do. As for faithful and true subject . . . he was one to talk!

'My lord of Leicester speaks truth,' Hatton ventured, only to have the Queen turn her head away. The meeting ended in stalemate.

Robert tried a new tactic – or rather, redeployed an old one. He went home to Leicester House and took to his bed, feigning sickness. It was a ploy that had worked before, and he was confident that it would bring Elizabeth hastening to his side. But she stayed stubbornly away, and when he finally got bored of waiting and returned to court, her manner towards him was chilly.

In August, still brooding on her councillors' shortcomings, she departed on a progress to the eastern shires. It was when she was in Norwich Cathedral, being shown the shields of her Boleyn ancestors high above the chancel, that news was brought to her that Anjou had not only invaded the Netherlands but had accepted an invitation to become governor of the Protestant states and defender of their liberties against what was termed the 'Spanish Tyranny'.

She simmered all through the dinner that had been laid on in the cloisters, and when she got back to the Bishop's palace, she exploded in rage.

'*You* allowed this to happen!' she shouted at her councillors.

'Madam, we have been begging you to take some action!' Robert protested.

'It was not *I* who did nothing to prevent what has happened!' she flung back. 'Now I shall have to placate Spain. I will write a message of support to King Philip. In the meantime, send word covertly to Anjou that we would speak with him of marriage.'

Her councillors released a collective sigh of relief.

*

The progress was a great success. Wherever Elizabeth went, she drew the hearts of the people after her. She had the common touch that came so easily to her family. Fêted, complimented and adored, she returned to London in a much better frame of mind.

Robert, however, did not enjoy a peaceful homecoming. There was Lettice, radiantly beautiful, her stomacher unlaced to accommodate her great belly, screeching yet again that she had been grossly slighted.

'I am the Countess of Leicester!' she declared. 'I will not be hidden away as if I have done something wrong. My father is not at all happy at the way I have been treated. He wants a public wedding, to make all things secure.'

'The Queen cannot break our marriage,' Robert said.

'I would not put it past her to try.' His wife was beside herself. 'Remember Katherine Grey! That is why my father is adamant that there must be a second ceremony, with all my kin present.'

'Listen, sweetheart,' Robert soothed, 'even Elizabeth cannot overturn a lawful marriage.'

'You think not? She has done it before. And she will not receive me, proof enough that she does not recognise me as your wife!'

'Did you expect her to receive you?' His patience was a little frayed now. 'In her eyes, you displaced her. Give her time. She may yet thaw towards you. You must stay calm and think of the child. Once it is born, things may well be different.' He doubted it, but he hated to see Lettice so distressed, and was prepared to say anything to calm her and have a quieter life. Was ever man so beset by two women? It was like living between Scylla and Charybdis!

'You don't help,' Lettice sniffed.

'I?' Robert was startled. 'What have I done?'

'You are seeing Douglass Sheffield and your bastard. Don't think I don't know.'

'It's true,' Robert admitted. 'Of course I have seen her. She is bringing up my son, whom I love. You would not deny my right to be a father to him, surely?'

'I have no quarrel with you seeing your son. For your sake, I would welcome him into our household and be as a mother to him. But I do not want you to see Lady Sheffield again.'

Robert knew that he had to put Lettice first in regard to his seeing Douglass, even if she was behaving increasingly unreasonably these days. He did not want her upsetting herself at this time; a happy outcome to her pregnancy was important to them both. He was forty-six, after all, and needed an heir. His heart had leapt when she suggested bringing his son to live with them. Of course, it was the ideal arrangement – and it showed how generous-hearted his dear wife was, and how much she loved him even to think of doing this for him. Only a very special woman would suggest raising her husband's bastard as her own.

'Are you very sure about my bringing Robin here?' he asked her, hoping he had heard aright. 'As a peer of the realm, I am within my rights to demand custody of my son, and nothing would please me more than to have young Robin live here with us. Then I would have no need to see Lady Sheffield again, and can break off all contact with her.'

'I meant it, my love,' Lettice replied, brightening and holding out her arms to him, and he went into them, profoundly grateful to her for providing a resolution to a situation that had been troubling him for some time. More than that, he could never resist her.

Lettice agreed that Robert should meet with Douglass one last time to make all plain to her. At his summons, Douglass came up to Greenwich Palace with young Robin, and he met her at the great gatehouse in the company of two of his servants, whom he had asked to act as witnesses.

Douglass noticed that Robert did not kiss her after she alighted from her barge, although he hugged young Robin warmly, but she suffered him to lead her a little way through the gardens to a bench painted with the royal arms. There she sat, increasingly dismayed, as he revealed the purpose of their meeting.

'I am releasing you from all obligations to me and the boy,' he said. 'I am offering you an annuity of seven hundred pounds, and in return I want you to surrender custody of our son to me.'

It was more or less what Douglass herself had envisaged happening one day, but even so she burst into tears. 'No,' she said.

'I can give our son every advantage,' Robert explained. 'And you did say that you would send him to me.'

'No!' Douglass repeated. 'He is my son too!'

'You have no right to him!' Robert shouted, losing his temper. Poor Robin was looking from one parent to the other, bewildered and about to cry.

'It was understood between us that I should take him at some stage,' Robert said, curbing his anger, and lifted the boy firmly on to his knee, as if he were taking possession of him. 'Do you want to come and live with me, Robin? I will raise you as a gentleman and you shall have many pretty toys and fine sports.'

'Yes, Sir,' Robin piped uncertainly. He knew that his father was a great and powerful man, and feared him a little; he also loved him, more than he loved his mother, for to his young mind Robert represented adventure and excitement.

Seeing them together, Douglass knew that her cause was lost.

'Very well, he is yours,' she said. 'But on one condition. You will help me to find a husband. It is no easy thing for me to do.'

Robert was ready to promise much in return for his son. 'It will be easier now that you are unencumbered, and have a greater fortune. I will help, I promise.' Already he had in mind the widowed Sir Edward Stafford, whose wife, Rosetta Robsart, had been a relation of Amy's.

'I pray you will, and I hope that I may see Robin from time to time,' Douglass said, looking sorrowfully at the boy.

'That can be arranged,' Robert told her, knowing that it probably would not be. He felt a pang at depriving the boy of his mother, but Robin would soon be of an age to be taken from the care of women and handed over to tutors, and in the meantime Lettice would play a mother's part. The child belonged with his father, who could give him the best start in life.

'Thank you,' Douglass said, her tone cool. 'And when will I get my annuity?'

'The first instalment is here.' Robert handed her a bag of gold coins. 'From next month it will be delivered to you by messenger. Now . . .' He stood up and took young Robin by the hand. 'Say goodbye to your lady mother.'

'Goodbye, Mamma,' the little voice piped up uncertainly. Douglass swooped on him and hugged him as if she would never let him go, covering his face with kisses. Then abruptly she put him from her, stood up and walked away, so that neither father nor son should see the tears streaming down her cheeks.

Robin soon settled happily at Leicester House, with Robert spoiling him and Lettice lavishing her frustrated maternal instincts on him. She missed her children by Essex, especially Robert, the eldest boy, a bright, lively lad whose spirited character outmatched her own. She often wondered how they were faring without her in Burghley's care. But here was little Robin, and because she feared that her own children would be pining for their mother, she was especially kind to him. She would sit for ages playing with the boy, or cuddling him to her as she rested on her bed, reading to him. As her pregnancy advanced she came to know a deep contentment.

She was overjoyed when Robert told her that they were to be married again in a public ceremony that would please her and satisfy her father. Robert had no wish to alienate Sir Francis Knollys, a true Protestant like himself, and a good man, and he was gratified when the Knollys family turned out in force for the wedding at Wanstead, along with his own brother,

Ambrose, and the Earl of Pembroke. It was a very merry occasion, and Robert knew that Elizabeth would have apoplexy if she could see them all toasting himself and Lettice and celebrating their union with a lavish feast.

Just two days later – as if by design (which indeed it was) – Elizabeth and her court descended on Wanstead on their way back to London after the summer progress. Robert had been given abrupt (and not nearly enough) notice of the Queen's coming and suspected that her visit was meant to be a test. Reluctantly, and speedily, he had packed off a furious Lettice, with Robin, to Leicester House, and ordered all evidence of the wedding to be cleared away. Then he set his mind to entertaining Elizabeth with his usual lavishness. He even commissioned a pastoral masque from his talented nephew, Sir Philip Sidney, in her honour, and Sidney worked through the night to finish it, as did an army of seamstresses stitching the costumes.

'It is called "The Lady in May",' Robert told the Queen, as he showed her to the great chair that had been set in front of the stage. 'It is about a lady who is being courted by rival lovers and must choose between them.'

Elizabeth's eyes twinkled wickedly. 'I seem to have heard that somewhere before, my lord!' she smiled.

There was a reason for her good humour. For weeks now she had been exchanging love letters with the Duke of Anjou, and his extravagant compliments and promises of undying devotion had revived her flagging spirits. No longer did she feel rejected and old. She thought she might even grasp the sow by the ear and finally marry. She was forty-five years old, and knew that in all probability this really would be her last chance. The marriage would bring peace between England and France; it would allow her to do more for the Huguenots; and it would show Robert that she was not pining for him.

Strong Protestant that he was – and not a little jealous, she hoped – he hated the idea of this union. The other councillors were in favour, however, and Burghley was so delighted at the prospect that he had turned romantic and was singing the praises of matrimony – and Anjou – at every turn. (Elizabeth wondered what his erudite wife, the stern-faced Mildred, made of this new Cecil, who suddenly seemed to have developed a talent for poetic turns of phrase, particularly in respect of the hymeneal couch and the pleasures that Psyche found with Cupid.) She could afford to ignore Robert's protests – which, of course, he had *no right* to make – and anyway he owed her this marriage, since he had forsaken her for *that woman*.

That woman, even as the Queen fumed, was brought to bed. Barred by her ladies, Robert could only pace up and down the gallery that led to her bedchamber, his nerves stretched taut by the screams that were issuing from within. What was going on, for God's sake? He was desperate to know.

Hours went by. He sat slumped on a window seat, drowning his fears in goblet after goblet of wine. The screaming had now abated to a low moaning – and then, suddenly, there was silence. He stood up, instantly sober, and began his pacing again. When would they tell him something? How dare they keep him in suspense like this?

Losing patience, he rapped loudly on the door. Immediately it opened and he found himself facing the midwife, a formidable village woman, skilled at her craft and with a good reputation. Normally her manner was brisk and reassuring, but now she looked frightened, diminished . . . Then he saw beyond her to the maid with the cloth bundle. He did not even dare think what it meant.

God forgive her, but when news reached Elizabeth that her adversary's child had been stillborn, she rejoiced. At least she would not have to endure the agony of thinking that Robert's son could have been hers.

1579

Anjou had sent an envoy, Baron Jean Simier, to finalise the negotiations. Elizabeth could not help taking to Simier at once. He had the dark good looks she so much admired; he was every inch the courtier, skilled in courtesy, compliments and flirtation – and he put all three talents to imaginative use when he was with her.

'Your Majesty, I am come to prepare you,' he sang, bowing low and doffing a hat with an outrageously large plume of feathers.

'To prepare me?' Elizabeth echoed.

'Yes, your Majesty, to prepare you for my master's frenzied wooing! He is *dying* of love for you. He languishes impatiently, *longing* for the day when he can behold your divine face.'

Steady on, thought Robert, scowling behind the throne.

Elizabeth beamed at Simier. 'And we long to see the Duke too, and to welcome him to England. You may tell your master that I was very impressed with his portrait.' The artist had left out the pockmarks, she'd noticed.

'I will tell him much more than that, Madame; I will speak of your celestial graces and dazzling beauty. If there be perfection in flesh and blood, undoubtedly it is in your Majesty.'

'Ah, my lord, methinks you are well named,' Elizabeth teased. 'You are a naughty monkey, and so I will nickname you! Of all the beasts, you are the most beautiful.'

'Who *exactly* is she meant to be marrying?' Sussex murmured, observing the banter between queen and envoy.

Robert was about to utter a caustic reply when Simier clapped his hands theatrically and a servant staggered in with a rich casket that was clearly very weighty.

'Your Majesty, I bring jewels worth twelve thousand crowns for your lords, as a gift from my master,' Simier cried with a flourish. 'They are a token of his good will and friendship.'

'And a bribe to make us like the marriage,' Robert muttered.

'Well I like it better every day,' Sussex whispered, ever ready to disagree with him.

'How very generous,' Elizabeth said, fluttering her eyelashes artfully at Simier. God, she was behaving like a skittish girl with her first lover, Robert thought. It was more than embarrassing.

Over the next days he watched, cringeing, as she flirted outrageously with the Baron, and went out of her way to show how eager she was for the marriage. She held a glittering court ball in Simier's honour; she had a masque performed for his enjoyment; she kept him constantly at her side; and she summoned him to talk with her – well, that was the official version of it – late at night. When Simier presented her with a gift from Anjou – a book with a jewelled binding – she went into transports of joy and declared she would keep it with her always. In return, she gave Simier gifts for the Duke: her portrait done in miniature and a pair of embroidered gloves.

'One day,' she told him archly, 'I hope to give Monsieur many more fine and valuable things, but for now these must suffice.'

Robert looked on, sighing, and wishing he was anywhere else. Yet he had to admire her audacity. In any other middle-aged woman such behaviour would have been ridiculous, but Elizabeth's courtiers had come to regard her almost as a semi-divine goddess with the gift of eternal youth. No one else could have carried it off, but she was not for nothing her mother's daughter, and although she was no longer beautiful or young, she had the gift of convincing people that she was. Robert himself had come under that spell. And people were clearly beginning to believe that this time the Queen was serious in her declared intention of marrying. It was hardly surprising that the court was gripped with excitement and abuzz with speculation.

Walsingham, like Robert, deplored the idea of the Queen marrying a Catholic, although he took a more pragmatic view.

Even so, his spies had uncovered disturbing intelligence about Simier, which he hastened to confide to Robert.

'He murdered his brother for having an affair with his wife, and she poisoned herself just before Simier left for England,' he said, his face grave.

'Don't ask me to tell the Queen,' Robert said. 'She'll only accuse me of trying to put her off the marriage.'

'She will likely say the same to me,' Walsingham sighed. 'No, we should say nothing, but be watchful.' Robert grunted. He was fed up with watching the pantomime of this strange courtship, and knew it boded no good for himself.

Elizabeth beamed at her Council. She had a paper in her hand.

'A letter has arrived from the Duke of Anjou. He tells me that if I consent to marry him I will restore him to life, as he has been languishing near death, existing only in hope of serving the goddess of the heavens. Isn't that touching?'

God help us, Robert thought. This is the man who might be our king.

'It is a fine thing for an old woman like me to be thinking of marriage!' Elizabeth laughed, provoking the inevitable chorus of denial, that she was not old but eternally youthful – a lady whom time had surprised, as Hatton said chivalrously.

She executed something approaching a *basse* dance on her way out of the council chamber, her step light; she was feeling utterly rejuvenated.

I shall have your words of love engraved in marble, she wrote to Anjou. *You may be assured of my eternal friendship and constancy, which is rare among royalty. You should know that I have never broken my word.* That was stretching it, but no matter. She had never *meant* to break her word.

Whenever Anjou was mentioned, her face lit up. Her councillors, her courtiers and her ladies grew weary of constantly hearing about his virtues and charms.

'I now believe that there is no greater happiness in the world than marriage,' she informed Burghley, who nearly fell off his chair in shock.

In truth, she added, she wished she had not wasted so much time. But privately she was tormented by doubts.

'Is your master interested in me for myself?' she asked Simier when they were closeted alone together, ostensibly discussing the terms of the marriage contract. 'Or does he just want to be king? I cannot rest until I know.'

'Your Majesty, he adores you!' Simier protested, hand on heart. 'How could you think otherwise?'

'But he has never met me,' Elizabeth reasoned. 'I can only find out what he really thinks of me if he visits me in person.'

'I assure you, Majesty, that there is no cause at all for concern.'

Maybe there wasn't, she told herself. All the same, she was not marrying Anjou until she had seen and approved of him.

When the Queen's councillors next gathered in the council chamber, Burghley's face was thunderous. There were no poetic metaphors now. 'It is scandalous!' he spluttered. 'Her Majesty told me herself that Simier had actually been in her bedchamber and taken her nightcap and handkerchief as trophies for the Duke,' he related, horrified. 'She also said that she went to Simier's lodging early one morning, and he was obliged to receive her wearing only a jerkin.'

'What was her Majesty thinking of?' Sussex asked, shaking his head.

'She seems to have taken leave of her senses,' Walsingham observed, his Puritan soul bristling with disapproval. He liked his Queen and was staunchly loyal to her, but at times like these he despaired of her.

They all looked at Robert.

'This seems to me an unmanly, unprincely, *French* kind of wooing,' he said, and the mood lightened as they all had to smile. 'God, I hate Simier,' he went on. 'I hate him for putting the Queen in this ridiculous position, and I hate having to be outwardly friendly towards him and entertain him at court.'

'I think everyone knows you hate him,' Burghley said. 'It is plain writ on your face.'

'And with good cause!' Robert was not jesting now. 'The word is that he uses love potions and other unlawful acts to procure the Queen for the Duke.'

'Unlawful acts?' Walsingham growled.

'They say that he has won his way not only to her heart, but also to her body,' Robert told him, wincing at the thought. 'And no, my lords, I am not jealous, although I know what is being said in the court. I am her loyal and loving servant and I will not see her reputation being traduced in this way.'

'Whose reputation?' interposed a strident voice. Like guilty schoolboys the councillors turned to see the Queen framed in the doorway, blazing with anger.

'Do you have a problem with my marriage plans, my lord?' she hissed, advancing on Robert and jabbing her finger in his chest. 'Do you think me so unlike myself and unmindful of my royal majesty that I would prefer you, my servant, whom I have raised, before the greatest prince of Christendom, in the honour of a husband?'

'I did not say so, Madam,' Robert replied. 'It is of Simier that we complain.' The others looked uncomfortable. To a man they were thinking that it might be preferable to face the armed might of Spain than the Queen in a temper.

'Pah!' Elizabeth spat. 'Simier has done nothing but show himself faithful to his master, and I have found him to be sage and discreet beyond his years in the conduct of these negotiations. I wish *I* had such a servant of whom I could make good use!' She glared at them all, then swept out, her skirts swishing imperiously. She could never have explained to them, if she had ten thousand years – and indeed she hardly liked to admit it to herself – that all her extravagant flirting with Simier was an elaborate ploy to preserve the illusion that she was an eternally young and eminently marriageable woman.

It was soon clear that Robert was decidedly out of favour, and he began to wonder what would become of him when Anjou was king, for the Duke was unlikely to think kindly of the man who had preceded him for so long in the Queen's affections.

For all the squabbling, the negotiations were advancing well. Some courtiers were even ordering their wedding outfits. Simier went about the court with a smile on his face. But there was much opposition from the Puritans and even from hard-line Anglican ministers, who got into a froth condemning the marriage from their pulpits. One brave, or possibly rash, clergy-man even dared to do so before the Queen.

'Marriages with foreigners will only result in ruin to the country!' he thundered, but that was as far as he got, as Elizabeth stalked out, then banned any sermons opposing the match. But the councillors were still divided. Even though Anjou was no fanatic, he was still a Catholic. He was also heir to the French throne until his brother had children – which seemed highly unlikely given Henri's dubious proclivities – so it was impossible for him to embrace the Protestant faith.

For all this, it looked very much as if the marriage might go ahead. But suddenly, as a result of one of Simier's more naughty asides, Elizabeth woke up to the fact that Anjou was a virile young man of twenty-four who really would want sex and children, and immediately she felt very scared. Hitherto, if she had brought herself to think of those aspects at all – and really, she had been hiding from the truth, for otherwise the marriage might never go ahead – she had been fooling herself. She had somehow deluded herself into believing that Anjou would be content with a marriage in name only; that he had not expected her to be capable of bearing sons; that theirs would be just a political union and that she would bend the Duke to her will after the wedding. But now reality was staring her in the face and making her confront what she did not want to confront. She knew she was very old to be contemplating motherhood, even though her courses still came regularly every month. And was it not dangerous, bearing children at her age? She was terrified of the risks involved, even more than before – and of facing the humiliation of a young man finding her wanting in bed, and less than desirable. And still she shrank from the prospect of surrendering her body.

She fretted about all this for a few days and then, gathering her courage, she summoned her physicians. After some searching and embarrassing questions, they all assured her that there was no reason why she should not bear a healthy heir to England (and maybe more than one, for there was still time for that), and that her fears were unfounded. All would be well.

Not convinced, by any means, Elizabeth recounted this to Robert, the only man to whom she could confide such intimate matters, and he took it upon himself to speak of her fears to his colleagues.

'The Duchess of Savoy bore a healthy prince at fifty, and lived,' Burghley observed. 'I have always thought that the Queen is a person of the most pure constitution, a well-shaped woman with all her limbs – and, er, her other parts – well proportioned. Nature, I am convinced, could not amend her in any way to make her more likely to conceive and bear children without peril.'

For all his brave words he *had* been worried. He had even commissioned a private report, for his eyes alone, on the risks involved, as he revealed to Leicester and Walsingham.

'I questioned her physicians, her ladies and her chamberers,' he said, keeping his voice low, 'and they all told me that her Majesty is well formed and has no lack of the functions that properly belong to the procreation of children.'

Robert hid a smile at the older man's modest choice of words.

'The doctors say that she has about six years left in which to bear children,' Burghley went on. 'And I believe that being married and having children will help to cure the pains she suffers in her face and the dolours that physicians impute to women for lack of a husband.'

'The pains are due to bad teeth,' Robert said, 'and she carries the great burden of sovereignty on her shoulders, and it is a taxing one. Who would not succumb to dolours in her position? But as for having children, there is no guarantee that she will conceive at her age.'

'I know you do not want this marriage, Robert, but I assure you that the benefits it brings will far outweigh the risks,' Burghley said reprovingly.

'I disagree,' Walsingham chimed in. 'Most of us fear that motherhood will place the Queen in extreme peril.'

There was a silence.

'Do we dare to risk our Queen's life?' Walsingham persisted. 'She has reigned over us and kept us safe from war these twenty years.'

'But what happens when she is no more?' Burghley asked. 'She needs an heir, and through this marriage she may get one. It is her last chance. Trust me, the physicians say that all will be well.'

Simier's eyes flashed fire, then he stalked out of the council chamber to find the Queen, whom he discovered walking in her privy garden.

'Beloved goddess,' he cried, bowing low, 'I hesitate to tell you that your councillors disapprove of this marriage that you desire so much. They refuse to agree that my master be crowned king after the wedding; they would deny him the power to grant lands and offices; and they will not approve his proposed allowance of sixty thousand pounds a year.'

'I am very sorry for that,' Elizabeth said, seething. 'They need not think that I will tolerate such obstructions!'

Furious, she sped back indoors and confronted her councillors.

'How dare you thwart me!' she screamed. 'I will not have my careful policies subverted like this!' And she ranted and raved at them so vociferously that she ended up having a coughing attack and they had to send for her ladies to calm her down. After that there was no more talk of limiting Anjou's power or his income; in fact no councillor now dared say a word against him.

Next it was the turn of the French to receive the lash of her tongue. They were making too many demands.

'*If* they had to deal with a princess who had some defect of body or nature, such stipulations might have been tolerated!' she shouted. 'But considering how it has pleased God to bestow on us gifts in good measure, we may in modesty think ourself as worthy of as great a prince as Monsieur without yielding to such conditions!'

She was gratified when Anjou himself stepped into the fray and told Simier not to insist on every condition being met. The Duke was now pressing for an invitation to come to England and meet his future wife. Elizabeth dithered. It did not do to seem *too* keen, yet she did so want to see this man that she might marry. After all, she had always said that she would not wed until she had met and approved of her future husband, and now here was one positively begging to come and be inspected.

Burghley and Sussex, eager to speed her up the aisle, urged her to extend the invitation. Not so Robert. To her astonished dismay, he prostrated himself full-length at her feet and begged her not to go through with the marriage. He was so obviously convinced that she was making the wrong decision that she procrastinated and wept for three days before giving in to pressure from the other councillors and issuing the invitation to Anjou, with a safe-conduct for his journey. Stung, Robert stormed off home to Wanstead and feigned illness once more, unable to bear watching Elizabeth hurtling towards what he believed to be certain disaster.

She followed him there, without fanfare. Her arrival caused a flurry as a furious Lettice made herself scarce and Robert raced around the house trying to remove all evidence of their life together. Then, with the Queen's party almost at the door, he rushed upstairs and scrambled into bed.

Elizabeth was not fooled.

'You don't look that ill to me!' she declared.

'It is my stomach,' Robert complained, rubbing it ostenta-tiously. And indeed he spoke truth. When he was stressed like this he did suffer griping pains.

'Hmm,' murmured Elizabeth. 'Methinks it is your obstinacy that does not want me to marry Monsieur.'

'If I spoke out against it, it was only from deep concern for your Majesty. But I will bow to your greater wisdom, and do all honour to the Duke when he comes.'

'It is no less than I expect, my lord,' Elizabeth said. 'Do you want some soup?' She had once spooned soup into his mouth when he was unwell. It was a peace offering, he knew.

'No, Madam, I thank you, the officers of my kitchen have their orders. Dinner will be ready by eleven. I trust that you will stay for it.'

She stayed two days, and when she had gone Lettice emerged from the smallest guest bedchamber spitting fire.

'I am the Countess of Leicester! I will not be shut away like some whore you should be ashamed of!' And more in that vein – in fact, the pent-up results of two days of seething. 'I am going to court whether she likes it or not!' she raged. 'I am her cousin, and I rank high among the foremost ladies of the land.' She rounded on Robert. 'This is your fault! You should have insisted that I be there at your side!'

'I dared not mention you,' Robert admitted.

'Well thank God one of us has some courage!' she flung back. 'Get ready. We are going to court!'

The presence chamber was crowded with gaily attired courtiers, some attendant on the Queen, many waiting for her to notice them; most were bearing gifts, in the hope that they might thereby induce her to be kind and generous. Elizabeth, however, was not looking their way. Her face concealed behind a huge fan of ostrich feathers, she was engaged in a conversation with Simier, punctuated by playful taps and giggles. But suddenly her smile, and the fan, dropped.

Leicester, looking as if he would rather be anywhere else, had just entered the room, and on his arm was – *no*, it couldn't be, thought the courtiers, but *yes*, it certainly was – his Countess, like a galleon in full sail in cloth of silver with a golden kirtle, slashed sleeves, a vast train and a ruff like a cartwheel. And behind her the bravest train of ladies and liveried servants ever seen following a lady not of royal blood.

Elizabeth stared. Her lips tightened. Her eyes glittered dangerously. Then she rose from her throne, stepped off the dais, bore down upon Lettice like an avenging angel and soundly boxed her ears. 'Get out!' she screamed. 'As but one sun lights the east, so I shall have but one queen in England!'

Her dignity in tatters, and her ears stinging, Lettice fled, leaving Robert standing there helpless, wanting to go after his wife and comfort her, but fearing Elizabeth's reaction if he did.

'Madam, she has done nothing wrong,' he pleaded. 'She but wanted to take her rightful place here as my Countess.'

'Her rightful place is out of my sight!' Elizabeth barked. 'Never let her cross my threshold again.'

'Madam, I beg of you,' Robert cried, noticing that the watching courtiers were not bothering to hide their glee at this unexpected drama.

'No,' Elizabeth said, glaring at him, 'and let that be an end to it!'

The King of France had objected to his brother coming a-courting to England, but that August Anjou came anyway, heavily disguised. His visit was meant to be a secret – hence the subterfuge – but in fact most people at court knew about it, even if they kept up the pretence that they did not.

To ensure secrecy – or the illusion if it – it had been decided that Anjou would lodge with Simier in a silken pavilion in the gardens of Greenwich Palace. Elizabeth was now burning with impatience for the Duke's coming; she did not cease bragging that it was her great beauty and accomplishments that had enticed him hither.

But then something happened that nearly put an end to everything.

Elizabeth was being rowed along the Thames on her way to visit and inspect the royal docks at Deptford, near Greenwich, at the same time as Master Appletree, a fowler, was shooting from his boat, hoping to bag something for his dinner. Like lightning a shot from his gun flashed past not six feet from where Elizabeth was sitting and passed straight through the brawny arm of one of her oarsmen, who shrieked and danced most pitifully in agony.

As his fellows leapt to help and staunch the blood, and the royal barge rocked dangerously, the Queen herself rose and swiftly clambered along the gangway to comfort the injured man, patting him on the shoulder and bidding him be of good cheer, for she would see that he never wanted for anything. Then she ordered that the terrified Appletree be fished out of his boat, arrested and tried. Condemned to be hanged, he was brought out some days later, shaking with fear, to the gallows that had been set up on the riverbank by the stretch of water where he had committed his crime. He was weeping pathetically as the hangman placed the rope around his neck. But then a shout came, 'Hold!' It was a messenger with the Queen's most gracious pardon.

'I meant only to teach him a stern lesson,' she explained to Robert afterwards. But the episode left her more conscious than ever of the frailty of human life, and strengthened her resolve to marry Anjou.

Simier came running to tell her, gesticulating wildly in delight. The Duke had arrived!

'Monsieur came early this morning and woke me up, *demanding* to see your Majesty. I explained that you were still asleep, but in vain! He was so eager to greet you that he insisted on going himself to wake you up and kiss your hand. I dissuaded him, of course, and put him between the sheets. Would to God, I thought, that it was by your side!'

'You are a bad man, Simier. I will not have such naughty talk!' Elizabeth's smile belied her words.

It had been arranged that she would dine privately with Anjou at sunset in the pavilion. She dressed with especial care. Her gown and stomacher were of silver damask, her huge puffed sleeves embroidered with gold, her kirtle of crimson silk. Her skirts over the stiff farthingale were fashionably wide, her waist tiny, as convention – and her whalebone corset – dictated. At her breast she wore her bejewelled pelican pendant, symbolising her role as a mother to her people – and, hopefully, the future heirs to England. On her elaborately bewigged head was a chaplet of roses and pearls. Thus gorgeously attired, she stole out of the palace with just one of her ladies in attendance, and sped on light feet down the gravel paths and across the verdant lawns.

What would Monsieur be like? She had heard unsettling reports that he was a misshapen dwarf, hideously scarred and disfigured by smallpox. Yet his portrait had shown a young man with pleasing features and none of those defects. Of course, artists flattered their sitters, it was well known. But with so much riding on that image, what was the point of such a deception? Well, she would soon know.

The elegant young man who rose at her coming and made a deep obeisance was small in stature, as she had been warned, but he was definitely attractive in a uniquely Gallic way, with the dark hair and eyes that had always appealed to her in men. His nose was straight, his lips full and his eyes warmly regarding her with no hint of dismay at her being so much older than he. Yes, his skin was pitted in places, but not that you would notice much. There was a look of the young Leicester about him, she decided – and even a resemblance to Thomas Seymour, that villain who had first captured her heart. But she would not think of him now, not when this paragon of manhood was standing before her and gallantly stooping to take her hand and kiss it.

'Welcome to England, Monsieur,' she said in perfect French. 'I trust you have had a good journey.'

'Your Majesty, I would have braved tempests to see you,' Anjou replied, his voice velvety and deep. 'And now that I am here, I am so, so glad that I came, for I see that reports of your beauty do not lie; in fact they do not do justice to the fairest of queens.'

This was better than she had ever expected, she thought, seating herself across the table from him and dipping her fingers into the rose-water in her finger-bowl. What was more, as the conversation and the drinks flowed – fine wine for him, good English watered beer for her – she discovered that she and Anjou had much in common. They both loved literature, poetry, music, dancing, hunting and long walks outdoors. She found to her delight that they shared a sense of humour and a sharp wit. She was delighted that he deferred to her at every turn and seemed eager to pay her the most flamboyant compliments. Above all, he spoke most tenderly of their coming marriage and the joy he knew that he would find in her. He could not wait to live in England, he declared.

She was no fool, nor did she delude herself. She knew that such talk did not normally proceed from so short an acquaintance, and that much of it was pure courtesy and – it had to be admitted – ambition. But there was something else, too, a rapport on which much could be built. She found herself looking forward enormously to nurturing the liking that had been born tonight.

As the wine sparkled in the candlelight, and the servitors silently came and went, bringing golden plates laden with exquisite food, Elizabeth sent up a silent prayer of thanks to God, who, in the late summer of her life, and with Robert lost for ever, had sent her this prince. By the end of the evening, she was telling herself that she had never seen a creature more agreeable to her.

She said much the same thing to her councillors and her ladies. She told Simier that she was captivated, overcome with love.

'I have never found a man whose nature and actions suited me better!' she declared.

'And Monsieur is as delighted with your Majesty as your Majesty is with him,' Simier told her, which gladdened her heart no end.

'I am pleased to have been able to get to know him,' she

enthused. 'I am much taken with his good looks, and admire him more than any man. For my part, I will not prevent his becoming my husband.'

There were more trysts in the pavilion, the very secrecy adding spice to the affair. Anjou proved an ardent suitor, pressing passionate kisses on her lips and drawing her tightly into an embrace that left her in no doubt of his desire for her.

'I shall call you my Frog,' she announced, making him laugh.

'Why Frog?'

'It is what the English call the French. In your case it is a great compliment. And you leapt like a frog across the Channel to see me.'

'And would leap into your bed,' he said with the boldness that she loved.

'No, my Frog, you must be patient,' she chided, but she was loving it all: the banter, the innuendo and the promise of passion to come. It was the breath of life to her.

They exchanged gifts: jewels, books and silver-gilt cups.

'I will love you for ever, my golden Queen,' Anjou vowed.

'And I will make you a true and faithful wife,' Elizabeth promised, 'and love you until death parts us.'

She went about the court with a broad, beatific smile on her face. Most of her courtiers knew the reason for it, and laughed behind their hands, but Elizabeth ignored them. Only Robert looked on balefully, sickened and shamed at what he had heard, on good authority, of what went on in that bloody pavilion. But he could do or say nothing, because officially Anjou was not in England. Most of the councillors were staying away from court as often as their duties permitted, to avoid being asked awkward questions. Robert had to content himself with cursing the French under his breath.

Robert had always loved literature and verse, and enjoyed a reputation as a great patron of letters. He had in his household a young poet, Edmund Spenser, a talented fellow who had come on the recommendation of the Sidneys. Spenser took pleasure in reminding Robert how Anjou's courtship of the

Queen was the talk of London and had scandalised the Puritans. Then Robert found out, to his horror, that Spenser, his own protégé, had circulated a satire, *Mother Hubbard's Tale*, which was less than flattering to Anjou, Simier and – Heaven protect him – Elizabeth herself. When he heard that she had read and publicly – and very hotly – condemned it, he was deeply mortified, and packed the foolish, hot-headed boy who had caused all the trouble off to Ireland.

Elizabeth guessed that Robert had had nothing to do with Spenser's offensive libel, but she let him stew for a while. She ignored the chorus of disapproval on the part of those who hated the Anjou marriage. She was enjoying her secret affair too much to pay them any heed. She decided to arrange a court ball, so that Anjou could see how well she danced.

'My poor Frog must stand behind the tapestries,' she told him. 'You will be able to see the dancing through the gaps.' Having had him smuggled in before the guests arrived, she showed off immoderately for his benefit, joining in many more dances than usual, executing dramatic leaps and twirls, and even smiling and waving in the direction of the tapestry. The court reverberated with silent mirth.

Two days later Robert asked to see her in private. He was dismayed to find her so cool towards him, but he persisted in his mission nonetheless.

'Madam, I am in great grief at the thought of this marriage,' he blurted out.

'Do not think to sway me with that,' Elizabeth retorted. 'I have had enough criticism from your camp.'

'I apologise for young Spenser,' Robert said. 'It was done without my knowledge.'

'I know,' she replied. 'But you would echo the sentiment.'

'I am not the only one,' he declared.

'I do not want to hear it!' she snapped. 'You should consider the weal of this realm and the happiness of your Queen!'

'I think of nothing else,' he averred, his blood up.

'Then you understand nothing.'

'I have your welfare at heart,' he protested angrily.

'As you did when you married *that woman?*' she flung back. 'No, my lord, I want none of your concern, so let that be an end to it.'

'I shall leave court,' Robert threatened, wounded to the heart.

'Is that a promise? Just go!'

He emerged from their meeting very distressed, and went to arrange for the packing of his gear and the saddling of horses. All he could hope for now was that Parliament would vote against the marriage.

At the end of August Anjou broke it to Elizabeth that he had to leave on the morrow. A bosom friend had been killed in a duel, and he was needed in France. Understanding the urgency, Elizabeth placed a fine ship at his disposal, and tried not to imagine that he might be making an excuse to abandon her.

She spent the last night of his visit lying wakeful and fretting, and in the morning Simier, come for his usual audience, told her that Anjou had done just the same.

'Monsieur was sighing and moaning all night, and hauled me out of bed at an ungodly hour to tell me about your Majesty's divine beauty. Then he swore a thousand oaths that, without hope of seeing your Majesty again, he cannot live another quarter of an hour!'

Tears sprang to Elizabeth's eyes. He did love her, her Frog. How could she have doubted it?

She went, disguised, to see him off from the great gatehouse at Greenwich, where waited the boat that would take him down to his ship at Dover.

'You are the gaoler of my heart and the mistress of my liberty,' he told her as he folded her in his arms, making her shiver with pleasure and misery at the thought of parting. They kissed tenderly, and soon he was gone from her sight. From Dover he wrote her three letters expressing his devotion in the most heart-rending terms, and soon afterwards, three more arrived from Boulogne.

I am desolate without you, she read, *and I can do nothing but wipe away my tears. I kiss your feet from the coast of the comfortless sea.* He had signed himself *the most faithful and affectionate slave in the world,* and enclosed in the packet a pendant formed as a little flower of gold with a frog crouching on it, which opened to reveal his miniature portrait.

She wept at that. She was in turmoil, all the worse for the fact that it could not be expressed, since his visit was a secret. She could speak of her sorrow to Simier, but with everyone else she had to maintain a smiling countenance. The one man to whom she might have unburdened herself was lost to her, sulking at Wanstead. For want of any human comfort, she found herself writing verses, which she entitled 'On Monsieur's Departure'. When she read them over, she realised that they expressed exactly how she felt.

> *I grieve and dare not show my discontent;*
> *I love, and yet am forced to seem to hate;*
> *I do, yet dare not say I ever meant;*
> *I seem stark mute, but inwardly do prate.*
> *I am, and not; I freeze and yet am burned,*
> *Since from myself another self I turned.*
>
> *My care is like my shadow in the sun —*
> *Follows me flying, flies when I pursue it,*
> *Stands, and lies by me, doth what I have done;*
> *His too familiar care doth make me rue it.*
> *No means I find to rid him from my breast,*
> *Till by the end of things it be suppressed.*
>
> *Some gentler passion slide into my mind,*
> *For I am soft and made of melting snow;*
> *Or be more cruel, Love, and so be kind.*
> *Let me or float or sink, be high or low;*
> *Or let me live with some more sweet content,*
> *Or die, and so forget what love e'er meant.*

Anjou had instructed Simier to finalise negotiations for the marriage, but by now the great swelling of opposition to it in London had spread to the shires. The Spanish ambassador feared that there would be a revolution in England if the wedding went ahead. Leicester's nephew, Sir Philip Sidney, even had the temerity to write Elizabeth a letter in which he reminded her of the horrors of the massacre of St Bartholomew's Eve and the perfidy of the French; Anjou's own mother, he begged to remind her, was the Jezebel of their age, and her son would be wholly unacceptable to Elizabeth's Protestant subjects.

Elizabeth cried tears of rage when she read it. By God, his uncle had put him up to this! Robert, though, was beyond reach of her temper, so she bawled out Sidney and banished him from court. But there was no trace of her fury and inner turmoil when she returned to London after her summer progress and went in procession through the City in a bid to win over her dissenting subjects. So radiant and gracious did she look on her fine Spanish horse, smiling and raising her hand in greeting, that the people marvelled and fell to their knees as she passed, honouring and indeed worshipping this veritable goddess who had come among them, and calling down on her a thousand blessings. The Virgin Mary might have been banished from English churches, but the Virgin Queen had now taken her place in the minds of loyal Englishmen.

Elizabeth was appalled therefore when a scurrilous pamphlet against her coming marriage, written by one of those damnable Puritans, John Stubbs, appeared on the streets of London and threatened her very precious popularity.

'This must be suppressed,' she demanded, banging her fist on the council board.

'Without doubt,' Burghley agreed. 'We cannot allow such offensive language against Monsieur.'

'Or the house of Valois,' Walsingham added. '*Rotten with disease and marked by divine vengeance for its cruelties,*' he read aloud. 'As for the assertion that the Duke is eaten by debauchery, that is an outright calumny.'

'I mean to punish the perpetrator severely, so that our allies the French see how we deal with those who cause such offence against them,' Elizabeth declared. 'Publish a proclamation condemning this pamphlet as lewd and seditious, and have all copies confiscated and burned. Then have a preacher go to Paul's Cross to assure my people that I have no intention of changing my religion when I marry. He must say that I have been brought up in Christ, and will live and die in Christ.'

When the people heard, they shouted out their thanks and appreciation, but they resented the criticism of Stubbs, whose words had awakened their ingrained distrust of the French. Alarmed, Elizabeth consulted her judges, and ordered that Stubbs be arrested and hanged for sedition, along with his publisher and his printer.

'But Madam, sedition is not a capital crime,' Burghley protested.

'Then they shall have their right hands cut off, and be sent to prison,' she decided. She took care to remind the people of her renowned clemency by pardoning the elderly printer, but declared that she would rather have her own hand cut off than mitigate the sentence against Stubbs and his publisher.

She was watching from a window when the two unfortunate men were brought to a scaffold that had been erected in front of Whitehall Palace. When the executioner brought down his cleaver and struck off the offending hand that had written the pamphlet, Stubbs took off his hat with his left hand, cried out, 'God save Queen Elizabeth!' and promptly fainted. Elizabeth was angered to see looks of sympathy and disapproval on the faces of the silent crowd. She felt gravely shaken. She could not bear to think that she had forfeited the good will of her subjects.

With this very much in mind, she prorogued the Parliament that had met to conclude the marriage treaty, asked her councillors for advice, and predictably plunged them into a heated debate. Robert and Hatton had mustered five of their colleagues to argue against the marriage, and Burghley had enlisted four others who were in favour of it. In the end, the councillors had to ask Elizabeth to open her mind to them as to her own inclinations.

'Madam, we lay this before you, as you seem not to be pleased with any person or any argument that appears to be against the marriage,' Burghley explained.

Elizabeth had already realised that it would be folly to go ahead with the treaty in the face of opposition from her councillors and her people. But it came to her that in not going ahead, she would probably be saying farewell to her last chance of marriage and motherhood, and to the dismay of all the men seated along the council board she suddenly burst into tears. It was the fault of those who had set out to wreck the negotiations! she sobbed. They were to blame!

'I marvel that you, my councillors, should think it doubtful whether there would be any greater surety for me and my realm than to have me marry and bear a child to inherit and continue the line of Henry VIII,' she wept, glaring daggers at Robert. 'I see that it was foolish of me to ask for your advice, but I had anticipated a universal request made to me to proceed in this marriage. I did not want to hear of any doubts!' She broke off there, too distressed to go on, having envisaged the empty, barren years ahead, and herself alone, advancing into old age without ever having known the consolations of wedlock and children. She really had meant to commit to marriage this time; she had done her best to conquer her fears of the nuptial bed and childbirth, even though they had threatened at times to overwhelm her – *and all for nothing!*

How could Robert have done this to her? He had made *his* choice and married where he would, so why had he tried so forcefully to prevent her from doing so? Was she not entitled to some happiness too? Anjou had been more than ready to make concessions; she could have loved him, she told herself, yea, and made a success of the match. But Robert had made it his business to suborn many who would have been in favour of it, *and* inflamed public opinion, she was sure. Her heart burned with resentment. She would not, could not, look at him, this man who had betrayed her more than once, and in so doing denied her the kind of happiness permitted to the meanest of her subjects.

She sat there weeping, the paint on her face blurring and streaking as the tears fell. Her councillors did not know whether to approach her, offer comfort or withdraw. In the end, they slunk away, deciding that it was best to leave her be for now, and summoned her ladies to attend her. To a man, they felt uncomfortable about what had happened. Even those who had supported the marriage felt guilty about placing their mistress in a situation where she had had to choose, especially after she had craved their advice. Robert could not have felt worse, yet he was still convinced that he had done the right thing for Elizabeth, and for England, in opposing this marriage.

Much arguing and deliberation followed, not to mention recriminations, and in the morning Elizabeth was surprised when the councillors asked to see her again. To their relief, they were told that she was dancing galliards, her usual morning exercise, and were pleased to find her in control of herself once more, with no trace of the emotional storm of the previous afternoon.

'Madam,' said Burghley, 'we are come to tell you that we are ready to offer you our wholehearted support in furtherance of the marriage with Monsieur, if it shall please you.'

'Well, this is a change of heart on the part of some of you,' she said, looking pointedly at Robert, who would not meet her eye.

'We have been moved to it by your Majesty's obvious desire to have issue, and because you have made it plain that you want the Duke for a husband,' Burghley explained.

'I marvel at those of you who were against the marriage!' Elizabeth reproved, her tone sharp. 'Had it not been for your eloquence, the majority would have been content for it to proceed.'

No one dared to say anything. At length Burghley broke the silence. 'Will your Majesty promise to give us an answer?'

'I will, after I have thought on it,' she consented at length, 'but I think it not meet to declare now what my decision will be.'

When they had gone, she felt inexpressibly sad, and this melancholy remained with her, a heavy pall cast over her former happiness. She felt cross with everyone and snapped at those who dared approach her. In truth, she was alarmed at the prospect of what would happen if she followed her inclinations and said yes, as she wanted to do. Anjou's handsome face kept coming to mind, and she could not help wistfully recalling their stimulating banter and his thrilling compliments. Should she give up her chance of happiness with him? If she seized it, would her subjects rebel, as they had rebelled when her sister Mary married Philip of Spain? The mood of the public was hostile towards Anjou and all he represented. There might be others, like Stubbs, who would speak out and inflame popular opinion. It even occurred to her that this marriage could potentially cost her her throne.

She attended the next council meeting, sitting stiffly at the head of the board, and made it clear from the first that she was not speaking to Robert. When Walsingham opened his mouth to say something, she flared at him, 'You had best go home, Francis, since you are good for nothing but protecting the interests of the Puritans. And you can go too, Christopher. You opposed me, and I don't want to see your face at court for at least a week.' Feeling like naughty schoolboys, the two men left the room.

'Why don't you banish me too?' Robert said suddenly.

'Shall we move on?' Elizabeth asked the rest, ignoring him and putting on her most statesmanlike manner. 'Now, my lords, it is clear to me that I cannot accept Anjou as a husband and retain the love of my subjects.' Some faces around the table registered relief; but Burghley looked ineffably sad. Twenty years of scheming to get the Queen wed had come to nothing, and England still did not have her heir.

'It is important, however,' Elizabeth was saying, 'that we

prolong the marriage negotiations to keep the French friendly. You will attend me in council three days hence, and bring with you the French ambassador.'

On the appointed day she dressed herself splendidly in virginal white satin, and placed on her elaborately be-wigged head a gossamer veil embroidered with gold fleurs-de-lis, the emblem of France. When she was seated in her chair of estate, she addressed the men before her. 'My lords, your Excellency, I am come to inform you that I am determined to marry and that you need say nothing more to bend me to it. I command you all to discuss what is necessary for concluding the treaty. Baron Simier and I have drawn up the marriage articles, and we will both sign them. I make one proviso: that I be allowed two months in which to dispose my subjects, as represented in Parliament, to agree to the marriage before I conclude the treaty. If I am unable so to dispose them, the agreement will be null and void.'

She was stalling, as of old, but this time she was half-hoping that Parliament would agree, even though she knew that there was little likelihood of it. It was at times like these that she felt very much the loneliness of her exalted position. There was no one impartial in whom she could confide. She remembered her father saying, long ago, that princes took in marriage spouses brought them by others, while only poor men made their own choices. She almost wished she was poor.

There was Anjou to think of too. She had led him to believe that she was sincere in her intentions, and hated to imagine that he might think ill of her for imposing this new condition. But there was a chance that he might be able to help. In some agony of mind, she wrote to him: *You realise, my dearest, that the greatest difficulties lie in making my people rejoice and approve. The public practice of the Roman religion so sticks in their hearts. I beg you to consider this deeply. For my part, I confess there is no prince in the world to whom I think myself more bound, nor with whom I would rather pass the years of my life, both for your rare virtues and sweet nature. With my commendations to my dearest Frog.* She smiled weakly at that. It conjured up so many happy memories.

Soon afterwards Simier went home to France, laden with gifts but leaving the marriage articles unsigned for now. And Anjou did not take the hint and abjure his faith.

Elizabeth never normally paid much attention to gossip unless it was about something worthy of her attention, but one day she overheard two of her maids of honour chattering in the linen closet next to her bedchamber. Had she heard correctly? Had they actually said that Douglass Sheffield had been secretly married to the Earl of Leicester?

'Where did you hear that?' she asked from the doorway.

They spun round in panic at her voice and dropped into curtseys.

'Answer me!' she demanded.

'Lady Frances Howard said it, Madam,' one piped up nervously.

'Did she indeed?' Satisfied, she dismissed them, knowing that they would repeat their gossip elsewhere, and with embellishments.

This was most interesting – and most gratifying. Frances Howard was a known tattler of tales, but she was Douglass Sheffield's sister and therefore in a position to know the truth about her. And if Robert had in fact been married to Douglass, he could not be lawfully married to *that woman.* Elizabeth had been longing to have her revenge on her traitorous niece, and now she saw her opportunity.

She summoned Burghley and told him, in the gravest tones, that she feared there was an impediment to the Earl of Leicester's marriage.

'I have it on reliable authority that he was married at the time to Lady Sheffield.'

'Married?' Burghley's bushy brows shot up. 'Forgive me, Madam, I knew she was his mistress and bore him a child, but this is news to me. If he was married, why did he not declare it? Why should a man deny his own son his rightful inheritance?'

'For fear of my just wrath, for marrying without my consent.'

'But Madam, he did just that with Lady Essex, and your Majesty graciously forgave him.'

She threw Burghley a contemptuous look. 'I had no choice in the matter. But William, this information comes from Lady Sheffield's sister, one of my own gentlewomen.'

'A known gossip,' he observed.

'But why should she lie?'

'For profit?' Burghley answered.

'Ah, my Spirit, you have grown cynical in your old age. It could be that she has broken her silence because she cannot bear to see her sister so wronged. And if Lady Sheffield has been wronged, I cannot allow the situation to continue. There must be an investigation. If there was a marriage between Robert and Lady Sheffield, we need to establish whether the ceremony was legal and binding.'

'And if it was?'

'Then I have resolved to give Robert an ultimatum: either he has his union with Lady Essex' – she nearly choked on the name – 'annulled – or he goes to the Tower.'

Burghley sighed. He knew why Elizabeth was doing this, and he was almost certain what the outcome would be. He also knew that she would not be gainsaid. 'Very well, I will arrange it,' he said wearily.

Sussex, being cousin to Douglass, was deputed to question her, and as soon as possible, because she had just married Sir Edward Stafford, England's ambassador in Paris, and was about to depart for France.

'She says that Robert ruined her and that she wants nothing more to do with him. She fears, of course, that talk of their affair will compromise her new marriage. She will admit nothing.' And off she had blithely gone to France.

Elizabeth was furious. It seemed that *that woman* was to

triumph at every turn, and that proved not to be all! When news came that she had borne Leicester a son, the Queen wept hot tears of frustration and fury. Not even a letter from Simier, tied with pink ribbon, could cheer her. *Be assured, on the faith of your Monkey, that your Frog lives in hope!* he had written. Already, she knew, the magical spell that Simier had woven around her was wearing off.

1580

Months later she was finding it hard to stay angry with Robert, although there were still times when she burned with fury towards him. Her feelings for him were desperately complicated; she loved him as fiercely as she hated him. But as she became mistress of herself once more, she came to realise that he was still the Robin she had known of old and cherished for so long, he was still devoted to her, and they might still share the interests, easy companionship and confidences that they had once done. The bonds between them had become so much of a habit that Elizabeth would find herself relapsing into the old ways without even noticing it. It could never be quite as it had been, though. There would always be what she saw as Robert's betrayal lying like a sword between them. She would never forgive him for marrying *that woman*, but there was nothing that she could do about that, and as he now made sure never to mention her faithless niece, she could pretend for most of the time that it had never happened – or that he was now the proud father of an heir. In the wake of that noble imp's birth, Robert had again ventured to ask Elizabeth to receive his wife, but she had responded so violently that he had never dared raise the subject again.

She had now come to see that Robert had been opposing the French marriage only in her interests, and from deeply held convictions, and when the French ambassador criticised him for placing obstacles in the way of it, she was stout in his defence.

'He was merely doing his duty as a councillor!' she snapped, as Robert stared at her in astonishment. More often than not he could do little to please her these days.

Otherwise, though, she was glacially distant to him, and the ice did not thaw until spring set in. By then, it was clear to everyone, Anjou included, that she was stalling in the matter of her marriage. The deadline for her to conclude the treaty had passed without her making any decision. Anjou, to demonstrate his good will to her subjects, had written begging her to free Stubbs from prison.

'I am beset on all sides!' Elizabeth complained to Burghley.

'I believe that your Majesty is disinclined to marry at all,' he observed sadly.

Elizabeth said nothing, yet her warring emotions were evident in her expression.

'If you do not intend to marry, you must undeceive Anjou at once,' he advised.

'I had hoped to keep him in correspondence indefinitely,' she said.

'The French will not take kindly to your treating him so shabbily,' Burghley warned.

'I am not interested in what they think,' she countered.

'Those that trick princes trick themselves,' he said sagely. Her face told him plainly that she did not like his bluntness.

She sent Anjou a steady stream of letters in which she implied, with increasing candour, that they should perhaps renounce each other, since her people objected to his hearing Mass. She asked for more time in which to convince her subjects of the benefits of the marriage. She kept praising the firm rock of his constancy, and repeatedly – and rather tactlessly – blamed all the delays on the French.

Our souls are meant to be united, she assured him, but left him wondering when, and how. Whenever the French ambassador was within earshot, she told people in a loud voice that she was still in love with Monsieur, and wore his frog pendant to prove it. She tucked the gloves he had given her into her belt and ostentatiously took them out and kissed them a hundred times a day. She almost managed to convince herself that this was no charade, but of course it was being played out purely for the ambassador's benefit.

Even her councillors began to wonder if she was serious. 'I would to God your Majesty would resolve one way or another touching the matter of her marriage,' Walsingham fretted. 'It would behove you to come to a speedy resolution, or you will breed greater dishonour than I dare imagine.'

'I will decide in my own time,' Elizabeth told him, her voice rising in ire. 'As for dishonour, may I remind you all that you and my lord of Leicester here did your best to prevent the marriage and stir up opinion against it.'

'Madam, we were but thinking of your welfare and the weal of the realm,' Robert protested.

'Your interference was most unwelcome!' she barked. 'I should have had you in the Tower!'

'Better for me to sell my lands and live a humble life than fall into this harsh disfavour,' he retorted. Was she never going to forgive him?

Elizabeth's sour humour became even more acidic after she received news from Rome that Pope Gregory XIII had reissued his predecessor's bull of excommunication against her. She knew, through Walsingham's intelligence network, that Jesuit priests, trained to undermine her rule and give succour to English Catholics, were infiltrating her realm. Her chief fear now was that they would organise Catholic resistance and even attempt her assassination.

To make matters worse she was sure that the Queen of Scots was plotting with the Spanish ambassador. Then word came that King Philip had annexed Portugal and so strengthened his naval power. The French were once again fighting their interminable wars of religion, and Elizabeth feared that they would not now be so readily able, or willing, to support her against this enhanced threat from Spain.

Immediately she offered to support Anjou's military venture in the Netherlands, and she invited his brother, King Henri, to send commissioners to England to conclude the marriage treaty as a matter of urgency.

There was no response. Anjou, it was clear, now had his

sights on becoming king of the Netherlands, of which there seemed to be more chance than becoming king of England. Elizabeth was stung by a cruel report from Paris that his ardour had cooled because of her advanced age and repulsive body. *Repulsive?* Oh no! It was a blow to her heart, and her pride, and she flung the offending letter into the fire. Had he really said that? Or was it her enemies spreading sedition?

Then came news that the Dutch had offered Anjou the crown.

'If the marriage goes ahead,' Burghley said, grave, 'it will be on condition that we give Monsieur an army to use against the Spaniards.'

'No!' Elizabeth snapped. 'It would be foolhardy to provoke King Philip thus, and I am not prepared to impoverish my subjects to fight a foreign war.' She was almost beside herself. 'I am not well used!' she complained. 'The nuptials would be savoured with my subjects' wealth, because the marriage would involve England in a costly enterprise. Have Monsieur informed that I am entirely against his becoming King of the Dutch.'

But Monsieur proved impervious to her angry protests. Defiantly he accepted the crown and was proclaimed Prince of the Netherlands.

Anjou had run out of money. Desperately needing to boost his resources, he suddenly remembered that he was in love, and dispatched commissioners to England to revive the marriage negotiations.

Elizabeth stared at the posy of wilting flowers that he had sent her.

'He picked them himself, your Majesty,' the envoys told her, looking justifiably abashed.

Elizabeth stared at the flowers again. She knew exactly why he had sent them. But did he think that a few dying blooms would soften her resolve and bring the might of England crashing over the Channel to his aid?

Nevertheless she wrote thanking him for the sweet flowers that his dear fingers had touched, promising him that no present was ever carried so gracefully. In fact she had carried it just for the time it took to get back to her privy chamber.

Shimmering in a gown of gold taffeta, she entertained the French envoys to a lavish banquet in a great pavilion with windows of real glass and a roof decorated with suns and stars, erected for the occasion. There followed feasts, masques, pageants and triumphs, as well as several council meetings at which the marriage was repeatedly debated.

At length Elizabeth summoned Anjou's commissioners.

'I must tell you that I am still concerned about the age gap between Monsieur and myself,' she informed them. 'I also fear that, were I to wed him, it would give unwelcome encouragement to English Catholics. Above all, I do not wish to become involved in a war with Spain. I should prefer to make an alliance with France rather than a marriage.'

The men before her appeared crestfallen. 'Your Majesty,' their spokesman said, 'we are not empowered to do anything other than conclude a marriage treaty.'

'I am sorry, but I have spoken,' Elizabeth declared, not without sympathy.

She did relent and take them with her to Deptford as guests of honour when she went to dine with Francis Drake on board his ship *The Golden Hind*, in which he had come home safely the year before after completing one of the most epic voyages ever made. Sailing around the world had been a tremendous feat, as he was only the second man to have done it – and he had stolen a lot of booty from Spanish ships during his three-year odyssey. Elizabeth liked the hearty, plain-spoken Drake, and – although she made the appropriate noises of outrage when King Philip complained about her pirates making away with his treasure – she was secretly cock-a-hoop about the gold that he had brought her.

The feast hosted by Drake on the deck of his brave galleon was sumptuous, with course after course of rich and succulent dishes, redolent of spices, sugar comfits and subtleties, and wine overflowing; people were saying that there had never been anything like it since King Harry's time. Elizabeth clapped loudest of all when the ship's crew appeared in Red Indian costumes with great head-dresses of feathers, and danced in a circle before her, giving strange whoops. She wanted to hear all about the New World and the many strange lands they had visited, and sat enraptured for four hours as Drake recounted his adventures for her, spicing them up with many pungent sea-dog's expressions, which made her laugh.

Afterwards, in the cool spring moonlight, he escorted her around the ship, and she was delighted to find herself bunching up her skirts and scaling ladders, and leaning over the forecastle looking down on the snout below and the black waters of the Thames.

'I was told, yer Majesty, that King Philip wanted me put to death for piracy,' Drake chuckled as they crossed the main deck and rejoined the company.

Elizabeth nodded to one of her guard, who handed her a sword that she had commanded to be brought to the feast. 'So should I use this to cut off your head?' she joked, making a clumsy attempt to swing it through the air, causing some of her courtiers to duck nervously.

'Depends whether I'm guilty or not!' Drake laughed.

'*I* think that you deserve a knighthood,' she declared, and summoned one of the Frenchmen to perform the ceremony for her, the better to rile King Philip. He would be hopping with fury when he heard, all his Spanish dignity forgotten!

Beaming with delight, the newly knighted Sir Francis Drake presented the Queen with a map of the great voyage and his personal diary of his adventures. As she thanked him, her golden garter slipped off, whereupon one of the envoys, seeing it lying on the planks in her wake, asked if they could have it for their master, Anjou.

'No!' she smiled. 'I need it to keep my stocking up.' But when she returned to Greenwich she relented and sent it to him after all. Then, keeping up the pretence that she had had a change of heart, she authorised the commissioners to draw up the treaty of marriage.

'But it *must* be endorsed by Monsieur himself!' she insisted, leaving the Frenchmen to depart for home disappointed and disgruntled.

Anjou did not come to England to append his signature – his proxies could do it, and he clearly felt he had better things to occupy his time – but by and by it became obvious that he was now even more desperate for money. Elizabeth was moved to send him a loan, and a letter with it assuring him that, although her body was her own, her soul was wholly dedicated to him. Let him make of that what he would!

She was enraged, therefore, when she heard that his interfering mother was up to her usual trickery, trying to make him wed a princess of Spain. If that happened, all Elizabeth's careful, tortuous diplomacy might be gone to waste! There was no overestimating the fickleness of the French.

'Go to France, good Moor,' she commanded Walsingham, 'and tell them that I really do mean to have the Duke. But try to negotiate an alliance that does not involve marriage.' Walsingham went, dragging his steps. The task seemed impossible, especially when Elizabeth sent after him a deluge of instructions, telling him to do first one thing and then quite another.

'He writes urging you to forget about the marriage,' Robert said. 'He is right, you know. I urge you to take his advice.' Hatton was nodding sagely.

'And *I* urge *you* to stop meddling, my lord,' Elizabeth said, tart.

'Madam,' Burghley intervened, shaking his head, 'Sir Francis is at the end of his tether. He writes that he would repute it a great favour to be committed to the Tower, unless your Majesty grows more certain of your intentions. He warns that, instead of the looked-for amity from the French, you will be the object only of enmity, and he will be much discomfited. King Henri, he says, is adamant that there will be no alliance without a marriage.'

Elizabeth replied, as she had done many times before when cornered, that she would think on the matter, making it plain that the discussion was at an end. Think she did, but still she bombarded Walsingham with conflicting orders. In the end, he wrote an exasperated letter telling her plainly that she would have to make up her mind.

So he wants me to marry Anjou after all! she concluded. I thought he opposed the match. He made enough fuss about it.

When, finally, a fraught Walsingham returned home, she was waiting for him.

'Well, you knave!' she chided. 'Why have you so often spoken ill of Monsieur? You veer round like a weathercock!'

'Madam,' he replied, 'had you been in my place, trying to interpret your commands and keep the French sweet, you would have come to wish that your Majesty would take the Devil himself as husband, so long as you made up your mind!'

*

354

It seemed to Elizabeth that there was now danger on every side. Intelligence reports told of hidden priests and secret agents furtively doing their utmost to subvert her rule. She gave her orders to Burghley and Walsingham. Houses were searched, people hunted down and arrested, and draconian new laws passed. There were arrests, interrogations and hangings. She found herself – much against her will – forced to sanction torture, so terrified was she of plots to kill her and overthrow all she had worked for. To add to her burdens, when King Philip heard of the treatment meted out to his fellow Catholics in England, he threatened war.

It was at this critical juncture that Anjou, hopeful of obtaining English support against the brutal Spanish presence in the Netherlands, came a-courting once more. At news that he was actually on his way to Richmond, Elizabeth felt her heart leaping – unexpectedly, for she had thought that her feelings for him had died. She chose a fine house for him in the palace precincts – being November, it was too cold for pavilions – and herself supervised the furnishing of it, taking pleasure in every last detail.

Anjou had matured into solid manhood since she had last seen him, and his greeting was more assured. She liked this grown-up Monsieur even better than the fledgling version, and welcomed him with genuine affection. Very soon they fell into their old intimacy. When Elizabeth showed him around his house, she even joked that he might recognise the bed. It was the one on which he and she had once tumbled, giggling, then looked at each other in realisation that something more serious might have been going on between them. How she wished now that she had been able to give in to that impulse. But never mind: he was back now, and who knew what might happen?

She gave him a golden key. 'It fits every door in my palace,' she revealed.

'Is that an invitation, Madame?' he asked, his eyebrows raised mischievously.

'It signifies that the doors of England are open to your Highness,' she smiled.

Anjou gave her in return a diamond ring of great price, with which she was inordinately pleased, even though it had probably been bought with her money. It was the thought that counted, after all, and thank goodness they were finished with wilting flowers. He even attempted to slip the ring on her betrothal finger, but she resisted him, firmly placing it on the other hand. 'That must wait!' she laughed.

They were back to being adoring sweethearts. He was once more her Frog and she his Divine Goddess. She had thought to have kissed goodbye to love and all its pleasures, but now she felt rejuvenated and the future no longer seemed bleak and lonely.

'You are the most constant of my lovers,' she told Anjou (forgetting Robert's twenty-three years of devotion, and the thirteen years in which the Archduke Charles had waited for an answer), at which Monsieur touched his lips to her hand most fervently. 'I shall call you Francis the Constant,' she beamed.

She took delight in showing him around Richmond Palace, that fairy-tale fantasy that had been built by her grandsire, Henry VII, to glorify the Tudor dynasty and adorned with pinnacles, domes, oriel windows and a plethora of royal badges wherever Grandfather could have them crammed in. She led her Frog through the maze of galleries and loggias framing gardens that were beautiful in all seasons; she danced him through the vast great hall, their footsteps echoing in that cavernous space.

She would not – *could* not – attend to any business; all she wanted was to be closeted with her Frog in her privy chamber, where they spent so many exciting and quite glorious hours. She knew that there was much gossip about them, that people were speculating as to what they did there, and that it was even being said that she brought Monsieur breakfast in bed. Anjou fuelled this talk by loudly declaring that he longed day and night to be in Elizabeth's bed, to show what a fine gentleman he could be. The court echoed with suppressed giggles.

Elizabeth had not forgotten that her subjects in general were against the marriage. She had Anjou accompany her to a service in St Paul's Cathedral, so that everyone could see how gracious and debonair he was, and made a point of kissing him in front of the entire congregation. But public opinion remained divided. The French thought that the marriage alliance was as good as sealed, but many Englishmen scoffed and said that the Duke was only after one thing, and that was money.

Anjou grew uneasy. He had been here in England for some weeks and nothing had been decided.

'I would pledge myself to you, my constant Frog,' Elizabeth murmured one day, as she lay in his arms, fully dressed, on the bed in his house.

'Then do so, *ma chérie!*' he urged. 'Make a public declaration of your intentions!'

'I cannot say anything publicly yet,' she said.

'Do not make a fool of me!' he pleaded. For all his ardent courtship, she knew that he wanted the treaty signed as a matter of urgency, as his money, even the sum that she had loaned him, had all but run out.

She was not ready to make a decision. She wanted him, yes – whether she wanted him enough to marry him was another matter entirely – but she did fear provoking her subjects. Not wanting to hurt or alienate Anjou, she staged a little charade for his benefit. She asked him to walk with her in the gallery at Whitehall, having commanded Leicester and Walsingham to be in attendance at a discreet distance. They had been the most vocal opponents of the marriage, so their presence would serve to give credence to what she meant to say.

She had been advised that the French ambassador would try to see her at this time (and she had a good idea what he was going to ask), and sure enough, as if on cue, he entered the gallery.

'Your Majesty, Monsieur,' he addressed her and Anjou, bowing low. 'Madame, we meet by a happy chance, for I have been instructed by my master to hear from your own lips your intention with regard to marrying Monsieur here.'

Elizabeth was ready with her answer. 'You may write this to the King, that the Duke of Anjou shall be my husband.' Then she turned to a delighted Anjou and boldly kissed him on the mouth, drawing a ring from her hand and placing it on his finger. 'This I give you as a pledge, my lord.'

Anjou looked deliriously happy – with love, triumph, or at the prospect of money, it was hard to tell. Hastily he gave her one of his rings in return, and vowed his undying adoration, kneeling in what looked like ecstasy and covering her hands with kisses.

'Now we may consider ourselves betrothed, the promise given and rings exchanged before witnesses,' Elizabeth declared, trying to look as delighted as a woman just betrothed should. She summoned her courtiers to the presence chamber, where, standing in front of her throne, she announced the happy news to them as Anjou beamed exultantly at her side, already dreaming of his coronation in Westminster Abbey and the gold that would soon be coming his way. But Leicester, Hatton and some of the Queen's ladies were seen to be weeping.

The announcement of the marriage sparked an immediate sensation at court. People were amazed that the Queen had finally decided to take a husband – and about time too! Church bells were rung. In his sickbed, laid up with gout, old Burghley cried, 'Praise the Lord!' Some of Elizabeth's courtiers leaped for joy; others, detesting the French and fearing the Catholics, wore their sorrow like a cloak. The mood in London was subdued.

By nightfall – it had not even been twelve hours since she gave her promise – Elizabeth was regretting what she had done. She had said more than she intended, she insisted, listening anxiously to the sounds of carousing and celebration going on around her in the palace. Long after the merrymaking had ceased, she sat up, pensive and doubtful, surrounded by her ladies, the incredulous targets of her laments. Some, catching her mood, were in tears at the prospect of their mistress making this terrible mistake.

'What will become of us?' they wailed. 'The King of Spain will make war on us for this.'

Elizabeth hushed them testily, but she knew that their fears were well founded. What had she been thinking of? She had betrothed herself before witnesses, just to keep the French on her side and Monsieur on the boil, and there was no going back now. She could not sleep for worrying about it. Of course, she told herself, the French King would refuse the terms she offered him, releasing her from her promise. But what if he did not? Well, she would just have to make impossible demands; it would not be the first time, after all. And if that did not have the desired effect, she could be certain that Parliament would veto the marriage. So she was safe. Or was she? Had she foreseen all contingencies?

Her feelings for Anjou now seemed insubstantial beside her reluctance to proceed with their marriage. She saw them, in the dark reaches of the night when stark truths rear their fearsome heads, for what they really were: an illusion born of the vanity of an ageing woman. They were feeble, illusory fantasies compared with the love she had cherished for Robert these twenty years and more. Anjou had fed her conceit; he had brought some long-needed excitement and gaiety into her life. But truth to tell, she was growing weary of the ritual courtship dance, the extravagant compliments, the pretence that this was true love. In fact she wanted nothing more at this moment than for him to go away.

She lay there wakeful until the late winter dawn broke, then stood wilting like a rag doll as her women dressed her. She felt ill, as if she would faint. When Anjou came to her she almost collapsed into his arms.

'I am very worried, dear Frog,' she confessed. 'I spoke out of passion yesterday, not wisdom, and if I endure two more such nights as the one I have just spent, I will be in my grave. You must not think that I do not love you. You must know that I want to marry you more than anything I have ever wanted in this life. My affection for you is undiminished. But

I have been forced to the conclusion that I cannot marry you at present. I must sacrifice my happiness for the welfare of my subjects.'

She felt Anjou stiffen in dismay before he relinquished her. She saw him swallow as he stood, cold-eyed, before her. 'I am utterly saddened and disappointed,' he said in a strangled voice. 'And now, forgive me, I must leave you in order to compose myself.'

He went, fuming, seething with humiliation. Had ever man been treated so contemptuously? She would not marry him after all. She meant to make him wait indefinitely, with no hope of a happy outcome. There would be no coronation, no money, and when this got out he would be covered in ignominy because of her rejection. He could wave goodbye to glory in the Netherlands too! All his careful courtship, all that romantic charade, had been for nothing!

Very well. He too could play games. If he could not get English gold by marrying the Queen, he would make her pay to get rid of him!

Seeing that the English Jezebel was intent on sealing a marriage alliance with his enemies, the French, King Philip began making friendly noises, offering to forgive her past transgressions against Spain. Elizabeth saw that she was now in a strong position, especially as far as France was concerned.

King Henri read the long list of demands she had sent him. Outrageous! He could not possibly consent to any of them.

He had rejected her demands out of hand! The marriage negotiations could now be considered terminated. Consumed with relief, Elizabeth thanked God for her deliverance, and felt that a celebration was called for, save that it would not have been appropriate, with the matter so sensitive. Because there was Anjou, glowering, having been told by the French ambassador what her terms had been. '*Mon Dieu!*' he was heard to exclaim. 'I cannot believe the lightness of women, or the inconstancy of these islanders.'

When this was reported to her, Elizabeth summoned him. She would show him a thing or two about the lightness of women. She smiled sweetly. 'If it pleases you to depart for the Netherlands, Monsieur, I will give you a loan of sixty thousand pounds to use against the Spaniards.'

'Divine Goddess,' he said, bending and kissing her hands, 'I cannot sufficiently express my gratitude. I accept your kind offer, of course, and will arrange to depart by Christmas.'

When he had gone Elizabeth danced for joy around her chamber. Sussex, bowing his way in, gaped.

'My lord,' she trilled, 'do you know something? I hate the idea of marriage more every day!'

Christmas came and went and Anjou was still at court.

'Do you not want to go to the Netherlands, my Frog?' Elizabeth demanded to know.

'Alas, I have found that I cannot face being apart from you,' he declared. 'I would rather die than leave England without marrying you.'

Elizabeth's mood abruptly changed. She knew what he was about! 'Do you mean to threaten a poor old woman in her own country?' she said sharply. 'I see I have been at fault, encouraging you in your courtship. Until matters are decided, you must try to think of me as a sister.'

At that, to her consternation, Anjou burst noisily into tears, a seemingly endless flood. God, he looked disgusting, with the snot running out of his nose. Exasperated, she handed him her lace handkerchief and walked off. She was desperate to be free of him.

'I never had any intention of marrying him,' she told her Council, 'but he insists on carrying on this courtship, and it is wearing me down.'

'Might I suggest offering him, as a bribe, an advance of twenty thousand pounds, on condition that he leaves England?' Robert ventured. 'It would be worth it to get rid of him at last.' There was a certain vehemence in his tone, Elizabeth noted, but mercifully he had stopped short of reminding her that he had been right about Anjou all along.

'The thought of wasting so much money on that little man appals me,' she said. 'Good Spirit, pray advise him to leave before the new year comes in. Say he will avoid the expense of buying me a gift.'

Back came Burghley. 'He has already got a gift for your Majesty.'

'Damn him!' Elizabeth swore. Was Anjou to confound her at every turn?

She was not pleased when he confronted her on New Year's Eve.

'You pledged yourself to me!' he reminded her, his tone plaintive, his face choleric.

'I have not forgotten,' she told him, 'and in token of that I will pay you ten thousand pounds of the money I promised to lend you.'

It was not enough, she could see by his expression. He knew very well that, if he left England, he would never see the rest of the loan. And she knew that, if he went now, the money would never be repaid.

Elizabeth's mind was gratefully diverted from the problem of Anjou by the arrival of a new gentleman at court. Walter Raleigh was a Devon man, and great-nephew to her beloved Kat Astley. He was courageous and dashing (he had fought with the Huguenots against the French), brilliant, versatile and dauntless, a poet and a man of many parts. He exuded virility, being tall and dark with penetrating eyes – the very mirror of all that Elizabeth considered attractive in men. She liked his forthright manner, his eloquent speech and his candid opinions. He had rather showily gained her attention when he had spread his cloak over a puddle into which she was about to step, but she had admired him for the panache with which he had done it. Rumour at court had it that he had even taken a diamond and scratched a message on a window in her gallery – *Fain would I climb yet fear I to fall.* And Elizabeth was said to have scored below it: *If thy heart fails thee, climb not at all.* It was typical of her, and all too believable, but no one could say exactly where the window was.

Raleigh's heart had not failed him. It seemed that he gained the Queen's ear in a trice, and within weeks he had risen to become one of her favourites. The turning point was when, one dark February afternoon he got a smut on his face from a brazier, and she offered to wipe it with her own handkerchief. The courtiers looked on in amazement. Elizabeth was captivated by him. The man could do no wrong.

These days it was Walter this and Walter that – or rather Warter this and Warter that, as she nicknamed him, mimicking his broad Devon accent. To him she was Cynthia, goddess of the moon and virgin huntress, and he fancied himself as Orion, the only man who had won Cynthia's heart.

Robert could not stand Warter, and he was not the only one. For Raleigh soon grew insufferably arrogant. He was a liar and a lecher. Robert seethed to see him installed in Durham House on London's Strand, and appearing at court in dazzling outfits each day, ridiculous plumage in his hat and gem-encrusted shoes on his feet. He could not bear to think that Elizabeth was showing favour to this adventurer, this wastrel, this . . . Words failed him. He was aware that he was jealous. He was fifty now, and feared, naturally enough, that his star might be eclipsed by this thirty-year-old upstart.

Hatton was jealous too. He sent Elizabeth a miniature gold bucket containing a letter complaining that 'Warter' was ousting him from his Queen's affections. She laughed when she read it, getting the pun, and hastened to reassure her Mutton.

'If princes were like gods, as they should be,' she told him, 'they would suffer no element to breed confusion. The beasts of the field are so dear to me that I have bounded my banks so sure as no water could ever be able to overthrow them. I am my Mutton's shepherd, and you should remember how dear my sheep is to me!'

She was not blind to Raleigh's faults. She made him captain of her personal guard, the Gentlemen Pensioners, but she told Robert, to mollify him, that she had resolved never to appoint Warter to high office, for he was too unstable, quarrelsome and unpopular.

She was aware that she had treated Robert badly. When she looked at him afresh after one of his absences from court, she was saddened to see a man who had grown old in her service. His long beard was quite white now, his head bald under the brave bonnet. He had put on more weight, his paunch straining his doublet. There was little left of the young and virile gallant who had captured her heart in the heady days after her accession. Yet the inner man remained, the one she would always love – her dearest Eyes, who was closer to her than any other.

He had given her good counsel on countless occasions, and he had been right in suggesting that twenty thousand pounds would be sufficient to make Anjou leave England. When the little Frenchman had presented her with a New Year gift of a brooch in the form of an anchor, symbolising hope and fidelity, she very speedily offered him another ten thousand, which he accepted with alacrity. It was worth every penny, for she had been having sleepless, feverish nights worrying about how to rid herself of her importunate suitor.

She was so relieved when Monsieur informed her that he was leaving early in February that she insisted on accompanying him as far as Canterbury, where they said their farewells in private in a house in the high street, commandeered for the purpose. She also gladly provided an escort of three English warships, and made Leicester and other lords go with the Duke all the way to the Netherlands, just to make sure that he did actually leave the realm.

'I would rather not go,' Robert had told her. 'I am suffering my old stomach pains.'

'Go you must,' she insisted, 'and you will suffer more if you do not treat respectfully the man I love most in the world!' Her lips twitched as she said it, and Robert had to smile. In a low voice, Elizabeth added, 'And I have a message for you to convey secretly to the Dutch. Ask them to ensure that the Duke never returns to England. And, Robin – come back to me safely!' She wrung his hands as she said this. He was surprised, and gratified to hear her using her old pet name for him after so long. At least some good had come out of the Anjou *débâcle*.

In public, and especially when the French ambassador was nearby, Elizabeth showed herself grief-stricken at Anjou's departure. 'I cannot go back to Whitehall,' she cried, 'because the place is full of memories of him with whom I have unwillingly parted.' She dabbed touchingly at her eyes. 'I do declare that I cannot live another hour were it not for the hope of seeing Monsieur again. Thank God he will be back in six weeks.' It was a lie, but no one was to know that. And six *years* would not be too soon.

She wore at her girdle a tiny prayer book set with miniatures of herself and the Duke, and told the astonished Spanish ambassador that she would give a million pounds to have her Frog swimming in the Thames once more (whereupon he immediately informed his master that he had heard it from the Queen's own lips that she was keen for the French marriage to go ahead). She wrote loving letters to her absent suitor, who in turn kept up the pretence that they were soon to be wed. He even pressed her to name the day. Elizabeth was determined to maintain this fictional courtship for as long as possible; her aim, as before, was to keep the French friendly and King Philip at bay.

Robert was soon back at court, looking pleased with himself for having, literally, seen off his rival for the Queen's affections. In full hearing of her courtiers, he could not resist taking a prod at Anjou. 'Some conqueror he looked like when we docked at Flushing! He resembled nothing so much as an old husk, run ashore, high and dry.'

Elizabeth screamed at him, for she feared he had ruined everything. 'Don't you dare be so insolent as to mock your future king, my lord! You are a traitor, like all your horrible family!'

Robert recoiled at her unexpected tirade. But Elizabeth's anger cooled as quickly as it had flared. Robert was right: Anjou was a husk of a man. Her spies informed her that he preferred to play tennis while the Spanish Duke of Parma took city after city. What was he thinking of?

Monsieur, are you quite mad? she thundered, her quill flying across the page. *You seem to believe that the means of keeping our friends is to weaken them!* After that, of course, there was no hope that Anjou would ever again contemplate coming back to England to claim her.

Anjou was back in France. He had been spectacularly repelled after foolishly turning on the Dutch rebels who had failed to support him, and had scuttled off home, his great ambitions in shreds.

'France never received so great a disgrace,' Walsingham pronounced.

Elizabeth said nothing. She sat brooding in her great chair. She felt no sense of triumph, only an intense sadness. All pretence that she would marry Anjou had been abandoned. She would not waste herself on a prince covered with ignominy. It did not trouble her. But she was now nearly fifty, and knew that her courting days were over.

'I am an old woman,' she said suddenly, 'and paternosters must suffice in place of nuptials.'

'Not so, Madam,' Burghley protested gallantly. 'You are our Hebe, the goddess of youth, eternally beautiful and raised above ordinary mortals.'

'My Lord Treasurer speaks truth,' Robert chimed in, his eyes warm and tender, and the other councillors chorused in assent.

Elizabeth smiled wanly, grateful to them for their courtesy and compliments. But face it she must: the Tudor dynasty would end with her, an ageing, barren woman, and instead of raising her own heirs, she would now have to grapple with the problem of the succession. Worse than that, she had lost her chief bargaining counter, which she had played to advantage – and at no small price to herself – for a quarter of a century: her hand in marriage. No longer was she the best match in her parish, as Walsingham had once called her. Youth had fled, and she was now probably past the age for bearing children. God grant at least that she outlived the Queen of Scots!

Marriage was no longer an option, but love and fidelity were just as important. She had persuaded herself that Robert's chief loyalty was still to her, and had resolutely ignored the likelihood that he had a prior loyalty to another, so she was furious when, that summer, he mentioned *that woman* – and as 'my lady wife', if you please – in her presence. In fact she was so incensed that she sent him from the court in disgrace, then went about telling everyone that Lettice – *that she-wolf* – had made him a cuckold.

'I will expose her in all the courts of Christendom for the bad woman she is,' she growled. But her inner voice of wisdom told her that she should not dare to provoke Robert that far, and by the end of August all was forgiven – at least on her part, for Robert was finding it hard to forgive Elizabeth for the unfounded calumny she had spread about Lettice – and he was back at court, in greater favour than he'd enjoyed for a long time. His place at the Queen's side was to remain unchallenged, because soon afterwards his old adversary Sussex died, and with him gone, Leicester's opponents lost their mouthpiece.

Robert was in favour, yes, but his power, like his health, was waning. He wanted – as he had wanted for so long – to lead an army into the Netherlands and drive out the Spaniards, while he still could, but Elizabeth would not hear of it. He was not well, she reminded him. She did not like the high, ruddy colour of his cheeks, and she worried a lot about the stomach pains he now suffered increasingly. She nagged him more than ever to eat a careful diet and made him visit Buxton once more to take the waters. Nothing seemed to help. Pain, and anxiety about his condition, made Robert short-tempered and intolerant of criticism; to hear him these days, you would think that every man was his enemy.

'What ails you, Robin?' Elizabeth asked, unable to conceal her fear. 'You always had a mild, amiable nature. I appeal from this lord of Leicester to my old lord of Leicester, who won the praise of so many. I want him back!'

He forced a smile. 'I am sorry I have been like an old bear, Bess. I'll be better in a few days. Just let me get back in the saddle and give the Spaniards a trouncing, and I will be a new man.'

'No!' she said, more vehemently than she intended. 'England cannot muster an army strong enough to overcome Parma's forces.'

'Tactics, Bess, tactics! What of Crécy and Agincourt? We were heavily outnumbered in both battles, but we won great victories.'

'I will not take the chance, and I will not risk your safety. You occupy a special place in my heart, Robin.'

'I know that, Bess.' He wished he could compete with her younger favourites, Raleigh and now young Charles Blount, newly come to court. Really, it was ridiculous to see a twenty-year-old boy fawning over a woman of fifty – and Charles was not the only one. All the youth of England seemed to be clamouring to be part of the charmed elite that clustered around the Queen. Already she was a legend, and her popularity had never been greater, especially in the wake of a horrifying plot to shoot her and put her head on a pole over London Bridge. The perpetrator had been a mad Catholic lad acting alone but inspired by Jesuit propaganda, and he had hanged himself in his cell at Newgate before they could put his head where he had meant to put his Queen's.

In the wake of this lucky escape, there was an upsurge of love and loyalty for Elizabeth. Wherever she went, crowds would gather, and people knelt by the wayside wishing her a thousand blessings, calling down curses on those evil persons who meant harm to her.

'I see clearly that I am not disliked by all,' she observed. She would have no children of her own, yet it was heartening to know that she was widely seen as a careful mother to her people, the small as well as the great, whom she had kept in safety and quietness these twenty-five years.

1585

The court was at Nonsuch Palace in Surrey, enjoying the brilliant July weather and the hunting to be had nearby, when a messenger arrived from Wanstead with the news that Robert's little son was dead of a fever. In an agony of grief, he saddled his horse and galloped homewards to console Lettice, not even pausing to ask Elizabeth's permission to depart. But she understood, and forgave him for it. She sent after him a courtier, Sir Henry Killigrew, with a heartfelt message of sympathy. Burghley, in turn, placed his house, Theobalds, at the disposal of the bereaved parents, so that they could mourn in private in a place where there were no reminders of their precious boy.

When Robert returned to court, having laid his only heir to rest in St Mary's Church at Warwick, he was a grievously changed and desolate man. He had aged ten years in as many weeks, and the pains in his stomach had intensified. Elizabeth did her best to console him, as did his colleagues on the Council, but all he could think of was the loss of his boy.

'My noble imp was just five years old,' he wept. 'He was too good for this world. Now all my wealth will go to my brother Warwick.' It was heart-rendingly clear that Robert would father no more children. Aged beyond his years at fifty-three, he plainly had not the vigour for it.

'I want to retire from public life,' he said abruptly.

'No, my Eyes,' said Elizabeth. 'I will not hear of it.'

'You are needed here, my lord,' Hatton told him. 'You cannot abandon us now.' He spoke truth, because the Queen of Scots had been found to have been actively plotting against Elizabeth, and it was evident that she was determined to overthrow her

370

and seize her throne; William of Orange, the brave leader of the Dutch Protestants, had been murdered on King Philip's orders; and Elizabeth's subjects were in terror lest she be next on Spain's list. With William gone – and Anjou dead this past year of malaria contracted in the Netherlands – nothing now stood between England and that great Spanish army in the Netherlands, and Parma was advancing relentlessly . . .

What would happen when there were no more cities left to take?

Elizabeth turned to Robert. 'Pull yourself together, old man. I am sending you to the Netherlands at the head of an army, to aid the Protestants there. I hope that cheers you!'

Robert turned his ravaged face to her in amazement. 'After all this time, you have consented to let me go?' he asked, unable quite to believe her.

'It is against my better judgement,' she said briskly, 'but I know that I can trust you, and that you are enthusiastic about the venture.'

Robert's eyes had lit up; she had known that this was the one thing that would rouse him from the torpor of grief. But yes, she had her qualms. His health was not good, and it was thirty years since he had seen action in the field. Warfare had changed in that time, and Parma was a great general. But she had made her decision not only for reasons of state, but also to divert Robert from his grief and restore his pride (and hers, if truth be told) in his manhood. Yet now that she had issued the order she would have given much to retract it.

Robert's spirits, however, had been revived by the prospect of trouncing the Spaniards. He would show those young bucks and gallants about the court what he was made of! He only wished that he was twenty years younger.

Seeing him busily occupied with preparations for the coming campaign, Elizabeth found her heart sinking. She could not face the prospect of parting from him. Something strange was happening to her, and had been for a year now. As her monthly courses had visited her less frequently, her moods had become ever more variable, and her temper more volatile. She could not help herself. She was more emotional these days, more given to irrational outbursts. To her horror, she was becoming what she had always despised, a clinging woman – and the man she was clinging on to was Robert.

In despair, she summoned him one night. She sounded pitiful, even to herself. 'Do not go to the Netherlands and leave me,' she pleaded. 'I – I fear I will not live long.' In truth, what she feared was that *he* would not live long, but she could not say that.

'That's nonsense!' he retorted. 'You have the constitution of an ox, and will outlive us all. Now, no more of this kind of talk. You know, none better, how much our English presence is needed over there. We will push back the Spaniards and then I will come home in triumph, and we will have a big celebration.'

'Yes,' she said, unconvinced.

'Do not worry, Bess,' Robert reassured her. 'All will be well.'

She was more cheerful after that. But how long this feeling would last was anyone's guess. One night Robert found himself being shaken awake by a groom in royal livery who informed him that it was the Queen's pleasure that he forbear to proceed with his military preparations until further notice.

What the hell was she playing at? Swearing great oaths, he pulled on some clothes and went in search of his fellow councillors, desperate to enlist their support. He found Walsingham working late in his closet, and slumped down on the stool facing him.

'Why, Robert, whatever ails you?' Walsingham said, laying down his pen and dragging his mind away from implementing the latest security measures against the Scottish Queen.

'I am weary of life and all,' Robert blurted out, and related what had happened.

'I shouldn't worry too much about it,' Walsingham said soothingly. 'You know what our mistress is like. She may be of another mind in the morning.'

And she was. She rescinded the order. Yet still she showed herself morose and irritable at the prospect of Robert's impending departure. And so it went on for days. Then she had another gripe.

'You are to be my Lieutenant General,' she informed him. It was an insult. He had expected to be accorded the highest rank, Captain General; it was his right, and it served a practical purpose, for it commanded the greatest respect.

'Why, in God's name?' he barked.

'I do not want you seeking your own glory rather than my true service,' Elizabeth said peevishly.

He was speechless. 'Any glory I win will naturally be yours,' he countered, trying to control his anger at yet another affront to his integrity.

'But the Dutch might not see it that way. And, my lord, you must never accept from them any title or role that implies my acceptance of the sovereignty of the Netherlands, for I do not want it.'

'You can rely on me, Madam,' he replied stiffly. Two could play at being formal. Her unfair assumption stung, and he felt that he must say something to counter it. 'Your Majesty puts me on trial to test how much I love you, and you even try to discourage me from your service, but I am resolved that nothing in this world shall draw me back from my faithful discharge of my duty towards you – even though you seem to hate me, which touches me very nearly, for suddenly I find no love or favour in you at all.'

Their eyes met, his wounded, hers filling with tears.

'Oh Robin, I just do not want you to go!' Elizabeth cried. 'Forgive me my unkindness. No queen ever had a more loyal servant.'

He stepped forward and drew her to him, gentling her against his breast. She had forgotten how good it felt to be in his embrace, and that made her weep even more.

'Fear not, Bess,' he murmured. 'I will take care of myself and all your brave soldiers. We will come back safely to you, covered in glory, you'll see!'

*

The kindness between them did not last. As befitted the Queen's commander in the Netherlands, Robert was to take with him a great household of one hundred and seventy persons, with his young stepson, the Earl of Essex, acting as his master of horse. But then it came to Elizabeth's ears that *that woman* was going too, and insisting on transporting with her a great train of ladies and a vast amount of baggage – magnificent gowns, furniture, tapestries, even her carriages!

'I did not send you to the Netherlands so that *your wife* could queen it over there!' Elizabeth shouted. 'Tell her to learn a little humility, or I will strip you of your command!'

Robert bore her histrionics stoically; he knew that they proceeded from jealousy, and the fear of losing him. He asked a simmering Lettice to scale down her preparations – 'This is war, and it is not meet that you keep great state,' he told her – and hoped that she would comply. One never knew with her; she was always itching to defy the Queen, whom she resented as bitterly as Elizabeth resented her. He sighed, and reflected for the umpteenth time that it was not easy being caught between two warring women! And now the Queen was refusing to take any further interest in his preparations because Lettice was going with him.

Finally he sailed, leaving his tearful sovereign behind – and immediately upon his arrival in the Netherlands ran into a problem. For the Dutch, so grateful to him for coming to their rescue, had arranged to send him on what amounted to a royal progress around their country, and were insisting that he consent to become their ruler, as Governor General.

He thought he might see the fireworks from Holland when news of *that* reached Elizabeth.

'How dare they?' Elizabeth spluttered. 'And how dare he accept!' She was shaking with a fury such as her councillors had never witnessed.

She dashed off a letter castigating Robert in the strongest terms for what she was pleased to call his childish dealing. 'You have made me infamous to all princes!' she ranted. 'On the duty of your allegiance, you will stand down, and fail not to obey my command, or you will answer for it at your utmost peril.'

Robert read her words with a heavy heart. He had believed – and still did – that he was acting in her best interests. He had sent William Davison, her secretary whom she had decreed must accompany him, back to England to tell her of the invitation to become Governor General, but Davison had been delayed by bad weather, and Robert had assumed that Elizabeth had voiced no objection. To be honest, he had wanted to accept the office. He knew now that he should have waited until he had heard from her himself, just to be sure that she was happy for him to do so.

Instead, a distressed Davison wrote that Elizabeth had lectured him in the most bitter and hard terms, refusing to let him speak in his or Robert's favour. Never, to Robert's knowledge, had she condemned a man before she heard him. He guessed that she was feeling the strain of his absence and the other worries that lay heavy on her shoulders. Walsingham wrote that she was daily becoming less able to bear any matter of weight, and his own brother, Warwick, informed him that her great rage against him had increased rather than diminished. She was even withholding pay from his soldiers out of pique.

'Her blasts are always sharpest towards those she loves the best, God be thanked,' Robert observed to Essex, sounding more confident than he felt.

His colleagues on the Council were anxious lest Elizabeth take it into her head to recall him, for it would never do for the Spaniards to see the English divided. They used every effort to calm her down and pacify her, telling her that Leicester had acted for the best, but it took a messenger bringing news that he was ill to make her accept the situation.

'He has offered to resign,' Burghley told her, 'but the Dutch have written begging your Majesty to reconsider. Madam, *I* will resign if he steps down, so God spares him to continue.' It was not often that her Lord Treasurer gave her ultimatums.

'Very well,' she said, gritting her teeth, 'he may remain as Governor General. But it must be made clear that he is not *my* deputy, and that he is in a subordinate position. He is a subject, not an equal prince.'

Robert accepted with relief. He would have agreed to any terms. He was overjoyed therefore when Raleigh wrote that the Queen was speaking favourably of him. *Thanks be to God, she is well pacified, and you are again her Sweet Robin.* He had to smile at that, coming from Warter.

England was still beset on three fronts. There was the danger from the Netherlands and from Spain, where Philip was amassing his great *armada*, having received the Pope's blessing on his planned enterprise of England. Then there was the Queen of Scots, plotting away at Chartley.

When Elizabeth told the Spanish ambassador, 'I know all that goes on in my kingdom,' she spoke the truth. For a trap had been laid for Mary, and the only people who knew about it were Elizabeth, Leicester and Walsingham; the latter's secretary, Thomas Phelippes, an expert cipher breaker; and a turncoat priest, Gilbert Gifford, a double agent in Walsingham's employ. Thanks to Gifford and Phelippes, Mary's letters were being secretly intercepted and deciphered, and they made for very interesting reading. One had urged King Philip to invade England as soon as possible. Another had revealed details of a Catholic rebellion, planned to coincide with the invasion. Thanks to this intelligence, Walsingham's spies were able to keep watch on the suspects.

The trail led to an idealistic but rather silly young Catholic gentleman, Anthony Babington, who was clearly half in love with Mary, whose page he had once been and to whom he aimed to present the crown of England. He and his friends were blithely plotting the assassination of the Queen Elizabeth, and had even been so rash as to have their group portrait painted for posterity. Then Babington wrote to Mary asking her to approve the plan and the 'tragical execution' of the usurper.

Walsingham and Elizabeth held their breath, waiting to see what Mary would do.

'If this matter is well handled, it will break the neck of all dangerous practices for the rest of your Majesty's reign,' Walsingham observed.

'I have every confidence in you, old Moor,' the Queen smiled.

Mary's reply finally arrived. In it she unequivocally approved Babington's plot and the assassination of Elizabeth. Phelippes deciphered her incriminating words and handed the letter to Walsingham, who saw that his secretary had drawn a gallows in one corner. Well satisfied, Walsingham took it to the Queen.

The year before, Parliament had passed an Act providing for any wicked person of whatever rank or nationality – meaning, obviously, the Queen of Scots – suspected of plotting treason to be tried and put to death.

'Can we now proceed against her?' Walsingham asked.

'Yes,' Elizabeth agreed. She knew that she could not afford to take any other course.

'Very well, Madam, I will gather the evidence and draw up an indictment.'

Elizabeth was panicking. Not so much at the prospect of Mary's imminent arrest, although she shrank from the notion of subjecting an anointed queen to trial (even if she had been forced to abdicate, Mary was still, in her eyes, Scotland's rightful Queen). That was bad enough, and she was not entirely sure of the legality of it. Nor did she relish the prospect of the natural consequence of a guilty verdict, which was Mary dying on the scaffold, as Anne Boleyn had done; and she was resolved never to allow it. Her conscience would not permit it. But now such concerns had been swept out of her head, for Robert had written urging her to accept the crown of the Netherlands, assuring her that it would be the surest way of winning the war.

'I dare not provoke King Philip!' she cried, knowing that Mary's arrest alone would be sufficient to do that – and that cold Spaniard already poised to send his *armada* against her.

Her councillors soothed her, telling her that she was under no obligation or need to accept the Dutch crown. It was her decision entirely. When she was calmer, she regretted her outburst, and wrote to Robert, trying to explain her immoderate reaction. *Rob, I am afraid that my wandering writings will make you suppose that a midsummer moon has taken possession of my brains, but you must take things as they come in my head. I do imagine that I still talk with you, and therefore am loath to say farewell, my Eyes, though ever I pray that God will bless you from all harm, and save you from your foes, and I send you my million and legion thanks for all your pains. As you know, ever the same, E.R.*

Robert smiled when he read this, a great warmth flooding his breast. It had taken seven months of storms and wrangling, but at last they were back on their old footing, and he was more relieved than he could say. He worried about Elizabeth, though, and he knew his fellow councillors shared his concerns. She was under so much strain that he feared it might break her. He wondered how the entrapment of the Queen of Scots was progressing. To think he might have married that dreadful daughter of debate, as Elizabeth had once called her!

*

In August Mary was arrested while hawking with her guards on the Staffordshire moors. Already her fellow conspirators – fourteen of them – had been rounded up and cast into the Tower.

When news of the arrests was announced, the bells pealed out in London and people danced and celebrated in the streets. In the Tower, Babington broke and confessed all, terrified of being put to the torture. His seven confessions incriminated Queen Mary and those others who had plotted with him to place a crown on her head.

'Your Majesty must summon Parliament to deal with the Queen of Scots,' Burghley said, determined to have the problem of this venomous princess dealt with once and for all.

'I will think on it,' Elizabeth said, stalling desperately. She knew that Parliament would insist on a trial and execution that it would expect her to sanction.

'Madam, you cannot be seen to be wavering,' Walsingham growled.

'Your Majesty *must* proceed against her,' Burghley insisted, his voice unwontedly stern. 'You must be seen to be just. If the lesser conspirators are to suffer the punishment the law demands for their treason, as surely they will, then the chief conspirator should not escape.'

'Very well.' Elizabeth capitulated, feeling sick to her stomach. 'I will summon Parliament.'

Babington and the other small fry had been condemned to a traitor's death. The agony facing them was unimaginable. They would be tied to hurdles and drawn by horses to the place of execution, for they had been deemed unfit to walk upon the earth; then each would be hanged by the neck, but they would not be allowed to choke to death, for before they passed into oblivion they would be cut down, and the butchery would begin. They would be castrated and disembowelled, have their hearts and entrails torn out, and all their vitals burned before their dying eyes. Only then would they be granted the mercy of beheading, and after that their bodies would be chopped into quarters, and the quarters and heads placed on spikes in public places, grim warnings to other would-be traitors.

'They plotted to murder me!' Elizabeth cried, shuddering in horror at the thought of the cold steel or the poisoned cup that had so nearly been her fate, and she a queen too. It had been treason of the worst kind. 'Is this sufficient punishment? I have heard that the executioner usually waits until his victims are dead before wielding the knife, but, William, I want a stern example made in the case of these traitors. Hanging, drawing and quartering is too good for them!'

'Madam,' Burghley said, wondering if she had ever seen a man being hanged, drawn and quartered, 'rest assured that the executions shall be duly and orderly executed by protracting the sentence to the extremity of the pain, and in the sight of the people. There will be no mercy shown. Believe me, the manner of death will be as terrible as any new punishment could be.'

Elizabeth looked doubtful, standing there gnawing her lip, but eventually Burghley persuaded her that the penalty provided for by the law was dreadful enough. And indeed the executions of Babington and six of his fellow conspirators were so uncommonly savage that the crowd turned away, sickened, and voices were raised in sympathy for the condemned.

Elizabeth knew that she had made a grave misjudgement. More than anything else she feared to lose the love of her people. Immediately she sent orders to the Tower: the remaining seven traitors, due to die the next day, were to hang by the neck until they were dead before the executioner began his grim work. Soon the people, ever fickle, were baying for their blood, and that of the murderous Queen of Scots. Ballads and pamphlets were circulated demanding Mary's head. Was not she the chief architect and focus of the late plot? Why should others suffer punishment and not her?

'I shrink from proceeding against her, my Spirit,' Elizabeth confided to Burghley, for Walsingham had no time for qualms, and Robert was of course abroad. 'She is an anointed queen, as am I.'

'Madam, there are many good reasons for letting the law take its course. There can now be no doubt that she plotted against your life, and we at last have evidence for it that can be produced in court. While the Queen of Scots lives, she will be a focus for Catholic rebellion. Her death will clear the way for a Protestant succession. The French have long since abandoned her cause, and King Philip can have no worse intentions towards us than those he already has.'

Elizabeth still looked distressed.

'Think of your people,' Burghley said kindly. 'They are unsettled and fearful after recent events, and a prey to rumour-mongers. At least let your Council debate the matter.'

'Very well,' she agreed, fearing that she might be hounded into a corner from which there was no honourable escape.

Her fears proved well founded. Her councillors, every man of them, wanted Mary in the Tower.

'No!' she protested, appalled. 'I will never consent to that.' It would have been too redolent of her mother's fate, and her own traumatic imprisonment in that grim place.

Other strongholds were suggested, but she vetoed them all. 'What of Fotheringhay Castle?' Walsingham wondered. Elizabeth considered. Fotheringhay was a good choice. It was the seat of her ancestors of the House of York, and well away from the capital; it also boasted ranges of royal apartments, and above all it was a secure stronghold.

'The apartments have hardly been used for a century,' she recalled, 'but they were still sufficiently palatial when I visited twenty years ago, even if they were somewhat musty and threadbare. Yes, Francis, Queen Mary shall go to Fotheringhay.'

'And there she will be tried?' Walsingham persisted.

Elizabeth paused. 'I agree that there is every justification for it. But the Queen of Scots is a foreigner who is not subject to English law, and in truth, as an anointed sovereign, she is answerable to God alone for her deeds.'

'But Madam, the question of your right to try her under the Act has already been laid before a panel of lawyers, who have debated the matter at length, and they have advised me that you may legally prosecute her. So are you now ready to give the order?'

The faces of the men ranged along the table were implacable, determined. They had cleared the way for this prosecution and were determined to press ahead with it. She felt an icy tingle of fear at what she was being forced to do.

'Very well,' she said. 'I authorise you to appoint commissioners, good men and true. Three dozen should be more than sufficient, for I will have justice seen to be done. And, William, you, Francis and Christopher are to be of their number.'

As if she had not suffered enough pressure, she received a letter from Robert. *I urge you to allow the law to take its course*, he wrote. *It is most certain that, if you would be safe, it must be done, for justice craves it beside policy.* His words left her weeping. She felt alone, utterly alone. This was what it was to be a queen.

The court assembled. Mary haughtily refused to acknowledge its competence to try her and, threatened with being tried in her absence, declared that she was no subject and would rather die a thousand deaths than acknowledge herself to be one.

Informed of this, Elizabeth wrote to Mary herself, her tone chill and peremptory. *You have in various ways and manners attempted to take my life and bring my kingdom to destruction by bloodshed. It is my will that you answer the nobles and peers of my kingdom, as if I were myself present.* At that, Mary capitulated, and the hearing commenced. She defended herself eloquently, but even she, accomplished intriguer that she was, could not rebut the evidence laid against her.

'Her guilt is established beyond doubt,' Burghley declared, and the commissioners saw their duty clear. But before they could pronounce Mary guilty, a letter arrived post-haste from Elizabeth, who had been racked with uncertainty and unable to sleep. The court must be adjourned to London, she commanded, where it would reconvene in the Star Chamber at Westminster.

Dutifully the commissioners returned south, leaving Mary at Fotheringhay in ignorance of her fate. But when they assembled in the Star Chamber and came to debate what was to be done with her, they found themselves subject to constant interference by the Queen.

'I would to God her Majesty would be content to refer these things to them that can best judge of them,' Walsingham muttered. Elizabeth was stalling again, he suspected.

There was no other possible verdict. With only one voice dissenting, the judges found the Queen of Scots guilty of entering a treasonable conspiracy against Queen Elizabeth's life, and of imagining and compassing the Queen's destruction.

The penalty, under the Act, was death. But the court did not presume to pass sentence. That would be a matter for the Queen and Parliament.

Elizabeth was distraught. The outcome she had feared above all had come to pass, and now she was faced with the most difficult decision of her life. Must she really give the order for her sister monarch to be put to death? Mary, like herself, had been hallowed by God; her person was sacred. Who was she, Elizabeth, to do violence upon her equal, even if the law did demand it?

She fretted and wept, tossing and turning in her bed. Was this not the most cruel decision to impose on her, whose own mother had died by the sword, and who had so narrowly escaped such a fate herself? She knew, none better, what it was like to live in terror of the summons to the scaffold, to imagine the deadly slicing of the blade. It had been dreadful enough having to send another cousin, Norfolk, to the block; but he had not been a sovereign ruler.

If she did what she was being pressured to do, what would the world think of her? Would she be reviled for acting outside the law? Would her Catholic subjects unite and rebel against her? Would Philip of Spain be moved to send his *armada* once the deed was done? Would the French, whose queen Mary had once been, be so incensed that they would rally in her cause, and perhaps even unite with Spain against Elizabeth? And what of the Scots? Mary's son, James VI, now twenty, had been brought up by Calvinists, and had abandoned the cause of the mother he had not seen since infancy, having been raised to believe that she had betrayed and murdered his father; he too looked to have the succession of the English crown, and feared on that account to offend Elizabeth. But even he might dredge up some filial feeling if Mary was put to death.

Elizabeth felt as a hare must feel when the hounds are gaining ground upon it. She could no longer rationalise her thoughts, and her sense of good judgement seemed to have deserted her. If only God would vouchsafe her a sign showing her the right thing to do.

All her instincts were screaming that she must let Mary live. And yet . . . and yet . . . Mary had had no scruples at all when it had come to plotting Elizabeth's death and the seizing of her throne. She had intrigued to that end all her adult life. The shadow she had cast these past nineteen years had darkened the lives of all Elizabeth's loyal subjects; she had been a focus for, if not the authoress of, conspiracy after conspiracy. She had sat there in her northern fastnesses like a great black spider, weaving an ever-widening web of treason and danger. And if she was let to live, she would not cease, that much was certain. Her sense of entitlement to the English throne was too deep-rooted. She would remain a magnet for Elizabeth's enemies, and a constant source of trouble and anxiety.

These were the thoughts that kept Elizabeth awake at night and plagued her by day. She knew not how to resolve the conflict within herself. She wished that her councillors would stop putting her under duress and bullying her. She wished that Robert was here to counsel her, although she knew what he would say, so there was no comfort to be missed there.

It was the thought of Robert that kept her going. He had

won a great victory at Zutphen, where both young Essex and Sir Philip Sidney had distinguished themselves. The heroic Sidney had been wounded, not badly, it was reported. Elizabeth had been touched when told that, lying wounded and parched on the battlefield, he had refused water and given it to a dying soldier nearby, saying, 'Thy need is greater than mine.' She had written to commend him for that, expecting to receive him when he returned a hero. But then came the tragic news that this brilliant young man – the best of courtiers and a great soldier and talented poet – had died. His death came hard on the heels of those of his parents, Elizabeth's old friends, Sir Henry and Lady Mary Sidney. Her grief for all three left her even more emotional. She ordered the court into mourning, and ordered that Sir Philip, that flower of English manhood, be accorded the honour of a state funeral in St Paul's Cathedral.

Meanwhile, a demoralised Robert had failed to capitalise on his victory. His men had begun to desert him, for he had well-nigh impoverished himself in the cause of Dutch independence, since the meagre funds Elizabeth had provided had been not nearly enough. It was obvious that his venture was doomed to ignominy and failure, and that his health could not sustain a winter of futile campaigning. When he asked for leave to come home, Elizabeth did not demur. In fact she was overjoyed at the prospect.

When Parliament finally sat, she took care to stay well away at Richmond.

'Are you not coming up to Whitehall as usual, Madam?' Burghley asked. 'We are to debate the fate of the Queen of Scots, a problem of more weight, peril and dangerous consequence than any of the other business that will be laid before Parliament.'

'I am loath to hear about that foul and grievous matter,' Elizabeth replied, frowning mutinously. 'I would have small pleasure in being there.'

But her staying away made no difference. As she had expected, the Lords and Commons demanded Mary's head.

Elizabeth was not pleased to find a deputation of them waiting on her at Richmond with a petition to have a just sentence on this daughter of sedition, as they put it, followed by a just execution. Yet they were so patently concerned for her own safety and the security of the realm – even warning her not to accept gifts of perfume, gloves or food, for fear of poison – that she could not find it in herself to be angry with them.

'I have never entertained any malice towards the Queen of Scots,' she told them. 'I have had great experience and trial of this world. I know what it is to be a subject, what to be a sovereign, what to have good neighbours or evil willers. I have found treason in trust, and seen great favours little regarded. I grieve that one of my own sex and kin should have plotted my death. I wrote to Queen Mary myself, promising her that, if she confessed all, I would cover her shame and save her from reproach, but she continued to deny her guilt. But even now, if she truly repented, I would be inclined to pardon her.' She saw dismay in the faces of many of the deputation.

'You have laid a hard hand on me, that I must give directions for her death,' she continued, her voice taut with emotion. 'It is a grievous and irksome burden to me. We princes are set on stages, in the sight and view of all the world. It behoves us to be careful, just and honourable in our proceedings. All I can say is that I will pray and consider the matter.'

'Delay is dangerous, Madam,' one gentleman ventured.

'I know that,' she told him. 'But I vow to you now that I will do inviolably what is right.' And God grant me the wisdom to know what that might be, she prayed to herself.

In the end, fearing to anger her loving subjects, she gave in.

Mary had been informed of the sentence passed on her, although she had been given no inkling of the agony of mind that Elizabeth had suffered before finally agreeing to bend to Parliament's will. Elizabeth forced herself to read the letter her cousin had sent her, thanking her for the happy tidings that she was to come to the end of her long and weary pilgrimage. *I must remind you,* Mary had ended, *that one day you will have to answer for your charge, and I desire that my blood be remembered in that time.*

This reduced Elizabeth to torrents of weeping, and she was in a very fragile state of mind when, at last, Robert returned home. When he obeyed the summons to come privily to her chamber, she threw herself into his arms and clung to him as a drowning man clings to a branch.

'Thank God! Thank God!' she cried. 'Oh Robin, how I have missed you!'

'Well, I do declare,' he smiled, tenderly disengaging himself and kneeling to kiss her hand. 'Never since I was born did I receive a more gracious welcome!'

She looked at him lovingly. He had aged in the year he had been away, and looked slightly shrunken. His beloved face was etched with more lines, and he carried himself stiffly. She wondered if he was still suffering stomach pains.

'How does my Queen?' he asked.

'That can wait,' she told him, knowing that if she unburdened herself to him the floodgates would open. 'More to the point, how are you, my Eyes?'

'Well enough,' he said. She let it go. There would be time for talking and healing, please God. She would fetch him the best doctors in the land if he needed them, aye, and pay for them.

He gave her the brief facts of his final days in the Netherlands, but she could see that the long journey had tired him, and reluctantly let him go to get some rest.

In council the next morning Burghley and Walsingham expressed genuine pleasure at having Leicester back. They would! Elizabeth thought venomously. They wanted his support for what was to come, knowing that she placed a high value on his opinions. Sure enough, Robert added his voice to theirs, and at a private supper in her chamber that evening he went creaking on his knees and begged her to have Mary's death warrant drawn up and sign it.

'You really have no choice, Bess,' he pleaded. 'It is only of you and this blessed kingdom that I think.'

The next morning Elizabeth announced that she would have the sentence on Mary publicly proclaimed. But that night she did not sleep at all, fearing that she had committed herself to the inevitable consequence of doing so. She groaned inwardly when, just before dinner, the French ambassador came seeking an audience and beseeched her to show clemency towards the Queen of Scots.

'Matters have gone too far for that,' she told him. 'This just sentence was passed on a bad woman protected by bad men. If I am to live, Queen Mary must die.' She was holding to her resolve – just.

Parliament sent another deputation urging her to have the sentence carried out. But now she showed herself distracted and undecided. 'Clearly it has been decided that my surety cannot be established without a princess's head. It is grievous that I, who have pardoned so many rebels and winked at so many treasons in my time, should be forced to this proceeding against such a personage. What will my enemies say?' she shrilled. 'That for the surety of her life, a maiden queen was content to spill the blood even of her own kinswoman? I should have cause for complaint if any man should think me given to such cruelty, when I am guiltless and innocent! Nay, I am so far from it that, for my own life, I would not touch her! If other means can be found, I would take more pleasure than in anything under the sun. I pray you, excuse my doubtfulness, and take in good part my answer answerless.'

She was barely existing, hardly eating and troubled by nightmares of severed heads and bloody axes. She found herself dwelling more on her poor mother than she had done for years, and resolved that no queen should go to the block by her hand.

Burghley, Walsingham, Hatton, Robert and the rest repeatedly used all their powers of persuasion to make her do what her people – and Parliament – expected of her. They were relentless. If she had thought that Robert would spare her, she had been badly mistaken. He was as firm as his fellows.

'If you do not order this execution, you will lose all credibility,' he warned her.

'And men will say that the weakness of your sex is clouding your judgement,' Burghley added, severe.

'Had I been born crested, not cloven, you would not speak thus to me!' Elizabeth retorted hotly. 'It is nothing to do with the weakness of my sex! It is about doing what is right!'

For all her misgivings, the sentence was proclaimed early in December, and in London there was a huge outburst of rejoicing. Bells pealed for joy, and the sky that night was lit up with the glow from a hundred celebratory bonfires.

Burghley laid the death warrant, drafted that day by Walsingham, before Elizabeth. 'For your Majesty to sign,' he said, in a voice that brooked no opposition.

'Not yet, good Spirit,' she said. 'Give me time.'

'Parliament has spoken, Madam. It has ratified the sentence. You *must* face the inevitable.'

Walsingham was equally adamant, as were Robert and all her other councillors. 'Sign! Sign!' was all they kept saying to her. Then she had to fend off the Scottish and French ambassadors, who were both urging her to show mercy. How could she refuse these two friendly kingdoms?

Out of the blue came a letter from King James, who had the temerity to tell her: *King Henry VIII's reputation was never judged but in the beheading of his bedfellow.* That infuriated her. Her father had been duped, the victim of evil men. Mary was a murderess and traitor who would have had her royal cousin assassinated. There was no comparison, none at all!

'He is making a token protest, that is all,' Robert opined. 'He is more concerned about securing the succession than saving his mother's life. He writes that honour constrains him to insist on her being spared. That sounds a bit half-hearted to me.'

'But some of the lords of Scotland are now threatening war on England if I have her executed,' Elizabeth said anxiously.

'Be minded of what their ambassador said, Madam,' Burghley put in. 'He said there is no sting in this death. And he should know.'

It was the most agonising decision of her life. She knew – and God knew it had been made clear to her often enough – where her duty lay, but could not bring herself to order Mary's death. The stress this caused affected her so profoundly that she feared she might go mad. She felt so alone, for everyone else was pressing her to sign the warrant, but as the weeks went past she was beginning to run out of excuses, and was weary of reciting her objections. Her soul's quietness had flown away. She was constantly on the verge of tears; she lost weight, as she could not eat; sleep came only fitfully, and she was plagued by the headaches that had manifested themselves so often, and increasingly viciously, in recent weeks. She felt ill, and dared not admit it to anyone, in case it be thought that old age was encroaching and she was losing her grip on affairs. *What was she to do?*

1587

Christmas had come and gone, and Elizabeth had hardly noticed. Still playing for time, she authorised Burghley to prepare a new warrant from Walsingham's original draft, and it was duly drawn up and given into the safe-keeping of her secretary, Davison. She told herself she did not mean to use it, but in fact resentment was building in her against Mary, who had caused her all this anguish on top of plotting her death. She found her resolve hardening.

Then the Scottish ambassador, Melville, came to her once more, pleading for Mary's life.

'There would be no need for your Majesty to order her execution were she formally to renounce her claim to the throne in favour of her son. King James is a Protestant, so he would never become a focus for Catholic plots against you.'

Ha! she thought. But he would attract malcontents and those who – even now – wanted a man on the throne; inevitably a faction would form around him. She had never forgotten how her sister's self-seeking courtiers had deserted her for the rising star, herself. Besides, she had not yet named anyone as her successor, and never would, for these reasons. The very idea put the fear of God – and treason – into her.

'By God's passion, that would be cutting my own throat!' she flared. 'No, by God! Your master shall never be in that place.'

'Then, Madam,' persisted Melville, trying, not very well, to suppress his anger, 'will you please consider delaying the execution, if only for one week.'

Elizabeth had worked herself up into a frenzy. 'Not for an hour!' she shouted.

Her bad temper was further fuelled by a message from King Henri of France, telling her that he would deem it a personal affront if she put Mary to death.

'Now that is the shortest way to make me dispatch the cause of so much mischief!' she growled. Yet still she would not sign the warrant.

'Is it not more than time to remove that eyesore?' Burghley asked testily, when next the fate of the Queen of Scots was debated in council.

The others grunted their exasperated assent.

'She has been at the centre of every conspiracy against your Majesty!' Walsingham reminded Elizabeth, who was grimacing at the head of the board.

'No!' she said again, and kept on saying it.

Later, after she had left the room following yet another outburst of distress, Robert stayed behind with his colleagues. 'She will not do it unless extreme fear compels her,' he told them.

'Then let us put about some rumours to frighten her and harden her resolve,' Hatton suggested. 'Spread it around that the Spaniards have invaded, or London is on fire, or the Queen of Scots has escaped.' The others nodded in assent, the gleam of conspiracy in their eyes.

The rumours, ignited in the most volatile places, caught hold like Greek fire, prompting widespread panic throughout the kingdom, and resulting in men donning their armour in case of invasion, and guards having to be posted on the main roads. Still Elizabeth was immovable, knowing that there were no real threats to justify the hysteria. But when the Council informed her that they had arrested and questioned the French ambassador in connection with a plot against her life that *almost certainly* involved the Queen of Scots, they swept away her fears of provoking the French by executing Mary.

'Suffer or strike!' she declared, anger surging against that black spider spinning yet another web of intrigue. 'In order not to be struck, *I* must strike!'

She summoned Davison. 'I am much disturbed by these reports,' she told him, 'and am resolved to sign the Queen of Scots' death warrant without further delay. Please bring it to me.'

Davison laid it before her. She read it over, picked up her quill and signed her name.

'I wish the execution to take place as soon as possible,' she told him. 'It is my pleasure that it be done in the great hall of Fotheringhay, not in the castle courtyard. Ask Sir Christopher Hatton to attach the Great Seal of England to the warrant, then have it shown to Sir Francis Walsingham. The grief of it will nearly kill him,' she jested grimly. 'Have the warrant sent to Fotheringhay with all speed. I do not wish to hear any more of it until it is done.'

As soon as a jubilant Davison had hastened off with the warrant to find Burghley and tell him the astounding news, Elizabeth regretted what she had done. Yet she dared not recall the offending document; her councillors would be in an uproar if she did that. But after another sleepless night, and another punishing megrim, she sent word to Davison that he was not to lay the warrant before Lord Chancellor Hatton until she had spoken with him again.

Davison came running. 'Madam, it has already been sealed,' he informed her. Of course; they would not have wasted time.

'Why is everyone in such a hurry?' she asked, her voice sharp with panic.

'They but wish to expedite your Majesty's bidding,' he told her. God grant that she was not about to change her mind!

'Swear on your life that you will not let the warrant out of your hands until I have expressly authorised you to do so,' she commanded.

'Very good, Madam,' Davison muttered, taking care not to swear anything.

'And Sir William . . .' The Queen's ringing tone stopped him in his tracks, but then she lowered her voice. 'Contact the Queen of Scots' gaoler, Sir Amyas Paulet. Ask him to ease me of my burden and quietly deal with her, so that I can announce that she has died of natural causes.'

Davison could not believe what he was hearing. Was the Queen really asking that stern, upright Puritan Paulet to commit murder for her? 'He would never consent to such an unworthy act!' he blurted out.

'Wiser persons than I have suggested it,' Elizabeth told him. 'My lord Burghley and my lord of Leicester think it a politic solution, and it would save us from the threat of reprisals from abroad. And Davison, I am answerable to none for my actions, but to Almighty God alone, and in this my conscience is clear. I follow Cicero's principle that we must strive for the highest good.'

'Yes, Madam, I am sorry, Madam. I will write to Sir Amyas,' Davison said reluctantly, knowing that it would be a wasted effort, for the answer would be a pious and outraged no.

Informed that the Queen might be wavering, Burghley summoned a secret emergency meeting of the Council.

'Do we, or do we not, dispatch the warrant without further reference to her Majesty?' he asked. The response was a unanimous yes; and to avoid Davison being blamed, all ten councillors present agreed to share responsibility for what they were about to do.

'Then it is agreed,' Burghley said decisively. 'But not one of you is to discuss the matter further with her Majesty until Queen Mary is dead, in case she thinks up some new concept of interrupting and staying the course of justice.' He then dashed off an order for the sentence to be carried out. 'Send this to Fotheringhay with the Queen's warrant,' he instructed Davison. 'Do it today!'

Elizabeth sent for Davison. 'I have had a nightmare about Queen Mary's execution,' she confided to him.

'But your Majesty still wishes to go ahead with it?' he asked, trying to conceal his alarm.

'Yes, by God!' she said. 'Even so, I might have wished things done in better form. Have you heard back from Sir Amyas?'

'I fear so,' Davison replied. 'I have his letter here. He says that his life is at your Majesty's disposition, but God forbid that he should make so foul a shipwreck of his conscience, or leave so great a blot to his own posterity, as to shed blood without law or warrant.'

'I wonder at his daintiness!' Elizabeth exclaimed. 'It is strange to me, the niceness of those who say great things about my surety, but in deeds perform nothing. Write a sharp note to Sir Amyas, complaining that the deed is not already done.'

'Madam, he will require a warrant from you.'

'No,' said Elizabeth. 'I cannot be seen to have a hand in this.' She sat and thought for a long space, frowning and drumming her fingers on the desk. 'It is best that we forget this plan,' she said at length. Two wrongs, she had concluded, do not make a right.

Davison was worried lest she bring up the subject of the death warrant, but she did not mention it, being too preoccupied with the other matter. She merely dismissed him with a sigh of frustration.

Elizabeth stared at Burghley in horror.

'Dead? She cannot be! I gave no order.'

'Madam, you signed the death warrant and we duly had it sent to Fotheringhay. The execution took place yesterday morning. All was done according to law.'

'I told Davison it was not to be dispatched without my express authority!' Elizabeth hissed.

'I knew nothing of that, Madam. I am sorry, but we, your loyal servants, acted only out of duty to your Majesty, thinking that it was your wish that the warrant be sent.'

She was on the verge of frenzy. She could not believe that Davison had defied her, although she certainly could believe that Burghley and the others, hot for Mary's elimination, had deliberately disobeyed her express command. The blood had drained from her face; she could barely speak. Then suddenly she burst into a torrent of tears, sinking to the floor and crying out incoherently. Alarmed, Burghley summoned her ladies, who had already heard the commotion and come running to see what ailed her. As they assisted her to her feet and towards her bedchamber, he could hear her ranting, swearing and threatening all manner of dire punishments. It took no great leap of the imagination to realise that he and his fellows were the target of her rage, and he hastened away to warn the others.

When she emerged from her apartments, Elizabeth looked ravaged. She had donned the deepest mourning, and could make no utterance without dissolving into sobs. She could not assimilate the horror of Mary's end, or even ask about it; she was consumed by fear of what that dreadful deed might engender, and did not cease to cry vengeance on the perpetrators.

When she met with her councillors it was only to hurl insults at them, making them quake in fear that she might, in her extreme tumult, condemn them to the same fate as Queen Mary. Burghley and Robert were banished from her presence. Davison was sent to the Tower for his gross disobedience. Walsingham fled home and feigned illness, hardly daring to poke his nose above the blankets in case he saw a detachment of the Queen's guards waiting at the foot of the bed to arrest him.

Burghley wrote repeatedly to Elizabeth, begging to be permitted to prostrate himself on the floor near her feet to catch some drops of her mercy to quench his sorrowful, panting heart. He even offered his resignation, but his letters were returned to him marked 'Not received'.

Elizabeth was barely functioning. Her remaining councillors begged her to think of the state of her health, but still she could not face food, or sleep at night. Her greatest fear was that God would punish her for Mary's death, and next to that she was in dread at what the world now thought of her. She was desperate to exonerate herself from blame.

Time proved, as always, a healer. When the worst outpourings of her grief and fury had subsided, she maintained the pretence that she was as racked as ever by emotion and regret. Her constant prayer was that her enemies would say that one so moved by the Queen of Scots' death could not possibly have ordered or compassed it. 'It will wring my heart as long as I live,' she declared, more than once.

Catholic Europe reviled her – she had expected that. She held her breath and waited for the clouds of war to gather, but nothing happened. James of Scotland made the appropriate protests against his mother's execution, but publicly accepted that Elizabeth had not intended it to go ahead.

In time she calmed down, forgave her councillors and took them back into favour. Soon they were back on their old footing, and Elizabeth again sent Robert to the Netherlands to trounce Parma. She was delighted when she heard that the Duke had sued for peace. Things were looking up! But Robert seemed incapable of reconciling his endless differences with his Dutch hosts, and before long he was begging to be recalled, since he could be of no further use to her.

'You are incompetent!' she berated him, as soon as he returned to court. 'You should have united with our allies in case Parma changes his mind and starts advancing.'

'I am very sorry for my shortcomings,' he apologised, his mien abject. 'With your Majesty's permission, I will resign my office of Master of the Horse and go home to Wanstead.'

Elizabeth was staggered. Robert had been her Master of Horse for nigh on thirty years.

'I will not allow that,' she barked.

'It is too much for me now,' he explained sadly. 'I pray you, Madam, bestow it on my stepson, Essex.'

Elizabeth was inordinately fond of young Essex, now one of the rising stars of the court. Even though she was more than thirty years his senior, he flattered her vanity with his ready compliments and took pride in demonstrating his prowess in the lists before her. Talk, dark, dashing and comely, he – like Robert, Hatton, Raleigh and (it could not be denied) Seymour before him – embodied all that she admired in a man, and although they were not blood kin, he reminded her a little of the young Robert, his loving stepfather and namesake.

Essex made her feel young again; she loved the sonnets he wrote her, the hours they spent playing draughts on her ebony board, or listening to her consort of musicians, or watching him perform in court masques. He played the young gallant with her, yet in some ways he was the son she would have liked to have had, and her feelings towards him were partly maternal.

She could not rid herself of the notion that Robert was making a gift to her of Essex; it occurred to her that he had been grooming him as his replacement in her affections. She prayed that Robert was not planning to retire from court permanently. She had meant only to show her displeasure. He knew that she could never be angry with him for long. But she feared that there might be some other, more sinister reason for his withdrawal. God grant it was not connected with his health! He had looked strained under his tanned skin, and no wonder, given the reception he'd received! Well, he had deserved it! Let him stay away and see if she cared!

There was no doubt now that King Philip would send his *armada* soon, or that Parma's intentions were as warlike as ever. Walsingham's intelligence reports revealed that the huge fleet of Spanish galleons was now almost ready to sail, its purpose being to vanquish the English navy and so clear the way for Parma to invade from the Netherlands. Elizabeth was to be deposed – and no doubt condemned to the same fate as Queen Mary – and Philip was planning to set up his daughter, the Infanta Isabella Clara Eugenia, as queen in her place; he himself already had enough to do governing Spain and her territories.

Orders had been given for England to look to its defences. Harbours were strengthened, new ships built, old ones repaired, and a chain of beacons prepared to give warning of the approach of the enemy.

'I do not want war,' Elizabeth declared. 'I do not crave military glory, and the expense in money and lives appals me. If diplomacy can achieve a solution, I will pursue it, and I will continue to sue for peace right up till the last moment!'

Peeved that he had made no attempt to beg forgiveness or even asked to see her, she had not invited Robert to court for Christmas, but now that the threat from Spain was manifest, he wrote at last, pleading her to behold with the eyes of princely clemency his wretched and depressed state. He wants to go to war! she thought, and because she needed his support desperately at this critical time, she sent for him at last.

She was shocked when she saw him. His clothes hung on him and there were deeply grooved lines in his face. He looked old and ill; there was nothing left in him of the Sweet Robin she had loved long ago. Yet he would not brook any discussion of his health, and insisted on dragging himself to every council meeting and immersing himself thoroughly in preparations for the coming invasion. When Elizabeth quailed at the bloodshed and financial outlay that war would necessitate, Robert spoke firmly and everyone paid heed.

'Diplomacy will not suffice!' he warned. 'Your Majesty must further strengthen your armed forces. As things stand, we are not ready and we will be outnumbered.'

Elizabeth ordered the refurbishment of more ships and gave orders for her forces to receive intensive training. Sir Francis Drake came to her, bullish and eager for action.

'Allow me to sail to Spain to sabotage the *armada*!' he urged.

'No, Francis.' She was adamant. 'If you failed, my ships might be damaged or lost when I most need them. Any conflict at sea must take place within sight of the shores of England, to remind our men what they are fighting for!'

She sent envoys to Parma to sue for peace, even as the great *armada* was setting sail. At Plymouth, the English fleet was poised at battle stations. Drake was playing bowls on Plymouth Hoe when word was brought to him that the armada was sighted.

'There is time to finish the game!' he chuckled, and went back to his play.

All across England the beacons were lighting up and men were hastening to arms. At Richmond Elizabeth received the news of the *armada*'s approach bravely, showing herself not in the least dismayed, and Robert took huge pleasure in spreading word of her courage and her resolute assurances that right would prevail. Everything possible had been done that could be done. Both the commander-in-chief, Admiral Howard of Effingham, and Sir Francis Drake, serving as second-in-command, had assured the Queen that the English fleet of nimble little ships stood every chance against the towering, cumbersome Spanish galleons. Thanking God for her confident commanders, Elizabeth sat down and composed a prayer of intercession to be read out in all churches.

A strange peace descended on the court. The nation waited, expectant, fearful and defiant. They were all in the hands of God now, Elizabeth said.

The shire levies had been mustered, and Leicester, now Lieutenant *and* Captain General of the Queen's Armies and Companies, assembled the troops at Tilbury Fort, in the mouth of the Thames, to guard London's eastern approaches.

'I myself shall ride to the south coast to be at the head of my southern levies,' Elizabeth announced. 'I mean to be ready to meet Parma when he comes!'

'Madam, we cannot allow it!' her councillors protested, horrified. 'Think of the risk to your Majesty's most precious person!'

'I want to go!' she insisted, and kept on insisting. They were aghast when she produced a silver breastplate and helmet that she had had made for herself, should the need for it arise. In desperation, they dashed off letters to Robert, asking for advice on how to stop the Queen plunging headlong into danger. He responded with an invitation to Elizabeth to visit Tilbury and comfort her army. *You shall, dear lady, behold as goodly, as loyal and as able men as any prince can own. I myself will vouchsafe for the safety of your person, the most dainty and sacred thing we have to care for in this world, so that a man must tremble when he thinks of it.* Her visit would enable her to feel that she was doing something useful, and it would divert her from dangerous thoughts of braving it out against Parma.

Elizabeth agreed to go to Tilbury. She could not refuse him. In the meantime, she wondered how her fleet was faring out there somewhere in the English Channel. Had her sailors encountered the *armada* yet? The waiting was gut-wrenching.

At last came news of victory! After a couple of skirmishes, the English fleet had shadowed the armada eastwards, where it anchored off Calais. Drake, seizing his opportunity, had sent in fireships, causing an inferno and widespread panic. The Spanish galleons that survived had been scattered, their careful crescent formation wrecked. Their commander had tried to regroup, but the brave little English ships now outnumbered his, and they had bombarded the great galleons.

It was at this point that divine intervention had decided the outcome of the battle.

'God blew with His winds and they were scattered,' Elizabeth jubilantly announced. 'Truly this was a Protestant wind!' It had sent the Spanish ships northwards, where they were lashed by terrible storms. Many foundered with their crew; a few limped on as far as Ireland and even Cornwall. Countless Spaniards perished, and a lot of the survivors would never see their homeland again. It was the most humiliating defeat in all the annals of Spain. And yet, Elizabeth was proud to hear, England had lost just a hundred men, and none of her ships.

'It is fitting that we render our most hearty thanks to Almighty God,' she declared, 'but there is still the threat from Parma to be dealt with. He waits only for a favourable wind to bring his forces across the Channel.'

It was time to take her barge to Tilbury Fort to rally her troops. Her councillors, still fearful for her safety – Parma could invade at any time, they warned – pleaded with her not to go, but she insisted that she would come to no harm, and told them that Robert himself had begged her not to alter her purpose and assured her that her person would be as secure as in London.

Fresh air and activity had done much for Robert; he was looking a lot better, and was clearly in his element in his new command. They embraced each other with their old warmth, and he showed her to the lodging that had been prepared for her. An hour later, she was ready to greet her soldiers.

Wearing a white velvet gown under her silver breastplate, and looking like a bright avenging angel, Elizabeth rode upon a snowy gelding. Before her went her page bearing her helmet on a cushion, and the Earl of Ormond carrying the sword of state, and beside her walked Robert, bare-headed, holding her bridle. The martial music of drums and pipes stirred the blood as her little procession advanced; pennants fluttered in the sea breeze, seagulls squawked and swooped overhead – and men stared in awe at this Amazon come among them.

Before Elizabeth were drawn up rank upon rank of her foot soldiers and cavalry. She blinked back tears at the sight of these brave, true men, come to defend her and the realm that they all held dear. As she advanced through their lines, calling out repeatedly, 'God bless you all!', many fell to their knees, pikes were lowered in deference, and there were hearty shouts of, 'Lord preserve our Queen!'

'Thank you with all my heart!' she cried.

The next morning she came again, receiving a burst of spontaneous applause so loud that it seemed like the rumble of thunder.

'I feel as if I am in the midst and heat of battle!' she told Robert, who was riding at her side. It was some time before the clamour died down, and then, at his command, the soldiers acted out a mock engagement so that the Queen should see their prowess. When it was over, and they had paraded in all their bravery before her, she addressed them from the saddle, her voice ringing out over the camp.

'My loving people,' she cried, 'we have been persuaded by some that are careful of our safety to take heed how we commit ourselves to armed multitudes, for fear of treachery; but I assure you I do not desire to live to distrust my faithful and loving people. Let tyrants fear. I have always so behaved myself that, under God, I have placed my chiefest strength and safeguard in the loyal hearts and good will of my subjects; and therefore I am come amongst you, as you see, at this time, not for my recreation and disport, but being resolved, in the midst and heat of the battle, to live and die amongst you all; to lay down for my God, and for my kingdom, and my people, my honour and my blood, even in the dust.'

She paused, her gaze roving over the sea of faces upturned to her, her heart full, her courage high. 'I know I have the body of a weak, feeble woman,' she went on, 'but I have the heart and stomach of a king, and of a king of England too, and think foul scorn that Parma or Spain, or any prince of Europe, should dare to invade the borders of my realm; to which rather than any dishonour shall grow by me, I myself will take up arms, I myself will be your general, judge, and rewarder of every one of your virtues in the field. I know already that for your forwardness you have deserved rewards and crowns; and we do assure you on a word of a prince, they shall be duly paid. In the meantime, my Lieutenant General shall be in my stead' – she smiled at Robert – 'than whom never prince commanded a more noble or worthy subject; not doubting but by your obedience to my general, by your concord in the camp, and your valour in the field, we shall shortly have a famous victory over these enemies of my God, of my kingdom, and of my people.'

There was a mighty roar of approval that reverberated around the fort, and shouts and cries of acclaim.

'I think your Majesty has so inflamed the hearts of your good subjects that the weakest among them will now be able to match the proudest Spaniard that dares land in England,' Robert said loudly, to more cheers. His eyes were warm with admiration – and love. It was as plain as day to her.

Her heart was soaring as he led her into his tent, where dinner was served. While they were eating, news was brought that Parma was about to set sail.

Robert stood up. 'Your Majesty must go back to London,' he insisted.

'Aye, Madam!' echoed his captains.

'I cannot in honour do so,' Elizabeth protested, 'for I have said that I will fight and die with my people.'

They were moved by her courage, she could see, but still they tried to dissuade her.

'Your safety and preservation is of the utmost importance,' Robert insisted. 'I fear that I cannot guarantee either.'

The argument dragged on, with Elizabeth refusing to leave. Outside the men went about their tasks quietly, knowing that the long period of waiting to see action was drawing to an end. How did it feel, she wondered, knowing that soon you would go into battle and might die or be horribly wounded? Her heart went out to them all.

Dusk fell. And then came a shout of joy. *'They're not coming!'*

It was true, the messenger confirmed, kneeling breathless before the Queen and the Earl of Leicester. Parma had refused to venture his army without the backing of the Spanish navy, which of course was mostly at the bottom of the sea. Robert had never seen such emotion in Elizabeth's face. It was radiant with joy and unshed tears.

'This is the Lord's doing,' she said, as she had said thirty years ago when they told her she was queen. 'It is marvellous in our eyes.' And she fell to her knees and folded her hands in thanksgiving.

It was over; the great enterprise of England, plotted over so many years, had been an abject failure. They had won! It had been one of the greatest victories in England's long and glorious history.

Elizabeth rode back to London in triumph, looking forward jubilantly to the City's welcome and the victory celebrations that were being planned. All along the roadside crowds gathered as she passed, calling down blessings on her, and everywhere the people were making merry. God be praised, that had sent this hour!

She made clear her determination to reward Robert with the office of Lieutenant Governor of England and Ireland, which would invest him with more power than had ever been given to a subject.

'Madam,' said Burghley, 'I beg you to think seriously before granting this. He will be a virtual viceroy.'

'Indeed!' chimed in Walsingham. So opposed were they to the appointment that she was forced to abandon her plan, wishing that Robert could know how highly she had wanted to honour him. But maybe his welcome by the cheering crowds in London was sufficient reward.

There were to be great national celebrations to mark the victory. In August, Essex staged a triumphal military review in Whitehall, followed by a joust in which he repeatedly excelled all others. When Elizabeth, come to watch the tournament, appeared at a window in the Cockpit Gate, the crowds below, catching sight of her, all knelt in reverence.

'God bless my people!' she called.

'God save the Queen!' they roared. And they remained kneeling until she made a sign for them to rise.

She stayed at that window, with Robert beside her, watching young Essex joust and applauding heartily. She and Robert had been much in each other's company since his return from Tilbury, and they had dined together in private every night. It was like the old times come again, Elizabeth thought, rejoicing that he should be here sharing these heady days with her.

But tonight, when dinner was served, he waved it away.

'I am not hungry,' he told her. 'I have eaten like a horse this week and should look to my diet.'

'Eaten like a horse?' Elizabeth echoed. 'You haven't finished a single meal. And you look tired, dear Eyes.'

'I am, Bess. These past weeks have been very demanding for an old man such as I.'

'Then you must rest!' She was suddenly alarmed for him. 'And take that physic that I had made up for you!'

'It is nothing to worry about, I assure my sweet lady. But I was going to crave leave to visit Buxton again to take the waters. They should restore me.' He smiled at her.

If he was prepared to make the long journey north to Buxton, surely there couldn't be that much wrong with him? 'Of course, Robin, you must go,' Elizabeth said, 'although I cannot tell you how deeply it grieves me to part with you at this time.'

'I will be back soon,' he promised. 'Certainly in time for the thanksgiving service at St Paul's.'

'But that is not until November!' she protested.

'Then I will tarry no longer than I have to.'

'When do you leave?' She dreaded hearing his reply.

'I thought tonight. If I go now I can be at Edgware by nightfall, and on the road towards Kenilworth tomorrow. The sooner I am on my way, the sooner the cure can be effected and I can return to you.'

'Then God go with you, Sweet Robin, and may He bring you safely back to me.'

Robert rose. He seemed to hesitate, then suddenly he bent forward, pulled Elizabeth to her feet, drew her into his embrace and kissed her most lovingly on the mouth. It was no perfunctory kiss of farewell, but a lover's kiss, such as he had not given her for years.

Then he stepped back, a smile playing on his lips. 'The true joy of my heart consists more in your Majesty's eyes than in any other worldly thing,' he said. 'I will think every absent hour a year until we are reunited.' Then he made an elegant bow, and was gone.

A few days later Elizabeth was overjoyed to receive a letter from him. It had been sent from Rycote in Oxfordshire, where he and she had often been guests of Lord and Lady Norris.

He had written: *I most humbly beseech your Majesty to pardon your poor old servant to be thus bold in sending to know how my gracious lady does, being the chief thing in the world I do pray for, for her to have good health and long life. For my own poor case, I continue still your medicine and find that it helps much better than any other thing that hath been given me. Thus, hoping to find a perfect cure at the bath, with the continuance of my usual prayer for your Majesty's most happy preservation, I humbly kiss your foot. From your old lodging at Rycote, this Thursday morning, ready to continue my journey, by your Majesty's most faithful and obedient servant, R. Leicester.*

He was the one who was unwell, and yet his chief concern was for *her* health. It was typical of him. She imagined him in company with the Norrises, enjoying their good hospitality. She hoped he was eating sensibly. It would not be long now before he reached Buxton.

She went about with a spring in her step. Already she was anticipating his return. The healing waters would do him good, she was certain of it. Meanwhile, she was planning a great portrait of herself, with the great Spanish armada – as they were calling it now – in the background, to commemorate the victory, and Hatton and Essex were busy organising lavish festivities with Sir Henry Lee, the Queen's Champion. There was to be a medal struck too, on her orders, with the legend *God blew with His winds, and they were scattered.* Elizabeth was in such a buoyant mood that she was moved to release the hapless Davison from the Tower.

The euphoric days of rejoicing passed in a hectic blur. Then one warm evening in early September Elizabeth, lute in hand, returned from a jaunt by barge along the Thames to find Burghley waiting for her in her privy chamber.

'Good Spirit, why such a dolorous face on this glorious day?' she teased him by way of greeting.

'Madam, I bring heavy news,' he said, his voice an unaccustomed croak.

'Not Parma?' she asked in alarm. God could not be so cruel as to snatch the victory from her now.

'No . . .' He hesitated. 'There is no kind way to say this, my dearest lady. Robert is dead.'

'No!' Elizabeth's anguished cry came from the depths of her soul. 'He cannot be! No! No!'

'I am so deeply sorry,' Burghley murmured.

Elizabeth had sunk down into her chair, her face cradled in her hands. Tears were pouring between her fingers. He was dead. He was dead, and all his glory gone. All his love for her, his tenderness, his care; his greatness, of which he had been so proud, and justly too, – all turned to nought. She would never see his dear face again. The book of his life was closed, the story ended.

Burghley stood silent as she wept copiously.

'Would you like me to go?' he asked gently. 'Shall I send for your ladies?'

She struggled to master herself. 'Tell me how it happened,' she stuttered, wondering how she was going to live without her beloved Eyes.

'He was on his way to Kenilworth, but was troubled by an ague on the way. It turned into a fever and he was obliged to make for his hunting lodge at Cornbury, where he took to his bed. He died this morning at four o'clock, almost alone. There was barely anyone in attendance to close his eyes.'

She wept again at that. All his greatness, all his wealth – and her precious Eyes had died virtually alone.

'I am more sorry than I can say, Madam,' Burghley murmured, breaking all the rules by laying a comforting hand on her shoulder. 'He had become a good friend and a colleague I greatly respected. He will be sorely missed.'

But by me most of all, she thought. How could Fate be so brutal?

'Leave me, William,' she said.

When Burghley had crept away, she went to her bedchamber and dismissed her waiting attendants. Then she locked the door. God had been cruel after all, plunging her into the deepest sorrow in her hour of triumph. She raged against Him, then stormed against those who had vilified Robert over the years, the vipers who had dragged his reputation in the dust with slurs of murder and poison and self-seeking – and all unfounded! It had been envy, pure envy, and he had not deserved it. She cried all the harder just thinking of it.

She could not face the world. She lay on her bed for two days, weeping pitifully, ignoring the increasingly urgent taps on her door.

'Madam, your Council awaits you.'

'Madam, your supper is ready.'

'Madam, are you all right?'

'Go away!' she cried, every time.

On the third day, Walsingham came to the door. 'Madam, forgive me for disturbing you at this time, but there is urgent business that needs your Majesty's attention.'

Silence.

'Madam?'

'I am unable to attend to state affairs,' Elizabeth wailed. 'I will not suffer anybody to have access to me. I am too grieved at the death of my lord of Leicester.'

Another day passed. She was sunk in misery, her stomach empty, her mouth dry. The room smelt horrible and stale. Yet still she did not want to face the world.

Burghley came knocking next. 'Madam, I speak to you as a father, as it were. You must take care of yourself. You cannot shut yourself away like this. Life has to go on – and this kingdom and all your loving subjects look to you for a mother's care. Will you not come out?'

'No!' Elizabeth cried. 'Go away, William!'

There was a muttering of voices outside.

'Madam,' said Burghley, more firmly, 'if you do not come out, we will have the door broken down, out of concern for you.'

'No!' she sobbed. She could not face the world yet.

'Do it,' she heard him say, and there was a heavy thud, then another, and then a crash as two burly grooms shouldered the door open. Burghley and Walsingham stood waiting outside, compassion in their lined faces.

She stood up shakily. Even *in extremis*, she was conscious that she had her dignity to preserve.

'Very well,' she said, hoarse and bitter. 'I see I must patiently endure my grief.' And with a supreme effort, she stepped through the doorway to begin living again.

In his will, Robert had left her a beautiful diamond and emerald pendant and a rope of six hundred perfect pearls. She wore the pearls when George Gower took her likeness for the Armada portrait, in which she was gratified to see that she appeared more like an icon than a queen of flesh and blood.

She did not attend the funeral at Warwick, where Robert was laid to rest beside his beloved noble imp in the exquisite

Beauchamp Chapel of St Mary's Church. She spared barely a thought for the anguish of his grieving widow, who had found herself saddled with debts of fifty thousand pounds, half the sum being owed to Elizabeth herself. The month after Robert's death she took back Kenilworth, and ordered Lettice to auction off all his possessions in his other houses. She was not surprised when the impoverished widow took another husband in a scandalously short time.

What really hurt Elizabeth was that, amid the victory celebrations, Robert's death passed almost unnoticed. No poets lauded his virtues, and the court mourning she insisted on was observed resentfully. The only person who really seemed to be grieving for him was herself.

He would barely recognise her now, she thought. His death had aged her and mantled her in melancholy. She had run the gauntlet of conflicting emotions – ecstatic joy and desperate sorrow – and she was spent. It was as much as she could do to put on a smiling face in public.

In November, her grief still raw after two months, she went in great state to St Paul's Cathedral for a special service of thanksgiving for the greatest English victory since Agincourt. She rode in a sumptuous canopied chariot drawn by two white horses, and her gown – the most splendid of the three thousand she owned – was of white satin encrusted with gold. Such a glittering procession had not been witnessed since her coronation thirty years before, and the people ran to see her as she passed, crowding behind barriers hung with blue cloth.

'God save your Majesty!' they cried in joy.

She bowed to left and right. 'You may well have a greater prince, but you may never have a more loving prince,' she declared to them, her voice filled with emotion. Her father would have been proud of her this day, she thought, as madrigals and ballads and pageants enlivened her way through London's festive streets. And her mother – surely Anne Boleyn would be rejoicing in Heaven now, knowing that she had cause to be proud of the daughter she had left disparaged and bastardised!

At the west door of the cathedral the Queen alighted and fell to her knees, thanking God in full sight of the crowds. Then, to the sound of the soaring anthem *Sing Joyfully*, composed by William Byrd, one of the gentlemen of her Chapel Royal, she proceeded into the great church, which was hung with captured Spanish banners. After the sermon had been preached, she read out a prayer she had herself composed, then addressed the congregation, enjoining them all to give thanks as she did for their glorious deliverance. Her words were received with a mighty shout of acclaim and loving voices wishing long life to her, to the confusion of her enemies. She wished – how she wished, the ever-ready tears not far from flowing – that Robert could have been here to share this triumph with her.

Her fame had spread far and wide. She was the Virgin Queen, Eliza Triumphant, her Sacred Majesty, a goddess on Earth whose praises were sung by princes and poets all over Christendom, and even – wonders would never cease – by the Ottoman Sultan and the Pope himself! People were saying that there had never been such a wise woman as Queen Elizabeth. God Himself had destined her to rule as absolute and sovereign mistress of her people, and this victory over the Armada was a signal manifestation of His divine will. He had kept her and her people safe, intervening in England's hour of need to preserve them all from harm. The threats from abroad were no more. The Anglican Church was stable, the Catholics quiet or in retreat, the people contented and confident. The marriage game was long at an end – although, by God, she wished she had it all to play again – but Elizabeth knew that she could now move forward and build on this peace, so that in time to come Englishmen would look back with pride on the golden age that had been her reign.

Epilogue: 1603

They had at last persuaded her to go to bed, helping her up from the cushions on which she had stubbornly lain, hoping to ward off death. She was sixty-nine years old, and she knew that the time was nigh for her to meet her Maker and give account of herself.

She was not afraid; she had done her best these forty-five years, and been blessed in her councillors and her captains. But they were all dead now — Burghley, Walsingham, Hatton, Drake . . . and Robin, of course. It was fifteen years now since she had looked upon her beloved Eyes. A new generation had taken their place, and the world seemed full of younger people. She knew that many of them were impatient of living under an ageing queen who hated change and new customs, and looked to her successor, whom she still had not named, but who would undoubtedly be James of Scotland. No fool, she knew that Robert Cecil, Burghley's brilliant son, who had become her chief minister in his place, had for years been paving the way for James's smooth accession, and no doubt a horse was already saddled, waiting to carry a messenger to Edinburgh with the news of her passing. They would take the coronation ring from her finger, and soon it would be shown to James as proof that she was dead.

The last years of her reign had not been happy ones. Bad harvests, vain attempts by her arch-enemy Philip — now dead himself — to send a second and then a third armada, factions squabbling at court, and then Essex. She still had no regrets about signing his death warrant. After all her favour shown to him, he had insulted her, wrangled with her — more than patience and her royal dignity could bear — and then risen against her,

413

or – so he claimed – against those who misruled in her name. It did not take a genius to see through that. She could not bear to think of the day when he had returned without leave from Ireland and burst in upon her as she sat in her thin chemise, her grey hair and wrinkles laid bare to his shocked gaze, the great charade of youthfulness exposed as the fraud it was. Sweet England's pride was gone, men said after the popular Essex had perished on the block, yet she could feel nothing but relief, for all that she had once looked upon him as the son she never had. He had been too rash and dangerous to be allowed to live.

But there had been good times too. England had flowered in many ways. Great houses – some built in the shape of the initial E as a compliment to herself – stood as testimony to the spirit of the age over which she had presided; drama and poetry had flourished. Elizabeth had taken particular pleasure in the plays of Mr Marlowe and Mr Shakespeare, especially the latter, whose *Twelfth Night* and *King Henry the Fourth* had recently been performed at court. She smiled even now at the memory of Falstaff, that great buffoon! She had bidden Mr Shakespeare write a play in which Falstaff fell in love – and he had obliged with *The Merry Wives of Windsor*.

It gladdened her heart that she had finally vindicated her mother's memory. Lord Hunsdon, her cousin, had brought to her attention his protégé George Wyatt, grandson of the poet Thomas Wyatt, who had once loved Anne Boleyn from afar. The younger Wyatt had a fund of information about Anne, lovingly collected over many years from his family and people who had known her. Elizabeth asked Hunsdon to bid Wyatt write a memoir of her mother, one that would proclaim Anne's innocence to the world. And so he had begun. And when Hunsdon died, Archbishop Whitgift, the Queen's great friend in her later years, had become Wyatt's patron at her request, and it was under his auspices that the work was continued. One day, Elizabeth knew, it would be published, and posterity would at last know the truth.

But it would not be in her lifetime. After striving for so long to ward off Death, she was now ready to go. It was not her desire to live or reign longer than was good for her subjects. It was the greatest measure of her love for them, the love she had carefully nurtured and cherished since youth. They might have mightier and wiser princes reigning over them, but she was certain they would never have any who loved them better than she did.

Whitgift was here now, praying at her bedside as she drifted in and out of sleep. There were others kneeling in the bedchamber too. She felt the Archbishop gently take hold of her hand, and was comforted. She turned her weary head almost imperceptibly towards her bedside table. On it stood a little coffer, inside which lay Robert's last letter and the jewels and pearls he had given her. These were all that she had of him now. But soon, soon, if God was good – and she had no reason to think that He would be lacking in mercy – they would be reunited in that Heaven in which there was, praise be, no giving or taking in marriage.

She felt herself slipping away; the drone of Whitgift's voice was becoming fainter. She turned her face to the wall, and drifted off to a place where none could reach her, dreaming of herself and Robert, young again, locked in each other's arms, playing hide and seek in the privy garden, and racing their steeds across the broad green breast of England, Elizabeth's red tresses flying out bravely behind her, her eyes shining with joy.

Presently her ladies leaned over her to see if she was asleep, and found that eternity had beckoned and that she had gone from them, mildly, easily, like an apple falling softly from a tree – and sweet England the poorer for it.

Author's Note

This novel is based closely on the historical record, although I have taken a few liberties. Conversations that took place over two or three meetings have in places been shown as taking place in one. Minor facts have been tweaked. Quotes have sometimes been taken out of context, or put into the mouths of others. Even so, they are accurate in spirit.

The use of language in a historical novel is always a challenge. Here I have made extensive use of the recorded sayings and exchanges of Elizabeth I and the people surrounding her, although I have modernised their words slightly in places, so that they remain accessible and in keeping with the narrative.

I have also made creative use of many of the legends associated with Elizabeth's reign: Drake playing bowls before the Armada, Raleigh spreading his cloak before Elizabeth; Lord Hunsdon drawing his dagger on Dr Burcot; and Elizabeth dancing around the cherry tree outside the Old Mitre Inn, although in the legend it was with Sir Christopher Hatton, not Robert Dudley. But, strange as it might seem, Elizabeth really did visit the Tower to ensure that all was in order for Norfolk's execution.

No one knows for certain why Elizabeth was reluctant to marry. There were probably a number of factors. The horror of her mother's fate, Katherine Howard's execution and that, seven years later, of Thomas Seymour, the divorces and matrimonial controversies within her own family, the deaths of two stepmothers in childbed, and her sister Mary I's disastrous union with Philip of Spain all probably contributed. In this novel I have taken a psychological view based on Elizabeth's own statements on marriage. She is on record as saying that she hated the idea of it for reasons that she would not divulge to her twin soul. And it is true that, at the age of eight, she informed Robert Dudley – as he recalled later – that she would never marry.

I believe that Elizabeth had an aversion to marriage for three reasons. First, having witnessed the breakdowns of several marriages within her own family, she did not see it as a secure state. Second, as she told Dudley, the man she probably loved more than any other, she had no intention of sharing sovereign power: 'I will have but one mistress here and no master!' Third, and most importantly, in Tudor times a monarch was regarded as holding supreme dominion over the state, but a husband was regarded as having total dominion over his wife. A queen regnant was still a novelty in England: Mary I had made an unpopular marriage with Philip of Spain, who, expecting to play the traditional authoritarian husband, had chafed against his wife's attempts to assert her regal authority. Elizabeth had no intention of embroiling herself in such an impossible relationship. 'I am already married to an husband, and that is the kingdom of England,' she was fond of declaring. She solved the dilemma over her marriage by taking a courageous decision, revolutionary for her time, not to marry or have heirs. Nevertheless, as 'the best match in her parish', she exploited her marriageability, using it as a weapon to the advantage of her realm.

She might not have married, but was she the Virgin Queen she claimed to be? The debate has been raging since the 1560s, and scurrilous rumours were rife throughout her reign, fuelled by Elizabeth's own behaviour, which was often condemned by her more sober subjects as scandalous. She would allow Leicester to enter her bedchamber to hand her her shift while her maids were dressing her. She was espied at her window in a state of undress on at least one occasion, and in old age she had a French ambassador squirming in embarrassment for two hours during a private audience by wearing a gown that exposed her wrinkled body to the navel.

Yet many ambassadors, at the behest of prospective royal husbands, made enquiries as to whether or not the Queen was virtuous, and in every case they concluded that she was. She herself could not understand why there should be so many racy tales about her, or claims that she had borne bastard children.

'I do not live in a corner,' she told a Spanish envoy. 'A thousand eyes see all I do, and calumny will not fasten on me for ever.' A French ambassador who knew her well claimed that the rumours were 'sheer inventions of the malicious to put off those who would have found an alliance with her useful'. Perhaps most tellingly of all, in 1562, when Elizabeth believed she was dying of smallpox and was about to face divine judgment, she spoke of her notorious relationship with Robert Dudley and swore before witnesses that nothing improper had ever passed between them. It is unlikely that she would have jeopardised her immortal soul by telling a lie at such a time.

As a historian, I believe that Elizabeth I was in all probability the Virgin Queen she claimed to be, technically at least – the evidence we have strongly suggests that she indulged in some intimacies with Dudley. However, in the prequel to this novel, *The Lady Elizabeth*, I explored the possibility that Thomas Seymour had actually seduced the adolescent Elizabeth, and that she had miscarried of the child that resulted. The 'what if' aspect of history is always fascinating, and there is some contemporary gossip on which to base this theory – had there not been, I would not have developed this storyline. I know that some readers took issue with it, but having written it in the first novel, I feel obliged to remain with it in the second, and so in *The Marriage Game*, Elizabeth has reinvented herself as the Virgin Queen, and her aversion to marriage stems largely – but not wholly – from the Seymour scandal of her youth.

I think that that scandal contributed crucially to Elizabeth's resolve never to marry. It is intriguing to find that most of the men with whom she later became involved were dark and dashing, even a little dangerous, like Seymour. But in reality she kept a tight rein on her emotions on hearing of his death, so we have no way of knowing how deeply it actually affected her. I do not believe that she gave herself fully to Robert Dudley; the evidence suggests that their private relationship was much as it is portrayed in this novel. But I think there is enough to show that Elizabeth's fears of marriage and sex were deep-seated, and I have developed that theme in this novel.

In 1604, after the Queen's death, Leicester's son, Robert Dudley, claimed that his parents had actually been married. Douglass Sheffield testified that the wedding had taken place before witnesses in 1573 at Esher, but her statement could not be supported because all the witnesses were dead. This was probably a ploy to secure an inheritance for Robert Dudley, even though Leicester had only ever referred to him as his 'base son', and both he and Douglass had married other people after they parted. So it is likely that they were never married at all.

George Wyatt's memoir of Anne Boleyn was never finished, hence there is no dedication to a patron. There is also no direct evidence that Elizabeth I asked him to write it, yet he implies that important persons encouraged him, and certainly no less a personage than John Whitgift, Archbishop of Canterbury, the close friend of the Queen, was one of them, replacing an earlier anonymous patron who had died; I have speculated that it might have been Lord Hunsdon. Thus it is possible that Wyatt's sympathetic defence of Anne, written in response to Catholic calumnies, reflects Elizabeth's own views.

I should like to thank my agent, Julian Alexander, and the historian Sarah Gristwood for reading the first draft of this novel, and for their very helpful and encouraging advice. Warm thanks are especially due to my editors, Anthony Whittome and Susanna Porter, for creative suggestions that have undoubtedly made this a better book. Thank you,

Anthony, for commissioning this book and for so many fruitful and enjoyable editorial sessions.

I am grateful also to the production team at Random House, especially Phil Brown, and to Rose Waddilove in the editorial department. Thanks also to Jocasta Hamilton, Publishing Director of Hutchinson, for her kind support, and to my publicist, Philippa Cotton, for her sterling efforts on my behalf.

Finally I want to thank my amazing husband Rankin for being my mainstay and constant support while I was writing the novel – and indeed, all my books so far!